Moon Bright

AURIANO CURSE SERIES
BOOK 3

PATRICIA BARLETTA

www.patriciabarletta.com

Published Internationally by Patricia Barletta
Boston, MA

Copyright © 2019 Patricia Barletta

Exclusive cover © 2019 inputux.com
Interior design by Tamara Cribley www.deliberatepage.com

PRINT ISBN 978-1-7324769-9-8
EBOOK ISBN 978-1-7324769-8-1

Editor: Joanna D'Angelo

This is a work of fiction. Names, characters, places and incidents are either the product of the author's imagination or are used fictitiously, and any resemblance to any person or persons, living or dead, events or locales is entirely coincidental.

Acknowledgments

We authors often get so caught up in writing our stories, watching our characters grow, and figuring out how to get those characters out of dilemmas, that we forget sometimes there's a world beyond the one we've created. But occasionally, we run into a snag, so we need to raise our heads to research a fact or brainstorm a plot point. Then, when we have finished that story, we must rely on the expertise of others to put that story out into the world. So this book would not have happened without the help of several people. First of all, my thanks to Joanna D'Angelo, my editor and go-to lady for all things publishing. I'd like a macro on my phone for "can u chat?" because I text it to her so many times. Next, my thanks to Steve Coppola for his design of my fabulous cover, because you *can* tell a book by its cover. Amy Sharp did a wonderful job as my proofreader, finding all those missing commas, repetitive words, and passive voice sentences. And Tamara Cribley at The Deliberate Page once again made the inside pages beautiful. Last, but certainly not least, my thanks to my critique group—Wendy L., Linda G., Wendy R., and DeAnna P.—who are generous with their praise as well as their criticism.

I want to give a special shout-out to Denise Blake, who came up with the Irish translation for the charm that Sebastian uses. She not only sent me the written translation, she also sent me an audio version so I'd be able to hear how those words sounded. I hope my phonetic transcription equaled her wonderful pronunciation. Denise, those few words you sent gave my story another dimension. I also wish to thank Annie Deppe, from the Stonecoast MFA program, for putting me in touch with her. Those Stonecoast connections are priceless.

I relied on quite a few resources while doing my research, but some that I found the most helpful are the ones below, and I feel their authors should get credit:

Jane Austen in Bath: Walking Tours of the Writer's City, by Katherine Reeve.

Stonehenge Decoded, by Gerald S. Hawkins in collaboration with John B. White.

The Druids, by Peter Berresford Ellis.

ALSO AVAILABLE

Moon Dark

BOOK 1 AURIANO CURSE SERIES

Moon Shadow

BOOK 2 AURIANO CURSE SERIES

Moon Bright

BOOK 3 AURIANO CURSE SERIES

The Duke Who Loved Me

BOOK 1 ON HIS MAJESTY'S SECRET SERVICE

The Duke's Dangerous Kiss

BOOK 2 ON HIS MAJESTY'S SECRET SERVICE

Sign up for Patricia's newsletter at patriciabarletta.com.
Follow Patricia Barletta on BookBub & Amazon.

Chapter 1

Somewhere near Bath, England, 1797

Sebastian Fox, Earl of Hawksmoor, dragged his mind out of the swamp of oblivion and tried to organize his wispy thoughts. His brain spun. He pulled in a breath and forced himself to take stock of his situation. He was standing, hanging by his wrists, actually. Manacled. But the iron bands were padded with something soft. His legs felt wobbly and useless. He could not see. Blindfolded. He smelled the mustiness of an underground chamber, the scent of bees-wax candles, the smokiness of a fire. Faint heat from that fire warmed him on one side.

Behind him, the dead cold of stone pressed against him from shoulders to buttocks. That meant he was naked. When had he lost his clothes? A fleeting sense of panic swept through him that he had also lost his signet ring and the gold torc that he wore around his neck. They were symbols of what he was, passed down to him through many generations. Then the vague memory that he had removed them calmed his anxiety.

Nothing hurt except the uncomfortable stretch of his shoulders, so he was not injured. Padded bands also circled his ankles, so he was chained to that stone wall. But the padded shackles confused him. He was spread across the stone wall like a tantalizing bite for some carnivorous monster. He wondered what strange torture lay ahead. Apprehension slithered through him.

He heard the faint rustle of clothing. A whiff of orange and some darker, headier scent teased his nose.

A woman?

He remained slumped, not wishing to alert whoever was with him that he was awake. He needed information about his situation, needed to know what his odds were for remaining alive. For escaping.

How did he get here?

Then he remembered.

He had gone to that tavern outside the city of Bath on an assignment from his superior in the Ministry. Young gentlemen had been disappearing for a day or two, only to turn up some place far from the tavern where they had started, unhurt, but naked, and not able to remember a thing about where they had been. He had been asked to look into the odd occurrences, so he had gone to the tavern and used himself as bait.

As soon as the barmaid had placed a tankard of ale before him, he'd smelled the potion in it. He could ward off its effects. That was part of his Gift. Arrogantly, thinking he could pretend unconsciousness and discover where the others had been taken, he drank. What he had not bargained for was the swirl of magic in the drink. Stupid. He should have detected it.

After only one swallow, he had lost consciousness. And awakened here—wherever here was—naked and chained.

"I see you are awake, *signore*." A woman spoke, low, melodic. Her words held a foreign accent, neither Italian nor French but a combination of both, although the appellation indicated Italian.

He felt the rim of a metal cup pressed against his lips. "Drink, *signore*. It will help the spinning in your head."

He straightened and turned away, not trusting his muddled senses, not wanting to imbibe anything else that might be dangerous.

"It is only water," she said. "Nothing harmful. Believe me, I want you fully awake."

The light trail of her finger down the middle of his chest made his skin quiver. Her touch felt like sunshine. When she held the cup to his lips again, he drank deeply. The water helped to clear his thoughts.

"Where am I?" he asked, his voice rusty after disuse. "Why have you brought me here?"

She chuckled, a pleasant ripple of sound. "You are naked and chained to the wall. I think you can guess why."

His muscles tightened as more than one reason ran through his head.

"As for where..." Her words trailed off and he sensed a shrug. "You don't need to know that."

He heard her move away, heard clothing rustle, then only silence. The blindfold annoyed him. He wanted to see her. Instead, he was forced to rely on his other senses — feeling, hearing, smelling, tasting. When she spoke again, she was once again before him.

"You are very handsome, but I'm sure you know that. And very arrogant, but what man worth having is not, *si?*"

That last word and the cadence of her speech pierced through the dregs of the clouds in his brain. He tried to recall any rumors or tidbits of information that included an Italian woman. He could remember nothing. But then, he had not been back home in England for very long.

She ran her hand down over his ribs, then up. Her touch sent heat spiraling into his groin, pleasant, unusually arousing. Too much, too quick. He sucked in a breath. He wanted more, knew he should not.

"Who are you?" he asked.

"Do you truly need to know?" Her question teased and deflected his query at the same time.

She circled one of his nipples with her finger. The intensity of the sensation made him grit his teeth. Either he was still drugged, or this woman was beyond normal.

"I'd like to know who is ravishing me," he explained, forcing his voice to remain level.

Chuckling again, she said, "Not ravish."

"What would you call it?" he challenged.

He felt the brush of her hair — silken enticement — against his chest as she leaned in toward him. "Seduction," she whispered close to his ear.

Her breath tickled his skin, riffled the hair on his neck, and sent a shiver through him. She had barely touched him, and he was already hard. Bloody hell, she was making him as randy as a goat in spring.

He continued the conversation in order not to make a fool of himself. "Why do you feel the need to seduce me?"

A heartbeat of silence, then, "Do you not enjoy being seduced, *signore*?"

"What if I said no?" He challenged her, wanting to know if she had scruples.

She sighed. "I would prefer that you did not."

So she had scruples, but was, perhaps, willing to ignore them to get what she wanted. He decided to bait her. "Did any of those other men refuse you?"

Her tiny intake of breath was barely audible, but he had hit his target.

"What other men?" she asked.

He heard the forced indifference in her words and hid his smile. "I've heard rumors."

"Rumors," she repeated, dismissively. A pause, then, "Do you truly believe a man would refuse me?" She ran her finger over his ribs again, tickling, creating heat where there should have been only the sense of skin on skin.

His mind flashed on scenes of making love, of sprawling across a bed with this woman writhing beneath him in passion, of her whimpers of pleasure. Who was she? What magic did she have that enticed with merely a touch? He forced his mind to focus on his assignment.

He probed for more information. "Do you think those men enjoyed being left naked by the side of the road?"

"I left their clothes. If they couldn't find them, that was their own failing." Her response was clipped.

So, she did not deny that she was behind the odd disappearances. Why would she need to kidnap so many men? She sounded beautiful. She smelled like heaven. She moved silently, so she must be graceful. Surely a woman like that could have any number of men without kidnapping them.

Her hand pressed flat against his chest. "Your mind is wandering, *signore*."

The touch focused his attention on her. The warmth from her palm spread across his skin, beneath it, circling down under his ribs, arrowing into his groin. He shifted to ease his growing need, to rein it in before everything else in his head was wiped out. He needed to delay the inevitable, to discover as much as he could about her before she seduced him. For he knew there was no escaping what she wanted. "What is your name, lady?"

"My name is anything you wish it to be," she purred. She arched her bare feet across each of his, which made her taller, brought her closer. Much closer. "It could be Mary." She pressed her legs along the length of his, shin to shin, knees to knees. "It could be Constance." Framing his face with her hands, she pressed her breasts against his chest. "It could be Alice." Her lips brushed across his mouth.

Sebastian stopped breathing. Naked. Dear God, she was naked. The feel of her against him was delicious. The smooth skin and taut muscles of her thighs promised delight. The soft heaviness of her breasts pressing against his chest made his fingers itch to cup them. But in exquisite torture, she kept a distance between her hips and his. If his hands had been free, he would have pulled her tightly to him, trapping her, inducing her to surrender. He gripped the chains attaching him to the wall.

"Are you slipping into madness, *signore*?" she taunted, her tone amused.

Not answering, he remembered to breathe. Yes, this was madness. He should be stronger, able to block her enticement. But he found he had no will to do so. His surrender would come with a price. At some point in the future, he would have to pay for this bit of paradise she offered. But right now, the cost seemed reasonable, whatever it might be. Resigned, he gave himself up to her seduction.

She fell fully against him, his erection fitting perfectly into the hollow of her hip. Not inside her, where he wanted to be, but nestled very nicely just the same. The light weight of her pressed him back into the rough stone. Despite the discomfort, he was glad for the support. His knees had gone weak again.

He exhaled, part sigh, part groan.

"You know denial only makes the release sweeter," she said.

He would not deny her. Could not. She could do as she wished, and he would follow willingly, either to heaven or hell. Her lips pressed against his, lingering, soft, delectable. He tasted wine on them, a heady vintage. Wanting to taste more, he angled his head, but she pulled away, refusing him. Her fingers trailed down his cheek, back along his jaw, to the pulse below his ear.

5

Something about the movement made him wary. Something warned him this was not ordinary seduction, no matter what she said or how sensuous she was. Something made him raise defensive walls in his mind.

"Do you want me?" she whispered.

Bloody hell, if he wanted her anymore, he would explode. "Yes."

"I want you, as well."

Her admission nearly disarmed him, but his instinct and his training kept those walled defenses in place.

"Let me pleasure you." Her voice, a whispery murmur, seeped into his head.

In his mind, he felt a gentle caress and another presence. Hers. Surprise flashed through him. She could enter his mind? Read his thoughts? Know his emotions? What sort of woman was this? Good or evil? Whichever she was, she was very powerful.

Reinforcing those walls of protection in his head, using his training, he doused his surprise and attempted to remain calm, not an easy task. While one part of him observed dispassionately, the other part burned with passion. He wanted her — all of her — her body, her mind, inside, outside. Recognizing his lust for what it was, he held very still and waited, allowing her to set the pace and the direction. He would remain detached, let her take what she would, but observe. He would learn all he could about her.

Her free arm snaked around his back and circled his waist, binding them together. Reflexively, he wanted to wrap his own arms around her, to press her close, enfold her. Despite his resolve to remain aloof, he jerked against the restraints at his wrists.

Her laughter rippled silently through his mind.

Careful, do not hurt yourself, he heard in his head.

Her silent words surprised him. This woman's ability amazed him. Her skill had obviously been honed from her early years. In defense, he reinforced those walls in his mind again.

He felt another caress through his brain. This time, the heat flowed down through his body, pooling between his hips, making his erection throb near the point of pain. A growl rumbled in his throat.

Her voice came again in his head. *Come, dance with me.*

Dance? The last thing he wanted to do was dance.

And then, in his mind, he saw her essence, golden, shining, glittering, with specks of colors that he could not name, had never seen before. She was a mass of sparkles that swirled inside his brain, alluring, enticing.

Dance with me, he heard again in silent invitation.

Without hesitation, he accepted.

Her misty cloud spiraled around him. He joined her, matching her twirl for twirl. They flowed upward, swooped down, tangled together until there were no boundaries. He could not tell where he ended and where she began. The pleasure of her flowed through him. He smelled spring. He tasted honey. He felt sunshine. He heard birdsong. And all he could see was the beauty of her.

She caressed every nerve ending until he was a quivering mass of desire. The sensation was pure arousal, yet behind that carnal lure, he sensed extreme sadness, pain, guilt, shame. At the edges of her golden beauty was a shadow of darkness. He wanted to wipe that darkness away, erase it, send it into oblivion.

At the thought, he felt her gratitude, so sweet it ached. Her twirling slowed, as if she examined him, as if she were puzzled at the experience of someone who wished to take away her pain. Despite his caution at allowing this woman into his mind, he let the barriers he had erected slip just the tiniest bit. His energy flowed around her, caressed her, cherished her for just a moment. That dark shadow faded for a heartbeat, and she sparkled even brighter than before. Her sigh of pure pleasure wafted across his mind, and then her spiral twined once more with his. He was swept up, higher. Higher. In his mind, he sensed her hands stroking, her lips kissing. He had never experienced anything as beautiful, marvelously sensual, erotic.

His body gathered itself, his muscles drawing in. He was so tight he thought he might crack. And then, with a roar, he exploded, breaking into a million pieces, a starburst of glittering colors. His. Hers. Mingled together. There was no him, no her, only them.

Awestruck, he rode the tidal wave of pleasure forever, to the edge of time and back again, until it ebbed into a soft, gray fog.

He was wrung out, depleted, boneless and limp. Slowly, he returned to the physical world around him. He felt her weight against him. Her forehead rested against his shoulder. Her fingers still pressed against his pulse. Her arm still wrapped about his waist. If he had not been manacled to the wall, he doubted he would have still been on his feet. In his head, her essence pulsed with soft light.

Grazie, signore, he heard her say silently.

For some reason, he kissed the top of her head.

Sleep, signore, she said. *When you awake, you will remember nothing of this.*

He had no energy to speak aloud. But he thought, *What if I wish to remember?*

She made a sound that might have passed for quiet laughter or for dismay. She had heard his thought. *Do not try to remember. You do not want to stray into things that are so dark.* She raised her head from his shoulder and pressed her lips softly against his mouth. *Sleep*, she said again without breaking the connection.

That soft gray fog swirled inside his head. It obscured everything. It broke his thoughts into bits and scattered them. He could have fought her, could have forced her away, but he refrained. He would give her this false sense of security, for he sensed her desperation. But he resolved he would discover who she was, why she needed to go to such extreme measures to find fulfillment.

The fog spread out, clouded his mind, and he let it. With a sigh, he allowed sleep to claim him.

But deep in a corner of his brain, he locked away the memory of her.

Sebastian stood in the dark on the veranda of the manor house and looked out over the formal gardens and the manicured lawn beyond. In the moonlight, the scene shimmered with a silvery glow. A couple strolled the stone path, then disappeared behind a hedge. Many shadowy places in the vista offered spots where two people could hide and indulge their desires. The thought of indulging his desires with one woman in particular made his blood race. But that was for later. He had to find her first.

Behind him, the orchestra played a light tune, and the crowd in the ballroom danced and laughed and gossiped and postured. He breathed in the cool evening air and relished the bit of solitude. In a moment, he would return to the crush to continue his search.

This was not the first place he had looked for the woman. He guessed she was gently reared, and he suspected she would be found amidst the glitter of the *ton* here in Bath. He had accepted invitations to every ball, every dinner, every gathering of society that had crossed his threshold. He had visited both the Lower Assembly Rooms and the Upper Assembly Rooms. He had gone to the Pump Room. He had seen no sign of her.

A week had passed since she had taken him, chained and naked, and left him spent and wrung out and slightly mad with wanting her. He was angry he had been so arrogantly foolish, so easily duped. He was disturbed that he still craved her. Even finding himself unclothed in the predawn chill out in the countryside the next morning had not driven away his need. The desire to know who she was and the hunger to have her drove him to engage in society when normally he would have shunned it. He had no time to engage in the empty frivolity when he was working on his assignment from the Ministry.

He knew her mind, knew he would recognize it as soon as he encountered it. Closing his eyes, he probed the guests in the ballroom behind him. Although unable to read thoughts, he could sense natures and personalities. There was the Baron Chauncey, dull and plodding. Sir George Frick, whose perverted lust made Sebastian swallow against his revulsion. The Earl of Graveson, solid and connected to his wife, who sat across the room. A group of young women, all light and sparkly. Two men together, one darkly layered, the other bland.

And then he found her. Luminous, golden, but with an undercurrent of torment. What caused her such agony? Was it her need to kidnap and seduce men? Or was it something more dangerous? He intended to find out.

Turning to face the ballroom, he held out his hand, palm up, and blew across it. A breeze picked up, swirled through the room heated by so many bodies. And on that breeze, he sent his message.

Come to me. Dance with me.

9

The message flew with the current of air, billowing the filmy drapes, tinkling crystals in the chandeliers. An inaudible sigh seemed to come from the guests, the breeze a relief from the heat of the crowded room. And as if she were a flame, he sensed her essence glow brighter with the breeze, and then fade back as the breeze passed. But she had heard his message.

Now all he had to do was wait.

Allegra Donatella Bianca Rosetta D'Este, Princess of Auriano, pushed open the door just enough to slip into the dark room. The only light came from the moon shining through the long windows. One wall was lined with shelves of books. A desk sat across a corner at the far end. A fireplace, unlit in the warmth of the summer night, and two chairs were to her right. But she could see no one in the room. What had drawn her here? Why had she sensed a summons to meet... someone, but who? Why had she been foolish enough to come?

But something called to her. Something she could not deny. She took another step into the room. She could sense no evil, nothing that would indicate the presence of the sorceress Nulkana, her family's enemy for generations. Still, she kept a firm grip on her closed fan. If she used it correctly, she could injure an attacker and give herself time to escape. It was her secret weapon and had saved her several times on the streets of Paris. Her Guide, Luisa, had charmed it as protection against Nulkana. She glanced around the room once more and peered into shadowed corners, but she saw no figure, either man or woman. She turned to leave.

"Running away?" a male voice asked.

Allegra froze. She knew that voice. Its smooth cadence, its velvet tone had haunted her for the past week. Slowly, she turned back. She searched the room once more. A man stepped into the rectangle of moonlight on the dark Persian carpet.

Yes, he was the same, except this time he was elegantly dressed in evening attire, not blindfolded, not naked with his skin gleaming in candlelight. His dark hair was skimmed tightly back into a queue now, not loose and free flowing like black satin about his shoulders. His black coat and breeches faded into the shadows, but the white of his shirt and neckcloth appeared to glow as he stood in the moonlight. One side of his face was outlined by the light, defining his cheekbone, the hollow beneath, the sharp angle of his jaw. The other side disappeared into the darkness.

Allegra flipped open her fan and fluttered it. "I was escaping the heat of the ballroom," she said. "I'm sorry if I intruded on your solitude, *signore*." She could not let him know she recognized him. Could not.

"I would gladly give up my solitude if it is to be broken by such a beautiful woman," he said with a small bow of his head.

"Such flattery, *signore*." She laughed lightly and turned to leave. "I will leave you to your solitary thoughts, *si*?"

"So, you *are* running away."

Allegra turned back at the challenge. "I am being sensible. A woman does not remain alone in the dark with a stranger, no matter how handsome."

"Then allow me to introduce myself. I am Sebastian Fox, Earl of Hawksmoor," he said with a formal bow.

She covered her shock by fluttering her fan more vigorously. She had kidnapped one of the most elusive, wealthy, sought-after, eligible bachelors in England. And one of the most disreputable and dangerous. He was rumored to have a mistress in every country on the Continent, to have killed twenty, thirty, forty men in duels, to have lost and won fortunes at the gaming tables, to be the head of a notorious band of smugglers, to spy for whichever country paid the most. The reality, of course, could not possibly be any of those things, but rumor was always generated from some truth. What had he been doing in that seedy tavern where she'd had him kidnapped?

Allegra lifted her nose a tiny bit into the air. "Learning your name, *signore*, does not reassure me of your intentions."

"Then perhaps I have gone about this all wrong. Perhaps I should have offered you something to drink." He held out a crystal wine glass that he must have been holding the whole time. It was filled with a clear liquid.

Suspicious, she said nothing and did not move to take the glass.

"It is only water," he said. "Nothing harmful. Believe me, I want you fully awake."

Allegra immediately recognized the very words she had spoken to him. She fought not to react, but her heart jumped. How could he remember? She had induced him to sleep, muddled his memories. He should not have remembered what had occurred between them.

He took a step forward, still holding out the glass. "Come, come, Mary. Or is it Constance? Or Alice? I never did learn your name. I am sure I will learn it eventually, especially since we will be spending very much more time together."

Allegra sniffed, covering her confusion. She had taunted him with those names. "You are being quite presumptuous, *signore*. I do not recall giving you leave to spend time with me."

He smiled. His teeth glowed white in the moonlight and gave him the appearance of some predatory cat, ready to pounce on its prey. "Lovely lady, we will be spending time together whether you give me leave or not." He sauntered to a small table next to the door and set down the glass.

He was closer to her now. His proximity and his words sent a shiver down her back. He was angry. She had made a mistake kidnapping him. At the time, he was all she wanted. As soon as she saw him strolling with feline grace down the street of Bath, she needed him, desired him, craved him with a ferocity that drove out any other thought from her head. The Hunger had clouded her brain. Serendipity or something more sinister had brought him to that tavern where he drank the charmed ale.

Now, all she wanted was to get away from him.

She backed away and pulled the door open a bit more so she could slip out. His arm came up, and he placed the flat of his hand on the door above her head. With a gentle shove, he closed the door fully and leaned his weight on his hand. She was shut in with him. Alone. In the dark. The orchestra and the babble of guests would drown out any calls for help. She took another step back, away from him, and came up against the wood of the door. His other arm rose, blocking her in, caging her against the door. His scent, piney, woodsy, clean male, teased her nose. The memory of his naked body flashed through her mind. No, no, no. She must not think of that.

She snapped her fan shut, gripped it tightly. "Let me go."

He shook his head. "I think not."

"I will scream." She dared him with her eyes.

He smiled again. "A useless exercise. You know as well as I that you would never be heard."

Desperate to get away from him, even just a few feet, she jabbed the end of her closed fan into his ribs.

He grunted and jerked away, but his hands remained firmly pressed on the door. "That was very unladylike," he said with a scowl.

"I am only reacting to your very ungentlemanly behavior," she countered.

"I never admitted to being a gentleman." He leaned in closer. "In fact, you tempt me to very poor behavior." He leaned closer still. "I find I have the irresistible urge to spread you across my bed and kiss every inch of your body until you whimper."

A hot-cold frisson flashed across her skin. Allegra gulped. "That is—"

"Seduction," he finished in a murmur. His fingers traced along her shoulder and up her neck. They circled the pulse below her ear. "I find myself suddenly in full agreement with the Bible: an eye for an eye, a tooth for a tooth. In this case, one seduction for another."

Madre di Dio. His touch felt like lightning. And something that she had missed when she had him chained, naked, washed over her. He had come into contact with a piece of the Sphere of Astarte, the artifact that would break the curse on her family. Right now, that meant nothing. Right now, she had to get away. His words sent fear thrumming through her. She trembled so hard her dress rustled against her ankles. What could she say or do to make him let her go?

"Please…" The word escaped. She had not meant to plead. But what was she asking for? Release? Or seduction?

"Hm. An interesting word for you to use." His lips brushed her ear. "How shall I answer? You did not ask when you had me chained to a wall."

She had to bluff. That was the only way out of this. Gathering her nerve, she stiffened her knees to stop their trembling. "*Signore!* I am shocked. That is an outrageous, offensive thing to say to a lady."

He straightened his arms and held himself above her. "A lady who drugs men and then seduces them. Ravishes them, to be precise."

His eyes held a tiny glint of hard light that seemed unusual in such a dark space, almost as if the full moon left an imprint on each pupil. Allegra decided it was a trick of the moonlight streaming through the window, for his eyes were shadowed in the dark of the room. Yet, something about him was extraordinary. That summons earlier, for instance. And something nagged at her about the night she had kidnapped him, something about his mind when she connected with him.

She opened her mouth to protest his accusation.

He spoke first. "Do not try to deny it. You are truly caught, lovely lady. You can protest until England sinks into the ocean, but I know what you have done."

"You know nothing," she said with a sniff. "You don't even know my name."

He shrugged off her argument. "An easy thing to discover. Our hostess must know who you are, and I am sure there are numerous men who would divulge the identity of a beautiful woman who speaks with foreign accents. Who has hair of chestnut with golden streaks, whose eyes are—" He stopped, turned her chin with gentle fingers. "Gold. Golden eyes. Beautiful, seductive eyes. Whose lips beg to be kissed. Who has a delightful dimple in her right cheek, and…yes, one in her left as well."

His murmured words skipped along her skin. His nearness both alarmed and enticed. What he said about discovering her identity was true. She had been foolish and had charmed too many men, all in her pursuit of the piece of the Sphere of Astarte.

"You can prove nothing," she said as she slipped beneath his arm and put some space between them. Her breath came easier now that she stood several paces away, but he still blocked the door. Flight was impossible.

He leaned his shoulder against the door and crossed one ankle over the other. "I don't have to prove anything. I could report you to the authorities. Even before you are caught and transported to a penal colony, rumor and innuendo can accomplish a great deal. What society maven will invite you to tea, to dinner, balls, and assemblies when it is whispered that you have been suspected of misdeeds, that you are not the unblemished flower you appear to be?"

Allegra flicked open her fan and fluttered it. She could not let on that she was afraid of what he threatened. If she were barred from society, she would no longer be able to single out the men for kidnapping, the men she needed to get through the Hunger, that period between Shadow and flesh when she was forced to feed her appetites. Damn the curse. And damn this man for finding her.

"If I run out of this room with my dress torn and screaming hysterically, then you will be the subject of scorn and censure, *signore*," she said coolly.

He laughed softly. "That would only reinforce my reputation as a blackguard and a rogue. People would think you foolish for entering a room alone with me."

"My family would be outraged," she said, with absolutely no intention of telling them.

"Who is your family?" One dark brow arched.

"They are very powerful. They could have you disappear. Perhaps your body might wash up on some distant shore." She gave a careless wave of her fan, despite the nervous flutter in her middle at the mention of her brothers. If either of them caught wind of what happened here, she would be locked away forever in Auriano, immediately after they dumped this man's body in the middle of the ocean.

"They would have to find and catch me first," he said. "And I have influential friends in very high places." Amusement rippled beneath his words.

What he said might be true, and neither brother was here in England to protect or chastise her. She attempted to convince him once more to allow her to leave. "At the very least, my family would force you to repair my reputation."

He shook his head. "The only way to repair what you suggest would be to wed. Would you really wish to be shackled to me for the rest of your life? I might be a monster."

She snapped her fan closed. "And I might be a shrew."

"Then we are evenly matched and at an impasse." A ripple of humor ran beneath his words.

Allegra wished she had never answered that odd summons which had brought her here. The man blocking the door was too wily, too dangerous. Too seductive. "What do you want, *signore*? Surely there are other more respectable means of getting a wife."

"I'm not looking for a wife, lovely lady. I'm looking for you." He pushed away from the door and took a step closer. "I want you to help me."

Surprised, Allegra did not immediately answer. But she saw that as he moved closer to her, he moved away from the door. She backed away one step, then two. If only she could move him far enough away, she could make her escape.

"No reply?" he asked.

She smiled coyly. "What would you need my help for, *signore*? The latest fashion in ladies' hats, perhaps? Or perhaps ladies' unmentionables." She nodded with conviction as she stepped back another two steps. "*Si*, that is it." With a sigh, she said, "I'm sorry, *signore*, I don't know you well enough to divulge that sort of information." She poised to spring past him.

Abruptly, he grabbed her wrist. "Don't run away, lovely lady. We haven't finished our conversation."

Allegra forced a laugh at the same time she tried to ignore the feel of his long, warm fingers wrapped around her wrist. "Whatever makes you think I was running away?"

He pulled her a step closer to him. Those tiny specks of light were very bright in his shadowed eyes. "Don't think for a moment that I am a fool. I know exactly what you did to me. And I know exactly what you can do. You will use your talent to help me, or..." His unfinished sentence hung in the air.

"Or what?" she whispered, unable to speak aloud.

Raising her wrist, he brought it to his mouth and placed a kiss against the pulse jumping there. "Or my punishment will be more than merely helping me." He licked across that pulse, once, twice.

Allegra thought her legs might have turned to aspic. Was it his threat, or the touch of his lips and tongue?

His eyes focused on her once more and held her as firmly as his hand. "Nothing to say again?" he murmured.

She pulled against his hold, but he did not release her. "I have no idea what it is you wish me to help you with, so how can I respond?" Her words were annoyingly breathless.

One corner of his mouth tilted up. "I need you to gather information for me, and I need you to do it surreptitiously."

Allegra caught her breath. "You wish me to spy?"

"That is such an ugly word," he said with a shake of his head.

"I can't. I won't." She wanted no part of his unsavory dealings. She had enough of her own to deal with.

"Then I shall have to contact the authorities." He expelled a sigh. "You will no doubt be transported to a penal colony. A shame to see such beauty wasted in such a place."

Cold swept through her. If she were sent to a prison colony, she would go mad and die on the voyage, if not before, for she would not be able to feed the Hunger. She attempted another argument. "I have never spied. I would not know how to go about it."

He tipped his head. "I don't believe you would need much coaching. After all, you are very adept at seduction."

Heat blossomed in Allegra's cheeks. If he only knew how much the seduction cost her in shameful guilt and despair after every episode of the Hunger. She turned away from those pinpoints of light in his eyes. "I—I will have to think about this."

"Then expect to be shunned at the next social event you attend as a reminder of what I can do." With a gentle tug, he had her up against his body. "I would enjoy being the only member of the *ton* who would socialize with you. It would afford me more opportunity to have you sprawled across my bed."

His hard body against her reminded her of the night she kidnapped him. She wanted him. Again. This time connected by more than just their minds. She found herself, indeed, wanting to be sprawled across his bed. The thought frightened her. Never before had she wanted any man after her time in the Hunger. And to want this man, who seemed to know more about what she could do with her mind than was safe, made her want to hide in some deep, dark hole.

His threat shook her. If she were shunned from all of society's events, she would be forced to find less desirable men to feed the

Hunger. She would be forced to run, to find some other place to hide. She would be forced to use peasant boys or search the stews of London for victims. That thought made her skin crawl.

Allegra jerked out of his grasp. She inched away, moving around him toward the door. "*Si*, all right," she said. "I'll gather information for you."

"I knew you would see the situation clearly." He pivoted toward her as she moved.

"You will, of course, have to tell me what information you are seeking," she said, as she sidled nearer to her exit.

"Of course."

She reached the door and stopped, attempting to fool him into thinking she would not run. He was still too close for her to feel safe.

"But you will have to find me first, *signore*." With an abrupt jerk, she had the door open, stepped through, and closed it behind her. Another dark room was directly across the hall. In four running steps, she was through the doorway. The moonlight shone through the windows at an oblique angle, but it lit the room enough that she could see. Quickly, she hid behind the floor-length draperies. All she had to do was wait for Hawksmoor to chase after her into the ballroom, and then she could slip away.

She heard him step into the hall. But she did not hear him move away. She held her breath.

Then, from the other side of the drapery, he said, "You can hide from me for now, lovely lady, but don't think you have escaped. I will find you and discover your identity. Until our next meeting…"

Allegra pressed a fist to her mouth to suppress a cry of dismay. How had he moved so silently? How had he known where she was?

She heard his light tread across the carpet, then his step into the hall. His footfalls retreated. Allegra let out her breath in a rush. She would have to hide from him, but how? She had to feed the Hunger when she turned from Shadow to flesh, and she had no time to find another place to settle before the moon slipped into its dark phase when the curse would take hold again. Besides, Sebastian Fox, Earl of Hawksmoor, had touched a piece of the Sphere of Astarte, the mystical artifact, broken apart and scattered by her ancestor generations ago, that would break the curse on her family. And that contradicted her desire to run.

If she wanted to find that piece of the Sphere, then she needed to stay near him. But if she wished to keep her soul, she needed to be far, far away.

For now, she would collect Luisa, her companion, her some-times-maid, her Guide, and flee to the abandoned priory where she found refuge during the Hunger. Later, tomorrow or the next day, she would figure out what to do about Sebastian Fox, Earl of Hawksmoor, the man who had come into contact with a piece of the magical Sphere of Astarte, the man who had touched her mind with gentleness, then threatened her with words of steel.

Chapter 2

The next morning, Allegra was on her knees in the herb garden behind the monastery, pulling weeds. Each time she yanked a clump out of the ground, she envisioned tearing out the hair on the Earl of Hawksmoor's very handsome head. Last evening had been a disaster. Instead of learning anything new about the Sphere of Astarte, she had been pulled into the intrigues of a very dangerous man. After a restless night of little sleep, she had escaped to the garden to vent her frustration.

"A princess pulling weeds is a rare sight."

Allegra shot to her feet and spun to the voice. The Earl of Hawksmoor stood on the other side of the crumbled garden wall. He lightly held the reins of a huge, black horse. With his dark good looks, in a deep red riding coat, with his horse snorting and huffing behind him, he could have been an incarnation of the devil. How had he approached without her hearing him?

"An earl who snoops about another's property is trespassing," Allegra retorted.

He grinned. "I believe if you look closely at the lease for this run-down monastery, you'll discover that it's actually my property."

"Impossible." Allegra frowned. "I was told it was owned by a business organization. Foxstone Limited."

He raised an amused brow.

Of course. Foxstone. His family name was Fox. He lived within several miles of Stonehenge, the standing stones. "That's you," she said, aggravated that she was tied to him in such a manner.

He bowed his acknowledgment. "If you must know, I was delighted to rent the property. I had plans to level the buildings, but somehow couldn't bring myself to do it."

"We will vacate immediately." Allegra had no idea where she would find another perfect place to hide during the Hunger, but she would not remain a moment longer than necessary on this man's property.

"Please don't," he said, as his gaze swept the old herb garden. "I see you've begun to revive the plants."

Allegra's gaze followed his, and she saw the small area of plots and trimmed pathways where she had weeded, surrounded by the wildness of the rest of the garden left untended for years, perhaps even decades. "I couldn't abide leaving these poor plants in such a state."

"A princess with a heart for horticulture," he murmured. "Rare, indeed."

Allegra realized what he was calling her. "How did you discover who I am?"

He grinned again. "I merely asked our hostess last evening."

She closed her eyes and swallowed at her stupidity. She should have been hiding her identity all this time. Instead, she thought using her name and title would gain her knowledge and access to a piece of the Sphere of Astarte.

"May I enter the garden of the Princess of Auriano?" he asked.

Her eyes snapped open. Although his question was polite, something deeper, darker, flowed beneath the words.

"If I denied you entrance, you would cross the wall anyway," she said.

Without waiting for his reply, she went to sit on an ancient stone bench beneath the shade of an equally ancient cherry tree. As she pulled off her gardening gloves, she watched him tie the reins of his horse to a wild bush, step over the fallen stones of the wall, and approach. The priory was warded, so if his intent had been evil, the spell would have repelled him. While he might not be malicious, she knew he was not completely benevolent from his threat the night before. He had the appearance of a fallen angel.

His stride was fluid and graceful, revealing that he exercised regularly with a blade. Alessandro and Antonio, her brothers, moved the same way. Their agility made her feel safe, but this man's made the fine hairs on her arms stand up. She rubbed her arms and decided the reaction was caused by the transition from the hot sun of the garden to the cool shade beneath the tree.

He stopped before her, and she had to crane her neck to look up at him. The sun was directly behind his shoulder and blinded her.

"Would the fair princess allow her lowly visitor to sit?" he teased.

She swept aside her skirt of coarse cotton. "It would be a relief from twisting my neck to look up at you."

When he sat beside her, she immediately regretted allowing him to do so. He was much too close. Her whole body was aware of him, and all she wanted was to get as far away as possible. But if she did that, she would be admitting that he had an effect on her, and she would not give him that satisfaction.

She gazed out at the garden. "Why did you come, *signore*?"

"I think you know the answer to that, Princess." His words, low and quiet, shimmied down her spine.

Feigning unconcern, she untied the ribbons on her sunbonnet and dropped the hat at her feet. "I have no experience in spying," she said. "You have propositioned the wrong person."

"I haven't propositioned anyone yet. I usually like to get better acquainted first. Although, I suppose, we've already bypassed that step in our relationship." Laughter rippled beneath his words.

When Allegra realized what she had said, a blush crawled up her cheeks and she ducked her head. She focused on his last statement. "We have no relationship, *Sior* Hawksmoor."

"I disagree. And our relationship is going to become much, much closer."

The serious tone of his voice alarmed her. She turned to look at him. She had never seen such thick lashes on a man, nor eyes such a true blue. "I can't—" she began, then lost the thread of her thought as she was caught and fell into that gaze.

As soon as she turned to him, Sebastian recognized her resemblance to her brothers. The golden eyes, the chestnut hair streaked with gold, the delightful dimples in her cheeks, the sensuous mouth. He could not believe he had not seen it sooner. Her claim the evening before about her family being powerful was quite true.

He had made the acquaintance of both her brothers, twins, each charming, handsome, and deadly with rapier and stiletto, and most likely other weapons as well. He knew without a doubt that if either of the men of the House of Auriano ever discovered how he planned to use their sister, they would slit his throat with no more thought than stepping on an annoying bug. He determined they would never learn the truth. Since both of them were on their wedding trips, he doubted any news from their sister would reach them while it mattered. And he doubted their sister would reveal her part. Much too embarrassing a thing to tattle to her older brothers. No, his task would be accomplished and the Princess of Auriano on her way back to her *castello* in the north of Italy before either of the men was the wiser.

But in the meantime, he planned to take full advantage of his association with the lovely Allegra. She was delectable and spirited. Her ability to enter his mind intrigued him. That shade he sensed beneath her essence made him want to enfold her in his arms and protect her. Her sweet curves drove him mad. And he wanted to kiss that luscious mouth in the worst way.

Damn. What he told her the night before was the truth: he *did* want her sprawled naked across his bed and whimpering with desire.

But he was a gentleman, at least in outward appearance, and gentlemen did not invite unmarried ladies into their bed chambers. There were, however, other opportunities for dalliance. Like now, for instance.

Their gazes locked. Her eyes were fathomless, and he thought if he looked deeply enough, he would be able to see to her soul. He knew she hid a dark secret—the curse on her family. And the other, more personal secret—taking young men and using them for her own pleasure. She might be virginal, but she was no innocent.

"Don't you think a relationship would be advantageous for us both, Princess?" he murmured.

She blinked but did not answer or drop her gaze.

He pressed, knowing he had her attention. "While you gather information for me, you might gain knowledge about the thing you seek." He reached up and brushed a stray tendril of hair from her cheek.

She blinked again and leaned away. "I am not searching for anything." With a little sniff, she turned her gaze on the garden.

"Of course not." He smiled. "You kidnap young men and seduce them merely to while away some time."

He watched pink color her cheeks. Her mouth thinned. She remained silent.

"Nothing to say?" he taunted.

She shot to her feet and spun on him. "What would you have me say, *Sior* Hawksmoor? That I am sorry I drugged you, chained you to a wall, and then—" She choked on her last words. Her lashes swept down and she twined her fingers together as if in prayer. "I'm sorry."

Sebastian knew her apology cost her. He was torn between satisfaction and compassion. But this was not the time to show mercy. Not when he needed her for her ability, not when his life and hers were in such danger.

Leaning back on one arm, he smiled up at her. "I'm not sorry in the least, Princess. You have given me a reason to exact some revenge, and I plan to exact it slowly and deliciously."

Taking her clasped hands, he brought them to his lips. When she tried to pull away, he would not let her. Gently, he sucked one delicate knuckle into his mouth. He ran his tongue over her finger. Her eyes darkened and her lips parted. Satisfied at her reaction, he released her. She put her hands behind her back and took a step away.

He allowed her to retreat because he had her completely in his net. "We are going to become an item, you and I," he said. "We will be the subject of all the gossips. Speculation about us will be their latest sport."

She shook her head. "No. I won't. I can't."

He rose to tower over her. "You will. Either that, or the authorities will learn the identity of the person behind the kidnappings in the area." He shrugged. "Your choice, Princess."

The look she sent him could have sliced ice. Those golden eyes were as hard as metal. Her chin went up. "You give me no choice," she said. "I find myself deciding between two types of imprisonment—one in a penal colony or one with a slave master."

"Chains of iron or chains of velvet, Princess," he murmured and traced his fingers along her jaw.

She jerked away. "Both are chains, *si*?"

"Perhaps, but my chains will never hurt you as long as you don't fight against them." Sebastian hoped he spoke the truth. He did not want to hurt her. He would protect her as long as it was in his power to do so. All she had to do was go along with his plan.

She turned her profile to him as she stared out across the garden. "What would you have me do?"

He hid his relief at her acquiescence, not sure what he would have done if she'd refused. "The Countess of Hetherington is having a garden party this evening."

"I have already declined the invitation," she said, facing him again.

He shrugged away her argument. "No matter. I'm sure the countess will be delighted that the lovely Princess of Auriano changed her mind about attending."

A scowl created a crease between her brows, but she said nothing.

Sebastian continued. "I will have the lady formally introduce us. We will dance and laugh and act as if we are thoroughly enjoying each other's company."

She gave an ironic little huff.

"Remember the penal colony," he threatened.

"How could I forget?" she said, her jaw set firmly. "You keep reminding me." She sighed. "You need not worry, *Sior* Hawksmoor. I will be as charming as I can be. Once we are a couple, then what? What will you have me do?"

"I will tell you that this evening." He had intimidated her enough for now.

The line between her brows reappeared.

He smoothed over it with his finger. "Don't frown so, lovely lady."

She knocked his hand away. "If I wish to frown, I will. Or is your order part of my slavery?"

"Ah, no slavery, Princess" he said with a shake of his head. "Merely the payment of a debt. Remember, one seduction for another." He met her gaze, snagging and holding it. Taking her hand, he gently kissed each finger. He expected her to jerk away, but she did not. Instead, he found her frozen, her lips parted and a look of utter confusion on her face.

Then she blinked, and the expression was erased. She took back her hand and lifted her chin. "If you wish me to appear presentable this evening, *Sior* Hawksmoor, then you will have to excuse me. We must return to my house in the city."

"By all means, Princess. I would not wish to keep you from your toilette." He bowed. "Until this evening."

He made his way back to where Vulcan, his horse, waited patiently. An unfamiliar anticipation gripped him at the thought of attending the evening's social event. The thought of verbally dueling with the lovely Princess Allegra made him smile. The possibility of having her spread across his bed made his blood quicken. He could not remember enjoying himself quite so much on any other assignment.

When Sebastian returned home, Quint, his butler, greeted him with the information that Sir Cyril Foley waited in the small drawing room. Foley was the last person he wished to entertain at the moment, but he hid his annoyance, asked Quint to serve a chilled wine, and entered the room with a smile.

"Sir Cyril," he said. "This is an unexpected pleasure."

The older man turned from his contemplation of Sebastian's garden. "This is not a social call, Hawksmoor. I have heard some very disturbing rumors, and I wish you to confirm or deny them."

Sebastian hid his grimace, gestured to a chair, then sat in the one across from it. "Please, have a seat and tell me what disturbs you."

Sir Cyril remained standing. "It has come to my attention that two of the pieces of the Sphere of Astarte have been recovered by the House of Auriano," he said, as he paced across Sebastian's line of vision. "It has also occurred to me that you had access to those pieces and let them slip from your grasp."

Quint arrived with the wine. Sebastian waited while his butler poured and served the beverage. As Quint closed the door behind him, Sebastian took a sip, relishing the chill on his tongue as he mused about where the undersecretary had obtained that information. He carefully placed the glass on the table next to his chair.

"If I had been able to retain those pieces of the Sphere, don't you think I would have?" he said.

He watched the Undersecretary of Foreign Affairs pace back and forth again across his Aubusson carpet from the unlit hearth to the opposite wall. Very few things could agitate the older gentleman enough to make him pace. Foley stopped and eyed him with a certain cool glint in his very dark eyes. Sebastian knew that look. It meant either of two things. He was about to be reprimanded, or about to be sent some place he had no wish to go.

"I did not hear of any physical harm coming to you in an attempt to hold on to those pieces," Foley said.

"I'm sorry to disappoint you," Sebastian murmured. "Next time, I'll be sure to get maimed or dismembered."

The undersecretary stared for a moment, a sure sign of his annoyance. With an abrupt gesture, he spun on his heel and sat in the chair across from Sebastian.

"I don't need insolence from you, pup," Foley said. "The intelligence that you brought back from France is disturbing. If the French decide to invade Egypt, they will be threatening our access to our resources in India. We cannot afford to fight both the French and the Legion of Baal. To have such a powerful artifact as the Sphere of Astarte in the Legion's hands could bring disaster to England. And who knows how long the House of Auriano will be able to hold onto the two pieces they have? We need to obtain all the pieces to keep them safe."

Sebastian wondered if the security of the pieces was the only reason the undersecretary wanted them. Their magic could be a powerful boon to England's influence in the world. But he kept his thought to himself as he observed, "We don't even know how many pieces there are."

Foley narrowed his eyes. "I thought you told me the Lord High of the Legion of Baal knew."

Sebastian shrugged. "I've been able to gain his confidence as The Messenger, but there are some things he keeps to himself. I rather doubt he knows."

The older man crossed his legs and ran his finger around the frame of a miniature portrait of Sebastian's mother sitting on the table at his elbow. "I saw your mother in London not too long ago," he said. "She is still a beautiful woman."

Sebastian remained silent, perplexed at the abrupt change of subject. His mother and Foley had some history between them, but he could never discover what it was. After his father died when Sebastian was twelve, Foley would arrive unannounced once or twice a year here at Blackbrake. He could remember his mother being charming, yet cool. Foley would take him hunting or riding or take him into Bath for the day. As a fatherless boy, Sebastian had developed a fondness for him. He became the distant uncle that Sebastian never had. As Sebastian became an adult, those visits dwindled and finally stopped altogether. When, bored to distraction, he had begun spending too much time drinking and gambling at his club and running his horses at the racing ovals, his mother had sent him to the undersecretary, who taught him subterfuge and deception. Who taught him how to be invisible while in plain sight. Who taught him to be one thing on the surface while something else entirely beneath. Who taught him how to be dangerously lethal. And then, Foley put him to work. Which was why the man was here in Blackbrake and sitting across from him.

Foley turned his dark eyes back to Sebastian. "I understand she runs up very high tabs at the dressmaker's and milliner's, not to mention the number of chits she owes for her extravagant gambling."

"I'm well aware of the countess's debts," Sebastian said tightly.

"She also seems to be keeping company with one or two members of a very fast crowd. One of them, a Mister Crowley, has been of interest to us for some time," Foley observed.

"What are you trying to say, Undersecretary?" Sebastian had a passing acquaintance with Crowley, who revolved around the outer fringes of society. More important, the man was also a member of the Legion of Baal. He never liked him. He wondered if Crowley's association with his mother happened by pure chance or if the man arranged it for some sinister reason.

The older man sighed heavily. "It would be a shame if your beautiful mother was caught up in any sort of disreputable doings.

Transportation does terrible things to a woman's complexion, not to mention her health. And seven years in Port Jackson is a very long time for a delicate flower like the countess."

Sebastian curled his fingers tightly over the arm of his chair to refrain from grabbing the man by his stock and shaking him until his eyes rattled. After several long breaths, he said, "My mother has no thought in her head except her own comfort and pleasure. She has done nothing to warrant a threat of transportation to New South Wales. If you feel the need to threaten anyone, it should be me. You will leave the countess out of this."

"I *am* threatening you, my boy," Foley said quietly. "I am finding your lack of results suspect. Do better or your mother..." He glanced at the portrait beside him. "You know this is not her first indiscretion."

Sebastian ground his teeth. "She was only trying to smuggle her modiste out of France to save the woman from the *sans-cullotes*."

Foley shrugged. "Still, there are those incriminating letters we intercepted on their way to France. Someone might decide she was trying to communicate in a secret code."

Sebastian glowered as he bit down on the very nasty words that wanted to escape. Despite the man's past connection with the countess, whatever it was, his threat was real. He was ruthless. Sebastian had learned to be just as fierce and merciless under Sir Cyril's tutelage. He had used the same threat of transportation with the lovely Princess Allegra only the night before. While his own threat had little substance, the irony forced him to hide a twitch of discomfort.

With a wave of dismissal, the undersecretary said briskly, "Well, I am only concerned for her welfare and warning you of what could happen. Find those pieces of the Sphere of Astarte and find them quickly."

"I am doing my best." Sebastian took a sip of wine to calm himself.

The man across from him abruptly changed the subject. "What have you learned about those kidnappings?"

Sebastian carefully placed his glass on the small table at his elbow. He had learned quite a bit. Who was behind them, and, now that he thought about it, the most likely place where the men were held — on his own property beneath the ancient monastery. But before he would ever reveal that to Sir Cyril, he needed to discover more about the lovely and mysterious Princess of Auriano. And he wanted to keep her away from the undersecretary's scrutiny as long as possible. Giving her up to the man sitting across from him made him very uncomfortable, a tactic he would use only as a last resort, perhaps not even then.

He released an exaggerated sigh. "I'm afraid I can share no further information. Whoever is behind the kidnappings is rather elusive. And really, the young men are not harmed, just a bit flustered at finding themselves naked in the countryside." He smiled inwardly at his own discomfort upon waking in the middle of a field of heather with his clothes strewn in a path that wended its way toward a well-traveled country road.

"Hmph. My thoughts exactly," Sir Cyril said. "But many of the young men are sons of members of Parliament, and their papas are none too happy."

"Has anyone been kidnapped recently?" Sebastian asked innocently.

The undersecretary shook his head. "No, not that I've heard." He stood. "The kidnappings are far less important than the pieces of the Sphere of Astarte. Find them, Hawksmoor." With that final imperative, he left.

Sebastian remained in his chair and absently twirled his wine glass by the stem. He had the feeling that Sir Cyril's threat against his mother went beyond merely an incentive to get him to find the pieces of the Sphere of Astarte quicker. Something about the man's demeanor indicated he was deeply, coldly angry. Sebastian had examined the man's essence, but all he'd sensed was an unclear, muddled swirl around a shiny, black center. Sebastian assumed it had something to do with the complex, sensitive position Foley held. After all, as Undersecretary of Foreign Affairs, he dealt in secrets and deception. But to threaten the unwitting countess with transportation was excessive. Sebastian was stuck in the situation for now, but he vowed as soon as the Lord High had been defeated, he would leave government service and Foley's manipulations.

But because of that service, he had discovered that the kidnappings and the delightful Princess of Auriano were all interwoven. Now all he had to do was figure out why she had decided to come to England, and specifically Bath. He would start by becoming better acquainted with the seductress who had drugged him, who had then ravished both his body and his soul. He would take his revenge. The vixen would be well and truly caught before she realized it, and back in the safety of her brothers' arms before she could do anything about it.

His mood lightened at the thought. With a satisfied curl to his lips, he rose to collect his valet and make the trip to Bath where he would engage in his gentle war.

Chapter 3

Allegra drifted across the lawn of Lady Hetherington's country manor outside the city of Bath. Torches lit a large area near the house, and farther into the gardens, fairy lights danced and twinkled in the breeze, marking paths where one might stroll. Music floated from the veranda where an orchestra played. The scene was magical, but Allegra was not enchanted. Instead, her insides jumped, and her head felt like lead. She wished she were far away, for soon she would be formally introduced to the Earl of Hawksmoor, that sly, manipulative, devastatingly handsome rogue.

Smiling and nodding, she greeted the few acquaintances she had made in her short time in England. Luisa, acting as her companion-chaperone, trailed behind her and muttered in Italian under her breath. Her Guide was not happy that Allegra had changed her mind about attending the garden party. Allegra sympathized. While she had not told Luisa the real reason, her Guide had caught a glimpse of Hawksmoor as he rode away that morning.

"Not for you," Luisa had scolded. "He is English. He knows nothing about the curse. Now we find that he owns this place. That is too close. We will have to find another."

"We have no time, Luisa," Allegra said. "The moon will be full in another two days."

Her Guide sighed dramatically. "I warned against taking him for the Hunger. Would you put that man in danger because you fancy him?" She shook her head. "Your brothers would not be pleased. They will find a proper husband for you when it is time, when the curse is broken."

Allegra had ignored the urge to argue about her brothers finding her a husband. She had decided either she would remain unwed because of the curse or find a husband on her own despite it. She also refrained from revealing that Hawksmoor remembered his kidnapping. Instead, she had used all of her wiles to convince Luisa that she had no interest in the Earl of Hawksmoor and merely wished to attend the countess's legendary affair. She certainly did not reveal the strange sensations he created in her when she was flesh and bone. Luisa had relented, but Allegra was not sure her Guide believed her.

Now, as she strolled toward the scattering of guests who were milling about Lady Hetherington's lawn, the visit that morning from the devilish rogue swirled around her brain. His threat to reveal her secret was the only reason she found herself being pleasant to these stuffed-up, pompous aristocrats. She glanced across the expanse of grass in the hope of catching a glimpse of him so she could prepare before he abruptly appeared before her. She saw no tall, dark, sleek figure anywhere.

"Oh, Princess Allegra!" a voice called from behind her.

Allegra turned and found her hostess hurrying toward her.

"I am so glad you came!" Lady Hetherington gushed.

Allegra nodded and smiled and murmured something appropriate. She glanced beyond her hostess's shoulder, but instead of the Earl of Hawksmoor, another man stood waiting to be introduced.

Lady Hetherington did the honors. "May I present Sir Cyril Foley, Undersecretary of Foreign Affairs? He is a very dear friend, and I so wished for the two of you to meet."

As Allegra offered her hand, she surreptitiously studied the man who bowed over it. He was older than Hawksmoor, nearing middle age, and a slight man. His hair was graying at the temples and stylishly cut short. His eyes were a chilly dark gray.

"Princess," he said with a bow, "It is a pleasure to finally meet you. I have traveled extensively in Italy and have been to Venice several times. It is a very beautiful city."

At his touch, Allegra discovered with surprise that he had also come into contact with a piece of the Sphere of Astarte. The coincidence intrigued and disturbed her, and she wondered if this man were somehow connected to the Earl of Hawksmoor. She would need to learn more about him. But something about his manner made her uncomfortable. She disengaged her hand from his cool fingers and forced a smile.

"I have seen little of Venice in the past few years," she said. "My family sent me away to school."

"They did not wish to keep you close?" he asked. "I would never have let such a beautiful young woman out of my sight and protection. Where did you do your schooling?"

Allegra hesitated, wondering how much information about herself she should disclose. Then deciding that revealing her past held no danger, she said, "I was in Paris. My family are quite progressive in their thinking."

"Ah, Paris," Sir Cyril sighed. "Such an exciting city. But one holding great dangers for a young woman alone."

"I was in a convent, *Signore* Foley," she said, tipping up her chin. "My family are progressive, not foolish."

"I think you have insulted the young lady, Sir Cyril," a deep, velvety voice said from behind her.

The tiny hairs on her arms stood up at the sound of Hawksmoor's words. While Lady Hetherington babbled over his arrival and he made the appropriate greeting, Allegra compared the two men. Sir Cyril exhibited wealth and breeding, but he was a gray ghost to Hawksmoor's vibrant, dark vitality. Something about Foley gave her the impression that he spent his time collecting secrets about people and lurking in the shadows to pounce on unsuspecting prey, but she had no idea why since she had just met him. Obviously, Foley and Hawksmoor knew each other, and she wondered how they had met, but then reasoned that English society was a small, select group. What intrigued her more was that both Foley and Hawksmoor had touched a piece of the Sphere of Astarte, which made her conclude that a piece must be in England. She would have to discover where and charm each of them to get the answer. But she'd have to be careful. Neither man could be trusted.

Lady Hetherington formally introduced Hawksmoor. When he bowed over Allegra's hand, he boldly touched his lips to her skin instead of kissing the air just above it and sent tiny shocks up her arm. When he straightened and smiled, her legs went rubbery.

"May I escort you and your guardian into supper?" he inquired with a charming smile in Luisa's direction.

Allegra introduced them. Her Guide gave Hawksmoor a speculative, searching look as he bowed to her, then she gave a terse nod.

Luisa sniffed. "Do not think you may capture the favors of *la principessa* because you are handsome and charming, *signore*," she said sternly. Then she relented. "But you may escort us."

"Perhaps I should charm you, mistress," Hawksmoor said to Luisa in Italian as he walked them across the lawn to the large tent where supper was being served. "Perhaps then you will allow me access to the princess."

Luisa sent him a sharp glance. "You know our tongue, *signore*?"

"*Molto bene.*" He grinned. Very well.

As Luisa sent him a tiny smile, Allegra ducked her head to hide her dismay that he was charming her Guide. And he was fluent in Italian. When she had been living in Paris, she and Luisa had conversed in that language when they wished their discussions to remain secret. Now they would be unable to do that when Hawksmoor was near.

That was not the only thing that disconcerted her. His arm beneath the fine wool of his coat was firm with muscle. The memory of that bare arm, chained and spread against a stone wall, tensing with strength as she seduced him during the Hunger, made her insides hot and jittery. Like the night before, when he had drawn her into that dark room, the knowledge that she wanted to be ravished by him scared her. She knew nothing about him except that he had touched a piece of the magical Sphere. And for the moment, he was blackmailing her into helping him do something that was dangerous and most likely illegal. She would comply for now, and in the meantime, learn everything she could about him.

"Are you enjoying your stay in England, Princess?"

Her head jerked up when she realized he had spoken to her. Smiling sweetly, she said, "I am discovering more about this lovely country every day, *Sior* Hawksmoor. I find it delightful, but I think there is intrigue and mystery beneath its charm, *si*?"

His lips twisted wryly. "Every place, every person has hidden depths, Princess, even those who seem the most innocent."

Allegra realized he had just stated a challenge. He would attempt to discover her secrets—the reason she kidnapped unsuspecting young men, the curse, and the Hunger. She wondered what she would have to do to keep him ignorant. If she could have, she would have fled England immediately, but she had no time. The curse would take hold soon, and she had nowhere to hide except in the ancient monastery that belonged to *him*. Besides that, she needed to remain because of the possibility that a piece of the magical Sphere of Astarte was in England. Frustration rose in her like a plume of smoke. She would have to tread very carefully through this thorny dilemma. And keep all thoughts of *Sior* Hawksmoor's magnificent body out of her head.

Sebastian caught the flash of alarm in the princess's eyes as he escorted the ladies into the supper tent. He wondered if her fear concerned more than her secret of kidnapping young men. He knew the House of Auriano was cursed, and he knew of the family's need to secure all the pieces of the magical Sphere of Astarte to break the evil hold on them. But he had no idea what happened when the curse took control. The Lord High of the Legion of Baal had been vague on the subject. Perhaps the Lord High had no idea, either.

He put aside all thought of the curse, the Legion, and its Machiavellian leader, and focused on the two ladies with him. He had been away from the social whirl of balls and dinners and assemblies for quite some time because he had been in other countries as he played The Messenger for the Lord High and gathered information for the undersecretary. When he was home, he shunned the glitter of society as much as possible because he found the events tedious, the conversations dull, and the ladies, for the most part, vapid. But the young lady on his arm was far from insipid or tedious. Despite her secrets, or perhaps because of them, he found her intriguing. More than merely for the double assignment he was supposed to complete, he wanted to learn all about the woman who kidnapped young men.

They sat at a small table with the dowager Marchioness of Hurrell, the dowager's companion, and the Baron and Baroness of Snelling. They engaged in small talk, with the marchioness quizzing the princess about the situation in France, especially Paris, with the French General Napoleon ranging across Italy and invading Venice. Tears glistened in the princess's eyes at mention of Venice being overrun by soldiers. He watched her blink them away. He wondered if this was artifice or her true feelings, for she had told Foley that she had spent little time in that city. If she were pretending, she would make a superlative spy. He needed to discover more—more besides the fact that she was alluring and beautiful and he wanted to put his hands and mouth all over her.

They finally finished the light supper. The music from the orchestra drifted across the lawn. Sebastian saw an opening when the marchioness engaged Luisa in conversation. He leaned the tiniest bit toward the princess. She smelled delightful, like oranges and vanilla, the same scent he remembered from the night she had kidnapped him.

"Come, dance with me," he murmured.

She regarded him with narrow look. Those luscious lips pursed. He smiled innocently, knowing full well he had used her words of enticement when she had him chained to the wall. When he saw she was about to refuse, he quirked up an eyebrow in challenge.

"It is only a dance," he said. "And you did agree to our arrangement." He held out his hand.

She looked away and down for a moment. When she turned back to him, her lips curved in a smile. But her eyes were chilly. She placed her hand in his.

"I would be pleased to dance with you, *Sior* Hawksmoor," she said. "But you must remember, I was raised in a convent and have not the advantage of knowing all the proper steps."

He stood and she rose with him. "Do not concern yourself, Princess. I will lead you through all of the dance."

Their words were polite and innocent to anyone who happened to overhear, but Sebastian knew that the beautiful woman strolling beside him was very aware of the double entendre of their conversation. He would like nothing more than to lead her through each step of every dance he could think of. As he escorted her across the lawn to the wide veranda where other couples were dancing, he smiled to himself. Teaching her new steps would be delightful.

Allegra argued with herself as Hawksmoor led her across the lawn. She could docilely dance with him and try to discover how and when he had touched the piece of the Sphere, or she could act as if he had insulted her and force him to relinquish his hold over her, at least in public. But his threat of her being shunned by society or transportation to a penal colony held her mired in indecision. They reached the veranda before she could act. The lure of the warm muscular arm beneath her hand tipped the balance. She would dance with him just this once, only to feel the strength of his magnificent body one more time. And then she would erase all those annoying fantasies about him. She would be the ice princess, comply with his blackmail, and at the same time, ferret out his secrets.

The specter of turning to Shadow in two days and the Hunger that followed hovered in the back of her mind. She told herself she would not crave the handsome, enigmatic Earl of Hawksmoor. Luisa would help her find another willing playmate. The man who walked beside her was not the only available man. With that decision made, she smiled up at him as he led her onto the dance floor.

The orchestra began a quadrille. As she curtsied and moved through the steps, she was relieved that there was little time to converse. Only when the dance required that they promenade was he able to dip his head and speak.

"The man standing near the potted plant," he murmured, "frequently travels between Dover and Calais. His movements are suspicious. His name is Hubert Crowley."

Allegra glanced at the man. The promenade ended and another set began that separated them. The man was as dark as the one who partnered her, but that was where the resemblance ended. While Hawksmoor was tall and sleek, the other was shorter in stature and broader, although not fat. The bone structure of his face was less angular and less striking than the earl's. He also lacked the earl's singular blue eyes and thick lashes. His hair was cut short and curled extravagantly in the new style, which made him look a bit ridiculous.

When they came together again, she asked, "You wish me to spy on him, *si*?"

"I wish you to gather information," he gently corrected.

She made a moue of annoyance. Spying was spying, no matter what it was named. "What information do you wish me to uncover?"

"Have you ever heard of an organization called the Legion of Baal?" he asked.

Allegra lost the rhythm of the music and nearly tripped over her own feet. "*Scusi*," she murmured distractedly as her mind raced. She had fled Paris because of that evil group. Surely, they had not followed her to England. If so, then she had run from one danger into another. She had to remain outwardly calm and reveal nothing. No one, especially members of the Legion of Baal, must learn of her secret and her need to discover the piece of the Sphere.

As she met Hawksmoor once more in the dance, she innocently said, "A curious name for a group of men, *si*? What is this Legion? And who is this Baal?"

The dance ended, and without responding, Hawksmoor led her to the other end of the veranda where a table was set up with various libations. He procured her a glass of lemonade and a glass of wine for himself.

"A gentleman should return the lady to her companion when the dance is finished," Allegra said with mild reproof. But she took a sip, glad for the tiny reprieve.

"A gentleman is allowed to offer the lady some refreshment after the dance if the lady allows." He responded with a small toast of his glass. "And we are to become an item, lovely lady, so stay and converse with me, and I will answer your questions."

She responded by demurely taking another sip of lemonade and peeked at Hawksmoor's prey. Her insides quaked at the thought of becoming friendly with a member of the Legion of Baal. Surely, the man would know who she was and that she searched for the magical

Sphere of Astarte. But then, perhaps he had no knowledge of who she was. And perhaps he knew where the artifact could be.

Hawksmoor directed her to a quiet corner of the veranda and explained, "The Legion of Baal is a secret cabal. It gets its name from the Phoenician god Ba'al, who was the Lord of High Places and the consort of the goddess Astarte. He was sometimes depicted in the form of a frog or toad. The Legion is an organization of men who worship this god and crave wealth and power. They are searching for an ancient artifact called the Sphere of Astarte, created by a magician as a gift to the goddess. The Sphere is rumored to be magical and will provide its owner with great power, wealth and immortality."

"How quaint," Allegra murmured. "If this Legion is a secret, then how do you come to know of it?"

"Rumors," he said with a tiny shrug. "Gentlemen's clubs are notorious places to exchange gossip."

"Then surely, this is all some dark fairy tale, *si*?" she teased, pretending playfulness when her insides clenched at the thought that the Legion was so close.

He tipped his head. "Don't you believe in magic and fairy tales, Princess?"

Allegra smiled to hide her unease. "When I was a child, I believed I would sail away to some exotic land that was being terrorized by a dragon. I would fight the dragon, but just before I killed it, I would discover it was truly a prince who had been placed under a spell by an evil sorcerer. I would break the spell, then marry the prince, and I would rule the land."

The sharp angles of his face softened in a smile. "So, you do believe in fairy tales."

"I was a child, *Sior* Hawksmoor," she reprimanded. "I do not believe in them now that I am grown."

"And what of magic?" he asked.

She shrugged one shoulder, pretending indifference. "Magic does not exist," she lied.

"I think you are not being truthful," he said.

Her heart jumped in panic. "*Scusi*?" She was prepared to slap him in feigned indignation and stalk away to keep her secret safe. The threat of expulsion from society be damned.

His brow quirked up in challenge. "How can you not believe in magic, being a Venetian? It is a magical city."

She glanced away and hid her relief with a soft laugh. "*Si*, you are right, *Sior* Hawksmoor. But you must remember, I spent much of my childhood in a convent in Paris."

He nodded. "Of course, where you learned of creatures like angels and devils, and saints who were taken bodily into Heaven."

"You mock me," she scolded as she tapped his arm with her fan.

"Perhaps a little." He smiled, but those blue eyes seemed to convey that he knew they played a game.

Allegra needed to turn the conversation away from her. "These men of the Legion of Baal, do they believe in magic?"

"They do," he replied. "And that makes them very dangerous."

"But why should that concern you?" she asked. "And why do you wish me to spy? Are you perhaps an agent of the government?"

"There are many reasons to gather information, Princess. For instance, if I had business interests on the Continent, I would want to know the political issues so that my interests would be safeguarded. Or, I might have a more personal reason—revenge, perhaps," he said smoothly.

Allegra's hand tightened on the delicate glass. His revenge on her would place her in danger.

His fingers lightly brushed across her white knuckles. "Careful, lovely lady. I wouldn't want your sweet hand disfigured with a scar from broken glass."

The warmth of his touch traveled nearly all the way up her arm. She fought the seduction of his caress and the opposite impulse to throw that glass at him. Instead, she placed it on the wall of the veranda.

She raised her chin in challenge. "I would never stand in the way of someone seeking revenge. You must arrange an introduction with this man so I may help you destroy him. I look forward to meeting him, for he must be urbane and witty if he takes so many journeys, *si*?"

Hawksmoor grinned. "I will let you form your own opinion on the type of man he is, Princess. And I think you will find he is a fountain of information."

Taking her hand, he raised it to his lips. Allegra would have pulled away, but his eyes caught and held hers. Once again, she thought she saw the moon in their depths. Merely a reflection, she told herself, of the torches and candles whose flames danced in the breeze. But she could not control the frisson that danced down her spine.

"I think tomorrow evening will be soon enough to make his acquaintance," Hawksmoor went on. "It is concert night at the Upper Assembly Rooms. I believe the orchestra is playing Handel's *Water Music*. Have you ever heard it?" He quirked an eyebrow in question.

"I have lived in a convent, *Sior* Hawksmoor," she said with a touch of exasperation. "When would I have had the opportunity?"

His lips twisted wryly. "When indeed?" he murmured, his words heavy with irony. "Come. I will return you to your companion." He tucked her hand into the crook of his arm and led her from the veranda.

Apprehension at Hawksmoor's implication that he knew she was dissembling distracted her. As they strolled across the lawn, he spoke of the interesting or infamous members of society that were visiting Bath that season. But her relief at being returned to Luisa's company was so strong that she barely heard his words.

When they reached her Guide, he said pointedly, "I hope to see you at the Assembly Rooms tomorrow evening, Princess."

Allegra merely flipped open her fan and fluttered it.

He bid her good evening and left with a gracious bow. Just as she was sinking onto a tiny chair next to Luisa, a servant approached and held out a note on a silver tray.

Puzzled, Allegra took the folded, sealed piece of parchment. When she opened it, four black words were scrawled across the creamy background:

I know your secret.

Her hand convulsed, crushing the note. She swallowed and took a breath to hide her fear.

"Who sent this?" she asked the servant.

"I do not know, your highness," he said. "Mr. Goody, the butler, asked me to deliver it."

Allegra scanned the lawn. People laughed and chatted, but no one seemed to be paying any particular attention to her. She saw Hawksmoor making his way through the guests as he exited the gathering. She decided the note could not have come from him because he already knew one of her terrible secrets, the one that forced her to the kidnappings whenever the moon waxed full or waned dark — the Hunger. But she did not think that he would resort to sending her a note. He would be much more direct, much more forceful. Much more seductive.

The note had to come from someone else. Someone who watched her in secret. Someone who knew of her family's curse. Perhaps someone from the Legion of Baal. Perhaps the man whom Hawksmoor wished her to spy upon. Or perhaps someone else within the organization.

Hawksmoor could be the key. He knew too much about the Legion. And he kept secrets of his own, like his ability to summon with the breeze, and that strange light in his eyes. She decided she would investigate Sebastian Fox, Earl of Hawksmoor. While he had a hold on her, she would use their association to her advantage.

She sensed Luisa's eyes on her.

"The curse," her Guide hissed. "We must leave at once."

Allegra looked down at her hand. Its form was becoming filmy and undefined. She glanced up at the moon, not quite full. Wide-eyed, she stared at Luisa. "It is too early, *si*?"

"*Si*." Luisa gave an emphatic nod. "Your prize is near. Come."

Her Guide hurried her through their goodbyes. By the time they were settled in their coach and rolling down the drive, Allegra had turned to Shadow.

Chapter 4

Sebastian ground his teeth as he galloped through the dark on the road to Blackbrake, his estate just outside of the city of Bath. The Princess Allegra had failed to appear at the Assembly Rooms this evening as he had prompted her to do. When he called at her house in the Royal Crescent, she was not there. He suspected she was hiding at the priory. Perhaps, she had kidnapped another young man and was even now seducing him as he was chained, helpless, against the wall. The thought sent heat raging through his veins. Anger? Jealousy? Arousal? He settled on anger because that was the safest.

He had wanted to meet with her again to discuss his request to spy on Crowley. That is what he told himself. Using her to get close to the man was safer than if he abruptly became friendly with the bounder, for they had never been particularly congenial. Now that Sebastian knew his mother was involved, he disliked the man even more. The urgency he felt to separate Crowley from the countess fueled his frustration at Allegra's absence. That was the only reason he had felt so displeased she had ignored his request. Not because she was the most intriguing woman he had ever met.

He entered the dark woods that gave his estate its name. The forest swept around the western boundary of his lands from north to south. The road was powdery, easy on the hooves of Vulcan, his horse, so he did not slow even though the trees shaded most of the light from the full moon. Movement in the shadows to his left caught his eye. Vulcan's ears twitched back, and his eyes rolled. Sebastian searched the dark as they galloped through the dappled moonlight. He saw nothing.

Vulcan shied abruptly, whinnied and reared. Sebastian fought to keep his seat and bring the huge animal under control. The horse landed with a jolt. Sebastian's teeth snapped together on the edge of his tongue. He cursed at the pain and the taste of blood.

As Vulcan danced in a circle, Sebastian tried to calm him with a soothing hand on his neck. At the same time, he peered into the woods and attempted to see what had spooked his horse. A small clearing lit by moonlight lay beyond a thin screen of brush that ran along the road. A shadow flitted along the edge of the clearing, then disappeared.

Sebastian blinked, straining to see. The shadow looked human, but it moved with an agility and speed that marked it as something more. Branches rustled farther along the road. He loosened his pistol in its saddle holster and trotted Vulcan closer. There was nothing to see except the black woods dappled by moonlight and the road disappearing into darkness. The chirp of crickets and the croak of frogs played their usual nighttime melodies. If something threatened, they would be still.

"I guess the wood nymphs are teasing us tonight, Vulcan," he said as he patted the horse's neck.

The animal snorted and bobbed its head in reply.

Sebastian urged the animal into a canter and headed toward the lighter end of the road where it opened into the fields. Just as the trees thinned and he was able to see across the meadows rolling away, he caught a glimpse of the dark figure again, this time in the full moonlight. It seemed to skim across a hillock and then it vanished down the far side. Vulcan had seen it, too, for his gait broke and he side-stepped.

Sebastian stared, wondering if his eyes were playing tricks. The figure had appeared female, lithe and graceful, with very long hair rippling about its form. It moved quickly, too quickly for a normal human female. It was all shadow, darker than the night, even under the light of the moon. He had never seen or heard of anything like it.

As much as Sebastian wanted to follow to investigate the creature, he was not about to force his favorite horse onto uneven ground riddled with rabbit and fox holes in the dark. Besides, he had a goal, the reason he was racing away from the city of Bath. He was going to pay a surprise visit on the Princess of Auriano. He would discover why she had refused to appear at the Assembly Rooms this evening. Then he would impress upon her the futility of evading him. And if she were "entertaining" a young man, he would make her understand that the only man she should entertain would be him, and on his terms.

Touching his heels to Vulcan's flank, he encouraged the animal forward, intent on completing his goal.

In the shadow of the hill where she crouched, Allegra's eyes narrowed in annoyance. She had not expected the Earl of Hawksmoor to leave the Assembly Rooms so soon, nor travel quite so fast. Her goal had been to get to his estate, discover as much about him as she could, and get away before he returned. She refused to acknowledge that something drew her to him as surely as the shore beckoned the waves. All she wanted, she told herself, was to learn how he could summon with the breeze and why the moon seemed to appear in his eyes. And what possible reason he could have for wanting her to spy for him.

She wondered if he had seen her. If he had, he no doubt thought she was some sort of magical creature. She smiled as she looked down at her hand, dark and shadowy. He was not far off the mark. Peeking above the hillock, she saw that he was trotting along the road as it meandered across the meadows.

She glanced over her shoulder. His mansion sat nestled on the far side of the rolling fields. A few lights twinkled from its windows. It looked like a little girl's extravagant dollhouse at this distance. She could out-race him at his present pace, do a quick search, and be gone before he arrived. Or, she could stay and observe him, an easy task in her present form. She would decide which later. Staying in the shadows, becoming one of them, she scampered across the meadow toward those twinkling lights.

Sebastian jerked off his coat as he strode into his bedchamber. His valet, trailing behind, caught it before it hit the floor.

"The gray garments, Soames," he said. "I'm going hunting."

"Hunting, m'lord?" Soames queried as he glanced to the dark windows.

"This is a very different sort of quarry, Soames." Sebastian handed the valet his waistcoat and stripped off the rest of his evening clothes. "One that needs a bit of observation and tracking."

"Yes, m'lord," Soames replied stoically as he collected falling garments with one hand and with the other, handed his employer a pale gray lawn shirt and soft buckskin breeches dyed a dark gray.

Sebastian pulled them on, then chose the gray superfine waistcoat over the suede one that Soames held out. As he buttoned it, he dismissed Soames for the night. He left the shirt open at the neck, then sat to pull on his jack boots, broken-in and comfortable. He would wear no coat. The evening was too warm. Besides, he was not paying a social call on the lady, so he did not need to dress up. He was going to watch the priory and try to discover if she had lured some unsuspecting buck into her clutches.

His mind churned as he considered the absence of the princess at the Assembly Rooms. He vacillated between forgiveness because she might have suddenly become indisposed, and anger because she had refused to fall in with his plan. Besides that, she had not even the courtesy to send a note of regret.

As he wriggled into his second boot, he felt something in the air currents of the room, a frisson against his skin. It was nothing that would have alerted anyone else, but his heightened abilities allowed him to sense things that others did not. Someone — some*thing* — was here. The impression he felt was not malicious, but neither was it friendly. It was more curious, perhaps even a bit nervous. And oddly, the impression was vaguely familiar.

Casually, he turned to the cheval glass to his right and held out his booted foot, as if admiring its form, but the reflection of the room behind him was what held his attention. Something moved toward the open window, then halted. He peered into the glass. The strong breeze made the flames on the candelabra shimmy, then they blew out. He blinked, trying to get his night vision and turned, peering into the darkness to his left where the reflection had come from. The full moon lit the room with a pale glow. A shadow, blacker than the rest of the space, seemed to hover in the corner.

He stood, and the shadow shrank back. It was denser than mere shadow and seemed to cancel all light within its outline. It appeared human in form — female, svelte, lithe. Entranced, he stared. This was the creature he had seen in the woods and meadow.

"What are you?" he breathed.

The creature raised her head, and he saw her eyes — glowing, glorious, like molten gold. She stepped forward. Her thigh-length hair flowed around her body. She was naked.

Dear God in Heaven, she was *naked!* And the most alluring creature he had ever seen.

"What are you?" he whispered again. "Who are you?" While one part of him was riveted, another part marked the distance to where his dagger lay beneath a pile of shirts in his wardrobe.

Does it matter what or who I am, signore? she answered silently in his head.

Sebastian fell back a step. "You are Italian."

Si.

"I only know of one other person who could speak to me in my mind," he said. "She is also Italian." Even as he said the words, he sensed the essence of her. And he knew.

That is a curious coincidence. A tiny ripple of amusement ran through her words. She moved closer. *But you know, there are others of us,* she said, as if imparting a secret.

"How many?" He started to edge toward his wardrobe. He did not think she was a threat, but he had experienced some of her powerful abilities. As Shadow, her human compunctions and principles might be compromised or even nonexistent. He had stayed alive this long because he was always alert to danger.

She gave a shrug. Then her eyes crinkled with humor. *Do you think I will hurt you, signore?*

He stopped. "Will you?"

This time a laugh tinkled through his brain. She held out her hand, and in the space before her, his dagger floated, as if held in place by some invisible string.

If I had wanted to hurt you, you would be bleeding by now. With a tiny motion of her fingers, his dagger twirled slowly in midair.

Both mesmerized and wary, Sebastian watched it closely. He had his own gifts, but this creature and her ability astonished him.

She moved her hand in a circle and then slashed it down through the air. The dagger spun and landed with a solid thunk in the floor, where it stuck, quivering. His butler and his housekeeper would not be pleased when they discovered the slash in the Turkish carpet and the gouge in the polished parquet beneath it. Sebastian released the breath he had been holding, relieved he had not had to dive out of the way of the sharp blade.

"If you're not here to do me harm," he asked, "why did you come?"

She was silent for so long that he thought she would not answer. Finally, she walked closer, hovering just above the surface of the floor. Her movements were fluid, graceful, mesmerizing. She stopped mere inches away.

Do you always question why, when you find a woman in your bedchamber, signore? she asked.

Despite her being Shadow, he could see the faint outline of her delicate, round cheeks and the plump mouth beneath a short, straight nose. That mouth curved in amusement. He desperately wanted to kiss it, then wondered how he could be so attracted to such a creature.

Her lips pouted. *You do not answer, so perhaps you do not like a woman in your bedchamber, si?*

Sebastian dragged his attention away from her lips and focused on her words. "I..." Even as he started to speak, he realized he had no thought except for that intense desire to kiss her.

Her sigh wafted through his head. *Ah mi, it is just as well. We should not consider the possibilities of my visit here.*

Her gaze dropped to the open neck of his shirt and sharpened. He had forgotten that the torc he wore as a symbol of who and what he was could be visible. She reached out a finger and touched the dragon head at one end of the gold circlet that came together at the hollow of his throat.

What is this? she asked. *I have never seen such a piece. I did not think men wore such jewelry.*

"A quirk of mine," he said with a shrug.

He damned himself for being so unmindful, for not covering the piece he held secret, except for those others like him. As he stepped back, her finger slipped off the piece and brushed his throat. Bright prickles erupted where her skin touched his. His breath caught, and he heard her tiny gasp in his head. Those golden eyes widened, and she stared.

What are you? she asked.

"What are *you*?" he returned, equally astonished. He reached out and gently ran his fingers down her cheek. She had substance, but it was fluid, like the surface of warm water. Tingles jumped in the pads of his fingers. They were intoxicating, like the bubbles in champagne. He wanted more.

As if his hands belonged to someone else, he watched as he cupped her face. Delightful tickles blossomed in his palms. Without another thought in his head, he lowered his mouth to those inviting lips.

Surprise turned to shock as Allegra stood absolutely still. The touch of his fingers, his palms, his lips created tingles everywhere his skin met hers. She had never before felt anything as Shadow. As soon as the curse took hold and she transformed, the sense of taste, smell, and touch disappeared, only to return in a rush during the Hunger when she regained her body and all her senses. Now, the ability to *feel* while Shadow was enough to enthrall her, but his lips and tongue, doing their erotic dance against her mouth, turned her insides to warm mush. She wanted nothing more than to press against him, curl herself around him, give herself up to him. The siren song of his touch wiped nearly everything else from her mind, except for one tiny glimmer of sanity.

She had come here because he was something beyond normal. She had come to discover what he was beyond the sleek, sophisticated, seductive Earl of Hawksmoor. She had come to find a way to extricate herself from his hold. She had come to learn when and how he had touched the magical Sphere of Astarte that would free her family from its curse.

She had not come for his seduction.

Using every ounce of her willpower, she stepped back, breaking their contact. She took a breath to regain her sense of self, but she felt bereft, as if she had just lost something precious. She clenched her fists, fighting the surge of need that swamped her. Her nails dug into her palms, but she felt nothing. That sense of touch, the ability to *feel*, had disappeared.

I did not give you permission to kiss me, signore, she said, summoning affront where there was none.

He stared as if he had not heard her. Then he blinked. His eyes focused, his gaze turning sardonic.

"And here I thought you had come to my bedchamber to frolic," he drawled.

Frolic? What an interesting idea, she said as she took another step back, her mind racing. She had to come up with a plausible reason for being in his bedchamber, besides trying to spy on him. *I thought only kittens and bunnies frolicked.*

His lips twisted in a sly smile. "Bunnies," he said, "frolic all the time. That's why there are so many of them." He took a step toward her, closing the distance she had put between them. His expression abruptly turned serious. "Why did you come here?" he demanded. "What do you want?"

Allegra shrugged. *Perhaps I only came to see the elusive Earl of Hawksmoor, si? I have heard that he is quite the catch for the young ladies. A man of prodigious abilities. A man who could be angel or devil.* She edged around him toward the open window.

"And what is your opinion?" Amused curiosity ran beneath his words.

Now that I have seen him for myself, I think perhaps he is only a man. She lied. She knew from that kiss that he was extraordinary. She knew from those tingles she had felt that he was much more than a

52

normal man. She knew from her first encounter with him as he was chained to the stone in the priory that she had to be careful of him. The problem was that she had no idea what he was. Annoyance at herself for not escaping him without being seen overcame her fear. She focused on that window, still several long steps away.

"Of course, I am only a man," he said, capturing her attention again. "What else could I be?"

His hand moved through the air in a dismissive motion. A sudden breeze shifted the heavy draperies at the closest window and wispy fog obscured the night beyond. Allegra realized with a jolt that the other draperies hanging at the rest of the open windows in the room had not moved, and moonlight still streamed through them, creating pale angular shapes on the floor. He had conjured the breeze and fog with merely a flick of his wrist.

She remembered that night at the ball, the summons on the breeze to the dark library, the sense of being called that she could not ignore. And when she had arrived, she had discovered him waiting for her. And then there were those spots of moonlight that appeared in his eyes. Fear stole her breath. She had to get out, away from him. Whatever he was, he was dangerous.

Summoning her courage, she said with disdain, *I think you are a man who likes to play tricks, si?* She stalked to the window and jumped up to the sill. The breeze stopped and the fog faded away. *I think I have seen enough.*

Just as she stepped out into the night, she heard him say, "I have a great deal more to show you. Until we meet again. *Princess.*"

Her breath whooshed away at his taunt, and she nearly fell as she landed on the soft grass two stories below. How had he known who she was? In her Shadow form, she was transformed into something other, nearly unrecognizable and invisible in the dark. Then she scowled. Her accent and her silent words in his head had most likely revealed who she was. Yet, beyond that, his powerful abilities confounded her, frightened her, for she had never seen the like. He could probably do more than merely create a breeze and fog, perhaps even a storm with strong wind and rain. She doubted even the ancient, evil sorceress, Nulkana, could do as much.

She raced across the lawns to the meadow and woods beyond as if the demons of hell chased her. She needed to be back at the priory where the crumbling walls evoked a sense of peace and safety, even if it were illusory. Most of all, she needed to be away from him, for her attraction was even more dangerous than his abilities.

But even as she ran through the night, the thought of his kiss, his touch, and those sparkling tingles chased through her mind like teasing fairies.

Chapter 5

The next night, Sebastian waited in the dark outside the gate of the priory. He knew now why the Princess Allegra had not appeared at the Assembly Rooms the night before. And he'd figured out the secret of the curse of the House of Auriano. For part of every month, the members of the family turned to Shadow. He had watched Allegra's brother, Antonio, Duke of Auriano, die and then return to life with a piece from the magical Sphere of Astarte. In between death and life, he had seen the duke's body become filmy and shadowy, but he was so focused on reviving the man that he thought he might have imagined the transformation. He knew now he had not. But even knowing the secret of the curse did not explain why the princess felt the need to kidnap young men and seduce them. He planned on uncovering the truth.

He had watched a small coach drive out of the priory gate at dusk. The driver wore a voluminous cape and his hat pulled down low, confounding any attempt to discover his identity. Shades had been drawn across the windows, but a faint light from within showed the silhouette of a woman, heavily cloaked, and larger than the princess. Sebastian surmised the figure was the formidable companion, Luisa. The two had to be on a mission to find an agreeable and suitable young man for the princess's pleasure.

Jealousy twisted through him at the thought that another man would feel her against him, would feel the softness of her skin, the heaviness of her breasts. That another man would experience the dance of her mind. The idea of her touching another nearly made him leap from his hiding place in the shadows beneath the trees and run after the coach to stop them from their quest. But common sense prevailed. That, and the knowledge that the princess was still safe and alone within the walls of the priory. He clenched his teeth and fought down his stupid urge.

He waited for full dark and the coach to be far away before he stirred. He moved out of the trees and scrambled across a crumbling part of the priory wall. The faint sizzle of a magical ward brushed his skin as he crossed the boundary, the same sensation he had felt when he first visited the princess in the garden. If he had been evil, the ward would have blocked him from entering. He was intrigued by the use of such magic, but not enough to explore it further. He wanted to find the princess and be gone before her guardian returned.

A large, nail-studded, wooden door marked the entrance into the building, but he was not going to knock to announce his presence. This would be a clandestine visit. He lifted the heavy latch and was surprised to find it unbarred. The door opened on silent hinges. He slipped inside. The interior of the priory, lit by the moon, was darkly medieval, with heavy beams across the high ceiling of a great hall. Cold, cavernous fireplaces stood sentry at each end of the room. The silence that greeted him was unnerving.

Even though he owned the property, he had not been inside for years. He had expected to find peeling plaster, fallen beams, and general decay and disarray, but was oddly pleased to discover it to be clean and fresh smelling. A comfortable seating area huddled around one of the hearths was made brighter by several candles and a colorful rug.

He turned in a circle as he contemplated where the princess might be hiding. Thinking back to his seduction, he remembered the manacles chaining him to the wall. The dungeon came to mind immediately. While dungeons were not a normal part of a religious building, this priory had become part of Henry VIII's holdings when he'd confiscated property belonging to the Catholic Church during his reign centuries ago. The dungeon was added to the cellars at that time in order to punish the monks who had lived at the priory and had refused to recognize Henry as head of the Church.

Memories of playing in the building as a child floated back to him, guiding his way to the refectory and the kitchen beyond. The cellars could be reached through a trap door in the kitchen floor, and if he remembered correctly, a small door carved in the stone wall of the last cellar gave into the maze of dungeons. He confiscated one of the candles in a heavy silver candlestick from the sitting area in the great hall and held it aloft as he followed his childhood footsteps.

His memory held true as he dropped through the kitchen trap door and into the cellars. A few mice skittered away as he made his way through the empty cellars, each one progressively smaller. He stopped at the last wall where dusty, cobwebbed, gnawed oak shelves stood. They were the only items left in the cellars. They barred his way, but he remembered that with a bit of effort, they slid neatly to the side and revealed the small door into the dungeons. He surmised the door had been put in place as an escape route for the monks, but the dungeon beyond told a tale of the irony of that.

With a grunt, he pushed the shelves out of the way, lifted the latch on the small door and stepped through. Cobwebs draped across his face and were so thick in the passageway that they seemed to be a solid wall. No one had passed here in decades. Perhaps the princess had another space for her seductions. Dust clogged his nose and he smothered a sneeze.

He was about to turn back when he heard a sound, partway between a cry and a moan, that echoed from deep in the maze. It was a woman's cry, and she sounded as if she were in great distress. *The princess!* She must have used another way into the cellars. The urge to rush to her aid washed over him. He pulled the candle from the candlestick and used the heavy silver piece to swipe through the webs.

He quickly traversed the narrow, low, stone passage. It opened up abruptly, and several stone cells gaped to his left and right, some with bits of rusted hinges and broken doors hanging at their openings. Light came from a doorway farther down the corridor. A low moan reached him, as if the princess were in some pain, and he ran the few yards to the room.

He stopped in the doorway of what must have once been the guards' room, for it was spacious in comparison to the cells. It was surely more comfortable now than when the guards took their leisure here centuries ago. The room was warmed by a fire on the hearth and softly lit by several candles. The stone wall to his left was bare except for a set of manacles hanging just above head height and another pair near the stone floor. A small bed, a comfortable chair and a side table were the only furniture. A thick Aubusson carpet covered the stone floor. But the room was not what held his attention.

The princess was pacing, the heels of her hands pressed to her temples and a line of anguish etched between her brows. Her hair was pulled back tightly into a single, thick, long braid that swung with every turn. She wore a loose robe of some satiny material belted at the waist that opened each time she took a step and revealed a long, shapely, naked leg. The soft, heavy fabric of the robe caressed every lovely curve of her very lovely body. Sebastian's own body stirred at the sight.

She saw him and stopped abruptly with a gasp. Her eyes were dark and haunted, not the beautiful golden color he remembered. Her lips parted.

"You!" she whispered. "You have come to me. You were *not* to come to me."

Her eyes squeezed shut, her lips compressed, and her face tightened as though she were in pain. A second later, her eyes flew open, wide, dark, hungry. Her gaze raked him from head to toe. She licked her lips as if he were a feast and she were starving. Without another word, she strode to him, knocked the candle and the candlestick from his hands, laced her fingers through his hair, and kissed him.

Shocked at first, Sebastian froze. Then his body reacted instinctively. He could not resist. He kissed her back. Her mouth was hot and inviting. Her tongue dueled with his. His arms went around her, his hands caressing her bottom and dragging her tightly against him. He realized that beneath the satiny robe, she wore nothing, like the last time they were in this chamber, but this time, there was no gentle seduction. Now there was only passion and heat and raw hunger.

Sebastian wanted her more than any woman he'd ever known. His hands ran over her curves, up her smooth back, down over her bottom to her thighs. His erection, pressed hard against her belly, pulsed with need. And all the while, their mouths sought and found and licked and sucked. He grabbed the back of her robe and tugged. It fell from her shoulders, opening in the front, baring her to the waist where the tie held it on. All he wanted was to feel her, touch her, be inside her. She whimpered and wriggled closer, as if she needed to crawl inside him.

Something, that whimper, that squirm, clicked in his head. This was wrong, wrong, *wrong*. Using every ounce of willpower, he took her shoulders and set her away.

Stunned, she stared at him. Her mouth was rosy and swollen from their kisses. Her hair was disheveled, strands trailing across her cheek and poking from her braid. Her cheeks were flushed. And her breasts were lush, the nipples pert and puckered and begging to be kissed.

Sebastian dragged in a breath. He tamped down his raging need. With shaking hands, he pulled her robe around her, mourning the loss of the sight of her.

"You do not want me?" she asked, her words flat with insult.

"I want you very much, Princess," he said, his voice strained with his restraint.

Her mouth thinned. Her face turned stony. Without warning, she slapped him.

Sebastian accepted it. Although he said one thing, his actions demonstrated another. He had rejected her. She was insulted. So, he remained calm and tried to put together some words that would explain, but he was not prepared for her onslaught of flailing fists. She pummeled his chest, punched wildly at him, landing a fist against his arm, another glancing off his ribs.

He backed two steps and blocked her blows as best he could without hurting her. He finally caught one of her wrists, but her other fist connected soundly with his cheek. While he shook off the dark spots that marred his vision, he realized the only way to quiet her was to kiss her. Again. The one thing he wanted to do above all else. The last thing he wanted to do. Because it seemed wrong.

Summoning up every shred of his training, putting up walls around the desire that flamed in his head and ignoring the desire that pulsed through his body, he stepped forward, caught her and kissed her.

As soon as Hawksmoor's mouth covered hers, Allegra stilled and the fires that crawled beneath her skin died. The Hunger this time had been nearly unbearable. Luisa had refused to kidnap the earl again, so Allegra had been forced to accept whatever young man her Guide could find. When Hawksmoor had appeared, she thought she might have been hallucinating. When she had kissed him, the fires beneath her skin had faded away until they merely became embers. The relief had been so intense she nearly cried, but her desire for him — just for him — had blotted out everything else.

When he had rejected her, her emotions were so out of control and jumbled, she could barely think straight. All she wanted was to punish him. For appearing in the doorway. For being the handsomest, most intriguing man she had ever met. For making her desire him beyond all thought. For evoking such a response from her. When he had put her away from him and pulled her robe back into place, the fiend's fury had possessed her, and she had lashed out at him.

Now, as he kissed her, she gained control over the fiend that lived in her brain. With effort, she slowly disengaged, but she held on to him, because the only relief she had was from touching him.

His eyes were wary, as if he thought she might attack him again. And he seemed a bit bemused.

"This is part of your curse," he said.

"Curse?" she said on a light laugh. "What curse? You do not find me desirable, *Sior* Hawksmoor?"

Allegra had been taught that she should never admit to being cursed. Despite the fire in her brain, that teaching prompted her to deny, even now, when every tiny bit of her clamored for relief, to tell him, to have him soothe the pain.

He frowned at her sudden shift in demeanor. "I find you more than desirable, Princess," he said. "I want you more than I have ever wanted another woman." His tone was so reasonable that she believed every word, and that sent a thrill through her. But he went on, "Yet, I think if we continue, this will not have a happy outcome."

Once again, she felt the rage surge through her at his resistance, but before she could react, a sharp voice from the doorway demanded, "What is this?"

It was Luisa, back from her trip to the tavern to find a young man to quench the Hunger. She held a small pistol aimed at Hawksmoor's heart.

The earl immediately dropped his hands from Allegra's shoulders and stepped away. She felt the separation like a tear in her soul. The Hunger surged up, threatening to take her over and wipe out all her humanity. She vaguely heard Luisa order the earl out. In a blurry fog, she watched him back away into the darkness beyond the doorway. Luisa kept her pistol trained on him. Allegra heard his footsteps recede into silence as he walked away. Desolation swamped her like a tidal flood, even as the prickling desire of the Hunger rose beneath her skin.

Ernesto entered with a man's body slung over his shoulder. Impatient, she paced, her skin crawling, her hands shaking, as Ernesto undressed the blindfolded, unconscious man. The fiend in her brain demanded satisfaction, writhing like a worm in its need. While she tried to force the fiend into submission, she felt her control slipping away. Her body was no longer her own. If she did not touch someone, anyone, she would go mad.

She barely allowed Ernesto time to attach the manacles before she threw a pitcher of wine in the young man's face to rouse him. And then she ripped off her robe and pressed herself against him. She was inside his groggy mind before he was aware he was chained against a stone wall and skin to skin with a naked woman.

The "dance" — of connecting with his mind, seducing him, bringing them both pleasure — lasted mere seconds. His cry of release was more surprise than pleasure. Her need was barely alleviated. She felt as if she were in the desert and dying of thirst with only a trickle of water to satisfy her.

With the Hunger slightly mollified, she backed away. But her relief was only a short respite before her skin was once again crawling with need and that fiend in her brain demanded satisfaction. She was on the young man again. And then once more after that. By the time she finished, the poor man was barely conscious, and not from any drug-laced, magic-imbued drink from the tavern.

A pervasive craving still pulsed dully beneath her skin, but her mind had cleared. She saw the young man hanging against the wall. His head drooped. His skin was pale. He was hardly breathing. Guilt, shame, and remorse rose in her so strongly that her legs gave out, and she collapsed into a ball with a moan of despair. She heard Luisa enter and felt her Guide's calming hand on her head.

"I have hurt him," Allegra whimpered. "I can't do this. It's not enough. I need — I need — " She dissolved into sobs.

"Shush, child," Luisa murmured. "Drink this. It will help to calm you."

Allegra took a shaky breath and sipped at the cup Luisa held to her lips. She tasted spiced wine but knew there was something more in the drink. She hoped the drug was enough to send her into oblivion, where the desires that surged through her body would be put to rest until the Hunger passed. but the cravings were different this time. They demanded something more.

Luisa helped her to her feet. "You must make him forget," her Guide murmured, referring to the poor man who hung at the wall.

Allegra wanted nothing more to do with him. She could not even look at him. "No," she groaned. "I can't."

Luisa gave her a little shake. "You must, or do you want him to spread tales of what went on here? Of the curse and the Hunger?"

The threat made her pull herself upright and drag her feet over to the young man. She dashed away her tears with the heels of her hands. Barely looking, she placed her fingers at the pulse in his throat, and touching him as little as possible, entered his mind once more. It appeared as a flat grassy plain, and heavily fogged over. Even in her exhausted, tormented state, she recognized the stodginess of his mind. It was not anything like the bright, complex mind of the man whom Luisa had sent away, who could call to her on a breeze, whose eyes seemed to hold the moon. She quickly induced the young man chained before her to forgetfulness and sleep. But that did not ease the shame at what she had done. It burned like an ember in her chest.

Luisa guided her to the bed, and the drug began to take effect. But it did not completely erase the cravings that crawled beneath her skin. As Allegra curled on the mattress and became drowsy, she knew what those cravings demanded.

Him.
Hawksmoor.
With his hard body.
With his blue, blue eyes where the moon shone.
With his gentle hands.
With his touch.

After Sebastian backed into the dark corridor, he hid in the dungeon where he had a clear view of the door of the room where the princess was. The older man and the companion left, and then he heard a shout of release from the young man. And again. And again. Each time, the sound grew weaker.

And each time he had to steel himself from running into the room to stop her. He hated the nameless young man manacled to the wall. He hated the fact that, instead of him, she had that young man at her disposal. And he hated the fact that he should feel such a ridiculously foolish thing. The princess meant little to him beyond a means to complete his assignment from the undersecretary and discover the pieces of the magical Sphere of Astarte. At least that was what he told himself, but he could not deny his clenched fists or the knots in his muscles that grew tighter with each shout of release.

His plan had been to stop the princess from her seduction, but he had seen her torment when he first entered her chamber and knew instinctively he could not. He had no idea what he would have done if her guardians had not appeared, but he knew that he would return to her as soon as he could.

The older man — Luisa had called him Ernesto — waited in the passageway with Luisa on the far side of the door to the room. Luisa had that pistol. He had no doubt she would use it on him if he interfered. Finally, they re-entered the room. He heard the murmuring of voices. Ernesto emerged carrying the young man, limp and most likely asleep, followed by Luisa. Their footsteps faded away into the dark. The princess did not appear, but weeping reached his ears.

The sound made his chest tighten. But he needed to focus on the reason he was here.

Time to go back to her and demand some answers.

She was on the small bed, covered to the neck with a blanket, and curled away from him in a tight ball. She shook as if she had the ague. Compassion made him reach out and touch her shoulder. She moaned as if in pain. He jerked his hand back, afraid he had made her torment worse. She rolled to face him, her eyes glazed, dark and haunted.

"I hoped you would return," she said, her words slurred and dreamy.

The blanket had slipped from her shoulder and showed bare skin. Sebastian swallowed in a dry throat. She was naked under the cover, and in his mind's eye, he saw her spread out beneath him and writhing in passion. He drew a shaky breath. No, he would not take advantage of her, not like this.

She reached out and took his hand. Her eyes closed and she sighed as if in relief. Her tremors quieted.

"Your touch," she whispered. "It comforts me."

She brought his hand to her cheek.

"I'm sorry I struck you," she murmured.

"It does not matter," he said. "You're ill."

"*Si*. No." She opened her eyes. "*Per favore*, stay with me."

"Princess—" he began and attempted to gently disengage his hand.

She gripped him tightly, as if she could not bear to let him go. "Please." Her eyes, clearer now but still not the glorious golden color he remembered, pleaded. She moved back to give him room on the narrow bed.

Sebastian was torn, wanting very much to hold her, but not trusting himself to refrain from his own seduction of her. His arousal from the wild kisses they had shared was a very near thing. He would need little to tip him over into the raging desire that hovered close to the surface.

She tugged on his hand. Her eyes held sadness and torment. A shiver ran through her. She hissed in a breath.

Her pain decided for him. He could not let her suffer. As he sat on the bed and pulled off his boots, a vague understanding of what was happening to her pushed at the edges of his mind. He would not try to decipher it now, but examine it later, when he could think more clearly.

He settled himself in a semi-reclining position. She cuddled close, her head against his chest, and rested her hand at his neck. The feel of her sent heat spiraling to his groin.

"Princess," he warned.

"Let me touch you, skin to skin," she said. She unbuttoned his waistcoat and shirt and pushed the garments from his shoulders, leaving him bare-chested. "Please…"

"Princess," he croaked.

She ignored him. She wrapped her arms around his waist and snuggled against him. One soft, lovely breast was crushed against his ribs. Her braid lay like a silky rope against his abdomen. Sebastian thought he might have to bite through his tongue in order not to flip her to her back and plunge into her.

With a sigh, she closed her eyes and a tiny smile curved her lips. The lines of tension around her eyes and mouth eased. Her shivers stopped. Gingerly, he put his arm around her shoulders and resigned himself to a night of torture.

"*Grazie,*" she murmured.

"My pleasure, Princess," he replied, noting the irony of that response.

She was quiet for a moment, then she said, "Allegra. My name is Allegra."

"I know, lovely lady." He whispered, because she was already asleep.

Sebastian awoke alone. The single candle beside the bed had burned down so low it was merely a wick floating in a tiny pool of wax. He had slept for several hours. His shirt and waistcoat lay perfectly arranged on a chair in the opposite corner with his boots tucked neatly beneath. Sometime in the night, he had obviously shed his garments, but he could not remember doing so. He wondered why he had heard nothing. He was a bit bemused that he had fallen asleep with such an alluring bed partner, but he found that he missed the comfort of her lush body curled around him, more than the loss of a passionate tumble beneath the covers.

He rolled off the bed and dressed, then went to find a way out. Torches spaced far apart lit the way through the underground tunnel in the opposite direction from which he had entered. He followed the lights to a set of stone steps. When he reached the top, he pushed open a trap door above his head and emerged behind the altar of the small, ancient chapel. Now he knew the alternate and cleaner route to the lair of the princess. The dim light of early morning filtered through the stained-glass windows, allowing him to make his way through the empty space. His footsteps echoed as he crossed the stone floor. He pushed open the small wooden door into the enclosed cloisters stretching to the right and left.

And was met by Princess Allegra , sitting calm and regal in an ornately carved wooden chair. She was dressed primly in a high-necked, long sleeved white dress, her hair piled in chestnut curls on her head. Her single accessory was a deadly rapier.

He halted.

"Princess," he said, giving a small bow. "You are looking well this morning."

"*Grazie.*" Tiny dimples appeared in her cheeks and then disappeared. She rose and sauntered closer — close enough that the rapier could easily stab him through with little effort on her part. "You are also looking well, *Sior* Hawksmoor."

"A good night's sleep is always beneficial," he said, noticing her eyes had returned to their glorious golden hue.

"*Si.*" She brought up the point of the rapier and rested it on his shoulder. "Now that we have those pleasantries out of the way, I think we should have a little chat, *si?*"

"I am at your service, Princess," he said, as he wondered if she were as skilled with the rapier as she was with a dagger.

"*Bene.*" She gave a decisive nod. "Then we shall have no trouble."

"I would never give a lovely lady like yourself any trouble," he said.

Her eyes narrowed. "You say one thing and do another, *Sior* Hawksmoor. I recall that you threatened transportation to a penal colony if I did not do as you asked. I think that might be *trouble*, as you say."

He shrugged, mindful of the blade resting on his shoulder. "Merely a bit of insurance, Princess."

Her lips tipped up in a cool smile. "Then I will require a bit of insurance as well." Her gaze slid away. "Last night was...unfortunate." She met his eyes again. "But what is done, is done, *si*?

"Yes." What was she up to?

"You were witness to something that no one knows about." She tapped his shoulder with the blade. "I want your word as a gentleman that you will tell no one."

"Princess, I—"

She cut him off with another tap of the rapier. "Your word, *Sior* Hawksmoor. *Si* or no."

"Of course. Yes. *Si*." His honor bound him. Now he would never betray the woman before him to the undersecretary. He would have to invent a plausible story about the naked young men.

"*Bene*," she said. "Now for that insurance." She tipped her head thoughtfully.

"You have my word, Princess," he said, hoping to sway her against demanding anything.

"*Si*, but I think this will bind us a bit more." She tapped the point of the rapier against his torc, clearly visible in the open neck of his shirt.

Sebastian fought not to react. The torc was a symbol of his position as a Druid priest, but it also helped to concentrate his powers. He was able to use those powers without it, but they weren't nearly as strong or focused. Giving up the torc could be dangerous in many ways.

Her eyes narrowed at his hesitation. "I do not know what you are, *Sior* Hawksmoor, but I think this is more than a silly bauble. And I think you most likely do not wish for others to know of this, *si*? So. You will give me this and tell no one of what you saw last night, and I will keep it and tell no one that I have it." The point of her blade slid to rest at the hollow of his throat.

The metal felt icy hot. He had the urge to swallow but dared not for fear that the rapier would pierce him. He did not think the beautiful woman standing before him was heartless enough to stab him with her blade, but she was wily and dangerous. At that moment, despite his precarious position, all he wanted was to kiss her mindless. He took a careful breath, and it helped his brain to function again. If she had the torc, then they were connected in another way besides his threat of blackmail. And he very much needed them connected if he were to protect her from the Legion of Baal and the sorceress Nulkana.

He smiled in defeat. "Very well, Princess, you may have it." He removed it and held it out.

Her gaze shifted from his eyes to the piece and back again. She dropped the point of the rapier and used it to hook the gold circlet. "*Grazie.*" The torc slid down the blade to the guard with a silky chime. She plucked it off with her free hand.

"This has nothing to do with our first agreement," he said. "I will expect to see you at the Assembly Rooms this evening."

Her mouth flattened.

Before she could argue, he added, "I'm sure you would not want to be shunned by the society matrons. Rumors of impropriety are so difficult to deny."

She muttered an obscenity in Italian. That golden gaze turned as piercing as the rapier she had just held against his throat.

"You are a very hard man, *signore*," she said.

He smiled, baiting her with his words. "I am as hard as I need to be. Allegra."

"Get out." Her low words were filled with fury. With a swish of her blade, she pointed to a door that he assumed led outside.

Sebastian swept her a sardonic bow, then sauntered to the door. He could feel her gaze between his shoulder blades, as sharp as the rapier she held. Before leaving, he turned and said, "I look forward to many dances with you this evening, Princess. Please don't overtax yourself working in the garden."

He heard her hiss of anger as he stepped outside. He found himself in a corner of the courtyard, and Vulcan, looking quite content, was saddled and tied to a hitching post near the gate. His extended visit with the princess and the nap they had shared had not been as secret as he believed. Her servants seemed to be aware of more than the ordinary retainer. But then, the princess was no ordinary mistress.

Sebastian allowed himself a tiny, satisfied smile. Despite losing the torc, he had discovered quite a bit about the alluring Princess Allegra. And he intended to discover more that evening when he could partner her in as many dances as was proper. And perhaps improper.

Chapter 6

Allegra fumed as she sat in a corner of the Tea Room in the Upper Assembly Rooms. Her view of the room was blocked by a large woman with multiple feathers bobbing above her pink turban, but Allegra did not care. She had little interest in which young miss attended this evening, or who escorted each young lady, or how many times the young lady danced with some besotted swain. She was trying to hide, and so she had chosen this table. It was wedged behind one of the columns that held up the gallery where the musicians sat, so it was not brightly lit by the three large chandeliers. The table was the least desirable in the Tea Room. All the worthy patrons shunned it.

She admitted to herself that hiding was a cowardly thing to do, but she had been coerced to appear at the Assembly Rooms by that rogue, the Earl of Hawksmoor. She feared if she did not, he would carry out his threat of ruining her. Then she would be compelled to find some other country in which to hide. She did not want to have to establish another place where she could indulge the Hunger. And, if she were brutally truthful, she did not want to run away from the man who had touched the Sphere of Astarte and seemed to have as many secrets as she did. Her need to break the curse held her in England. Her desire to remain had absolutely nothing to do with her curiosity about the man. At least, that is what she told herself.

Her reaction to the Earl of Hawksmoor during the Hunger brought heat to her cheeks and a craving for him that felt as if she were still in the grip of the fiend that inhabited her brain. Normally, her memory of that time between Shadow and flesh was foggy and vague, but this time, when all effects of the Hunger should have disappeared, the thought of his kisses, his broad chest, his clear blue eyes, and his gentle embrace made her body throb. She needed to discover why. And perhaps indulge that craving.

Luisa had gone to use the necessary, and so Allegra had a few moments to herself. She tried to put the previous night out of her mind but was only partially successful. She wondered if her brothers had ever had the same reaction to a woman when not suffering through the Hunger. She missed them terribly. A simmering resentment at their prolonged absence and their last enigmatic responses to her letters made her jaw tighten. She hadn't heard from them in two months. A combination of concern and aggravation made her fingers clench on the thin handle of her delicate teacup. She hated tea and had the sudden urge to fling the piece of porcelain across the Tea Room. Instead, she took a breath and pasted a pleasant smile on her lips.

She sensed someone approach from behind and she glanced up, expecting to see Luisa. Instead, a woman of dramatic beauty slid onto the tiny chair across from her. Her black hair, piled on her head in intricate curls, reflected the candlelight with blue highlights. Heavy black lashes shadowed her black eyes. She smiled with lips of crimson.

Allegra stared. She had never seen anyone with such striking, well-defined features. The woman's perfection made her feel dowdy and drab. But while the woman's face glowed with health and perfection, the rest of her seemed a bit out of focus, as if a faint haze surrounded her. Despite that, Allegra was drawn to her, and she smiled back.

"I do not believe we have met, *carina mia*," the woman said.

The woman's words sent a thrill through Allegra. "You are from Italy, *signora?*"

The woman smiled more broadly. "*Si.* From *Venezia*, like you. When I hear that the Princess Allegra is here in this very town that I am visiting, I say to myself that I must make myself known."

"I am so very happy you did," Allegra said, lapsing into Italian.

The woman leaned closer. "So, you are here hiding in plain sight, *si?*"

Taken aback at the woman's correct assumption, Allegra fluttered her fan to give herself time to think. She forced a little laugh. "Why do you think I'm hiding?"

The woman cocked her head. "You are not in *Venezia* or in Auriano. I have heard many whispers that misfortune stalks your family."

Something about the woman seemed strange. That first feeling of connection seeped away. Becoming wary, Allegra feigned surprise. "Misfortune? *Signora,* these are stories made up by my family's enemies. Surely, you cannot believe them."

The woman smiled, but this time it chilled. "Many times, rumors are based in truth." She leaned in, and her voice lowered. "Would you believe that I caused your misfortune, *Principessa?*"

Fear snaked its way down Allegra's spine. The woman sitting before her could not be the one who had caused her family's misfortune. This could not be the evil sorceress Nulkana who had placed the curse on her family so many generations ago.

Whoever this woman was, Allegra wanted to flee from her. She started to rise. "Pardon me, *signora,* but I must find my companion."

The woman reached out and touched the back of her hand, the motion uneven, as if moving her arm caused her some pain. "No, don't go. We have barely met, *carina mia,* and I want to learn all about you."

Allegra sank back into her chair, her knees suddenly weak. A chill crept into her hand where the woman's fingers touched her skin. It seeped into her bones and twined up her arm. She tried to pull away, but her arm seemed frozen. The chill entered her chest and circled her heart. She fought for breath as an icy pain stabbed her.

"Nulkana," she gasped.

Nulkana's smile was serene. "It is a pleasure to finally meet you, *Principessa.*"

"How did you find me?" Allegra strained to speak. Her heart congealed into slush.

The sorceress gave a negligent shrug. "I have ways."

"Spies," Allegra spat.

"If you wish, yes." Nulkana nodded. "I heard you were here. This city is quite fascinating. But I do not understand why it is so fashionable. The waters, they make one distressed. And so many spirits and deities here." She gave a delicate shudder. "I suppose you thought the waters might keep you safe." Her lips tipped up in an evil smile. "But it was rather easy to find you."

Allegra wished she had never revealed her true identity when she first arrived on England's shores. That had been *stupido*. The pain in her chest throbbed and her arm went numb. She forced herself to focus. "You sent me the note. About knowing my secret."

"Yes, yes." Nulkana waved away the accusation. "I do so enjoy my little games. I think you will provide quite a bit of amusement."

"What do you mean to do?" Despite her fear and the frozen numbness in her arm, Allegra wanted to keep Nulkana talking to distract her. If she were quick enough, she could stab the sorceress with her fan that she clutched in the hand resting on her lap, and escape. That fan had been charmed by Luisa as protection against sorcery. But even as she had the thought, the iciness oozed down her other arm, freezing the muscles, paralyzing her hand.

Nulkana tsked. "Do you really believe your little weapon can hurt me?" Her smile was colder than the chill surrounding Allegra's heart.

"You wouldn't dare do anything here," Allegra said, bravely hoping she was right.

"No, not here. The time is not ripe." The sorceress's eyes took on a greedy glint. "But soon enough you will be Shadow. When you return to flesh and bone, I plan on watching you suffer through the Hunger. And then…" She paused, gluttony turning her face ugly. "Then I plan on sucking the life out of you." She licked her red lips. "I have waited a long time for a taste of an Auriano female whelp. Your mother was quite delicious."

Rage surged through Allegra at the mention of her mother. She had been only eight years old, but the memory of watching the sorceress attack her mother was very clear. The sorceress had looked different then, old and desiccated. She wanted to stab Nulkana through the heart until the sorceress's blood ran like water, but she was so frozen she could not move.

A shadow fell over the little table. Allegra jumped, expecting some other nightmare to appear. Instead, she caught the scent of pine and woods. Hawksmoor. A different fear clutched at her. Despite their differences, she did not want him harmed by the sorceress.

Go away, she sent silently.

"There you are, Princess," he said, obviously ignoring her plea.

Nulkana glanced up. Her eyes narrowed and turned colder than two stones in winter. "What do you want?"

"I believe I have the next dance with the Princess Allegra," Hawksmoor replied in a smooth tone.

Allegra closed her eyes, partly in relief and partly in exasperation at the man's persistence.

"We are talking," Nulkana snapped. "Leave us."

"I don't believe I will," Hawksmoor said. "And I don't believe you wish to allow everyone to see your true appearance."

Surprise hit Allegra with a jolt as she realized he knew who Nulkana was. The sorceress snatched back her hand, leaving a tiny scratch on Allegra's skin. At her release, immediate warmth seeped into Allegra's muscles. Nulkana stood, her body hidden by a cloak of swirling gray mist.

"This is not the end, Priest," the sorceress hissed. She turned and stalked away, becoming more indistinct as she melded into the crowd, then she disappeared.

Shivers shook Allegra and her heart hurt, but she was finally able to move. She looked up into Hawksmoor's blue eyes. "*Grazie.*" It was the only word she could manage.

His warm gaze was punctuated by the imprint of the moon. "My pleasure."

The iciness around her heart seeped away, but she could not seem to get warm. She felt as if the sorceress had drained all the heat from her blood. The only warmth she could find was in those blue eyes that regarded her with concern.

Allegra fell into that gaze. Her own eyes grew heavy. She wanted to ask him something, but she hurt too much and she could not form a thought. Before she realized what was happening, he had scooped her out of the chair and into his arms. His warm strength comforted despite the niggling notion that she should not allow him such liberties. She murmured a wordless objection.

"We are leaving here, lovely lady, whether you wish it or not," Hawksmoor whispered. "You have just encountered a very evil woman, and you are shivering as if you have the ague. You have been brave enough for one evening."

She did not have the energy to debate. Around them, excited exclamations erupted in the crowd at his brazen behavior. He ignored them and opened a path to the door with murmured apologies and glares. Allegra hid her face against his shoulder as she fought icy shivers. She might have even fainted, for the next thing she knew, she was seated in a coach, wrapped in a fur throw, and hugged close to a muscular chest. The scent of him filled her nose. Clean pine and warm, earthy woods. She burrowed into that warmth, knowing she was being extremely improper but reluctant to dissolve the cocoon of safety. The memory of Nulkana's touch still chilled her.

Someone rapped on the door of the coach. An indignant voice demanded entrance. The door swung open.

"Do you intend to destroy the reputation of *la principessa, Sior* Hawksmoor?" Luisa demanded.

Allegra shot upright as guilt at her intimate position swept through her. The world spun and she grabbed the first thing she could — the muscular arm of the man who had rescued her. He covered her hand with his large one and whispered something. His touch and the intimate murmur soothed her spinning head.

"Do not chastise him, Luisa," she said. "He saved me."

Luisa scowled at Hawksmoor's protective hand.

"Please, *Donna* Luisa, come sit with us," he said.

"I am not *la donna*," Luisa muttered, but she picked up her skirts and entered the coach. Ernesto, who had hovered at her shoulder, remained outside and shut the door behind her. When she had settled herself in the seat across from them, she asked, "So. How did this man save you? And from what?"

"Nulkana." Allegra spoke the name with a shiver, but she was feeling warmer and safer.

Luisa went very still. Her gaze cut to Hawksmoor.

"The sorceress seemed afraid of him," Allegra said as she turned speculative eyes on the man beside her.

He shrugged. "Nulkana was more concerned about revealing who she was in the middle of the Assembly Rooms and her true appearance."

"But she called you *Priest*," Allegra persisted.

He smiled and waved away her comment.

"She called him *Priest*, because he is," her Guide said. "He is a Druid." Luisa pinned him with her gaze. "*Si?*"

A muscle jumped in his jaw and his eyes chilled. Allegra immediately thought of the times when those beautiful blue eyes seemed to hold the moon in them. And the time she had heard a summons on the breeze. And the way he had remembered their connection during the Hunger despite her inducing him to forget.

She knew her Guide spoke the truth. Druids were powerful, able to control the elementals — air, earth, fire, and water — and possibly demons from Hell, although no one had proven that. Their mental abilities were astounding. They could be strong allies or harsh enemies, depending upon their whim. Until she determined on which side this man fell, she would need to be very careful about what she said and how she acted with him. She pulled her hand from beneath his and slid onto the seat opposite him, next to Luisa. She ignored the loss of warmth from his body.

"Does that gold circlet I borrowed have a connection to your power?" she asked.

He raised a cool brow. "It is called a torc, lovely lady, and you did not borrow it. You *stole* it."

Allegra noticed he did not answer her question. And he never acknowledged Luisa's accusation. But silence indicated affirmation. She smiled. "It is a guarantee for keeping a secret, *si?*"

His eyes narrowed. "What shall I *borrow* from you to keep my secret?"

Luisa spoke up. "You will borrow nothing, *Sior* Hawksmoor." The small feather in her turban vibrated with indignation. "*La principessa* does not gossip, nor does she reveal secrets that are given into her care." She rapped on the door of the coach. It swung open immediately. "Come, *principessa*. We are done."

Allegra watched as Ernesto, who obviously had been standing guard outside, handed Luisa out of the coach. Then with an impudent grin at Hawksmoor, she followed her Guide.

Stunned at the swift turn the conversation had taken and the quick exit of the two ladies, Sebastian stared at the closed door of his coach. The princess's chaperone had somehow divined that he was a Druid. Extraordinary. Even if Allegra had shown her the torc, he would not have guessed that she knew what it signified, for it was a closely guarded secret. *Signora* Luisa was more than a chaperone for the princess. Much more. He was reminded of his very brief, unexpected encounter with the coachman of the princess's brother, Prince Alessandro, in Milan, when the servant had surprised him in the stables. While the man had been perfectly civil, something about him put Sebastian on alert. He surmised the man had some uncommon ability but had paid it little attention. Many people were imbued with minor, untapped faculties. Now, he realized that both the prince and the princess had people around them who were more than servants and protected them with more than their physical presence. Very likely, the duke, the prince's twin and Allegra's other brother, also had a protector.

He rapped on the ceiling of his coach, indicating that he was ready to leave. As the vehicle lurched into motion, he mused about this new wrinkle in his association with the lovely Princess Allegra. He would have to be careful. If his secret — *secrets* — were ever revealed, he would end up dead. And his death would not be an easy one.

He put that thought out of his head as he contemplated how to disarm the princess into returning his torc. It was safe in her hands for now, as long as she did not discover its secrets. but with the appearance of Nulkana this evening, he would have need of it soon. He surmised the sorceress was not yet able to tap her full power, otherwise, she would not have been surrounding herself in that misty cloud. He remembered the last time he had seen her at the mansion of the Marquis de Vernoux in Paris, when she had incinerated Le Chacal, the King of Thieves of Paris. She had only been a projection, and a very powerful one, but she had been hurt.

Tonight, had not been a projection. He knew that from the way her touch had affected the Princess Allegra. If the sorceress regained her full potential for evil, the princess and everyone around her would be in terrible danger, more than they were now. And the Legion of Baal would have a full-blown war with her, not the surreptitious race they were running to find the magical Sphere of Astarte.

No matter what happened, he knew he was on the front line of this battle, even though he conducted his maneuvers in the background. And in order to keep the princess safe, he had to keep himself safe while walking a dangerous tightrope.

He sighed as a headache began to pulse behind his eyes, but when his coach turned into the drive of his house, he sat up abruptly. The windows were lit up as if a ball were in progress. Since he had invited no one, he could not imagine why Quint had decided to illuminate all the rooms.

His coach had barely come to a stop as he bounded up the stairs. Quint stood in the open door. Sebastian's butler bowed and greeted him solemnly, but he had a dazed look in his eyes.

"Quint," Sebastian demanded. "What goes on here?"

"My lord," his butler intoned. "Your lady mother has arrived home."

Sebastian bit back his groan. The headache that had merely been a pulsing annoyance became a decided pounding. He loved his mother dearly, and he enjoyed her as long as she behaved. He could tolerate her company in small doses. But she was demanding of his attention when she was near, even though he was far from her thoughts when she was away. She was charming and vivacious and in constant motion, at the same time she was profligate and self-centered, and from what Sir Cyril had told him, ran with a wild crowd in London. She was his father's third wife, the only one who had provided him with a living heir, and so his father had doted on her every whim. His father was dead, so she expected her beloved son—Sebastian—to indulge her. Which he was very happy to do as long as he could do it from a distance.

He stepped into the foyer and heard the rush of servants at the back of the house and below stairs. Only his mother, arriving unaccompanied and unannounced, could create such commotion among the staff. He handed Quint his hat and gloves. At the same time, he mentally armored himself against whatever capricious mood his mother decided to indulge.

"The Countess of Hawksmoor is in the upper drawing room, my lord," Quint said.

Sebastian eyed the stairs as if he were examining ground held by an opposing army. Then drawing a bracing breath, he went to greet his mother.

He found her, not in the upper drawing room, where tea and toast were laid out for her, but in her sitting room, reclining on a fainting couch, with a cool compress over her eyes. Her maid, competent and long-suffering, hovered near with a replacement cloth. The smell of rose water hung heavy in the air.

"Mother," he said to gain her attention.

She pulled the cloth from her face and blinked, revealing eyes just as blue as his own. A weak smile curved her lips. He noticed her pale cheeks, a sure sign she was suffering one of her megrims. She waved away her maid, who disappeared through the door into the dressing room.

"Sebastian, love, come give your mother a kiss." Her voice matched her cheeks.

Dutifully, he crossed the space between them and gently kissed her on the forehead.

"I must have missed the message that you were coming to visit," he said.

Her eyes crinkled in amusement. "You know I sent no message. I wished to surprise you."

"You have accomplished what you set out to do." He pulled up a chair and sat. "Why are you here, Mother?"

She glanced away and picked at the lace on her dressing gown. "Can't I just come to see my son? Must I have a reason?"

Sebastian was not going to fall for her deception. "I know how you hate the country, and Bath in particular. You made it quite clear that you find London much more to your liking."

"London does not like me," she mumbled.

Sebastian surmised her profligate spending had brought her running back to Blackbrake. Usually, she merely sent a letter asking for funds. To bestir herself and travel must mean that her situation was quite dire.

"Too many chits at the gaming tables? Too many debts at the dressmaker's?" At each of his suggestions, the line between her brows deepened.

"I should not have to explain myself," she sniffed. "And certainly not to my son."

"Especially to your son." He contradicted gently because he remembered Sir Cyril's report that his mother was socializing with Crowley, a member of the Legion of Baal, and not one of his favorite people. The association could be purely innocuous, a way for Crowley to consort with those higher up the social scale and gather crumbs of respectability, but he tended to think that Crowley was plotting something devious. What better way to get to The Messenger than through his mother? The last thing he wanted was to put his mother in danger by alerting her to the precarious situation, because then she would do something foolish, like try to protect him.

But Crowley had already appeared in Bath, days before the countess. He had been present at Lady Hetherington's garden party. And Sebastian had suggested that the lovely Princess Allegra should spy on Crowley as part of their bargain. At the time, he thought it was a safe way to demonstrate the truth of his disreputable reputation, and at the same time give her a chance to gain information about the Sphere of Astarte for her own benefit. He also thought he might learn the reason why Crowley had ingratiated himself with the countess. Now, with his mother's arrival, he suspected a darker plot was in motion. But he had no idea what it might be.

His mother concentrated on folding and refolding the cloth she had pulled from her eyes.

"How much do you owe at the modiste's?" he asked.

"Really, Sebastian," she said, affronted. "I haven't bought a decent gown in months."

"Then?" he prodded.

She let out an exasperated breath. "If you must know, I lost the curricle."

Sebastian forced himself not to react. Even though he had contemplated replacing the vehicle, the loss was an aggravation he did not want to deal with at the moment.

"I see," he said. "At faro? Whist?"

She swallowed. "Dice," she said, barely above a whisper.

Sebastian choked. "Mother! You were at a gaming hell?"

The countess waved away his protest and sent him a parental look warning him to watch his tongue. Then she went back to folding the cloth. Something else was bothering her besides the loss of the curricle. After several moments, she raised her head and met his gaze.

"I find myself in a bit of a bother, Sebastian," she said. "It seems I let drop a bit of information about something I shouldn't."

He reminded himself not to jump to conclusions. His mother could have merely revealed what Prince George's paramour might be wearing at the next ball, which would certainly cast a pall over her social standing for a time but would not put her in danger.

Forcing his voice to remain level, he asked, "What did you reveal?"

"Well, you know how those French émigrés love to turn up their noses at our fashions." She waved her hand dismissively, as if what she had to say was inconsequential. "I may have mentioned to the Vicomtesse D'Aramitz that you had recently traveled to Italy and France and were certainly up to the mark."

On the surface, her comment to the lady about his haberdashery was innocent enough, merely stating that he was traveling on the Continent as many men of means were wont to do. But if anyone gave the remark any thought at all, it would reveal that he had been traveling in one country where the French had successfully invaded Milan and Venice, and then traveled in the very country the English looked upon as an enemy. Because of the war, travel by Englishmen in both Italy and France was difficult and restricted. Anyone with a suspicious mind or anyone who happened to be watching him might deduce the truth: that he was working for the undersecretary to gather information. His other, more clandestine reason for being in those countries — that he was The Messenger for the Lord High of the Legion of Baal — might be harder to deduce, but still...

His mother looked guilt-ridden and miserable. He had made her promise not to reveal where he was traveling. While she did not know the specifics of where he had been, she knew he had been in both Italy and France on a "diplomatic mission." He had to keep her unaware of how serious her mistake had been. If she knew, she would isolate herself as penance, thus prompting speculation and gossip among her peers. Gossip could be deadly and change into something else as it snaked its way through the *ton* and landed on ears that harbored malevolent plots. She had to behave normally, and he had to act as if her slip did not matter. Otherwise, both their lives could be in jeopardy, along with that of the lovely Princess Allegra.

He forced a smile. "I appreciate that you spoke for me, mother. I will be sure to pass along your compliment to my valet and my haberdasher."

Relief eased his mother's features. "Oh, I am so glad. I truly thought…"

As he waved away her concern, he said, "I have been thinking that this house has been quiet for too long. We should entertain."

His mother brightened, her headache completely forgotten. "Oh, that is a wonderful idea! A ball. Yes! I will start planning right away."

As his mother prattled about who to invite, and what they should serve and all the details she would have to oversee, Sebastian congratulated himself. Having a ball would divert attention away from any speculation that he was in hiding. At the same time, his mother would be occupied with the planning, and he would be free to spend time with the Princess Allegra. He might even suggest that his mother involve her in the preparations, a convenient way to have the princess close. He would be able to watch over her and perhaps learn more about her secrets.

And having the princess close by would be a delightful diversion.

But as he took leave of his mother, the memory of Nulkana's appearance at the Assembly Rooms sent a chill down his spine. The sorceress was becoming bold, perhaps even desperate. She had been injured in the confrontation in Paris, and that might have been the reason for her brazen appearance in public this evening seeking sustenance from Allegra. But then she had left when he confronted her. That raised his suspicions, for he had expected some resistance and had been prepared to use his gifts to protect the princess. He had not seen much of the conversation between the two, but the physical reaction of the princess told him that Nulkana had used her evil power in some way. His concern over the well-being of the princess made him resolve that he would pay her a visit the next day. Whether he was welcome or not.

Chapter 7

The next morning, after a night spent tossing and turning, Sebastian rode toward the priory. He tried to convince himself his sleeplessness stemmed from concern over the well-being of the princess. An encounter with Nulkana was not an occurrence to take lightly. But as he flopped over first one way and then another in his solitary bed, the cheeky grin she tossed at him as she exited his coach seemed to be imprinted on the inside of his eyelids. That, and the memory of her luscious body snuggled against him as she recovered from her ordeal. When he rose that morning feeling out of sorts and decidedly unsatisfied, he determined the only way to rectify the situation was to pay a visit to the lovely lady.

He was not sure if she had remained in Bath for the night, but the memory of their encounter in the priory garden drew him like a siren's song to the run-down place. If she were not at the priory, then he would ride into the city. He told himself he merely wanted to be sure of her safety after the encounter with Nulkana. But he knew his decision to follow the overgrown lane across the meadow had more than gentlemanly concern behind it.

The day was misty, so he did not expect to see the princess in her garden. When he saw a slight figure wrapped in a voluminous cloak standing in the middle of a tangle of huge weeds, he was surprised. She turned at his approach.

He could not see her face, shadowed within the cowl, but he sensed her distress. Something was clearly wrong.

He stopped at the crumbled wall. "Princess." He greeted her with a bow of his head.

She took a step forward, hesitated, then retreated. She seemed to be cradling one arm with the other. "Luisa will not be pleased to find you in my garden, *Sior* Hawksmoor," she said, her words low and flat.

He refused to become annoyed at her poor manners. Instead, he forced his response to mildness. "I came to see how you fared, Princess."

"I am well," she said.

He did not believe her. He let his gaze wander around the misty ground. "The weather doesn't seem conducive to a stroll in the garden."

Her shoulders rose and fell with a small shrug. "I was in need of some air." But then she could not quite conceal the shiver that followed her words.

"Princess, you are cold." He dismounted and looped the reins around a wild bush. "Allow me to help you inside where you will be warm."

She nodded, giving permission to cross the crumbling wall, so he stepped over the stones and ignored the slight sizzle of the wards. But the tight lines of pain around her eyes made him stop abruptly.

"I cannot be warm, *Sior* Hawksmoor," she said. She turned from him. "Go away. I can never be warm again."

Her desolate words stabbed through him. Despite her wish for solitude, he moved closer. Another shiver slid through her.

"Princess," he said again as he stopped before her.

She raised her head. Shadowed by the cowl, he saw pain clouding her eyes and sharpening her features.

"Do you never do as you are asked, *Sior* Hawksmoor?" she snapped. But then she shivered again, and she grimaced.

"You are hurt." He reached out and took her by the elbow to steady her. She gasped in pain. Without another thought, he scooped her up to carry her inside.

"Put me down. *Subito!*" she hissed.

He was not about to put her down, immediately or otherwise. Anger at her guardian for allowing the princess to wander in the damp garden rose up in him. He ignored the weak wriggling of the woman in his arms as he moved to the door. And he ignored the reaction of his body to the feel of her soft curves clutched against his chest. His intent focused on seeing to the comfort of the princess and then to have a word or two with the woman who cared for her.

The door stood slightly ajar and opened easily with a nudge of his boot. He stepped into the kitchen, clean and warmed by a fire in the large hearth. A young servant girl stirred something in a pot over the flames. She turned to him with a gasp. At his brusque request, she pointed him in the direction of the princess's bed chamber.

As he strode through the great hall and up a winding flight of stone steps, the princess murmured, "You should not...You can't..." Her words faded with another shiver.

"Shush, lovely lady. We need to get you warm." He hurried up the last few steps and to a landing at the top of the small turret in the priory.

A fire burned in the hearth. A cushioned chair and footstool sat before it. He crossed the room and gently set her down in the chair. A large bed with dark blue hangings and coverlet sat in one corner. He grabbed the coverlet and tucked it around her.

"You are ill," he said. "Where is your companion? Why does Mistress Luisa allow you to roam about in the chilly garden when you should be in bed?"

She tilted up her chin and gave him an impish smile. "Because she did not know I was outside."

Her grin did something to the muscles in his chest.

Before he could collect his thoughts enough to respond, her smile faded and turned upside down. "I wished to see the garden one last time."

Sebastian's brow crinkled. "What are you saying?"

She turned away. "Nulkana—" Her voice broke. She swallowed and started again. "Nulkana did something. My hand..."

He knelt before her as fear wormed its way through him. "Show me."

She hesitated a moment. Then she moved beneath the coverlet and a small, bandaged hand appeared.

"Luisa did all she could," she said. "She says it will get better— or not—in a few days."

He did not hesitate. "I may be able to help," he said. After all, he reasoned, she already knew what he was.

"How can you help?" she demanded. "Luisa has had much experience with this evil. While I know little of your experience, *si*?"

He met her gaze and allowed her to see some of his power. Despite not having his torc, his power thrummed deep inside him, dormant and not quite as powerful as he wished, yet ready to gather at his call. Her lips parted, and her eyes darkened in response to what she saw in his eyes. He knew nothing of Luisa's ability, but if he could overlay his ability with hers, they might be able to help the princess.

He cradled her hand in his as he unwrapped the linen strips. They were wound up to her elbow. Her skin beneath was icy to the touch and held a bluish tinge. The veins stood out darkly indigo, nearly black. The scent of various herbs teased his nose, telling him Luisa had used healing balms and potions. Beneath that scent was another thread, faint but distinctive, singing of magic. So, the woman who guarded the princess had some ability. The knowledge reassured him.

"I can feel nothing in my hand or arm," the princess said, as she gazed down forlornly at her poor limb. "Almost as if—"

"As if what, Princess?" he prompted.

She shook her head. "It matters little."

He knew it mattered more than a little, for he suspected what she had been about to say. Ancient Nulkana remained alive by sucking the life out of beautiful young women. The princess's arm looked as if the sorceress had attempted that the night before. He was not going to let that happen again, and his resolve to protect the woman before him strengthened.

"Allow me to help you." He lifted her hand to his lips and gently pressed a kiss to her cold, cold skin.

As soon as his lips touched her, Allegra felt a pulse of warmth. Her breath hitched at the sweetness of it. Her hand and forearm had been numb and icy all night. All sensation had leeched from her during the trip back to the priory after leaving Hawksmoor's coach outside the Assembly Rooms. By the time she reached her bed chamber, she had no feeling from the fingertips of her left hand to her elbow. She was afraid she was prematurely turning to Shadow, when she had no sense of touch, but the rest of her remained normal. Then she realized that this was not part of the curse, and fear gripped her belly. Nulkana had done this to her.

That fleeting warmth from Hawksmoor's lips gave her hope that perhaps he could help. Or perhaps she had imagined it, her mind playing tricks and making her feel something that was not there. For she did very much want to be able to feel his lips against her skin. But that was not an option for her. Not when part of her had turned to ice. Not when she turned to Shadow twice during the moon's cycle. And she certainly would never tell him what she craved, for he might hold that as leverage over her. But perhaps he held the answer to solving the problem of her icy arm.

She wondered if she could trust him. She had kidnapped him, chained him against a wall, and seduced him. He had retaliated by forcing her into a disagreeable arrangement of spying for him, although she had yet to perform that task. But he had been solicitous after the meeting with Nulkana, and now he seemed truly troubled by her condition. Perhaps he did wish to help her, if only for his own purposes.

"I feel I was ungracious at your arrival, *Sior* Hawksmoor. Forgive me. If you could do something," she said, "I would be grateful."

"There is nothing to forgive, princess. You are feeling poorly." A corner of his mouth quirked up in a wry smile. "We will explore your gratitude later, after you are feeling better." Then he became serious as he rose to his feet and strode to the bell pull.

Luisa appeared in the doorway soon after. She stiffened and her brows drew together when she saw the earl. "You are not welcome here, *signore*, especially not in *la principessa's* bed chamber."

"Luisa, *per piacere*, let him help." Allegra's words were polite, but they held command as well.

"How do you know he will not use dark magic to turn you to his will?" her Guide demanded. "He is a Druid priest."

Allegra drew herself up, ignoring the chill that ran through her. "Your balms have done little. I say he can help." She relented when she saw the hurt reflected in her Guide's eyes. "Please Luisa."

Hawksmoor stepped forward. "If I wished to harm the princess, I could have done so before now."

"But that does not say you will not harm her in the future," Luisa snapped.

"None of us knows what will happen in the future," he said mildly.

A deep, throbbing ache in Allegra's elbow drew an involuntary moan from her. She felt as if her forearm would fall off. And then she lost sensation in the joint.

Hawksmoor sent a concerned glance her way, then turned back to her Guide. "We are wasting time, *signora*. As we stand here arguing, the princess grows worse."

Allegra saw the indecision on her Guide's face. Despite her own misgivings about the earl, fear made her reckless, wanting to try any solution to her growing problem—even trusting Hawksmoor enough that she would let him use his Druid magic.

"Luisa. Enough." Her reprimand sounded more like a plea.

Her Guide hesitated, then bowed her head in compliance. "What do you need, *Sior* Hawksmoor?"

"I'll need ivy," he said with relief in his voice. "And pine needles."

Luisa sent him a skeptical look, but she retreated to collect the items.

Hawksmoor knelt before Allegra. He took her hand in his much larger one. She wished she could feel him, for he held her hand as if it were priceless porcelain. The loss of touch while she was Shadow was hard to endure, but having the condition while she was flesh and bone was even more difficult.

"Thank you for allowing me to help you," he said.

Her lips twisted wryly. "I have little choice, *si*?"

"We always have a choice." His blue eyes seemed to bore into her. "Do you trust me, Princess?"

Her previous misgivings flitted through her head. But his actions seemed to contradict them. For some reason she did trust him, at least in this. But she could not give him the power of knowing that. She remained mute.

He waited for her answer, his gaze probing. When she said nothing, his head bowed over her hand. "I would never harm you," he said, his voice muffled.

And then he placed his lips against her skin once more.

The pulse of warmth on the back of her hand was unmistakable. She fought not to react, but she could not hide the breath she sucked into her lungs. And there, where his mouth had touched, was a small spot of pink skin again. She watched, fascinated, dismayed, as it slowly disappeared, and her hand was once more tinged an icy blue-white.

But for that fleeting moment, she was able to feel him.

Sebastian heard her tiny intake of breath and saw the pale pink spot where his lips left an imprint on the back of her hand. He watched it slowly fade. From her reaction, he assumed she had been able to feel him. He wondered at the connection between them, as fleeting as it was, that broke through whatever curse or charm Nulkana had placed on her.

Luisa returned then with two baskets, one overflowing with pine needles and the other trailing ivy vines. She placed them beside him on the floor.

"As you requested, *Sior* Hawksmoor," she said. "Ivy and pine." Her tone was chilly. "If you harm the princess —"

"Luisa," the princess interrupted. "Please leave us."

The woman sent a glare at Sebastian, gave a sniff, turned on her heel and left.

"Please, *Sior* Hawksmoor, continue," the princess said. Hope brightened her eyes.

Sebastian first took his hair out of its queue and twined it into a single long braid. The twist of the braid would confuse whatever spell Nulkana had placed on the princess. He drew a breath and let it out slowly to clear his mind. Taking the ivy, he wrapped it around the small hand resting in his palm. Then he twined more up her arm beyond her elbow. After resting her arm along his and placing his hand on top, he took another breath and released it.

His power began to gather. Runes danced in the air before his eyes. The forces he called upon were dangerous. They could be capricious, benevolent one moment, fiendish the next. Apprehension slid through him. He missed his torc. Not only did it focus his power, it also protected him from charms bouncing back and harming him. He pushed away his misgivings and focused. This was not the time for cowardly qualms.

He could feel Nulkana's evil as a discordant thrum through the sluggish pulse in the slight arm beneath his hand. And he could sense the fear of the woman before him. She was afraid of what was happening to her. And she was afraid of him. He wanted to erase that fear but knew he would not. That fear kept her alive, at least for now. He hated himself for deceiving her. When she learned what he kept secret, she would despise him. He wanted to postpone that as long as possible, for he enjoyed the princess. Despite *her* secrets.

Allegra had no feeling in the arm that rested upon Hawksmoor's, but as soon as he wrapped the ivy around it, her shivers stopped. His strength and calm soothed her, despite her apprehension. The moon appeared in his eyes, and she thought she glimpsed strange symbols hanging in the air. And then he began to chant.

"*Tóg ar shiúl an phian. Imigh uaim a dheamhan.*"

The syllables made no sense to her, but they sounded like: *Toag aer sool um pe-un. Emmay oon a jow-en.*

His voice was low and quiet. The chant wound around her, calming her with its rhythm. She felt herself drifting on the pure tone. He chanted the same syllables over and over.

"*Tóg ar shiúl an phian. Imigh uaim a dheamhan.*"

She became drowsy. Her eyes slipped shut. A sense of peace draped over her. His voice curled around her, enveloping her in its warmth, lulling her with his words.

"Tóg ar shiúl an phian. Imigh uaim a dheamhan."

Her hand and arm began to throb with a dull, deep-seated ache. Prickles, like pins and needles, ran along the surface of her skin. She gritted her teeth at the discomfort. She would not make a sound, not if his healing brought her sensation.

He continued his chant. *"Tóg ar shiúl an phian. Imigh uaim a dheamhan."*

Heat pulsed in her arm, obliterating the throb and pricklings. She welcomed the sensation. But it became hotter and hotter. The throbbing ache intensified, became a pounding in her veins, beneath her skin. The tingles became knife pricks, each one a minute stab of sharp pain. Without thinking, she grabbed his wrist with her free hand, the tips of her fingers against his pulse. And she fell into his mind.

She saw him standing in a small glen before a large fire. He was dressed in a kilt and nothing else. His bare chest gleamed in the light from the flames. His arms were spread, and his palms were open in supplication. His head was thrown back, his hair completely plaited in many thin braids and hanging down his back in a black spill. He looked like a pagan priest from antiquity, supplicating a barbaric god. He chanted, the same chant that wound around her. Dark runes and symbols appeared on his biceps and across his chest, scrolling, winding, curling into intricate designs, then fading to nothing, only to appear and grow once more.

She was transfixed by his beauty. She was in awe of the power that flowed from him. His body was magnificent, muscular and honed. She had the urge to go to him, to wrap her arms around his waist and lick him. Appalled at the thought, she focused on his chant instead. She heard it as he pronounced it before her, and she heard it in her head. It filled her with its potent energy. For the first time since Nulkana had done this thing to her, she felt some optimism. The man before her could help her. He was powerful.

He suddenly looked at her across the flames. His eyes were no longer a true, clear blue, but black, with that disk of the moon in them. She knew he saw her, but most of his attention was focused inward. She sensed his displeasure at her presence, and then he seemed to dismiss her, returning once again to his chanting, his head thrown back, his strong throat exposed in the firelight.

And then, abruptly, a curtain of nothingness fell before her and she was closed off from him. He had pushed her out of his mind. She gasped at his ability to do that and her eyes flew open.

She was in her bed chamber and he knelt before her. He was fully and elegantly clothed. She expected him to glance at her, acknowledge what had happened. But his concentration never wavered from her arm. He continued to chant as if nothing had happened.

"Tóg ar shiúl an phian. Imigh uaim a dheamhan."

The discomfort in her arm became unbearable. She squeezed her eyes shut, squeezed his wrist, and ground her teeth together to hold in her cries of pain. And then, in an instant, it all disappeared — the pain, the throbbing ache, the pins and needles, the intense heat.

He paused in his chanting and took a breath. He gently laid her arm on her knee and disengaged his wrist from her tight grip. Without a word to her, he scooped up a huge handful of pine needles, stood, and threw them into the fire. As they caught the flames in a whoosh, he repeated his chant once more in a deep, booming voice.

"Tóg ar shiúl an phian. Imigh uaim a dheamhan."

And then silence. He remained turned to the fire, his fists clenched by his sides. He stood in profile to her. The skin over his jaw and cheekbone was stretched tight, as if the bones beneath had been sculpted from stone.

Allegra drew a breath and glanced down at her arm, now completely back to normal beneath the wreathing of ivy. No iciness claimed it. Her skin was warm and tinged a healthy hue. Her blood pulsed with life through her veins. She stared at him, amazed that he had been able to heal her. And amazed, as well, at his ability to push her from his mind when she had unconsciously used Thought-Binding.

"My arm... It's healed." Tears threatened and she swallowed them down. *"Grazie,"* she said in awe when he turned back to her.

His eyes had lost the moon and returned to their normal color, but their blue seemed to have taken on an icy tinge. His expression had turned stark.

He nodded. "You're quite welcome, princess."

"I have never seen... I didn't know... Your ability is quite powerful," she said.

A cool brow quirked up. "As is yours."

His manner had changed, becoming remote and distant, as if they had never exchanged a word, as if they had never been skin to skin, as if they had never experienced an erotic dance of their minds. Allegra was unsure how to proceed, but she knew that she wanted his cool, remote manner gone. She wanted to tell him how beautiful he was in his kilt, with his braided hair hanging free and his skin gleaming in the firelight. But years of keeping her distance from any man held her tongue.

Instead, she said, "The chant was beautiful. What does it mean?"

He was silent a moment, his gaze seeming to bore into her thoughts. Finally, he gave a small shrug, as if the chant were of little consequence. "Take away the pain. Begone evil spirit."

Such simple words to achieve so much. She glanced down at her hand, pink and healthy, and marveled again at his ability. To overcome Nulkana's sorcery was no small feat. Wanting to know more about him, she tipped up her head in challenge. "Perhaps we should discuss our abilities."

"Perhaps we should." He stepped back, and the action emphasized the distance between them. "But another time. You should rest now." He bowed. "I will take my leave."

When he turned to go, reluctant to let him, she said, "*Sior* Hawksmoor, you never gave the reason for your visit here this morning."

He stopped halfway to the door. He seemed to be struggling with something, although he was trying very hard to hide it. Slowly, he turned back to her. "I came to see how you fared, lovely lady, and to tell you that my mother is planning a ball. She would be delighted if you could come for tea, if that would please you. She would be most interested in hearing of the balls and masquerades from your homeland."

Allegra felt a pleasant thrill at his warm term for her and the fact that he wanted her to help his mother. So, she was not the reason for his chilly manner. She smiled.

"I would be honored to visit your mother," she said, then held up her healed arm. "And I am very grateful—more than grateful for your help."

He bowed again, but this time, a corner of his mouth curled up just the slightest bit. "I am always ready to help a lady in distress."

With that, he was gone.

Allegra felt the loss of his warm presence keenly, as if a chilly breeze had swirled through the room. But her arm seemed to be healed, and his mother had invited her to tea. She smiled. Her life held few positive moments, so she relished them when they came. But her thoughts snagged abruptly.

How could she face *Sior* Hawksmoor's mother after what she'd done to him? She had kidnapped him, chained him to a wall, and shared that erotic dance. The memory of that made her cheeks heat as well as other parts of her body.

But perhaps his mother might reveal some of his secrets. Like why the moon appeared in his eyes. And how he had been able to heal her arm. And why he seemed to be the only one who satisfied her craving when she entered the Hunger. No, she would not ask his mother about that last.

She ran her fingers over her arm, savoring the warmth of her skin. Dealing with the embarrassment of facing his mother would be worth the discomfort if she could get the answers to her questions. If he could help protect her from Nulkana, she would definitely stay close to him. Not an unpleasant task. She enjoyed his company. The thought of being with him evoked a warmth inside her that had nothing to do with the heat from the fire.

She smiled in anticipation. Despite the dreariness of the weather, despite the malignant threat of the evil sorceress, her day held a tiny ray of sunshine.

Sebastian could not escape from the priory fast enough. He swung up onto Vulcan and spurred him into a gallop. But he did not head back to Blackbrake. Instead he headed into the woods.

The chill that had invaded the arm of the princess had some-how seeped into his soul. He had been foolish to attempt to cure her without his torc. He should have asked her for it. Instead, he had stupidly, arrogantly forged ahead without it.

Branches whipped across his face as he plunged deep into the woods. He did not slow until he came to a barrow, its mound tree-less but covered in a thick layer of moss. A small opening near its bottom, hidden by vines, allowed entrance. He flung himself from Vulcan's back and ducked through into complete darkness. The interior would have been dim on a sunny day, but with the mist and heavy clouds, no light penetrated the gloom. He stepped carefully, using his memory as his guide. When his boot scraped across a large, flat stone, he stopped.

He pounded his heel against the stone three times, waited a heart-beat, then three more times. The sound of leather on stone rang deep in the ground far below. It was oddly muted in the space around him. He waited. One heartbeat. Two. Five. Eleven. He began to despair that his visit would be in vain. If his summons were ignored, he was not sure he could last through the day. Whatever Nulkana had done to the princess was affecting him far more than he ever could have imagined.

Finally, a faint glow appeared in the space before him. Slowly, it became brighter and larger. It swirled a bit, and then coalesced into three distinct human forms. His father, his grandfather, his great-grandfather. All dead, but powerful Druids.

Sebastian bowed low before them. "My apologies for disturbing your rest, Great Ones. I need your help."

"Of course, you do," his father said, his tone dry. "Why else would you come to us?"

"Leave the boy be, Michael," his great-grandfather said. "He looks to be in some distress."

The three spirits floated closer. Sebastian felt their energy like a warm breeze across his skin. If only he could draw that into his freezing soul.

"What ails you, boy?" Edward, his grandfather, circled around him. "Your aura is wrong."

Sebastian sucked a breath into his lungs. He felt as if his chest were congealing into a solid mass. "Nulkana," he forced out.

The three spirits reared back. Then they all crowded close and spoke at once.

"How...?"

"When...?"

"I knew it...

"Were you daft to...?"

"What possessed you to...?"

"How did you...?"

"I cannot believe after all we taught you..."

Sebastian sank to one knee, unable to remain upright. "Stop, please," he gasped. "Can you help me?"

Michael, his father, floated closer. Sebastian felt his hand, like a touch of sunlight, land on his head.

"Of course, we can help you," Michael said. And then he jerked back his hand. "Where is your torc?" he asked in dismay.

Sebastian knew they would be able to sense its absence sooner or later. He just wished it had been later, after they had helped him.

"I lost it," he confessed.

That sent the three spirits into another round of questions, all running together, none of which he had the energy to separate and answer. Finally, Richard, his great-grandfather, put a stop to it all with a single word.

"You know better than to use charms without it," Michael admonished.

"We will deal with the boy's carelessness later," Richard said. "Tell us quickly what happened."

In as few words as possible, in short phrases, Sebastian related the appearance of the sorceress and what had happened to the Princess Allegra. And then he told them of the events that brought him to their sanctuary.

"He was brave," Richard said.

"We would have done the same," Edward conceded.

"And he did braid his hair," Michael admitted.

Sebastian felt his braid lifted and a hand run down its length before it fell heavily against his back. He knew they would scold and delay for a while before they granted his request for help, because he had done something unforgivably stupid. He just wished they would hurry. His heart felt as if it were congealing into a chilled, jellied lump.

After some silent discussion, the three men finally moved into a triangle around him.

"We can help you," his grandfather said.

"But you must reclaim your torc," his father said. "I suppose you lost it to that woman you saved."

"You were no better, Michael, worse even, offering yours to that milkmaid when you were twenty-two," his great-grandfather scolded.

"She was…" Michael cupped his hands around an imaginary voluptuous female form.

Sebastian perked up at that bit of information, and he wished he did not feel quite so icy so that he could ask about it. But all he could do was shiver.

"Enough," Edward commanded, and the other two spirits subsided. "We can dispel the evil from you, and we can give you some protection. But this shield will only work once. Do you understand, boy?"

Sebastian managed a nod and a whispered, "Yes."

The three spirits seemed satisfied with his answer. They crowded closer.

"I hope the woman was beautiful," Edward whispered.

Sebastian gave a weak smile. Oh, yes, she was very beautiful. And alluring and mysterious and headstrong and intelligent, and she smelled like oranges and vanilla. And she was cursed, he could not forget that. If he could just get through this nightmare, he would try to help her with that curse and then seduce her into his bed. Because he wanted her more than he had ever wanted a woman.

His great-grandfather distracted him from those wayward thoughts when he began to chant in a voice so low and deep, the ancient words were unintelligible. Then his grandfather picked up the chant in the middle of a phrase and started at the beginning. Finally, his father joined in. They chanted in a roundel, their voices melding and twining in harmony. The words wound around him and created a cocoon of soothing sound. As the three spirits intoned the words, the chant had no start or finish, the words seeming to run together in a cascade of syllables.

The notes began to appear as delicate spots of light—one here near his shoulder, another there near his knee, and another and another, until they joined into several strands of filmy light. The strands danced and circled, weaving together into a soft basket that cushioned and supported him. Sebastian felt as if he were floating on the music. The icy constriction in his chest began to loosen and thaw. He was able to take a breath without pain. The dark chill in his soul seeped away.

Just as he was beginning to feel comfortable, just as relief eased through him, he felt warmth on the insides of both forearms. The heat built as the chanting of the spirits became louder, quicker, darker. The discomfort grew until it seared him. His eyes squeezed shut. He wanted to cry out in anguish but knew he should not. Instead, he bit down on the inside of his cheek, drawing blood. The taste of the blood mingled with the pain, flooding him, blotting out everything else. The pain rose and fell with the chant of the spirits. It became so intense, fear niggled at the back of his brain. Surely the spirits would not harm him. These were his relatives, men he had known and trusted when they were alive, men he had seen die in their beds. But still his arms burned.

Perhaps this was punishment for his stupidity. If it was, then he would accept it, for he had been rash and careless in trying to break an affliction of evil without the protection of his torc. He would know better next time — if there were to be a next time. And he would endure the pain.

Then abruptly, everything stopped.

Silence.

He unclenched his jaw, opened his eyes. He was alone in complete darkness, lying on his side and curled into a ball. The spirits of his ancestors had disappeared. The inside of his forearms ached and stung, but the intense burning pain was gone. The iciness in his soul had thawed.

"Thank you," he murmured, knowing the three spirits would hear him.

He rolled to his hands and knees and struggled to stand, then staggered out into daylight. Weakened by the ordeal, he collapsed onto the soft, wet grass. He took several long breaths, then examined his sore arms. The lower part of the sleeves of his coat and the shirt beneath were ragged, torn and singed, and completely burned away in places, revealing the bare skin beneath. On the inside of both forearms was a tattoo scorched onto his skin. The tattoos were identical, a round design divided into four quarters, each showing intricate knots connecting one to the other. They were shield knots of protection.

He let his arms fall to his sides while the irony of that played through him. As The Messenger for the Legion of Baal, he was the one who tattooed the members of the group with their frog glyph, a minor protection against Nulkana. He had never wanted to be marked as a member, had, in fact, avoided it whenever he was questioned by the Lord High. He had truthfully claimed he did not need it because of his power. Now he was marked with Druid tattoos of protection by spirits older and more powerful than he was.

His relief mingled with appreciation of the spirits' wit, as well as gratitude for their help. Lying flat on his back, he laughed up into the sky. He could already feel the energy of the tattoos running through him. Then he sobered. His ancestors' spirits had given him protection, but he remembered they had said it would only work once. If he were to help the lovely Princess Allegra, keep her safe and keep both of them alive, then he had to retrieve his torc, for that would provide protection until he needed those tattoos. In order to protect her, he would need to arrange to be near her quite often, not easy with such an independent, strong-willed woman. That was a problem for another day, one that he looked forward to with anticipation, for sparring with the princess delighted and energized him.

He picked himself up and ruefully examined the ruined sleeves of his coat. He decided he should return home and let his valet deal with the disaster of his haberdashery.

Then he would see about getting back what was his from the beautiful Circe who had taken it from him.

Chapter 8

"Ah, my Messenger."

The modulated voice of the Lord High echoed in the cavernous crypt below the stone country church several miles outside Bath. Sebastian bowed his head, acting the obedient servant. Usually, when he was in this chamber, it was populated with others who were members of the Legion of Baal, present for one of their ceremonies. He had always puzzled over the brazen use of such a space. Surely, the rector of the church would not allow such sacrilegious services, unless he had been coerced. Or perhaps the rector was not as spiritual as he appeared to be. But Sebastian could not confront him, because that would reveal his true allegiance. Where the Legion was concerned, he trusted no one.

Several days had passed since he had healed the princess and then been forced to seek help from his ancestors. Fortunately, his arms had healed and the imprint of the moon in his eyes had faded. Those tattoos needed to be kept secret, to be used in a life or death situation. If the Lord High ever discovered he had them, Sebastian was sure the man would make some horribly repulsive request of him. He had already performed too many unsavory, disagreeable tasks for the man. He hoped the point of this meeting was for something benign.

Usually, when he privately met the leader of the Legion of Baal, their conversations were held in a dark room at an inn on the other side of Bath, so he was curious about the change. Nothing good ever happened in this chamber. He had been witness to members being summoned here to speak alone with the Lord High. They might leave the meeting, terror-stricken and submissive, or they might leave lifeless as a rag doll. As The Messenger of the Lord High, he had been called upon to demonstrate their leader's authority. Men used to a sheltered, soft life were often terrified to death with a show of his Druidic power, coupled by the Lord High's implied threat. Occasionally, he had been called upon to be the Lord High's assassin, a role that sucked the life from his soul. He salved his conscience with the fact that he was a soldier in a secret war. The men were enemies and no loss to society, each depraved and corrupt in his own way. But in some respects, he felt he was no better than they were.

He was the undersecretary's secret agent inside the Legion of Baal, acting as if the Legion's goals were his own. The duplicity gnawed at him. There were times when he wanted nothing more than to reveal his true feelings to the depraved man before him, an act of defiance that would surely endanger his life more than it was already.

Sebastian doubted his life was in danger this night, for that would deprive the Lord High of his spy and executioner. He had ironically made himself nearly indispensable to the man. So, he wondered at the reason for the summons.

He greeted the Lord High. "Sire."

The use of the honorary title annoyed him. Only His Majesty, King George, had the right to it. But the Lord High demanded it of the members of the Legion, and they obeyed, some out of fear, and others grudgingly. The identity of the man was a mystery. Not even Sebastian had been able to learn who he was. He ruled the Legion with a ruthless, iron fist. Sebastian had gained his trust through guile and charm. And perhaps the man's desire to have authority over one of the aristocracy. He suspected the Lord High had no claim to any title.

The Lord High sauntered closer, seeming to float in his floor-length, black satin robe. It was embroidered on one shoulder in purple silk with the iconic frog glyph. As usual, his face was obscured by the gold mask within his cowl. The face it portrayed was expressionless and bland. Sebastian suspected the face of flesh beneath was just the opposite. The light from the flame of the Legion's eternal fire in the center of the crypt caused shadows to waver across the mask, creating expression where there was none, a macabre sensation.

The Lord High stopped several feet away from Sebastian and was silent for a moment. Sebastian felt the man's regard like a prickly sensation across his skin. An occasional flicker of the flame between them reflected eerily in the man's eyes, shaded by the mask. But he knew those eyes held no power. The man's power came from elsewhere, mainly his ability to control and coerce through fear, and it also came from the collected energy of the rest of the members of the Legion when they gathered in this space. And, Sebastian had to admit, from the frog glyph he had tattooed on the man's wrist.

"Messenger," the Lord High said. "It has come to my attention that one of the Auriano brats has arrived on England's shores. Why was I not told of this?"

"I have only recently learned of this myself, Sire." Sebastian had purposely not revealed the presence of the princess in Bath. He kept his tone neutral, wanting instead to thrash the man. He scorned the man's arrogant tyranny and quest for power in the race to find the magical Sphere of Astarte. And he was revolted by the man's driving hunger to sacrifice the members of the House of Auriano to the god Ba'al, especially now since meeting the lovely Princess Allegra.

"You know I have plans for them," the man said. "Have I not made myself clear that I wish them out of the way? Our quest for the Sphere of Astarte and the power it will bestow has been hindered by their interference."

"Perhaps they interfere because they seek only to break the curse Nulkana has placed on them," Sebastian suggested mildly, keeping the sarcasm out of his voice.

"Nevertheless, I wish them eliminated." The Lord High waved his hand, as if he held a magic wand and could make them disappear in a poof of smoke. "I was very disappointed that you did not know there were twins, and that they had been deceiving the entire world into believing one had been killed in that fire at their *castello*."

"My apologies, Sire," Sebastian murmured.

"Well, at least one of them is dead now," the Lord High said with relief. His eyes sharpened behind his mask. "You are sure one of them died in Paris?"

Sebastian gave a brief nod. "I saw him stabbed through the heart." What he did not reveal was that he had also brought the man back to life with a piece of the Sphere of Astarte.

"Good, good." The Lord High paused, turned and wandered away a few steps, then swung back to face Sebastian. "I want you to deliver the Auriano bitch to me. Since her brothers are inaccessible, she will have to do." His eyes turned feverish behind the mask. "Yes," he said, excitement turning his word into a hiss. "I think she will be perfect for what I have in mind."

Sebastian swallowed back his revulsion. Whatever the man was planning, he suspected it would involve some form of evil debauchery. He could not wait to be done with this assignment, and perhaps send this creature to Hell where he belonged.

"I will do my best to bring her to you, Sire," he said, placating at the same time he tried to come up with a plan to stall. "It will take some time."

"I want her for our next conclave, Messenger." The Lord High's words were command more than request. "It will be a magnificent, international gathering at the ring of sacred stones."

Sebastian forced himself to remain calm. The Lord High referred to Stonehenge, the ancient circle of stones that held tremendous power. While that power would feed his own, it would also call to Nulkana, who was already growing stronger. With the Legion present as well, the clash of forces could be cataclysmic. Besides keeping the princess away from the Lord High, Sebastian was determined to keep her out of that stone ring. The conclave was at the next full moon, not much time to convince the lovely princess to leave England for someplace safer.

Sebastian took a breath while he scrambled to come up with an excuse to delay. "That may not be possible, Sire. I will have to gain the lady's trust before she will consent to go anywhere with me, and that will take time. Surely, you don't want me to kidnap her. If she suddenly disappears, questions will be asked. It must appear that she left the area to travel elsewhere. Preparations must be made."

"Yes, of course. Arrange it." The Lord High gave a dismissive swipe of his hand.

"Sire." Sebastian bowed, expecting to be allowed to leave, wanting to get away from the man as quickly as possible. He took a step back.

"Messenger." The man's deceptively silky tone put Sebastian on guard.

"Yes, Sire?" He forced his face to remain expressionless, but he dreaded whatever was coming next.

The Lord High slipped his hands into the sleeves of his robe. "I received an interesting letter from the Baron von Frei. He mentions when he was in Paris, he came into contact with a brother and sister who both have unusual powers. It seems they are descendants of Halima, sister to Nulkana. Von Frei mentions that you inducted the brother into the Legion. Why did you not tell me of this?"

The Lord High spoke of Solange, the beauty who had wed Antonio, the Duke of Auriano, and her brother, Gide. Sebastian had hoped he would not have to reveal what occurred in Paris.

"It was a messy business," he said. "The young man disappeared, and I did not want to waste time searching for him because you wished me to return to England for the conclave. Besides, he had become…unstable. And the young woman had been used by the Marquis de Vernoux. You know de Vernoux's preferences. I did not think you wanted spoiled goods." He gave a disinterested shrug. "I cannot tell what happened to her." And that was the truth, because he would never tell this man what had happened.

"They would have been great assets to our group. You should have been more diligent in keeping track of them," the Lord High scolded.

"Sire, I agreed to be your eyes and ears," Sebastian said with a small bow. "My duties don't include chasing runaway children."

The Lord High's eyes narrowed behind his mask. "Children? I understood them to be adults." He gave his head a small shake. "Nevertheless, we could have raised them up as followers to our cause."

Sebastian exaggerated. Solange and Gide were not truly children, merely a few years younger than he was. But the idea of raising children to the beliefs of the Legion of Baal turned Sebastian's stomach. He bowed again to hide his disgust.

"My apologies, Sire, for disappointing you." He kept his tone as soothing and bland as he could.

The Lord High took a menacing step forward. "You have disappointed me not just once, but twice, Messenger. You not only lost these assets, but you seem to have also misplaced the Crystal Dagger."

Sebastian hid his alarm at the man's knowledge of that bit of information. The Crystal Dagger was a magical weapon that had been created centuries earlier by the Legion of Baal in order to kill their enemy, the ancient sorceress Nulkana. Except it had a flaw. It would only work if it was imbued with the power of a descendant of Halima. That had occurred in Paris when it had fallen into the possession of the brother and sister whose fates he was unwilling to share with the Lord High. He was glad it was out of the grasp of the Lord High, but concerned about Gide, who now held it. The connection the young man had with the Dagger seemed to have an adverse effect on him. But Sebastian was not about to tell any of that to the man on the other side of the flame.

He chose his next words carefully. "I learned that the French general, Napoleon, had the Dagger in his possession for a while. It is possible that he still has it."

"The French? The French have the Dagger?" The voice of the Lord High went up a half octave, indicating his outrage. Although the man craved universal power, one thing he could not abide was insult to England, an ironic, slightly unbalanced foible.

"I believe the Dagger is out of our reach at present," Sebastian said. He wanted to keep the weapon out of the hands of the Lord High for as long as possible.

The man stomped away in agitation, stopped for the space of five heartbeats, then stomped back to confront Sebastian once more. "This is unacceptable, Messenger."

Sebastian bowed his acknowledgment of the criticism. "As you say, Sire. But as you have told me, we now have a member of the House of Auriano within our grasp. Surely, her sacrifice will make up for the loss of the Dagger and two descendants of Halima." Speaking the words made Sebastian want to gag.

"Yes, yes!" The Lord High nearly jumped in his excitement. "She will be the perfect sacrifice to the god." His eyes turned crafty behind his mask. "Perhaps the god will grant us our every desire, and our search for the pieces of the Sphere of Astarte will be irrelevant. He will have a new consort in the Auriano bitch. I understand she is quite comely."

"I'm sure that will please him, Sire," Sebastian murmured.

"Hm." The man wandered away into the shadows, deep in thought. "I must plan this ceremony," he said, his voice vague and echoing in the chamber. "It must be perfect. Yes, perfect." He swung back to Sebastian. "You will bring her to our conclave at the full moon. Do not disappoint me."

"Of course not, Sire." Even as Sebastian agreed, he planned to keep the princess as far away from Stonehenge as possible.

As he took his leave, the Lord High's voice reached out with silky menace. "If you fail me, not even The Messenger of the Legion of Baal will be absolved from punishment."

After submissively bowing, Sebastian escaped into the night. He drew air deep into his lungs, the first complete breath he had taken since entering the crypt. The moon's grin mocked him. All he had was a little more than two weeks to foil the plans of the Lord High and placate the undersecretary with information or an arrest. In the meantime, he needed to keep Allegra safe and prevent her from kidnapping any more young men to satisfy her craving. But before he would do any of that, he would return to Blackbrake and have his valet draw a bath. He wanted to wash away the filth of his meeting with the Lord High of the Legion of Baal.

Hubert Crowley used the end of his quirt to knock on the door of the cottage set far back from the lane. The crescent moon was high in the sky, and ghostly shadows from the surrounding woods made him think of unearthly creatures watching with glowing eyes and dripping fangs. He never should have answered the strange invitation, but he thought it had come from the Lord High. No one ever ignored a summons from *him*. Even so, he wished to be someplace else, like the Card Room in the Upper Assembly Rooms, or even listening to some young miss warble off-key at Mrs. Osborne's weekly salon. But he was here, and so must make the best of it.

The cottage was a lonely place, far beyond the boundaries of Bath, merely a curiosity on a pleasant ride through the country during the day.

It had been abandoned for years, overgrown and dilapidated. But from what he could see in the dark, some of the weeds had been cut back and a few repairs had been made. A single candle burned in the window.

He waited, listening for footsteps that told him someone would be answering his knock. He heard nothing. Without warning, the door opened on silent hinges. Crowley stepped back in surprise, not sure who — or what — might be standing on the other side. A tall, thin man, skeletal in appearance, dressed in a dark brown, cassock-like garment from neck to toes, bowed before him.

"Welcome, sir," the man said in foreign accents. "I am Kek. We are quite pleased you could visit." He motioned for Crowley to enter.

Crowley wondered who else Kek referred to, as he stepped into the dark interior of the house. In the dim candlelight from that single taper in the window, he saw the poor furnishings of the parlor of a farmer's cottage: a single stuffed chair, its covering worn very thin, several rustic wooden chairs, a table holding an unlit lamp, and a cold fireplace opening along the side wall. Kek led the way through the parlor but stopped halfway across the space. With a bow, he waved Crowley forward.

Confusion and a touch of trepidation wrinkled Crowley's brow. He saw nothing inviting in the rest of the room, and no one else was present. The man, Kek, was strange and a bit unnerving. As he stared, the air before him seemed to shimmer.

"It is a glamour, sir," Kek said. "Harmless." He pushed his hand through. His arm disappeared halfway to his elbow. Ripples expanded out through the air, as if he had stuck his hand into a still pool. When he pulled his hand back, he showed that it was unharmed. He smiled, the effect more like a grimace.

Crowley wondered at the magical power that could create such a glamour. He wanted to turn around and leave, get on his horse and gallop far away. But he sensed that Kek, whoever he might be, would not allow that. Besides, he told himself, he was a member of the Legion of Baal. He had that frog glyph tattooed on the inside of his wrist, protection against sorcery. Gulping and gripping his quirt tightly, he stepped through the shimmering air.

The poor parlor fell away and became a drawing room of large but pleasing proportions. It was lit by many candles in wall sconces and a central chandelier of wrought iron and Murano glass flowers. Chairs and settees upholstered in brocade and raw silk were placed in groups near small tables whose surfaces gleamed with beeswax. A fire burned merrily on the hearth.

He was in awe of the space, but his attention was riveted by the woman who approached. She was unbelievably beautiful, with ebony curls piled on her head, some escaping in artful abandon, dark, flashing eyes, and ruby lips that pouted. She walked with a provocative sway to her hips, accentuated by a clinging dress in red satin, whose neckline plunged to a breath-taking depth.

"Mr. Crowley," she said with a barely perceptive accent, "I am so glad you accepted my invitation."

He was struck mute, but his good manners forced him into a bow. The frog glyph on his arm began to itch, a curious sensation. As the woman came closer, the itch turned into a burn. It forced several things to click into place in his brain at once—the strange man, Kek, the shimmer of air he stepped through, the elegant space appearing where it should not. And the perfectly beautiful woman before him.

This was Nulkana, the ancient, evil sorceress.

He stumbled back several steps, away from her advance. She halted, and a crafty smile curved her lips.

"You are…You are…," he stammered.

"Yes, I am Nulkana." Her smile teased. "I think, perhaps, you have heard of me."

He raised his arm, revealing the frog glyph. "Don't come any closer."

She laughed with pure amusement. "That little picture on your arm will do nothing." She took another step closer and coyly looked down at her henna-tinged fingernail tracing the edge of the table next to her. "But I did not invite you here to fight, Mr. Crowley." She glanced up at him from beneath her thick, dark lashes. "Do you not wish to know why I sent you an invitation?"

Crowley's arm dipped, but he remained wary.

"Of course, you do," she said, stepping closer.

A cloud of fragrance engulfed him. It was rich, spicy-sweet, musky, like nothing he had ever encountered before, but he thought he detected a whiff of decay beneath the beauty. The scent fogged his senses until everything dissolved except for the woman before him.

"I...ah..." Crowley could not find any words. His brain seemed to have shut down.

She smiled up at him. "I like a man of few words." She stepped even closer.

Crowley felt as if all he had ever wanted in his whole life was to be with this woman standing mere inches away and smiling at him. He opened his mouth and closed it again, like a fish gasping for water.

"I have a favor to ask of you," she said. "Will you do this for me?"

He had no idea what she might ask, but his head bobbed up and down in agreement.

She leaned in. "I want you to bring the Princess of Auriano to me," she whispered.

Her words rustled gently inside his head. The request seemed innocent, but deep in his brain a tiny warning bell rang just once. He had no compunction about turning the princess over to this woman. After all, the Auriano offspring were the Legion's opponents in the race to find the Sphere. But he knew of the evil sorceress and the tales of her malice. What else would she ask of him? And what would she do once she had what she wanted? The rules of etiquette, drilled into him since childhood, gave him a chance to stall.

"I have not been formally introduced to the princess," he said, somewhat pompously.

She made a little moue, turned and walked away. Her disappointment cut through him. The loss of her attention made him want to please her.

"I could arrange an introduction," he said.

She swung back to him and her eyes sparkled in delight. "That would be wonderful."

"There's just one small problem," he added. "The Earl of Hawksmoor seems to have formed an attachment with her."

He saw a flash of something vicious and frightful in her eyes. Then it disappeared and he thought he must have imagined it. She stepped closer again, and her scent wafted into his head.

"I know what you desire more than anything," she murmured. "I can make it happen for you."

Her fingers circled his wrist, the one that had the tattoo of the frog glyph. He registered that she showed no ill effects, but the thought flew away as quickly as it came. Around him, he saw piles of gold coins and men bowing to him as if he were a king. Wealth and power. He had always wanted to be rich. He had never had the resources of Hawksmoor or the other members of the *ton*. And power. He wanted that very much. In school, he had been the brunt of jokes and cruel teasing, the toady, running errands for the other boys so he would be included. Even now, he fawned over the others in his crowd and escorted widows and other older women, including Hawksmoor's mother, so he could gather up whatever dregs they might toss his way. And the pittance he received from that French harpy, the Vicomtesse D'Aramitz, for passing along tidbits of information would not keep a dog in bones for a week. But what Nulkana showed him was beyond what he'd ever imagined. It was glorious. He would be accepted in the most exclusive clubs, invited to the most exclusive gatherings, have men and women jostle for his attention.

He had joined the Legion of Baal for that very reason because the Lord High had promised it all, as soon as they had the pieces of the magical Sphere of Astarte. According to the Lord High, the sorceress Nulkana was their enemy. But finding the pieces was taking too long, and the woman standing before him offered everything he had ever wanted without the Sphere. Perhaps he had joined the wrong camp in this secret war.

She pouted, and the desire to kiss those lips rose up in him so strongly it wiped out his visions of wealth and power.

"I do not think you will give me the other thing that I want," she said on a sigh.

"What is it?" he demanded. "Anything."

"When you bring me the Princess of Auriano, I want you to kill Hawksmoor."

Her words fell on his ears like a caress, but once they entered his brain, they sounded like a thunderclap. She wanted him to kill The Messenger of the Legion of Baal, the man who was the eyes and ears of the Lord High, the man who could appear and disappear as if he were made of smoke, the man who was more formidable with blade and pistol than anyone. The thought made sweat trickle down his back.

She stepped so close that she rubbed against him. "Surely, you could perform this little favor for me."

His head bobbed up and down in agreement again, as if it were not attached to the rest of him that was terrified of the idea. But at the same time, he realized that performing that task would help him gain everything he ever wanted.

She smiled. "When you have done this favor for me, then perhaps I will give you a bonus." Her hips gyrated against his.

Immediate lust clenched the muscles in his groin so tightly that pleasure bordered on pain. He grabbed for her, but she backed away with a chuckle.

"No, no, Mr. Crowley." She wagged her finger at him. "You will get your reward when you have done as I ask." Her demeanor turned cold and imperious. "Now say that you agree."

He blinked, taken aback by her swift change. But he wanted whatever she offered more than anything he had ever desired. "Yes," he said. "Yes."

When he spoke, he sensed a faint feeling of disappointment coming from the corner of the room. He glanced in that direction, and deep in the shadows, saw a robed, hooded figure that he had not noticed before. As soon as he became aware of the figure, the feeling vanished. In its place, he felt Nulkana's ire, a burning, spiky sensation inside his chest.

"Get out, Mr. Crowley," she ordered. "I will be watching."

Crowley was stunned at the abrupt dismissal, but glad to leave. He pushed his way back through the shimmer of air into the poor parlor of the farmer's cottage. The strange man, Kek, seemed to have disappeared. He staggered out into the night. The air had never felt so fresh. The stars had never shone so brightly. He mounted his horse in a daze. As he turned toward Bath, he wondered if he had dreamt the whole incident. An owl swooped overhead, and he had the uncanny sense that he was being watched.

In shock, he realized that he had just made a bargain with the evil Nulkana. He dug his heels into his horse's flank and urged it into a gallop. He suddenly wanted to be as far away from that abandoned cottage as fast as he could. Tomorrow, he would decide how — if — he would do Nulkana's bidding.

He completely ignored the fact that he had already agreed.

As soon as Crowley left, Nulkana waved her arm, and the gracious drawing room disappeared. The poor parlor of a farmer's cottage was revealed again in the dim light from a single taper. Nulkana sank onto one of the rustic, wooden chairs as her appearance shifted from a beautiful, sensuous creature to that of a wrinkled crone. Kek rushed to her, but she waved him off.

"You need to feed, mistress," he said.

"Not yet." Nulkana examined her arm. Her hand and forearm were those of a young woman. The skin was flush with color and plump, not wrinkled and desiccated like the rest of her.

"Look at this, Kek," she said, awe tinging her tone.

Kek moved closer and squinted at the limb. "It is quite remarkable, mistress."

"This is from touching that Auriano chit." She turned thoughtful. "I had planned on killing her — along with her brothers. But her brothers…" She hissed in aggravation and let her arm fall to her lap. "I will get all of the Auriano whelps eventually. But I have a better use for *her*." Her eyes gleamed with malicious anticipation. "Her force is strong. I am going to use her to make me whole, Kek. I will feed from her whenever I need."

A rustle from a dark corner of the room drew her attention.

Her eyes slitted with malevolence. "Don't you like that idea, worm?"

The black-robed, cowled figure made no acknowledgment.

Nulkana gave an evil little laugh. "I think I'll have you watch every time, worm. Every time I suck some life from her. And you will keep her alive and bring her to me whenever I wish."

The figure in the corner seemed to stiffen, but in fact made no movement.

"Oh, yes, mistress," Kek said with relish.

She glared at Kek, then turned back to the robed figure. "I need to feed, worm. Go!"

The figure jerked, as if in pain, then bowed low and glided from the room. When he was gone, Kek handed her a delicate wine glass filled with a viscous, purple liquid that emitted a poisonous-looking, violet vapor.

"Your medicine, mistress," he said.

She eyed it with distaste. "Why do your concoctions always taste so vile?"

Kek bowed in apology. "It is from the magical ingredients, mistress. They are the only ones that will heal your injuries."

Nulkana placed her hand on her side and winced. "Damn those Auriano whelps and their sluts. They've been trouble ever since they were born." She glanced toward the dark kitchen. "Where's my meal, worm?" she yelled, her voice booming through the tiny cottage and shaking the windows.

The far-away screams of young women reached her, as if they came from somewhere far below. She licked her lips. "First, my medicine and then a sweetmeat, eh Kek?"

She raised the glass to her lips and smiled as the screams landed like delightful music on her ears.

Chapter 9

Allegra stood outside the jewelry shop and examined the trinkets displayed behind the window. Earbobs and necklaces glittered against black velvet cloth, each one vying for the attention of the passersby. But rather than the sparkly pieces, her attention was held by a walking stick propped in one corner. It was made of some dark, exotic wood, ebony perhaps, and set into its brass knob was an enormous blue stone, most likely a sapphire, nearly the color of a pair of eyes that she had come to know quite well. The item was sleek and sophisticated, restrained, just like the man it brought to mind. When held, the blue stone would be hidden, like the magical light in those blue eyes, until he wished to reveal it.

She had not thanked him properly for healing her, and she contemplated buying the walking stick for him. Gifting him with such an item was highly improper, but she was a princess, and she remained within the bounds of propriety only when they suited her. Nearly a week had passed since he had arrived at the priory and healed her arm, and she had not seen him in all that time. He had not been at the Pump Room or either of the Assembly Rooms. She had not seen him riding down Great Pulteney Street nor strolling the streets of the city. Of course, he could have been in those places and she could have missed him, but she doubted that was the case. Why had he absented himself from society? Then she remembered his strange coolness when he left the priory. Perhaps he wished to have nothing more to do with her. Sorrow twisted through her, for she would miss him and his teasing. He was the most handsome, most charismatic man she had ever met, despite being one of the most aggravating. He reminded her of her brothers, but he made her feel things that her brothers never would.

She focused once more on the walking stick. Perhaps she would have a fine rapier concealed within its length. Weapons were banned from the streets of Bath, but a man who held so many secrets might have need of a secret blade. It would make a lovely gift. Before she could act on her decision, a voice from behind her made her skin tingle and warmth spread down through her core.

"Thinking of buying a bauble, Princess?" Hawksmoor asked.

Reflected in the glass of the display, he stood at her right shoulder. She refused to let him see the effect he had on her. Once again, he had moved so silently she had not heard him. She tipped her head as if examining the trinkets on display.

"I am merely passing the time, *Sior* Hawksmoor, before my companion returns from the milliner's," she said, as she indicated the shop next door.

"I am glad to hear that, because I would think you have enough baubles to amuse you," he said coolly. "Especially those that belong to someone else."

Allegra gritted her teeth. He was referring to his torc, of course, which she still had in her possession. And that, she reminded herself, would keep his silence about the Hunger until she deigned to return it. She turned to him with a smile.

"I am only keeping the bauble safe," she said, coming up with a flimsy excuse. "After all, you would not want it to slip into the wrong hands. You never know when some misfortune might befall you, *si*?"

His eyes narrowed on her. She noticed they held a flinty edge to their color that was not present before, and she was reminded of the iciness in them after he had healed her arm. She wondered if he had been touched by Nulkana's evil. That idea frightened and saddened her, for she would never wish that misery on anyone, especially the man standing before her. But otherwise, he seemed perfectly fine.

"I will certainly be mindful of any danger that might present itself." His tone was cool and measured, as if he could not contemplate anything ruffling his smooth existence.

His calm annoyed her. While her insides jittered heatedly at his proximity, he seemed unaffected. She could not deny that she wanted to Thought Bind with him again, to dance with his mind, to touch him skin to skin. The thought of touching him skin to skin made her want more than Thought Binding. She wanted him all over her, touching, licking, tasting. She wanted him inside her. The impulse confused her, for she had never had such a yearning for anyone she had connected with during the Hunger. She felt as if she were still in the claws of that madness.

With effort, she turned back to the shop display and attempted to appear unaffected by his closeness. "I do admire those earbobs," she said, trying to divert his attention. The earbobs were, in fact, the most ostentatious and gaudy pieces she had ever seen, and she would never wear them.

He stepped up next to her, as if he were also admiring the baubles on display. "Your life is in danger, Princess," he said quietly.

Her tiny laugh was brittle. "Do you think I don't know that *Sior* Hawksmoor? Nulkana attacked me in the middle of the Assembly Rooms."

He made a sound of impatience. "Nulkana is not the only one who wants your life, lovely lady."

His words sent a chill through her. Allegra stared at the walking stick without really seeing it. "The Legion of Baal," she murmured, not realizing she spoke aloud, as the fear that had made her flee from Paris grabbed at her.

She felt his searching glance. Then he turned back to the display. "You say that as if you already know of them. Yet, you claimed ignorance at Lady Hetherington's lawn party."

She winced, knowing he had caught her in her fabrication. Her only recourse was to take the offensive. She swung to him. "What do *you* know of them, *Sior* Hawksmoor?"

He shrugged. "One hears rumors."

Suspicious of his vague answer, she studied him, but he would not meet her eyes. Before she could question him further, Luisa emerged from the milliner's with her package of ribbons. Hawksmoor tipped his hat to her Guide, then held out his arm to Allegra.

"Shall we walk, Princess?" he invited, as if they had been discussing nothing more disturbing than the weather.

His proffered arm both invited and deterred. Allegra hesitated. She wanted to walk with him, to be near him, to feel his muscled arm beneath her hand, to know that every other woman in sight envied her. But walking with him brought her into close proximity with him, made her want him more, confused her senses, and assaulted the walls she kept around her emotions. Besides, he had secrets, and he had forced her into that outrageous bargain to spy for him so that he might remain silent about his abduction.

She wondered how he knew that the menacing Legion threatened her. And she wondered how much he knew about that vicious group, or if he were actually involved with it. But she remembered he did not have the tell-tale frog glyph tattooed on his arm. He had healed her and protected her when Nulkana attacked. If he had wanted to take her life, then he would have let her slowly turn to ice.

Accepting his invitation would put them in the midst of shoppers and those strolling in the sunshine. She did not think he could do anything unseemly or dangerous in the middle of a crowd. She slipped her hand into the crook of his arm. From behind, her Guide gave a tsk of disapproval. Allegra ignored it.

Pleased and relieved that she accepted his invitation, Sebastian smiled down at the Princess Allegra. Her small hand resting in the crook of his arm felt like it belonged there. Her proximity soothed something inside him that had been jagged and irritated ever since he had healed her, despite the help from his three ancestors.

He led her down Milsom Street, past the shops and through the throng of shoppers. His destination was Sydney Gardens where they could appear as any other couple out for a stroll, but where they might have a private conversation and still remain within propriety's bounds. Sometimes, the most private places were those in plain sight.

"I am glad to see you are feeling better, Princess," he said.

She held her hand out before her and made an experimental fist, then dropped it. "*Grazie, Sior* Hawksmoor. I fear I might have completely turned to ice if you had not come." She peeked up at him from under her bonnet. "Did you have no ill effects?"

120

"Nothing of any consequence," he said.

He certainly would not tell her of the chill in his soul, nor his visit to that hidden barrow and the three shades of his ancestors. And he certainly would not tell her of the twin tattoos he had received as a result of that visit. That revelation would only come in a life or death situation, one he hoped he would never need.

While they strolled past the bookshop, he changed the subject. "I see there is a reprint of Ann Radcliffe's novel, *The Mysteries of Udolpho*. Have you read it?"

"I found the heroine, Emily, to be a bit too naive," she said. "Imagine believing that everyone you know is a villain."

He huffed a laugh at her irony. "Yes, just imagine."

"But a good romance story is always *delizioso, si?*" she added with a sly peek up at him.

"*Si,*" he said, smiling.

Romance *was* always delicious. He felt that romance with this woman would be especially tasty. When he glanced down at her, he was caught by the humor in her golden eyes and struck by this woman's courage. She teased and made jokes when two of the most evil forces in the world wanted her life. If he accomplished nothing else, he would do his utmost to keep her safe. He just had not quite figured out how to do that and still satisfy the demands made on him.

He certainly was not going to obey the command of the Lord High and bring him the beautiful woman beside him. The leader of the Legion of Baal needed to die, but not before he revealed where the piece of the Sphere of Astarte was hidden. After Sebastian retrieved it, he would deliver it to the undersecretary. Or perhaps not. Perhaps he could arrange for it to fall into the hands of the beautiful Princess Allegra, whose family had owned it long before anyone else became aware of its magical qualities.

The thought of Sir Cyril brought to mind the real reason why he wished to speak to the princess in private. The kidnapping of young men had to stop. They had reached Bridge Street, and the Pulteney Bridge over the River Avon opened before them. The bridge was lined with shops, so he and the princess could mingle with those who had come to examine and sample the wares.

Just before they entered the bridge, the princess asked, "What is that odd construction in the middle of the river?" She had to raise her voice to be heard over the rush of water.

"It's called a weir," he explained. "It's a sort of low dam, used to control the flow of the river for the mills and to help prevent floods."

She strolled to the edge of the high riverbank. The water surged across the top of the weir to crash and boil a couple of feet below. As she eased forward another few inches to see better, her foot slipped on the loose dirt. Soil and pebbles slid off the bank and rained down on the river below. He grabbed her arm to jerk her back onto more solid ground. As he did, a black squiggle of rune snapped into existence in the space between his hand and her sleeve. Instinctively, he snuffed it out, but its appearance surprised him. Those tattoos were only to be used once to save a life. Perhaps his concern about the threat of both Nulkana and the Legion of Baal which the princess faced made them appear. He hoped neither the princess nor her companion had seen the rune.

"You must be careful, Princess," he said, quickly focusing attention away from his hand. "The riverbank can be treacherous."

She blinked up at him, the scare she received still evident in her eyes. "I will certainly stay away from the edge. Anyone falling into the river and tipping over the weir would surely drown."

"Quite an unpleasant way to die," he agreed. "Come, let us stroll across the bridge, a much safer way to navigate the river." As he made the suggestion, he could feel the eyes of Mistress Luisa boring into his back.

Allegra had caught a glimpse of something in the air when Hawksmoor pulled her back from the edge of the riverbank. His hand landing on her arm sent a cool wash of energy flowing over her skin. She wanted to ask him about it, but a flash of confusion in his gaze followed by a chill withdrawal had warned her off, despite his solicitous words. But whatever she had seen, along with the frisson that excited her nerves, made her suspect his power was growing beyond what had been displayed when he healed her arm.

As he led her onto Pulteney Bridge with its tiny shops, he distracted her with amusing comments about an outrageous bonnet displayed in one shop, or the delicious-looking delicacies in the bakery. He was entertaining, and the strange occurrences at the river's edge soon faded away. The bridge was crowded, so they became separated from Luisa. Allegra could see her behind several other groups of shoppers.

Hawksmoor kept her hand tucked into the crook of his arm. She should have felt uncomfortable in such close proximity to a man with such unusual and strong power, but instead, she felt safe. That confused her, for he could, with only a whisper into a hostess's ear, begin rumors and destroy the fragile life and gossamer veil of respectability she had created in England. She wished for her brothers' guidance, but in the very next thought, wished they would never appear. They would surely drag her back to Auriano and confine her within its walls. As much as she loved her home and her brothers, she wanted her freedom more.

She had grown up hiding away in that convent in Paris, trusting only a few — her brothers, Luisa and Ernesto, the Mother Superior — because of the curse and because of the danger from Nulkana. She wanted to trust Hawksmoor, but he held so many secrets, she was afraid of what they might be. A young woman's laughter from across the way caught her attention. A couple conversed, and as she watched, the young man raised the lady's hand to his lips and kissed her fingers. Even at a distance, Allegra could see they were in love. Envy stole through her. She wanted very much to be loved like that, to be able to love in return. She wanted to be able to trust, but until the curse was broken, she had to be wary of everyone, even the man who walked beside her, the man who had healed her frozen arm. Especially the man who walked beside her, for he had so many secrets.

They exited the bridge. When Allegra glanced behind her, Luisa was lost in the crowd. Apprehension tightened her hand on the handle of her parasol. Had Hawksmoor intentionally lost her Guide? When he brought her to a bench where strollers could rest, she realized she was being too suspicious.

He glanced up at the sky. "There will be a new moon in a few days," he said.

His tone was conversational, but his words sent a chill through her. "I did not know you were a student of astronomy." She gazed up at the blue sky as she forced herself to remain calm. The moon was visible as a pale, thin, white crescent against the backdrop of azure. Soon it would disappear, dark against the night sky.

He turned to her. "We both know the curse will be taking you over."

Her heart sped up. "How do you know that?" she demanded.

"Simple calculation," he said coolly. "Approximately two weeks passed between the time you had me chained to your wall and the next time you kidnapped a young man, when I found your secret chamber—the time between the last new moon and the full moon. The moon will be new again in a few days' time. Logic tells me that as soon as the moon goes dark, you will need to—"

"You know nothing about the curse," she broke in, knowing as soon as she spoke that her words were false. He knew a great deal about the curse on her family. Too much.

His eyes narrowed on her. "I think I know enough, lovely lady, that tells me you will be spiriting one or more young men into your secret chamber and using them."

Allegra turned away, ashamed and mortified at what she was forced to do when the moon waxed and waned. "What I do or do not do, *Sior* Hawksmoor, is none of your business."

"It is very much my business," he said. "Do you think that the occurrences of young men finding themselves naked and someplace other than where they started, with no memory of where they have been, have gone unnoticed?" He shook his head sadly. "If you believe that, then you have been living in a fantasy."

She huffed. "My whole life is a fantasy, but one that resembles a nightmare."

"Yes, that is very true, and I am quite sorry," he said with compassion. "But you cannot kidnap any more young men."

"I have no choice, *Sior* Hawksmoor," she snapped, angry at the unnatural life she was forced to live.

"If you continue, the authorities will soon find you and send you to Newgate Prison," he said, his words relentless.

Fear made her challenge him. "What would you have me do? If I do not—" She stopped, unable to continue around the lump in her throat. If she could not feed her appetites during the Hunger, she would remain Shadow for the rest of her life. That frightened her more than having her secret revealed. But she was caught in the curse with no way out.

He covered the tightly clenched fist in her lap with his strong, warm hand. "I will come to you when you have the need," he said quietly. "You may use me as you wish."

Allegra gasped and choked. "No. *Madre di Dio!* No!" The idea of Thought Binding with him again sent waves of fear streaking through her. She wanted it too much. His mind was a mystical, magical place that enticed and excited at the same time it comforted. She could see herself becoming addicted to its sweet lure. Besides that, the feel of his body next to her was the most wonderful sensation she could imagine. She wanted him, craved him like no other man. But her desire was too strong. She felt as if she were still in the Hunger with the fiend living in her brain. The thought of being with him, naked, skin to skin, made that delicious ache throb deep inside, and made the moisture weep between her thighs.

She could not have him. She would destroy him. Once she entered his mind during Thought Binding, she was not sure she could control her desire. She wanted him too much. Her great need might incinerate his brain. That would be devastating, a tragedy from which she would never recover.

And with his power that seemed to be growing, he could destroy her. He still had too many secrets. The ability to heal her. The ability to call to her on a breeze. The ability to have the moon appear in his eyes. What would he do once their minds were connected? Before, she had the advantage of surprise, but if she used Thought Binding with his knowledge of what she did, he might use his powerful abilities against her.

She pulled her fist from beneath his hand and met his clear blue gaze with a level stare. "No," she said again. "You will not come to me."

He tipped his head and narrowed his eyes as if he studied her. "Hm." His wordless response was more that of a scholar discovering an unusual bit of information rather than a rejected lover. "I believe you will find my suggestion is the only solution, Princess. Unless, of course, you wish for a long ocean voyage as you are transported to a penal colony, or a long holiday in Newgate Prison. I think Mistress Luisa will agree with me." He glanced over his shoulder. "Ah, there she is now. I will go speak with her."

Horrified, Allegra snapped out again, "No!"

But he had risen and was already striding toward her Guide, who was just emerging from the Pulteney Bridge. She watched him approach Luisa, tip his hat, and escort her to the side of the lane, where he spoke earnestly with her. Luisa occasionally sent a scowl in Allegra's direction, but she listened intently to Hawksmoor. She finally gave a curt nod.

Hawksmoor turned to Allegra, smiled and tipped his hat. She felt her stomach drop. Her Guide had agreed to Hawksmoor's proposal. In a few days, she would not only have to endure the curse, but the overwhelming magnetic pull of the most intriguing, dynamic, sensuous man she had ever encountered.

Her life, complicated already, had just tipped into a tangled labyrinth, where, at its center, much like the mythical Minotaur, sat the enigmatic, dangerous Earl of Hawksmoor.

Allegra was furious. Not only had she been maneuvered into a terrible situation, her Guide had betrayed her, beguiled by a handsome face and smooth words. As she watched Hawksmoor stroll away toward the bridge, Luisa sat next to her on the bench.

"How could you agree to his suggestion?" Allegra demanded.

"It was the best solution," Luisa said.

"It was not." Allegra drew in a breath between clenched teeth. "We could have found another way."

Luisa's glance was sharp. "Another way? And have you arrested and transported? Do you know what happens if you do not get what you need during the Hunger?"

Allegra turned away and refused to answer. She knew she had to feed her cravings, but she had only a vague notion of what would happen if she did not, just that it was life-threatening.

"Let me tell you," Luisa went on relentlessly. "You will never return fully from Shadow form. But that is the easy part. In between, when your body craves, during the time of the Hunger, there is incredible, horrific pain, when you flash from Shadow, to flesh and bone, and back again. And it happens over and over again, at every cycle of the moon."

Allegra felt the blood drain from her cheeks. The pins and needles she felt every time she turned from Shadow to flesh and bone were irritating and uncomfortable, and they quickly disappeared. But to endure them over and over for an extended period would drive her mad. "I had no idea. Why did you not tell me this before?"

"I wanted to spare you." Luisa's face softened, and she gently touched the back of Allegra's hand with her fingers. "If I may say, Princess, you have been like a daughter to me."

Allegra ducked her head, ashamed she had rebuked her Guide for protecting her. She turned up her hand and clutched Luisa's fingers. "*Grazie*, Luisa."

Although she was grateful, she was still not happy with Hawksmoor's manipulation. Her glance went beyond Luisa to the crowd milling about the end of the bridge. She saw Hawksmoor stop to speak to a couple — that man, Crowley, and a woman of middle-age, but still quite lovely. Something about her seemed familiar, then Allegra saw the family resemblance. The woman had to be Hawksmoor's mother.

The earl stood stiffly, and even from this distance, Allegra could see he was uncomfortable. He barely acknowledged Crowley. She watched them exchange a few words, then Crowley bent close to the woman and murmured something. Hawksmoor became rigid. As the couple moved off, the earl clenched one hand into a fist.

Allegra immediately came to a decision. If Hawksmoor wanted her to spy on Crowley, then she would. She would learn everything she could about the man. And she would discover why there was such animosity between the two men.

She smiled to herself. She would be Shadow in another two days. What better time to hide in the dark and discover a man's secrets? And after, when she entered the Hunger, she could reveal what she had learned to the man who would come to her.

An exquisite thrill rippled through her.

Chapter 10

Two nights later, Sebastian eased open the door to Crowley's suite of rooms in the White Hart Hotel in Stall Street, a respectable address but less fashionable than the Pelican on Walcott and far down the scale from the York House on George Street. Even so, it was above Crowley's means. Sebastian wondered at the man's ability to afford such extravagance. In the next thought, he wondered if any of his mother's allowance was going towards Crowley's living expenses. If that were happening, he would stop it immediately. But for now, he focused on the task before him.

After meeting his mother and Crowley at the Pulteney Bridge, he had decided he would learn as much as he could about the man. He did not like the way Crowley had seemed so possessive with the countess. Besides the age difference, which he found distasteful, he sensed the cur was after something. He intended to find out what that was.

He had learned from his mother that tonight she and Crowley would be at the gaming tables and knew from experience that would keep both of them occupied until the early hours. He had plenty of time to look through Crowley's things.

The moon had gone dark, so only starlight came through the window. He had brought a dark lantern, a piece of equipment he used often in his role as The Messenger. It allowed him to shut off the candle's light without extinguishing the candle itself. He slid open the lantern's shutter and examined his surroundings. Most of the area was in deep shadow, but he could see enough to move around.

He stood in a small sitting area that contained a chair, upholstered and looking a bit tired, a small table with two wooden chairs, and a writing desk. Clothing draped across the back of one of the chairs. A narrow fireplace opened in the middle of one wall. In an alcove to the back and left was a rumpled bed and shaving stand. Crowley's traveling case stood at the foot of the bed.

Sebastian moved to the writing desk first. He found some unpaid receipts from the tailor, another from the cobbler, and a few gambling chits, but nothing that revealed Crowley for anything more than what he was — a cur who did not pay his bills and who lived off wealthy women. The desk held no secret compartments where an unscrupulous person might hide a scrap of paper with a bit of secret information. He turned slowly, allowing his light to illuminate small sections of the room. The fireplace might be a possible place to look. He would leave that for last. He did not mind getting dirty but sifting through ashes and feeling the inside of the sooty flue were never pleasant.

He moved to the chest, placed his lamp on the floor and went down on one knee. Just as he was about to lift the cover, he sensed movement behind him. He froze.

What are you doing here?

The woman's words slapped into his mind. He knew of only one woman who could speak to him silently. Slowly, he rose to his feet and turned.

He could make out her form, a lithe Shadow darker than the rest of the shadows in the far corner. Her eyes were clearly visible, and they glowed like molten gold, just as hot, just as beautiful. She should not be in this room. He had told her to leave Crowley alone. But of course, she would not pay any attention.

"I should ask what *you* are doing here, Princess," he said, forcing his voice to calmness.

I am spying, as you said I must. Her eyes narrowed.

"But I specifically told you to stay away from Crowley." He took a few steps toward her.

And I wondered why you did. So, I came to see for myself. She moved out of the deep shadows, but barely enough for the indirect lamplight to reveal her shape.

He noted that her unbound hair, reaching to the top of her thighs, fell in dark, thick, mysterious waves and covered most of her. She was glorious in this form, like some nymph from mythology. And she was angry. Whether that was because he had commanded her to stay away or because he had caught her where she was not supposed to be made no difference. Because he was angry as well.

"I told you to stay away because of the danger," he said, ignoring the pleasurable clenching of his muscles at the sight of her.

You told me to stay away because you wish to take your revenge at a later date. Each of her words landed like a hot brand in his brain.

Her accusation was untrue, and that angered him even more than finding her in Crowley's rooms. But what made his temper soar was the frustration at being unable to reveal that he truly wished her no harm. He had to make her believe he was still a threat to keep her safe.

"I have no need to control you, Princess," he said, heat seething beneath his words, "because you are bound by your own limitations."

As soon as he spoke, he knew he had gone too far. He had insulted and hurt her by referring to the curse. She went perfectly still. And then she surged forward and slapped him across the face.

The blow rocked him but did not hurt. It had force behind it, more than what she would have had in her flesh and bone form, so he knew she had used her mind as well as her Shadowy body. But he also felt a delightful tingle on his cheek where her palm had landed. Wide-eyed, she stared at him, looking both shocked and appalled. He covered the imprint of her hand on his cheek, expecting to find his skin singed, but he was unharmed. Fascinated, he reached out and touched her cheek. Those sparkly tingles erupted beneath his fingers. Her gasp rustled through his mind.

Touching her felt like touching warm, thick fluid, enveloping and supporting at the same time. Yet he felt tension, so his fingers went no further than the surface where those tingles occurred. Beneath, he could feel the firmness of her delicate bones, yet even those were not truly solid. The sensation intrigued him.

Her lips parted. *I can feel nothing when I am Shadow. But I can feel you.* Her voice whispered through his head in astonishment.

"And you feel…" He could find no words to describe how she felt to him.

He wanted to feel more. His anger became secondary to his curiosity. His need. She was only inches away. With gentle pressure, he brought her closer. And lowered his mouth to cover her lips. Her sigh slipped through his head.

Those tingles danced and sparkled wherever he touched her. He felt her arms slip around his neck, tingles spurting like a magical necklace. She swayed against him. Her lips parted beneath his, inviting him in. He took advantage without thought to where they were — in the middle of another man's rooms, there to secretly gather information. Because kissing her, touching her in this state was the most erotic sensation he had ever experienced.

Although she had no weight, he knew the exact moment she went boneless, giving herself up to the kiss. And then she wound one leg around his hip. With another little leap, she had wrapped both legs around him. He supported her bottom, weightless in his hands, and tingles leapt from his palms, up his arms. He drowned in her. He wanted nothing more than to strip off his clothes and bury himself in her. But he could not. She was Shadow. Cursed. And virginal.

A silent sound, part sigh, part moan, wafted through his head. Her tongue tangled with his. He heard her whimper. She was as lost as he was. But one of them had to keep their wits. He struggled to maintain his sanity. That was difficult when sparkling tingles burst and danced where their tongues battled. It became harder when she wriggled her bottom against his hands. All he wanted was to touch her. All over.

He trailed one hand across her hip, up her ribs, and cupped her delightful breast. He felt the nipple pout against his palm, even in her Shadowy state. He teased it between thumb and finger. Another moan curled through his head. She tensed. And then she threw back her head and flew apart in his arms.

He watched, awestruck.

Allegra returned to reality very slowly. The delicious sensations that had coiled and exploded through her still pulsed faintly. She was not sure where she was or what had happened, except that she had never felt anything quite so wonderful — and certainly never while she was Shadow. She never felt *anything* as Shadow. But she had felt that amazing, wonderful release. And she had felt Hawksmoor. Could still feel him. His hand on her bottom. His fingers at her breast.

And that meant he was holding her.

She opened her eyes. They were mere inches from each other, their noses nearly touching. Her legs were wrapped around his hips. Intimately. Those tingles tickled on her skin.

He wore a very satisfied grin. Embarrassment made her want to squirm, but she realized that would only encourage him. And she realized what had happened to her. With only a kiss and a little caress. *Dio!* What had she done? And what would happen when he came to her while she was in the Hunger? She did not want to think about that.

She frowned, covering her discomfort with anger. *Put me down, per favore.*

"But you were the one who climbed up." His smooth words teased.

She suspected that wriggling her way out of his grasp would only make his hold tighter and delight him even more. She straightened as far away from him as she could.

If you do not wish me to turn your mind to porridge the next time we meet, you will do as I ask, she said.

"I was only trying to accommodate a lady." His grin turned wicked. "But if the lady wishes to deny herself any pleasure, then I bow to her wishes."

With aggravating slowness, he loosened his grip on her bottom and allowed her to slip to her feet. She stepped back from him as soon as she could. He continued to grin.

She raised her chin. *There will be no more kissing.*

"As the lady wishes," he said with a flourishing bow, but she heard a distinct chuckle.

We will each search this place, she commanded. *I will search over there, and you, Sior Hawksmoor, will search here.* She wanted as much space as possible between them, but she refused to leave until she had done his spying for him. She began to move toward her designated area.

"Perhaps, after what we just shared, you might start calling me Sebastian," he drawled.

His words stopped her. *Why would I do that?*

A cool brow went up. "Because, lovely lady—Allegra—that is my name."

Bah. The sound of exasperation burst from her mind, and she turned on her heel, dismissing his suggestion. Calling him by his given name was much too intimate, and she was not about to be intimate with him again. But then she remembered the Hunger and the agreement he had made with Luisa. He would come to her then to alleviate her need, most likely tomorrow when she transformed from Shadow to flesh and bone. And that would be very intimate.

No. It would *not* be intimate. It was merely a balm, a medication, a remedy, something similar to what a physician might prescribe for an illness. Something that would alleviate her pain. She would hold her nose and drink it down like any vile medicine.

But in the back of her mind, she knew it would not be vile. It would be glorious, luxurious, delicious. Sensuous. She pushed away that niggling anticipation and forced herself to focus on her task.

Allegra stalked away to the far side of the room. She was still aroused from their kiss, despite that glorious release in his arms. But she was not about to let him know she still wanted him. So, she feigned affront. His amusement at her subterfuge came as a soft huff.

She concentrated on her search and ignored him. He eventually turned away to do his own search. As she turned in a circle, she tried to envision where a man like Crowley might hide something. She had no idea what she was looking for, but she would know as soon as she saw it. The fireplace surround captured her attention. It was made of plain bricks in a herringbone pattern, but one brick was slightly out of line with the others. With a tiny gesture, she loosened the brick, pulled it out and allowed it to gently float to the floor. A black hole gaped where the brick had been. Her eyesight in the dark was acute in her Shadowy state, and she saw that something lay in the hole. With a flick of her fingers, she pulled it out and opened it, so it floated a minuscule space above her palm. It was a letter, dated thirty-six years earlier. She read:

Madam,

I sympathize with your predicament, but, unfortunately, you are not of my station and I am required to wed another. I have made arrangements to have you wed the Most Reverend Reginald Crowley. He will adopt your child and raise your son as his own. From this point forward, I will no longer acknowledge any connection between us, nor will I acknowledge the child as mine. I wish you a good life.

Michael Fox, Earl of Hawksmoor

Allegra read it again, not grasping what was before her. Then in a flash, she realized a piece of the puzzle that was Sebastian Fox was revealed in the letter. Crowley was his father's illegitimate son.

Madre di Dio! The words erupted in her brain, spilling out, landing wherever another might pick them up.

Across the room, having caught her words, Hawksmoor shot to his feet, ready to defend. Aggression rippled off him. One part of her appreciated his protection, but the greater part resented his assumption that she needed protection. And she was annoyed that she had revealed her astonishment. Of course, he would want her to spy on his half-brother. Anger at his manipulative secrecy coursed through her.

No one is attacking, Sior Hawksmoor, she said, her words crisp. *But I found this.* She held out her hand with the parchment floating above her palm.

He picked up his lantern, strode to her and plucked the parchment out of the air. His lips thinned as he read. A tiny tremor in his hand made the paper stir. He met her gaze. She saw shock and disbelief in those midnight eyes.

I believe I just learned another of your secrets, Sior Hawksmoor, she said.

He shook his head. "I had no idea," he said. "How did I not know? Crowley is my half-brother."

His surprise seemed real, but she was not sure she believed him. *He courts your mother.* Distaste twisted through her words.

He carefully refolded the letter on its well-worn creases. "He must want something."

Abruptly, he bent down and picked something from the ashes. It was a fragment of foolscap, mostly burned. Allegra craned her neck to see, but she could read only a few words: *dangerous…Egypt… information…countess*. It appeared to be correspondence that Crowley wanted kept secret. Perhaps he was more than Hawksmoor's illegitimate half-brother. Perhaps he was a French spy.

What have you found? she probed.

He pocketed the foolscap. "Nothing of any importance."

Her eyes narrowed on him. The bit of paper was quite important.

He held out the folded parchment to distract her. "You must put this back exactly where you found it. And, please, say nothing about any of this."

Another bargain, Sior Hawksmoor? she taunted. *We seem to be the keeper of each other's secrets.*

He raised a cool brow. "One secret for another, lovely lady."

She smirked as she turned to replace the letter. *I think I might be ahead in that bargain.*

He was quiet and deep in thought when she finished replacing the brick. Taking advantage, she hopped to the windowsill.

Buona notte, Sior Hawksmoor, she tossed out as she dropped to the alley, two stories below.

She heard his footsteps rush to the open window. "When should I come to you?" he called quietly, referring to the arrangement when she transformed back to flesh and bone.

She sent a tiny poke of annoyance into his head. *You will wait until I summon you. Patience is a virtue, si?*

Then she ran into the night as she tried not to imagine what coming together with him during the Hunger would be like.

Chapter 11

The next day, Sebastian procrastinated until nearly teatime before he gained the courage to speak with the countess. He had spent hours with his estate agent, had taken Vulcan for a long and vigorous ride, had eaten his midday meal at the tavern just beyond the boundary of Blackbrake, and, indulging his valet, had gone through his wardrobe. He could not put off the conversation with his mother any longer. He found her writing letters in the small drawing room.

She looked up from her correspondence with a welcoming smile. "Sebastian, my dear, you have been absent nearly the whole day. I have missed you."

"Madam," he began.

Her smile faltered at his formal greeting.

He cleared his throat and started over. "Mother." He paused, unsure of how to proceed. "May I sit?"

She waved him to a chair near her. He chose one a bit farther away.

A crease appeared between her brows. "Hawksmoor, the only time you refused to sit next to me was when you were little and had done something unbelievably naughty. What have you done?" Her use of his title name indicated her displeasure.

He glanced away and gathered his courage. "It is not I who has done something, Mother. I believe the man, Crowley, is a knave and a scoundrel."

Her frown deepened. "Whatever do you mean?"

He clenched his fist to refrain from blurting the sordid truth. He did not want to have to deal with his mother's megrims. "I believe he is playing you false."

She tossed down her quill. "How can you say such a thing? He has been engaging and a gentleman." She put her hand to her forehead. "I feel a megrim coming on."

His attempt to be gentle and diplomatic was not working. "Mother, you are not getting a megrim." Sebastian forcibly unclenched his teeth. "Hear me out. I believe he will claim some sort of family connection."

The countess dropped her hand and broke into a smile. "Why, of course! He is a distant cousin on your father's side."

Sebastian blinked. "I beg your pardon. I'm not sure I heard correctly."

"He informed me when we first met that he was distantly related." His mother nearly beamed. "I told him that I would allow him to take me on rides through Hyde Park, and escort me to less formal affairs and the theater and gaming hells. Naturally, certain houses would be closed to him."

"Naturally," he mumbled. Crowley had his mother completely hoodwinked. "Has he asked you to cover his gambling chits or tailor's bills?"

His mother waved a dismissive hand. "Pin money." She glared at him. "Do not dare to presume you will take over the allowance your father provided for me. It is mine to do with as I wish."

Her directive angered and insulted him, and, if he were honest, hurt, for he would never do that. But she needed to see that he was concerned for her. Crowley was dangerous.

He stood, too upset to remain seated. "Mother, he is a parasite. I should forbid you to see him."

"You'll do no such thing." She tightened her jaw assertively.

He drew a breath to respond, but it was interrupted by a knock on the door.

Quint entered and intoned, "Mr. Crowley to see you, my lady." He held out a silver salver with a note. "For you, my lord."

Sebastian took the note, a small parchment simply folded with the unusual seal of a circle broken into three parts and a shaft of lightning through its center. He broke the wax and read: *Come now.*

He knew who the note was from and what it meant. The princess had transformed from Shadow into flesh and bone. He had to go to

138

her immediately. His conversation with his mother would have to be continued at another time. He mumbled his apologies.

As he strode toward the door, Crowley entered. He vaguely heard his mother's charming greeting to the man. But as he passed the blackguard, their glances met. Crowley's eyes went hard and cold for just an instant before he raised his pleasant façade once more. Sebastian's ability to sense a person's essence clicked in. A sickly yellow-gray fog surrounded Crowley, with a faint sweep of something dark edging one side. That threatening smudge made Sebastian uneasy. It hinted at malevolence. He was more determined than ever to unmask the villain before he could harm the countess.

But first, he had to tame the beautiful creature who waited for him.

Allegra paced across the secret room below the priory. She could not remain still. But motion was an agony. With every movement, the thin, silk robe she wore slid against her in an exquisite torture of her senses. The soft swish of the material screamed like the rush of a tempest wind. The touch of it as it billowed and settled created a sensation of pleasure-pain beneath her skin. She thought she might go mad. She needed — craved — the touch of a man. But not just any man. Him. Hawksmoor. Sebastian.

Just thinking his name made her gasp as a throb of desire pulsed through her. She curled her fingers into a fist, the nails biting into her palm, creating pain now that she was flesh and bone. She should not want him that much. She should tell Luisa to keep him away. But that thought sizzled to nothing as the fiend that lived in her during the Hunger took over.

Want.

Touch.

She stopped in the middle of the room and drew a breath, at the same time pushing that fiend to a tiny corner of her mind. She could hurt Sebastian, destroy him when she entered his mind. Her need was too great, and her ability to control her Thought Binding not as strong as she wanted it to be. Luisa should never have agreed to have him come to her. They would have thought of another way to feed the Hunger. But she knew there was no other option.

She paced again. Where was he? She needed him. Needed his soothing touch. She hated this. Hated the curse that turned her to Shadow. Hated the cravings of the Hunger as she returned to flesh and bone. Why couldn't she be a normal woman with normal desires?

The fiend rose up again. Wanting, desiring, needing, demanding. She threw her head back as she strangled a cry. She thought she might crawl out of her skin. And then—

"Allegra."

Her breath caught. His voice sent a shiver through her. She turned slowly. He stood in the doorway, the shadows from the firelight flickering over him, highlighting the swell of a muscled arm, the sharpness of a cheekbone, the hollow at the base of his throat. He was dressed in a simple white shirt, open at the neck, and buckskin breeches that outlined the muscles of his hips and thighs. A bulge at his groin showed the stirrings of his arousal. His feet were bare. His hair was unbound, a fall of black silk down his back. He could not have looked more desirable nor more masculine. Her feet remained glued to the floor while every tiny bit of her wanted to surge forward and engulf him. The tips of her fingers pulsed with need. Her mouth went dry.

"Allegra," he said again, this time her name a mere murmur.

touch. Touch. TOUCH.

The fiend's demand forced her a step forward. The movement made her brain click into awareness. She stopped.

"Come in, *Sior* Hawksmoor." She refrained from running to him and putting her hands all over him. Her restraint caused something close to pain to zing through her.

Want.

Need.

The fiend's impatience clawed at her.

He moved into the room. One step. Then two, three, four. She counted each one, forcing herself to remain immobile, until her muscles burned. He finally stood before her, but not quite near enough to touch. She took the last step that brought her closer, and her relief came out as a sigh.

He frowned. "You're in pain, lovely lady."

She shook her head, denying it all. She could not let him see how much she wanted him, needed him, craved him. How much her desire to touch him consumed her. She reached out and placed her palm against his chest. The tips of her fingers brushed against the skin exposed by the open neck of his shirt. The contact provided an instant of relief so swift, so sharp, she whimpered, tears coming to her eyes. And it broke her control.

Her fingers curled into his shirt and ripped it, the sound deafening in the silence of the room. She heard his quick intake of breath and sensed rather than saw the flash of surprise in his eyes. Her other hand pressed against his shoulder and she pushed him back, back against the wall where the shackles hung. Taken unaware, his steps staggered, and he nearly lost his balance until he came into solid contact with the stone wall. Those incredible eyes narrowed, their blue turning to midnight. He wrapped his fingers around her wrists and forced her hands to her sides.

"You'll not chain me," he growled. "Not this time. This time I am here freely."

He defied her, would fight what she wanted, needed, but the fiend in her knew what to do. She swayed against him, hip to hip, letting him feel what she had to offer.

"Don't you want to dance with me?" she purred.

His gaze turned crafty. "Oh, yes, I want to dance with you, but this time, I lead."

With a motion so swift she lost her breath, he swung her around, reversing their positions. She felt the chill of the stone wall through her thin robe. The circle of his warm fingers at her wrists was a sensual counterpoint. She sucked in his scent—piney, woodsy. It momentarily calmed the fiend.

He leaned in, his body trapping her. "I know what you want," he whispered. "I know what you need."

His breath was warm against her ear. And then she felt the tip of his tongue caress her earlobe. His lips kissed the pulse beneath. Her eyes slipped closed and her breath released in a sigh. His touch was heaven.

Sebastian knew she was in an agony of arousal. She vibrated with her need. As soon as he had seen her in her thin silk robe, his own desire escalated from anticipation to heat. He wanted her. And he would have her. But not like this. Not when she was in a fog of need so great it destroyed her rational thought. He would help the princess through this and deny his own needs.

But he was not entirely selfless. He had made the arrangement with Mistress Luisa so that the kidnappings would stop, but he had other reasons as well. He had promised payback for his own kidnapping and seduction in this very place. He was getting his payback most delightfully. And he wanted the return of his torc. Perhaps he could persuade the princess to return his property.

With one finger he traced a path from her jaw, down her throat, across her collarbone, and along the edge of her robe where it gaped, teasing him with a glimpse of the valley between her breasts. Her head fell back against the stone and a low moan escaped her throat. While she was distracted, he slipped a manacle around one of her wrists.

Her eyes flew open. Heat flared in them. "What do you do to me?" Her words were husky.

"Don't you remember, lovely lady?" he said as he manacled her other wrist. "I promised you one seduction for another."

"But I didn't...That is...You can't...Ahh." Her protests ended as he slipped his hand under the flimsy silk robe and cupped her breast.

The firm mound fit perfectly in his palm, as if it had been molded just for him. He was already hard, and the feel of her beneath his hand made his muscles clench even tighter. He rubbed his thumb across the pouty tip and was rewarded with a moan. She licked her bottom lip, and he decided he wanted that lip as well. He lowered his head and ran his tongue along the same route.

"You taste like strawberries," he murmured. "Sweet. Juicy. Delicious."

He wanted to take possession of that luscious mouth. Her lips parted beneath his teasing and invited him in. He slipped one arm around her waist and pulled her close, her curves fitting him exactly.

Their tongues tangled in an intricate dance. Her hips gyrated against his groin. He was so hard he thought he might burst. He wanted to slip inside her and lose himself.

He was already lost.

Abruptly, she broke away. With a growl, he cupped the back of her head to hold her. He wanted more of her. She dodged his mouth.

"Thought Binding," she gasped. "I must Thought Bind with you."

He blinked. The fog of desire cleared enough that he realized he had nearly mauled her. That was not what he had planned at all. With effort, he regained control of his senses. He would have payback for what she had done. One seduction for another.

He rubbed his thumb across her nipple. "Why must you Thought Bind with me? What if you don't?"

Her eyes widened as if the idea had never entered her head. "I... ah." Her lashes swept down and her head fell back as he pinched the bud.

"What if I could give you what you need without Thought Binding?" he whispered next to her ear.

She remained silent as he massaged her breast, her breath suspended.

"Tell me why you need to Thought Bind," he pressed in a murmur. "What is it that you need?"

She licked her lips. "Touch." Her eyes opened. "I need touch."

He smiled. "I can touch you. Here." He gave her breast a gentle squeeze, then ran his fingers to her breastbone and followed the edge of her robe down. And here." He dragged his fingers down farther, separating the two sides until he reached the tie. With a flick, he slipped the tie loose. And here." His fingers dipped lower across her belly, circled her navel. He was rewarded with her tiny gasp and a shiver. "I can even touch you here." He cupped the soft curls between her thighs where she was warm and already moist. Her breath hitched. "And when I touch you here—" He slipped one finger across her wetness. "— I will give you every-thing you need."

She groaned and rocked her hips against his hand. Then she stiffened. She stared at him with those dark, haunted eyes.

"I cannot." She swallowed, the words seeming to be difficult to speak. "Luisa said I should never…" She swallowed again. "A man should never…"

"You are a virgin," he said.

"*Sì*." The word came out strangled. Her glance slid away. Heat bloomed in her cheeks.

He wanted very much to be the one to rectify that condition. Instead, he leaned close and murmured, "Ah, Princess, there are ways to touch that will not change that." He demonstrated by swiping his thumb across her moist nub.

She sucked in a breath. "Do that again." Her eyes were glazed and hot.

Sebastian's mouth tipped up. She needed release. He would give her that, but first he needed to bargain a bit. "If I give you what you want, will you return my property?"

Confusion drew a line between her brows. He saw the moment she knew exactly what he meant.

"I don't—" she began.

He pulled his hand away.

"Wait." She closed her eyes, licked her lips, and gave a little shiver. "Luisa has it. Your torc. For safe-keeping."

"Don't lie to me, Princess." He trailed his fingers up across her belly, then let his hand fall away.

"I do not lie." She squeezed her eyes shut even tighter.

He knew very well she was lying. She would not look at him. He remained silent and pulled back from her.

Her eyes opened, darkened with pain. "Please, help me."

He squashed his sting of conscience by falling in with her lie. "Then we will discuss its return with Mistress Luisa." His statement was more of a command.

Behind the need in her eyes, he saw something crafty. Her lips curved in a tiny smile.

"Whenever you wish, *Sior* Hawksmoor," she said.

She was plotting something. Sebastian knew he should be wary, but he looked forward to whatever tricks she wished to play.

He wanted her.

He had wanted her from the time when he had first become conscious in this room and heard her voice, smelled her scent of oranges tinged with vanilla. But he also wanted her to want *him*, and not just because he was a convenient male body. That thought surprised and appalled him. He had never thought about a woman wanting *him* for more than a pleasurable interlude. He had never thought about wanting a woman for more than that. But he found he wanted to know more about her than just her luscious body. He wanted to know her likes and dislikes, what amused her, what made her sad. But that was for later.

"Please," she said again. "Help me." She pressed forward and ran her tongue across his lips. "Thought Bind with me and I can take you to Heaven."

"Or Hell," he added, as his arousal strained against the buttons on his breeches.

Her witchy smile enticed. "If that's where you wish to go."

"Perhaps there's an alternative." He pushed his finger deep inside her.

She released a little whimper of pleasure. "*Si*," she said and undulated her hips. "Wherever that is, I wish to go."

Allegra had never felt anything quite so wonderful. His fingers were magical. No man had ever touched her there. She had never wanted another man to touch her there. Thought Binding had been enough to relieve the terrible cravings of the Hunger. But this man made her want more. She wanted his hands on her. All over. And she wanted her hands on him.

With a quick thought, she unlocked the manacles. The freedom made her smile in anticipation of touching him. She let her robe slip to puddle on the floor.

His breath of surprise was followed by a chuckle. "Vixen," he murmured, then brought his mouth down to claim her lips.

She slipped her hands inside his torn shirt, across his ribs, around to his back. His mouth, his tongue, his fingers combined to make her blood rush in her veins, to make heat flare in her skin, to make her muscles pulse and clench.

And then his mouth was gone. His fingers stopped. He kissed his way down her throat, across her chest. His lips fastened on her nipple and he sucked. She heard a deep moan, then, appalled, knew she had made that sound. In a flash of sanity, she understood she wanted him too much. Why? What made this man different from all the rest? Afraid of the answer, afraid of what she felt, she shrank away against the wall.

Confusion made his eyes narrow. He stepped back. That strange imprint of the moon appeared. The focus of his gaze was intense, deadly, aroused with heat.

"What's wrong?" he asked.

She already missed the feel of him. "Nothing," she whispered. "Nothing is wrong."

The only thing wrong was her and her damned curse. But her self-pity seared away in her need. The absence of his fingers, his hands, his mouth, his skin made the fiend rear up in blazing fury. *TOUCH. NEED.* With a cry, she took the single step that brought her close to him. Wrapping her arms around his waist, she pressed against his body. Relief flowed through her followed by a throb of desire so strong it shook her.

He growled deep in his throat. His lips pressed against her shoulder. "Let me give you relief."

At the touch of his mouth, she felt her muscles go slack. He pushed her back the single step that brought her up against the wall. With quick, efficient movements, he had the shackles around her wrists again.

"Leave them," he said, the command more of a caress. "I lead, remember, lovely lady?" He trailed his fingers down her arms and wrapped his hands around her ribs, his thumbs just beneath her breasts. He placed a gentle kiss at one corner of her mouth. "I will never hurt you."

A shiver went through her at his words. *Madre di Dio,* she believed him, trusted him, this man whom she'd kidnapped and seduced, which made no sense. Even though she felt exposed, vulnerable, spread before him like a feast, her body arched up, aching for his touch, for those delicious sensations he created.

She trembled in desire, but the madness that usually clouded her brain during the Hunger had calmed. The fiend had always been in control, pushing her to touch, to take, demanding she satisfy the cravings of her body. Now, it seemed to wait, as if giving up control, as if the touch of this man might fulfill its needs.

But it was not only the fiend who wanted his touch. Her soul wanted it as well.

"Touch me," she whispered.

Sebastian smiled at her words. He would touch her. But not in the way she thought.

He leaned in and kissed the elegant curve between her neck and shoulder. Then he placed kisses across her collar bone. Finally, he took the rosy tip of her breast into his mouth and sucked.

"Oh, *Dio mio*," she gasped. The jingle of the chains connecting her to the wall punctuated her words.

He smiled again and slipped one hand down to her hip. "Is that how you want me to touch you?"

"*Si. No. Si.*" Her eyes closed and her tongue flicked out, wetting her bottom lip. "Is that allowed?"

"Allowed?" he echoed, confused at her question.

She swallowed, and her cheeks, already rosy from their love-making, flushed even warmer. "Is that what men do to women?"

Stunned at her naiveté, he was wordless for a moment. How could this woman, who kidnapped young men and seduced them, be so innocent, despite her being a virgin? He would have to proceed very gently. But the idea of introducing her to true passion made the blood pound through his veins.

He brushed a strand of hair away from her cheek. "Men do that who wish to make love to a woman."

Her eyes opened and met his gaze. "Then make love to me."

"Ah, Princess, your wish is my command."

He circled her waist with his hands and kissed the valley between her breasts. Then he trailed butterfly kisses down across her ribs. Kneeling before her, he worshiped her body with his mouth, swirling his tongue in her navel, licking the hollow of her right hip and then her left. Finally, he lapped her where she was wet, warm, and ready. She gasped as he tickled and sucked on her nub.

The manacles clinked against the wall, and then her fingers tangled in his hair, massaging, gripping, a mix of pleasure-pain. She had used her mind to unlock the manacles — again. The minx. The sensation of her hands on his scalp urged him on. Her hips rotated in rhythm with his tongue. She whimpered. Her breath stopped. And then her release came on a wild cry.

Allegra's knees gave out and she collapsed on top of him. He fell back onto the floor and took her with him. Her head rested on his shoulder. His arms wrapped around her, enveloping in their warmth. The fiend was quiet. Her brain was calm. For the first time ever since the curse had taken her over, when she suffered through the Hunger, she felt peace.

"*Grazie, Sior* Hawksmoor," she said.

Amusement rumbled in his chest. "My pleasure, Princess." He placed a gentle kiss on her temple. "You taste delicious."

His words stirred something deep inside. The fiend roused. Her peace fled. She squirmed against him.

His arms tightened around her. "You will unman me if you keep on like that." His words were hoarse.

"I need to touch you. All of you." She clutched at his shirt. She would rip it to tatters if he did not take it off.

The fiend was demanding again. *Want. Need. Touch.* It was insatiable. But not in the way of the last Hunger, when she had nearly destroyed the young man chained to the wall. This time, the fiend wanted *this* man. Only this man. His skin. His breath. His being.

"Are you sure?" While his words showed doubt, a stream of dark intent swirled beneath them.

She wanted to wade in that stream, splash and wallow in it. But she had to convince him to let her. She sat up, straddling him, her fingers still curled in his shirt. "Your skin. I need —"

He rolled her over, looming above her, not allowing her to finish. "Are you sure?" he repeated. "This time, I'm not chained to the wall."

He pulled her arms over her head, pushed her legs apart with his feet. She was spread-eagled beneath him, and he covered her like the most sensuous blanket she had ever experienced. His weight imprinted every single ridge and valley of his muscles, tendons, and sinews on her body. The fiend reared up.

Skin.

Touch.

Want.

She groaned, her need nearly unbearable. She had to have him. Without thinking, she bit his shoulder. Hard.

He hissed and jerked away. The sound snapped her back to sanity for an instant.

The feel of his flesh between her teeth calmed the fiend, but she was appalled at what she had done.

"*Dio mio,*" she gasped. "Forgive me." At the same time she begged forgiveness, she wriggled beneath him. His arousal pressed against her belly, huge, hard, pulsing.

His eyes narrowed. That odd imprint of the moon glittered between his lashes. And then in a single fluid movement he was off her and standing, pulling her to her feet, backing her up. His hand spread across her chest just below her neck, like a living necklace. His skin was warm, and tendrils of energy curled down to tangle in a knot deep in her core. With a gentle shove, he pushed her to the bed. She flopped onto her back.

He stood above her, those eyes so blue they nearly glowed, and locked on hers as he ripped off the tatters of his shirt, unbuttoned his breeches and pushed them down. He wore no undergarments. When he straightened, he remained still, allowing her to drink him in. He was magnificent, as perfectly formed as she remembered from that first night when she'd had him chained. That time, he'd had no tattoos. Now, he sported one on the inside of each forearm, a delicate intertwining of lines that formed a sort of square knot. She was reminded of that glimpse she'd had of him as a Druid priest when he had healed her, magnificent, powerful, when dark runes had scrolled across his skin and then disappeared. He was not an image in her brain now. He was solid, with heat rolling off him and desire in his eyes. The sleek, sophisticated Earl of Hawksmoor was gone, and in his place was a wild male who looked like he could devour her.

She scooted back on the bed. While the fiend sang its litany of need, the sane part of her quivered with apprehension. She had always been the one controlling, urged on by the Hunger. She had always taken. Now, this man wanted to take. She was unsure if she could give, afraid if she did, she would lose herself. Then the fiend screamed its commands, blocking out everything else.

TOUCH.

TAKE.

WANT.

NEED.

Her body responded to the fiend. Coherent thought was gone, incinerated in the blaze of fires beneath her skin. Instinct, embedded and ancient, took over. She spread out on the bed, offering herself. He would come to her — *had* to come to her. If this man did not touch her, she would go mad.

The bed dipped with his weight. And then he loomed above her on hands and knees.

"I know the game you play, lovely lady," he said, warning running through his words. "I know the dance. Beware how you use me. Remember, I lead this time." He placed a gentle kiss on her jaw.

She released a sigh at his touch. The fires beneath her skin diminished, giving her relief, but not enough to vanquish the need that throbbed and demanded. The fiend knew very well how to use him. The man straddled above her might think he led, but the dance was hers. Cupping his neck, she pressed her palm against the pulse below his ear. Between one breath and the next, she matched her heartbeat with his.

And walked into the majestic palace of his mind.

Chapter 12

Allegra found herself in an entry hall of sorts, as if it were part of an enormous house. Doors of all shapes and sizes and of different materials like stone and wood and gleaming metal were scattered around its perimeter. The usual plaster and paint of walls was mingled with beautiful moss and vines. Tall trees held up a roof so far above her it disappeared into darkness. Flat and curved stones acted as chairs and tables and mixed with the usual furniture. Swirls of pebbles and tiny flowers decorated the floor. When she had first connected with his mind, when he was chained against the wall, she had only been aware of the vague essence of the man. Even then she had realized he was complex. But this was more than she ever could have imagined.

Abruptly, Sebastian, Earl of Hawksmoor, was standing before her.

And he was not happy.

He was dressed as she had seen him when he had healed her, in only his plaid, feet and chest bare. His hair fell free, twisted into many tiny braids. That imprint of the moon shone from his eyes, a bright pinpoint of light surrounded by true blue.

I did not give you permission to be here, he said.

She wanted to look away, but she could not, caught as she was inside his mind. *I had no choice. I need to Thought Bind with you.*

He took a step toward her, his power rippling off him in waves of energy. Twined with that was the heat of his arousal. *I told you I would take care of you. That I would lead this dance. Trust me.*

She had trusted very few people in her life. Her brothers, even though they had sent her away. Luisa and Ernesto. To a lesser extent the Mother Superior of the convent school in Paris. But she was unsure about this man. He had healed and protected her, but she did not know why. He wanted her to spy for him. And he had so many secrets, evidenced by all those closed doors. He had touched a piece of the Sphere of Astarte, so that could make him enemy or ally.

The fiend in her grew impatient. The Hunger forced her to disregard logic. It urged, demanded. She closed the distance between them.

Please. She gazed up into those blue, blue eyes. *Let me be here.*

He studied her. She could sense him analyzing, probing. Then he held out his hand.

I will dance with you.

Beneath his words, she heard a deep, rhythmic throb, like the beat of a drum. It was primitive, savage, and it made her want to move. It reminded her of the chant he had used when he had healed her, but this was quicker, lower. She wanted to absorb its rhythm. She placed her hand in his.

Together they dissolved, each becoming their essence, swirling mists of color and energy. His was bright and dark, powerful hues that held softness between. She had seen it before and been entranced by it then, but this time, the beauty of it, its strength and mysticism took her breath. It swirled around her, as she had done to him the first time, inviting her in. She accepted the invitation, merged with it.

In another part of her, she felt his body wrap around her, skin against skin.

Warmth. Comfort. Safety. Refuge.

Heat. Excitement. Arousal.

They danced. Whirling together. Spiraling up and up. Becoming so entangled in each other she could not tell where he ended and where she began. Colors sparkled around them and created starbursts. Music pulsed and throbbed in time to their dips and curls. Scents of gardens, forests, and seas teased her nose.

Each of her senses flooded. The dark shadow of her guilt was blotted out by the brightness of her desire, of his unflinching gift of himself. He slowed their dance at her gratitude, his pleasure a warm glow. She felt a rumble of happiness in the chest pressed tightly against hers.

He whirled her faster, higher, up and up and up, titillating every single nerve in her body. Her muscles clenched and trembled. And then her release came in a showering explosion of multi-colored stars, delicious and exquisite.

At the same time, she watched as he exploded as well, their bursts of lights and colors mingling. Against the skin of her belly, she felt his warm ejaculation.

Slowly, dreamily, she slipped her hand from his pulse in his neck and broke the Thought Binding. The fiend had been banished. Every inch of her was sated.

"*Grazie*, Sebastian," she murmured.

He placed a kiss at her temple. "You are very welcome, Allegra."

She sighed in contentment. Her body was replete. The Hunger was gone. She snuggled closer and fell asleep, the two of them tangled together.

Sebastian was startled out of sleep by something landing on his chest. He grabbed for the dagger he kept beneath his pillow. But the space was empty. In a flash, he remembered where he was. And why. And what had happened before he fell into the best sleep of his life.

"You need to leave."

The sharp words snapped his eyes open. The Princess Allegra stood over him. She was fully dressed in a prim, high-necked, long sleeved, white day dress sprinkled with embroidered pink rosebuds. Her hair was pulled back into a decorous bun and tied with a pink ribbon. She appeared cool and remote, but a hint of anxiety tightened the corners of her mouth.

Annoyed at his abrupt awakening, he decided to provoke her. He smiled lazily. "You are looking well, Princess. All recovered, I see."

She frowned. "You will get dressed and leave. Quickly, *si*?"

He glanced down at his chest. The pile of his clothes landing there had awakened him. "That's not very gracious of you. Particularly after your warm reception last night."

Color heated her cheeks. "*Per favore*. Please." She made a frantic little gesture urging him up.

He stretched, then curled his arm behind his head as if he were settling in for a long conversation. "I find I'm quite comfortable. Perhaps I'll just rest here for a while. After all, we were quite energetic last night."

Panic widened her eyes. "You cannot. Please."

Despite her obvious anxiety, her lack of gratitude for his help with the Hunger irritated him. He raised a cool brow. "What if I refuse?"

She sucked in a breath and clasped her hands before her. "If you refuse—" Glancing away, she drew in another breath, this time slow and measured. "If they find you, that will be on your head." Her glance cut back to him, chilly as golden nuggets.

He shrugged. "Mistress Luisa already knows that I'm here."

"*Scemo.* Fool. Not Luisa and Ernesto," she hissed. "My brothers."

Sebastian forced himself not to react. Her brothers were a problem. He had come into contact with both of them. To one, he had been a disembodied voice in the dark who had held him at sword point and knocked him unconscious. To the other, he had been The Messenger of the Legion of Baal, a deadly foe. Both of them would look upon him as an adversary, if not an outright enemy. He had no desire to meet either of them, particularly in his present state, and certainly not as the man who had given relief to their sister during the Hunger, no matter how much she had needed it. But he was not about to reveal any of that to the woman standing before him.

He affected unconcern. "I think I should like to meet them. Perhaps they are more honorable than their sister and will return my torc."

Her eyes narrowed. "They will gut you and then throw you to the fishes if they find you here."

"That is rather uncivil of them, particularly after I helped their sister through a very difficult time," he said, pretending insult. He watched her cheeks pinken and decided to relent, but not entirely. "Ah, well, I suppose I should take my leave then, before I become fish food." He moved his clothes off his chest, threw back the covers and rose, not bothering to cover his nakedness.

Her gaze ran the length of him, stuttered over his semi-aroused state, skimmed across his chest, rose to his face, then skittered away.

She made a little strangled noise, her cheeks went bright red, and she turned her back.

He planted his feet and his hands went to his hips. "This is a little late to become missish, Princess. You certainly saw me unclothed last night."

Slowly, she turned to face him. "Last night," she said, gluing her gaze to his face, "was different."

His mouth quirked up. "Yes, it was, and quite enjoyable. I'm looking forward to our next encounter."

A line appeared between her brows. "There will be no next time if you do not get dressed and leave, *si?*"

"I'll leave, lovely lady, because you are obviously distressed about your brothers finding me here." He casually closed the space between them. "But I would like a token to remember our time together."

She stepped back and showed him her empty hands. "I have nothing to give you."

He clasped his fingers around her wrist to prevent her from fleeing. "Of course, you do," he murmured and pulled her against him. Without giving her time to think, he wrapped his arms around her and kissed her.

She melted beneath his mouth, and he exulted in the feel of her soft curves, but the sensation was short-lived. With a mighty shove, she pushed him away. He keenly felt the loss of her body pressed to him.

"You take liberties, *Sior* Hawksmoor," she said indignantly. "I did not give you permission to kiss me. I told you I had nothing to give you."

He laughed and held up the ribbon from her hair. "A token, Princess. I will treasure it."

Her eyes narrowed. "I should have brought my blade."

"No need, lovely lady," he said as he reached for his breeches. "I will soon be on my way and leave you to your brothers."

She turned her back again as he donned his clothes. Amusement at her modesty kept him entertained and kept him from contemplating what would happen to him if her brothers did find him with her. When he was dressed and had done his best with his shirt that she had ripped to ribbons, he cleared his throat.

"It's safe to turn around, lovely lady," he said.

She ran a critical eye over him, then gave a short nod. "Come," she said. "You must leave through the cellars."

He followed her out of the chamber. She took a torch from a wall bracket and motioned to the blackness of the cells beyond. It was the way he had first entered her secret room.

"That way," she said. "*Andiamo!*" Let's go!

They had just passed the first cell when the indistinct sound of voices came to them from the floor above. She shoved the torch at him.

"Hurry," she said, as a line of tension creased her brow. "I must go."

As she spun, about to flee in the opposite direction, he curled his hand around the nape of her neck and swung her against him. Before she had time to think, he brought his mouth down on hers. It was a kiss that branded her, marking her as his. For a moment, she blossomed beneath him. Then she pushed against his chest and flounced back a step.

He grinned at her tight mouth and stormy eyes. "Something to remember me by, Princess," he murmured.

Her response was an unintelligible little growl of words.

He chuckled and flourished a bow, then turned and sauntered into the dark cellars. He heard her rush away in the opposite direction, no doubt to greet her formidable brothers. He had no wish to run into the twins. He had a feeling they would be distracted by their delightfully charming and wily sister, but he wasted no time wending his way through the dark.

As for himself, he could not wait to be distracted by her again.

Allegra emerged from the trapdoor behind the altar and hurried through the chapel. Her lips still throbbed from Hawksmoor's kiss. She should have known he would not leave like a gentleman. But his kiss had been delicious. A bit alarming in its intensity. Like none she had ever had before, even from him. It made her insides tingle down to her toes. She liked it. Too much. Even now, just the thought of it made her body pulse.

She had never before remembered details of her time during the Hunger, but each time Hawksmoor had given her relief, the memories were sharp and very explicit. And each time, it seemed, she craved him more than the time before. Even when the curse did not rule her, she wanted him. The sensations were unnerving and frightening. She should not want a man that much. Especially that man.

She came to the door of the chapel and slowed her steps. Her brothers could not see her so unsettled. If they discovered the reason, they would demand she find another way to assuage the Hunger — without Hawksmoor. Her interludes during the Hunger were to be anonymous in order to preserve her reputation. Her interludes with Hawksmoor were far from anonymous. Her brothers would force her to give him up. That could not happen. For some reason, he had given her the most relief she had ever had during the terrible time of transition between Shadow and flesh and bone. He made her feel whole, normal, not as if part of her were floating in air unable to connect with the rest of her. She was not about to lose that.

In gratitude for what he did for her, she had arranged for that sleek walking stick to be delivered to him. To her delight, she discovered that it already hid a thin, lethal blade, as if the item had indeed been made just for him. And, it seemed, the large blue stone in its knob had a story as well, which the jeweler related to her with relish. A little thrill ran through her in anticipation of relating it to him. The stone and blade were perfect accessories to the walking stick. She had a feeling he would need it now that Nulkana knew of his existence.

Stopping before the entrance to the great hall, she smoothed her skirts and took a breath. She needed to be composed when she greeted Alessandro and Antonio. She might be their little sister, but she was a grown woman now. They had left her on her own for too long to be obedient and compliant. While her brothers might wish for a report of her life since she had last seen them, they also had to make an accounting of theirs. They had been gone far longer than ever before, reticent about their absence, and silent concerning news of home. She would demand answers. But right now, she would be their perfect, loving sister. With a smile, she stepped into the vast space of the great hall.

Her twin brothers stood on either side of Luisa, who was graciously indicating a small repast set out on a table before the settee. Allegra took a moment to drink in the sight of them — strong, handsome, with coloring matching her own, and mirror images of each other. Then she walked forward and curtsied.

"*Buongiorno*, Prince Alessandro and Duke Antonio," she said. "It is my pleasure to welcome you."

Her brothers bowed in unison. "Princess Allegra." When they straightened, they grinned, a dimple showing on each of them in opposite cheeks.

Tossing away any decorum, with a cry, Allegra rushed forward and hugged them both. They enveloped her in their arms. She reveled in their security and their affection and the fact that they had finally come to help her. Ever since she had met the sleek Earl of Hawksmoor, she had felt her life tilted out of center. She hoped having them close would give her some stability. But she could not have them too close. They could not learn of the effect Hawksmoor had on her. Besides, she was angry they had abandoned her for so long.

Stepping out of their embrace, she scowled and gave each of them a punch on the shoulder. "You left me on my own!" she scolded. "Where have you been? I have barely heard from you."

The two men exchanged a glance. Alessandro's mouth flattened. Antonio shrugged.

"She needs to know, Sandro," Tonio said.

Allegra placed her hands on her hips. "Know what? You cannot protect me by staying silent. I have been on my own for too long."

Alessandro sighed. "Well, if you must know, Alli…" His words trailed off and he sighed again. "Well," he said, then paused.

Allegra nearly screamed at his reticence. She was ready to demand an explanation, when Tonio waved to the space behind her.

"We are wed, Alli," he said.

His words did not make sense to her immediately. Then her eyes widened, and she swung around to where he indicated. Behind her, in a corner of the hall that was shadowed, stood two beautiful women. One was petite and dark-haired. And perhaps with child? The other was taller and blonde. Both women dipped a small curtsey.

Alessandro spoke first. "May I present my wife, the Princess Sabrina." He indicated the dark-haired woman. "And her son, Master Evan Barclay."

A boy of about five or six years stepped from behind the woman and made a perfect bow. Allegra was immediately charmed.

"And may I present my wife, the Duchess Solange," Antonio added, with a nod at the blonde woman.

"I have sisters," Allegra said in amazement. "And a nephew." She rushed forward and gave each of them a hug. "I have never had a sister, nor a nephew."

"Nor I," Sabrina said with a smile, and a very English accent.

"I have only a brother," Solange sighed with mock affliction, her words accented with French.

Allegra sensed that true sorrow lay beneath Solange's words, but felt uneasy questioning her. Perhaps when they came to know each other better, she would learn her story. She turned back to her brothers to demand how each of them found wives, but then she was struck by another thought.

One of her brothers should have been under the effect of the curse, either as Shadow or experiencing the Hunger. The curse caused each of them to turn to Shadow at opposite times of the cycle of the moon, and for the hours in between when they were both flesh and bone, one of them experienced the Hunger. But both twins stood before her, flesh and bone at the same time, and neither one was showing any sign of the dark cravings of the Hunger. It was during the short period when each brother transformed that she turned to Shadow, experiencing that state twice during the moon's cycle, as it became full, and when it went dark. She had already been Shadow and gone through the Hunger for the moon's latest cycle, so she could not understand why both brothers stood before her, handsome, graceful, muscles rippling beneath their clothes, seemingly untouched by the curse.

"How can you both be here, together?" she demanded.

The twins exchanged a look.

She stepped forward and scowled. "Don't even think about holding a silent conversation without me."

A ripple of supportive laughter came from one of the women behind her, possibly Sabrina. Allegra loved her for it.

"We have a great deal to tell you, Alli," Sandro said.

"Obviously." Her single word could have made a desert seem damp.

Tonio shifted, glanced at his twin, then turned back to her. Excitement made his eyes glow. "We have each found a piece of the Sphere."

Allegra's breath caught. He spoke of the Sphere of Astarte, the magical artifact that would end the curse on their family. The Sphere had been broken apart and the pieces dispersed by their ancestor so that Nulkana would never get her hands on it.

"How did that happen?" she asked, her eyes wide.

"With the help of Sabrina and Solange," Sandro said. His gaze turned soft as he glanced at his wife.

"They are descendants of Halima, Nulkana's good sister," Tonio added.

Allegra turned and stared at the women. She saw nothing extraordinary about them except for their beauty. Then she realized her rudeness. "Forgive me," she said as she blushed and lowered her eyes.

Both women moved forward and each took one of her hands.

"There is nothing to forgive," Sabrina said.

"We only just learned of our heritage," Solange added. "We were amazed as well."

When they touched, Allegra felt the throb of Halima's power that ran through them, and another force as well. They had both held pieces of the Sphere of Astarte, most likely when they helped her brothers, so that was not surprising. What made her duck her head was the memory of that same force running beneath the skin of the Earl of Hawksmoor. *He* had touched a piece of the Sphere. She had missed it when she had kidnapped him because she had been in the Hunger. After that, when they had danced, and when he had healed her, she had been so distracted that it had never registered. And then later, she had attributed it to his power as a Druid. Now, she knew.

162

He was hiding one more thing, another secret to add to the cache he hoarded, like a sly, seductive dragon amassing his treasure. But she would be the one to discover how Hawksmoor had come into contact with the magical Sphere, not her brothers.

The boy, Evan, stepped up beside her and slipped his hand into hers. Immediately, Allegra sensed the vivid power running through him.

"Are you my aunt now?" he asked.

Charmed by his artless question, she dropped to one knee to be on the same level. "I believe I am," she said. "And you are my nephew. I have never had a nephew before."

"I have never had aunts before." He turned to look at the beautiful women standing at his shoulder, one his mother and one his other new aunt. "And now I have two." He grinned. When he again met Allegra's gaze, he became very solemn and his eyes became unfocused. His small fingers gripped her hand very hard. "You will find the truth in the stones," he intoned.

Everyone stilled. No one spoke or moved for a very long moment, all stunned at the pronouncement.

Alessandro broke the silence. "Another prophecy."

Allegra glanced up at her brother. "What does it mean?"

Antonio reached into his pocket and pulled out a pendant, a blue moonstone in a delicate setting. "It probably means this." The pendant swung gently on its chain and caught the light. "I was bringing this to you in Paris when I was delayed." He sent a sly glance at Solange who blushed a deep red.

Allegra assumed a story was behind that exchange.

Alessandro took his wife's hand and said, "It's part of a single stone that belonged to Sabrina," he said. "It broke into three, one for each of us. It dampens the effects of the Hunger."

From the protective way her brother held Sabrina's hand, Allegra sensed the two had their own tale to tell.

"Take it, Alli," Tonio urged. "It helps."

Allegra closed her fingers around the pendant. As soon as she did, she felt a sharp shock. But it faded immediately, and a sense of peace filled her. She had not felt that well in a very long time. The possibility that her brothers had begun to find a way past the horrible affliction that plagued them made tears come to her eyes. She met Evan's gaze.

"Thank you," she said, buoyed by the possibility of seeing the end of their quest.

His attention wandered to the pot of chocolate, scones, jellies, berries, cheeses, and bread laid out on the nearby table.

"You must be hungry after making that prophecy," she said. She slipped the pendant over her head and stood. While Evan eagerly filled a plate, she said to her family, "We must all have some refreshment, and you can tell me about finding the pieces of the Sphere. I'm sure you had many adventures. And then I want to hear everything about your weddings."

As they gathered around the table of refreshments, Allegra realized that if the pendant worked as her brothers said, she would have no reason for the Earl of Hawksmoor to come to her during the Hunger. The thought opened a void in the vicinity of her heart. But if she could keep the pendant a secret, she could be with him as a normal woman. She wanted that more than anything. What would that be like? To lazily trace the contours of his body, to listen to his gasps as she softly caressed him. To feel the heat build slowly between them. The idea made her heart jump and her body clench in delicious excitement.

And perhaps, as she kept her secret, she might be able to separate the enigmatic Earl of Hawksmoor from at least one of his.

Later that morning, Allegra walked in the garden with her two brothers. After devouring the small repast, they had excused themselves from Sabrina and Solange so they could have some time together to become reacquainted and exchange their thoughts and ideas on the curse, the magical Sphere, and all that had happened in the last few months. She loved having them close, one on each side of her. She felt protected and loved. The sun shone, and the garden, which she had come to think of as hers, was flourishing. For the moment, her world was perfect.

"How is it with you and the curse, Alli?" Sandro asked. "Is Luisa able to help you?"

With that one question, anxiety bloomed in her chest. She would never reveal the balm that Hawksmoor provided. She smiled up at her brother.

"Luisa provides comfort when I need it." She hoped her words sounded convincing. Luisa *had* provided comfort, for she and Ernesto had brought all those men and the earl—especially the earl—to the secret chamber below the priory.

"And the Hunger?" Tonio probed.

Her anxiety jumped up a notch. "I manage."

"Luisa writes that you are still… intact," Sandro said.

A slow burn of anger wended through her at confidences that should have been hers to share or not. "Yes, I am still a virgin," she snapped.

"You must be careful to have no accident," he said.

"Accident?" she repeated, her voice tight. She knew exactly what he meant but was incensed and embarrassed that he would counsel her in such a way.

"We must find you a husband soon," her brother went on, oblivious to her ire.

She dropped their arms, stepped away and turned on them. "Do you mean before I am *ruined*?"

"Well—" Sandro began.

Allegra interrupted. "First of all, I am not *ruined* if I decide to…to do that." She waved her hand in a vague movement. "Neither of you considered yourself ruined after you…did *that* during the Hunger." She repeated the vague wave of her hand. "And why should you find me a husband? Don't you think I can find one on my own? Did anyone find Sabrina for you, Sandro? And you, Tonio, did someone find Solange for you?"

Her brothers' mouths dropped open and, speechless, they stared at her. Then they gaped at each other. Then they stared back at her.

Allegra ignored their shock and dismay. "I am perfectly capable of finding a husband on my own. But perhaps I don't want a husband. I have been living quite alone since you sent me away when I was nine years old, fourteen years ago." She folded her arms and glared at them.

Sandro scowled. "But you must marry."

"Why?" she challenged.

As Sandro's scowl became darker, Tonio put a placating hand on his brother's arm. "Alli, we sent you away to keep you safe."

"Thank you." She gave a short nod. "But Nulkana has found me anyway."

"What?!"

"When?"

"How?"

"What happened?"

"Did she hurt you?"

The twins' questions tumbled over each other. Their stilettos, normally hidden up their sleeves, appeared in their hands.

Allegra looked from one to the other. Exasperation battled with love at their reaction. She knew they wanted to protect her, but they still thought of her as their little sister. Besides that, they were men, privileged and arrogant, who thought they knew better than anyone, especially her.

"Put away your weapons, dear brothers," she said. "I am well, and, as you can see, unharmed." Allegra was not about to reveal how she came to be well with the help of the Druid priest, Hawksmoor. "I will tell you the tale later." Much later, she decided, after she had extracted a promise from Luisa not to disclose what had happened. And after she could embroider her tale so that it appeared only an insignificant meeting with the evil sorceress.

A tickle, a twitch between her shoulder blades warned her of eyes watching. A streak of panic shot through her at the thought that just talking about Nulkana had made her appear. Allegra swung around and sought the source of that tickle, beyond the garden wall to the grassy knoll that overlooked the valley where the priory nestled. A rider sat, strong and graceful, silhouetted against the clear sky. Hawksmoor. She let out a silent breath of relief. From this distance, she could not tell if he saw them, but she felt sure those blue, blue eyes were focused on the three of them. Her brothers followed her gaze.

"Who is that?" Tonio asked.

Allegra shaded her eyes as if she tried to discern the rider's identity. "I'm not sure," Allegra lied. "It could be the owner of this property. I understand he has a large estate across the valley."

Tonio kept staring. "He seems familiar for some reason."

She remembered that Hawksmoor had been to Venice and Paris. And her brothers spent time in both cities. She wondered if either brother had come into contact with the earl, which would have been quite a coincidence in such large cities. But she was not about to let Tonio ponder the matter.

"I don't know why you should think he is familiar," she said. "He is quite English."

"We should pay our respects," Sandro suggested.

The last thing she wanted was for her brothers to meet the man who had brought her such relief during the Hunger. The situation was too embarrassing and too tangled to relate to them. Demanding equality during her time in the Hunger was one thing but revealing what she had actually done made her squirm. She came up with another lie.

"I have heard he is a recluse and shuns company," she said. Then the Devil took over her brain as she added, "Perhaps I'll take him for a husband. He will keep me secluded and then you won't have to worry about me."

The twins shared a look and they groaned.

Allegra gave them a mischievous grin.

"Come, Alli," Tonio said, chuckling as he tucked her hand in the crook of his arm. "No more talk of husbands."

Sandro tucked her other hand in the crook of his arm. "And no more talk of Nulkana for now. Tell us about what passes for society in this town. Our wives are craving some entertainment."

Allegra kept her satisfied smile to herself. She would give them all the information about the city they demanded, and in the meantime, she would come up with a plausible tale of her time in Bath, leaving out certain pertinent details.

Chapter 13

Several days later, Allegra arrived at Mrs. Abney's dinner party accompanied only by Luisa. She had offered to let the hostess know that her brothers and their wives had arrived so that they might be included, but Sandro and Tonio had both declined, saying they wished to get settled in their rooms in the city. Allegra was relieved they had decided to stay at the York House and not at the priory, and her own rooms in the city were too small to accommodate them all. She had no desire to have them close by and hovering when she next experienced the curse. She especially did not wish to explain the reason for the visit of the Earl of Hawksmoor when she entered the Hunger.

But perhaps that might not happen. She had the moonstone pendant now, which her brothers said would help alleviate the curse. While she did not think they exaggerated about the moonstone's power, she had become so used to turning to Shadow and then enduring the Hunger that she could not envision a time when the curse would not take effect.

She wore the pendant now, an odd blue stone set in intricate gold filigree, that seemed to contain the moon's glow, similar to that glow she had seen in Hawksmoor's eyes. Both Alessandro and Antonio had hinted that they each had a tale connected to their pieces of the moonstone. Allegra wanted very much to know what escapades her brothers and their wives had experienced, and she decided she would corner them all at the first opportunity and demand a telling.

As she handed over her wrap to the butler, he informed her most of the other guests had already arrived. It was a relatively intimate affair of only about twenty or thirty people, and Allegra had been introduced to all of them at one time or another during her time in Bath. Her hostess, Mrs. Abney, whisked her immediately into the salon where the guests mingled before going into dinner.

"Oh, my dear Princess," she gushed. "We have the most extraordinary luck this evening. The Earl of Hawksmoor accepted my invitation! You know he hardly attends these affairs."

Allegra murmured an appropriately astonished response, while inside, she cringed. Why had he suddenly decided to become engaged in society? He knew too much about her, especially her abominable behavior during the Hunger. And after their last time together, when they had shared passion, when she had tricked him to Thought Bind with him, she was not sure she could look him in the face and not blush, revealing to everyone present what they had done.

Mrs. Abney leaned close as she whispered, "We all heard how he carried you from the Upper Rooms when you became indisposed." Her voice dropped into a dramatic pitch. "And then he put you in his coach."

Allegra gave a small wave of her hand. "I had merely become faint with the heat, and he was kind enough to bring me into the fresh air. My companion, Luisa, was present. It was all very proper, *si?*"

"Of course." The lady's hand went to her chest as if to keep her fluttering heart from flying away. "But oh, my dear, it was s-o-o romantic."

Allegra managed a weak smile. She thanked all the angels in Heaven that the woman had no idea what had actually transpired inside that coach, or what had caused Hawksmoor to carry her from the Assembly Rooms. The memory of her encounter with Nulkana made a chill trickle down her spine. In reflex, she wrapped her fingers around the moonstone pendant and found it was slightly warm to the touch, warmer than from her body heat. Focused on that, she was startled to realize they had already entered the salon, where the guests mingled before dinner.

Mrs. Abney confided, "I have asked that he escort you into dinner."

Allegra nodded and tried to look pleased, the exact opposite of what she actually felt. If society kept throwing her together with Hawksmoor, her brothers were bound to demand an introduction.

That would have a disastrous outcome. How could she explain to them that he knew her secrets—all of them? If she told her brothers about Hawksmoor's threat of exposure, they would do something rash, like dumping him in the middle of the ocean as she had threatened him during that first encounter at Lady Bardsley's ball. The thought of losing him forever made her heart ache. That unsettled her. She didn't trust him. She had been taught never to trust anyone beyond her family and their Guides. But he had rescued her from Nulkana and cured her arm. And whenever he was near, her body reacted in such unfamiliar ways, not anything like her reactions during the Hunger. They were just as intense, but gentler, sweeter. She was so confused. She wanted to be far away from him, and at the same time very near to him. He was the one person who could give her relief during the Hunger. And the one man who confused her senses. What a muddle.

And then that very man, sleek and sophisticated, was bowing over her hand.

"Princess," he said in that smooth, deep voice that landed like velvet on her ears. "I am so very pleased to see you. And Mrs. Abney has asked that I escort you into dinner. How delightful. Will you allow me the honor?" His eyes glinted mischievously with shared secrets—too many embarrassing secrets.

Allegra wanted to kiss him, and she wanted to punch him, not necessarily in that order. Good manners required that she accept, despite her desire to run the other way. Mrs. Abney hovered at Allegra's elbow. She could sense that the lady was nearly bursting with the coup of having Hawksmoor attend her dinner party and the accomplishment of pairing them together at table. Instead of creating more gossip and unwilling to disappoint the lady, Allegra forced her lips to curve into a smile.

"Of course, *Sior* Hawksmoor," she said. "I can tell you about the arrival of my brothers from Italy. They arrived only a few days ago and are very anxious to acquaint themselves with Bath. Perhaps I could arrange for you to meet them, *si?*"

The slightest narrowing of his eyes indicated that he caught her subtle warning. But his smile was gracious as he said, "I would be delighted to make their acquaintance, Princess. We must make arrangements."

Mrs. Abney clasped her hands and sighed in contentment. Before she could comment, the dinner bell chimed, and the butler announced that the meal was being served. Hawksmoor offered his arm. Allegra placed her hand on the soft superfine of his coat and tried to look pleasant, not an easy task when his smile reminded her of a satisfied cat—a cat with muscles of iron beneath its silky fur and claws of steel hidden in its soft paws.

As they strolled toward the dining room, he said, "That is an interesting piece of jewelry you're wearing."

Allegra touched the pendant with her fingers and decided tormenting him would be much more entertaining than keeping the secret of the piece. "It is a gift from my brothers." Her tone was playful as she said, "They told me it is magical and wards off the effects of a curse. There is a verse that goes with it."

"That is quite fanciful," he said. "You must share this verse with me."

She leaned close and whispered in his ear:

"Feed the hunger;
Feed the pain.
Wear the moonstone;
Lose the shame."

She sent him a smile loaded with daggers. "So, you see, *Sior* Hawksmoor, our *arrangement* is no longer needed." Even as she said the words, she felt a tiny pinprick of regret.

His return smile was just as feral. "But we have so many other connections, Princess."

Allegra ducked her head. His reminder of the hold he had on her because he knew her secrets made anxiety clutch at her chest. She was saved from answering because they had reached the table and her seat to Mrs. Abney's immediate right.

"Enjoy your meal, Princess," he murmured, as he left to take his own seat directly across from her.

Heat rose in her cheeks. Her nails bit into her palm as anxiety turned to frustration. She needed desperately to negate his hold. The flurry of the guests finding their seats gave her enough time to compose herself. By the time Mrs. Abney had seated herself and the gentlemen at the table followed suit, Allegra was able to send Hawksmoor a cool smile.

His lips twitched and he acknowledged her with a slight nod.

A small commotion at the door to the room distracted her. A very late guest had arrived. It was Hubert Crowley. In dismay, Allegra realized the only empty seat at the table was next to her. She wondered how a man like Crowley could win a seat so close to the hostess. Then she saw that the man whose name appeared on the place card had seated himself far down the table next to a young lady who blushed and fumbled with her napkin.

"Mr. Crowley," Mrs. Abney said as Crowley made his way into the room and bowed his excuses. "It seems you have won a seat next to our delightful Princess Allegra."

Allegra pasted a gracious smile on her face, even though she knew the man was unscrupulous. Her search with Hawksmoor through Crowley's rooms had revealed one secret, but she had the feeling that the blackguard was hiding many more. This was her opportunity to get close and discover them.

As the servants began to bring in the trays and dishes of food, she said, "Mr. Crowley, I hear you have friends in Paris and Venice. You must tell me their names. Perhaps we have acquaintances in common, *si*?"

Crowley's eyes lit up. "I would be very happy to share their names with you, Princess. Perhaps you already know one gracious lady who has come to live on England's shores, the Vicomtesse D'Aramitz. She fled the terrible executions in Paris several years ago."

"I do not know this lady," Allegra said, "but perhaps you can arrange an introduction, *si*?"

"It would be my pleasure," he replied.

As Crowley went on about the lady's virtues, she could sense Hawksmoor's scowl even without looking. The earl looked so displeased, that Mrs. Abney asked if Hawksmoor found the soup not to his liking, Allegra had to cover her chuckle with a cough and her napkin. As a result, she missed his response, but not the undercurrent of irritation in his tone.

When she had recovered from her "coughing fit," she sent Hawksmoor a sly glance and said to her hostess, "I found the soup *delizioso*. You must have your chef share his recipe, *si*?" She turned to Crowley. "I am visiting the Pump Room tomorrow. I am so happy when I meet dear friends there." She smiled warmly and hoped Crowley was not too dense to understand that she was asking him to join her.

His eyes widened and a flush washed his cheeks. His mouth opened and closed twice before he found his voice. "I had planned on going there myself," he croaked.

"What a coincidence," Hawksmoor interjected smoothly. "My plans tomorrow included the Pump Room as well. We shall make it a jolly outing."

Allegra sent a narrow glance across the table. She surmised that Hawksmoor had no previous intention of going to the Pump Room, and she suspected that he never went near the establishment to take the waters with their reputation for healing. He was far too healthy. Further, she had never heard him use the word *jolly* for anything. He was the complete opposite of jolly. Sardonic, definitely. Droll, perhaps. Wry, most certainly. And the very definition of sleek and sophisticated. He mocked her little plot while appearing totally innocent. She had the urge to kick him. Instead, she smiled sweetly.

"*Splendido!*" she said, then turned to her hostess. "*Signora* Abney, you must join us. As *Sior* Hawksmoor has said, it will be *jolly*."

Hawksmoor's jaw worked as if he chewed his soup. He wanted her nowhere near Crowley, and her inclusion of Mrs. Abney was a complication, as Allegra knew it would be. She hid her smile of satisfaction. She would meet with Crowley and the French vicomtesse and discover all she could. Then she would pass the information to Hawksmoor and be done with this bargain she had with him. Her brothers were in England now, and they would fight Nulkana together without the earl's help.

Then again, she still needed to stay close to Hawksmoor. She tamped down the thrill of excitement that coursed through her at the thought and told herself it was because he had touched a piece of the Sphere of Astarte. She needed to discover when and where that had happened, and if he knew the location of the piece. A very pleasant idea drifted through her mind. Perhaps she could have one more assignation with him in that secret room below the priory and learn everything he knew about the lost piece. She might not be in the throes of the Hunger, but she knew the art of seduction. A quick journey into his mind with Thought Binding could reveal everything she wanted to know. She sent him a very warm smile.

Confusion, then suspicion entered those blue eyes. Allegra's smile became wider. Having the confident Earl of Hawksmoor uncertain of her made her giddy with anticipation. She would get whatever information she could from Crowley, and then set her plan in motion. She picked up her wine glass and saluted the man across the table. Soon they would be together, skin to skin. She would Thought Bind with him, unlock some of those doors in that majestic mind and learn at least one of his secrets. The idea made her insides clench in pleasurable expectation.

The next morning Allegra wandered through the spacious establishment known as the Pump Room. It was an elegant space, decorated with Corinthian columns and long windows that let in plenty of light. Benches and chairs were scattered about for the comfort of visitors. At one end in an alcove high in the wall, was a statue of Beau Nash, placed so he could watch over the interactions of the society that he had organized so well. A man called the pumper stood before the fountain and dispensed the healing waters. Around her, Bath's elite strolled and conversed, exchanging news, chatting with friends and acquaintances, and deciding which newcomers were worthy of attention, while a small orchestra played soothing music.

Earlier, her brothers had sent round an invitation to join them for a stroll in Sydney Gardens. She had begged off, claiming an appointment with her modiste. To salve her conscience for her lie, she had suggested an afternoon outing when she would show them the sights of the city. They could begin with a meal at Sally Lunn's. When they had agreed, she had sighed in relief. This was not the time for her brothers and Hawksmoor to meet, not when she was spying for him.

As she strolled around the Pump Room, Luisa trailed half a step behind her and grumbled. "I don't know why you think you should meet this man, Crowley," she said for at least the tenth time. "I saw him at the garden party. I did not like his looks."

"*Zitto*, Luisa," Allegra whispered. "There he is."

As she said this, he entered the room with a very attractive woman on his arm. She was of an indeterminate age, but certainly older than he. After seeing his sparse lodgings, she was convinced he aligned himself with wealthy, older women in order to filch them out of their pin money. She had the feeling that Hawksmoor certainly thought so. Knowing about the letter that could prove Crowley's relationship to Hawksmoor gave her a queasy stomach. She wanted nothing to do with the man, but she had set herself the task of gaining any tidbit of information she could from him. When he glanced around the room and spotted her, she gave him a nod of recognition.

"I think I require a draft of the healing waters of this place," she said to Luisa.

"I think you require the waters dumped over your *stupida* head," Luisa grumbled, but she took herself off to fulfill Allegra's request.

Allegra watched her Guide wend her way through the crowd toward the fountain where the hot springs spouted forth. She could sense Crowley's advance toward her from the opposite direction, but she refused to look. He must be made to work for her attention. When she finally granted it, he would be grateful enough to reveal any tidbit. She disliked playing the tease, but she disliked the man more.

"Princess," he said at her elbow.

She turned slowly and bestowed a warm smile on him. "*Signore* Crowley. This is a surprise meeting you here, *si*?" She would have been surprised if he had not come.

As he bent over Allegra's hand, his sleeve inched up. The edge of a tattoo peeked from beneath his cuff. Her blood ran cold. It was a frog glyph that signified Crowley was a member of the vicious Legion of Baal. She wanted to pull away her hand and wash it beneath the fountain. Instead, she smiled politely as Crowley introduced her to the woman on his arm.

176

He said, "The Vicomtesse D'Aramitz has come from Paris to brighten England's shores."

The vicomtesse was an elegant woman with dark curls and dark flashing eyes, and her clothes were of the latest fashion. Earbobs of large pearls with a matching choker indicated her wealth. Allegra wondered how much of that wealth she bestowed on Crowley.

The vicomtesse bounced a small curtsey. "I am zo 'appy to meet you," she said. "*Monsieur* Crowley has told me zat you lived a *trés* long time in Paree, *oui*? I miss France zo much. You must tell me zee news."

As they began to stroll about the room, Allegra asked, "Have you no one left in France?"

Suspicion flashed through the woman's eyes but was quickly replaced with a sad shake of her head. "*Non*. My family, everyone, zey all perish in zee Terror." She gave a delicate shiver and dabbed at an imaginary tear with her handkerchief.

"But there is one person you write to," Crowley said.

Allegra felt rather than saw the angry glance of the vicomtesse, but when the woman spoke, her voice was calm.

"Ah, *oui*," she admitted. "An old friend. She is like an aunt to me. But she lives far out in zee country and does not care of zee news in Paree."

Allegra suspected that this "old friend" was most likely passing along English secrets to the French Directory. She turned to Crowley. "Do you deliver these letters, *Signore*? I have heard that you often travel to the Continent. But travel to France from England is restricted, *si*?"

Crowley glanced down his nose at her. His eyes turned hard with suspicion, and his arm with the tattoo twitched. She felt an uncomfortable tingle along her side nearest to him, as if he were about to unleash some power. Then he smiled as though she had merely asked him about the weather. The tingle disappeared like it had never been.

"I have dear friends in other countries on the Continent," he said smoothly. "It's an easy matter to deliver a letter to France when I visit them."

Allegra was about to ask where these friends lived and when he had last visited to discover if he was connected to the gathering of the Legion of Baal from which she had fled. But Crowley abruptly halted their stroll, forcing both the vicomtesse and Allegra to stop as well. A couple stepped through the door — Hawksmoor with his mother on his arm. She noted he carried the walking stick she had sent him, and a warm feeling fluttered in her chest. The earl's gaze swept the room until it landed on her small group to his immediate left. She had the distinct impression that he knew where she was from the moment his toes crossed the threshold, perhaps even before that.

He smiled as soon their eyes met. "Princess! What a coincidence! I am very happy to find you here." His enthusiasm was so out of character and his surprise so contrived that Allegra nearly laughed. "May I present my mother, the Lady Evelyn, Countess of Hawksmoor."

As they greeted each other, Allegra saw how much Hawksmoor took after his mother. Her eyes were the same incredible blue, but her hair was auburn instead of the nearly black shade of her son's. The straight nose and sharp cheekbones that made Hawksmoor so attractive came from her. She was striking and must have been a stunning beauty in her youth.

She smiled and said, "Hawksmoor has told me all about you. I am so happy to finally make your acquaintance."

"And I am happy to make yours," Allegra said, charmed by the woman, at the same time wondering what her son had revealed.

Then the lady coolly greeted the vicomtesse and offered her hand to Crowley. Hawksmoor watched with narrowed gaze as the man kissed his mother's hand.

"I am glad we have met at the Pump Room," Allegra said before Hawksmoor could make any sort of cutting remark to Crowley. "We will have a jolly time, *si*?" She sent a sideways glance at him and said silently, *I am spying on Signore Crowley and you will not interfere.*

Hawksmoor raised an eyebrow at her.

"The vicomtesse was just telling me how much she misses France," she said, "and that the only news she gets is from an old woman who lives too far outside Paris to know what is going on."

"That is unfortunate," Hawksmoor murmured, his words loaded with irony that only she understood, for she had just given him the route of a French spy network.

"But *Signore* Crowley kindly delivers her letters when he travels to the Continent," she said with a smile.

Hawksmoor's mouth tightened just the tiniest bit as he absorbed the fact that she implicated the man who could be his half-brother as a member of the spy ring.

"A most chivalrous man," his mother declared with a warm glance at Crowley. "We will cheer up the vicomtesse at my ball." She turned to Allegra. "And of course, you must come. It will be a masquerade ball, just as they have in Venice. It will be a most splendid affair and make everyone forget they are sad. Princess, I have heard your brothers have arrived in Bath. I will send them an invitation. You must urge them to come."

Allegra caught the slight tick in Hawksmoor's jaw at the mention of her brothers. Even though she would never reveal to them that the earl had relieved her cravings during the Hunger, she could not help the little smile at the prospect of the three of them meeting. But then the idea of them meeting sent panic rippling through her.

"You must come for tea," Lady Evelyn said, regaining her attention. "I welcome any advice you might have for decorations. I will send around a note."

Allegra accepted her invitation, genuinely touched by her warmth. They continued to stroll around the room. Hawksmoor somehow maneuvered his way next to her as the others fell behind. To anyone merely glancing at him, he appeared smiling and relaxed, but she could feel the anger rippling off him.

"What are you trying to do?" he demanded in an undertone.

"I told you I was spying," she hissed back.

"I told you not to go near Crowley," he nearly growled. "Several times."

"*Si*. After you suggested I should spy on him so you would not send me to a penal colony," she shot back.

"That was—" he began.

"And if I had not," she interrupted, "you would not know that the Vicomtesse D'Amaritz regularly writes to someone in France, *si*?" she added.

She could hear him grind his teeth. They took several steps in silence.

Allegra made her second point. "And you would not know that *Signore* Crowley travels to France, most likely to connect with other members of the Legion of Baal."

He did not react immediately, which she thought a bit strange since he had warned her of the Legion. Perhaps he already knew about Crowley's travels. He finally gave a short nod.

"Thank you for that information," he said, his words tight. "But you do not know how dangerous he is, nor how dangerous the Frenchwoman is."

She silently acknowledged she knew nothing about the vicomtesse, but she knew Crowley was dangerous from the frog glyph on his arm. Rather than admit what she knew, she demanded, "Could either of them be any more dangerous than Nulkana?"

He remained silent, but his arm hardened beneath her hand.

"So, *Sior* Hawksmoor," she went on, "I wonder why you wished me to spy at all. I think perhaps you are involved in more than going to garden parties and attending the Assembly Rooms, *si*? I think the reason you wished me to spy on *Signore* Crowley is because you are a spy yourself."

Hawksmoor was again quiet for two steps. She could sense him tamping down his anger. Then he said quietly, "Thank you for your gift. It was quite a pleasant surprise."

His abrupt change of subject said more than if he had shouted his affirmative answer. He was a spy, but for whom? Did the spying have any connection to his knowledge of the Legion of Baal and Nulkana? Or was he merely an agent of the English Crown? He was a complex enigma of secrets.

In a graceful movement, he tossed up the walking stick, caught it in the middle, and let it slide through his fingers, capturing it so the large blue stone was covered by his palm. The tip made a small click against the floor.

The elegance of his acknowledgment of the Gift and abrupt switch from anger surprised her into graciousness. "The jeweler told me a tale about the stone. It is called the Druid's Sapphire."

"That is quite interesting," he murmured.

She peeked up at him from beneath her lashes. "A coincidence, *si*?"

"Hm," was all he said.

With a tiny smile, she said, "The stone gives the owner power over the spirits in the air, water, and underworld."

He refused to look at her. "That is quite amazing." His tone implied disinterest. She knew he was totally engrossed.

"*Si.*" She barely contained her laugh. "It is magical."

"A legendary myth, surely." A corner of his mouth deepened. "We all know there is no such thing as magic. I believe you have said so yourself."

Allegra was saved from answering when Mrs. Abney, followed by two other women, rushed through the door in a very awkward entrance. The lady hastened up to their small party.

"Oh, my goodness," she said, waving a handkerchief in front of her flushed face. "I was so afraid I'd missed you. We had some difficulty with a wheel on my carriage."

After everyone murmured their commiseration, Allegra took the opportunity to escape. As soon as she stepped out the door, she breathed a sigh of relief, glad to be away from both the Earl of Hawksmoor and Crowley. The earl sent her senses reeling with his cool blue gaze, his suave demeanor, his sharp mind, and the memory of his hard body beneath the elegant clothes. Crowley made her skin crawl. But she had accomplished what she had set out to do, and more besides. She had spied for Hawksmoor, completing her side of the bargain with him, and learned that Crowley was a member of the dangerous Legion of Baal.

As she and her Guide strolled down the street, she said, "I believe the morning was quite profitable, Luisa."

Luisa grunted. "If I drank any more of that water, I think I might have burst. If that Druid priest had not arrived, I might have been forced to use a hairpin on the French witch and her toady."

Allegra laughed at the same time the tiny hairs on her arms shifted. Her Guide could use a hairpin with deadly force. She silently thanked Heaven that Luisa was on her side.

Allegra and Luisa had not gone more than a few yards down the road when Crowley hailed her from behind. She turned, curious about what the man had to say. Luisa hovered close behind her shoulder. With a jerk of his chin, he indicated her Guide should back away. Allegra could feel Luisa stiffen at the insult, ready to protect and give argument, but she placed a hand on her Guide's arm and nodded to do as Crowley wanted.

She turned back to him. "What is so urgent or secretive that you must be rude to my companion, *Signore* Crowley?" she demanded.

A smug smile crossed his face. "I know the ancient artifact you seek, Princess."

Allegra blinked, then moved her parasol as if the sun were in her eyes. Calmly, she asked, "Why would I seek an ancient artifact?" She made a moue of distaste. "Most likely it is covered in dust and cobwebs, *si*?"

He smirked. "I know your secret."

Allegra forced herself to remain calm. Nulkana had sent her a note with those exact words. Did he refer to her curse, or that she had kidnapped young men to feed the Hunger? She gave a tiny laugh. "*Signore* Crowley, all women have secrets, even those who are young and innocent."

He waved away her argument. "I know why you crave to possess this artifact." His voice lowered dramatically. "And I know where it is." He nodded in triumph, as if he had just won a round of chess.

She opened her mouth to protest craving anything, an outright lie, but he spoke before she had the chance.

"A piece of the Sphere of Astarte, Princess," he said. "Wouldn't you like to own it to break the curse on your family?"

Behind Allegra, Luisa drew in a breath, hardly noticeable to anyone who did not know her. Allegra understood it for the warning it was.

She tipped her head as if very curious. "A curse? I do not know where you might have heard such a ridiculous thing, but surely you cannot believe it. My brothers are powerful, one a prince and the other a duke. Certainly, you cannot say they are cursed, *si*?"

He gave a shrug, as if he did not care, but his eyes said otherwise. "I am only trying to help, Princess. I know you are curious, at least. We can both profit from an exchange. I will send a message to let you know where and when we can meet to discuss this further." He glanced around at the busy street. "This is not the place for such things." He bowed to take his leave. "I hope you consider well my proposal."

Allegra watched him return the way he had come and re-enter the Pump Room. She did not trust him, but he had just offered the one thing that would turn her into a normal woman. Alessandro and Antonio had told her how they had each found a piece of the Sphere of Astarte, and how it had alleviated most of the curse. If she could find the third piece, perhaps the curse would be completely broken. But Crowley was a member of the Legion of Baal whose members wanted the Sphere for themselves.

"He offers you water in a sieve," Luisa said. "Do not believe him."

"What if he does know where the piece of the Sphere is?" Allegra asked as she began walking again.

Luisa shook her head. "He will want something very dear in return."

Allegra stopped and stared at her Guide. "What if I could find the last piece and break the curse?"

Her question hung in the air, for they both knew the magnitude of the answer.

Crowley sauntered back into the Pump Room. He refrained from rubbing his hands together in glee. He could see his future laid out before him as if a glittering road wended its way toward a castle nestled among the clouds. Obviously, Fate was smiling on him, and it had started the night before at that horrible woman's dinner party when he had found himself seated, not near the foot of the table, but right next to the princess. When she had first expressed a desire to meet his French friend and then had made it known she would be at the Pump Room, he could not believe his good fortune. His astonishment came not from being included in the outing because of the honor, but because she had so naively expedited his plan.

Now that she had publicly acknowledged him as a member of her circle, he could send a note to her. He knew she was interested in the piece of the Sphere, despite her denial. He would entice the princess to a secluded spot with that bait and capture her. Then he would send a note to the arrogant Earl of Hawksmoor and lure him with a threat of violence to his little Italian whore. Oh, yes, he had seen how they sparked together, obvious to anyone who cared to look closely that they were lovers. Even if they were not, the most honorable earl would run to protect the woman. He would kill the earl and turn over the princess to Nulkana, who would reward him with all he ever desired. The bonus in his plan would be that he would become the next Earl of Hawksmoor as the only living male in the family. He would take possession of the estate and turn out the dowager countess. Perhaps he might spare her a few coins for a coach ride back to London.

He had even manipulated another little extra by revealing that the vicomtesse corresponded with someone in France. Hawksmoor had to see that for what it was: passing secrets back to the Directory in Paris. The earl would inform the proper authorities, D'Amaritz would be arrested as a spy, and she would be gone. She had become much too tiresome. He wanted a young woman on his arm for a change. A wealthy heiress would do nicely.

He stopped in the doorway to the Pump Room and looked over the crowd. Soon, everyone would stop and gawk at him when he entered a room. He smiled. As his gaze landed on the vicomtesse in conversation with some other old hag, she smiled back, thinking that he was pleased to see her. If she only knew. Hawksmoor and his mother were no longer in attendance. Soon they would be gone forever. His smile widened as he moved through the crowd toward his rainbow's end.

Chapter 14

A week later, Allegra stepped down from her coach onto the gravel drive that curved in front of the imposing stairway and main entrance of Blackbrake. She had come to call on Hawksmoor's mother and take tea with her. Luisa stepped down beside her.

"It is quite imposing, yes?" Allegra said as she gazed up at the three cupolas that crowned the three sections of the house. Two wings stretched away to either side of the main section with its crenellated roof and three stories of multi-paned windows glinting in the sun. The last time she had been here, the house had been dark, and she had been Shadow.

Luisa grunted. "Not as imposing as Auriano."

Allegra grinned. "You will never think any place is as imposing as Auriano." Then she sighed. "It has been long since we have been home. Perhaps now that Alessandro and Antonio are here, we will finish this and be able to go back."

Luisa said nothing. Allegra knew from her silence that her Guide held no such optimistic view of the future. But the only way to get to any future was to move ahead, and the only way to do that was to take tea with the Countess of Hawksmoor. She stepped forward toward the entrance of the home of Sebastian Fox, Earl of Hawksmoor. Perhaps this meeting would provide some insight into the man.

They were greeted by a very proper butler who showed them into a pleasant drawing room. Long windows allowed in plenty of light, and French doors opened at the back of the room onto a veranda that overlooked formal gardens. Hand-painted wallpaper depicting exotic birds and flowers covered the walls and brought the gardens inside. Two settees faced each other before the hearth, and various other chairs and tables were scattered about the room. But the countess was not there to greet them. Allegra sat on one of the settees to wait, while Luisa retreated to a chair in a corner of the room.

Not long after, the door opened. It was not the countess who entered, but Hawksmoor. Allegra's breath hitched. She was unsure if her reaction was from surprise, or from seeing the beauty of the man. Why couldn't she be immune to his magnetism by now? He had certainly challenged and exasperated her enough. Frowning, she smoothed her skirt.

"Princess Allegra, Mistress Luisa," he said, giving a small bow. "Permit me to extend my apologies. I'm afraid my mother, the countess, is indisposed, and won't be joining you. But allow me to extend the hospitality of Blackbrake to you."

Allegra's temper soared. Her hands tightened into fists. "This is a very poor ruse to get me alone inside your domain, *Sior* Hawksmoor," she said. "I imagine you compelled your mother to send that invitation to tea."

He blinked as if she had struck him. His tone was bland as he said, "I assure you, Princess, my mother is quite unwell. She has suffered from the megrims her whole life."

Taken aback, realizing her gaff, she ducked her head. "I'm sorry," she said contritely. "And please extend my wishes for your mother's speedy recovery."

His smile wiped out the remorse she felt. Instead, warmth flooded her, like the sun breaking through clouds after a chill rain.

"I will certainly do so, Princess," he said. "She will be pleased." He gestured toward the doors at the back of the room. "I thought we might stroll through the gardens before we take tea." He held out his hand.

With only a tiny hesitation, she nodded. He tucked her hand in the crook of his arm and led her outside.

The day was very warm, and so Luisa opted to sit on a stone bench beneath the shade of a large oak tree that towered over one side of the garden. Allegra appreciated her Guide's discretion, keeping them in sight while allowing them some privacy, all quite proper. Hawksmoor guided her into a maze. The hedge had been clipped low, a bit above knee-high, so the fountain in the middle was visible.

But the path to get there wound back and forth upon itself many times, sometimes curving close to the middle and then veering away toward the outside edge.

"This is quite unusual," she said, intrigued as they strolled close enough to the fountain to be able to feel its light spray. She stopped, admiring the statue. It was a figure of a bearded man, naked except for a cape of feathers, crowned by leaves and sprouting antlers. His head tipped back as he blew a long, curved horn where the water spouted.

"Some believe he is the Green Man, protector of the forests, also known as Cernunnos, Celtic god of nature," he said, as he began to walk again.

"Is that what Druids believe?" she asked.

"The Druids call him "Antler Man." He grinned down at her. "He represents fertility."

Heat rose in Allegra's cheeks. She was not about to be baited into some risqué conversation, so she glanced out across the intricate pattern of bushes. "I suppose the maze has some hidden meaning as well, *si*?"

"It symbolizes the spirit journey to the underworld and then rebirth. Druids use it as part of the initiation ceremony," he said.

She looked around at the calming, graceful curves of the maze and wondered what ritual was conducted within its pathways. As a Druid, the man beside her had some very dark and lethal powers, some of which she'd seen when he healed her. She had the feeling that a Druid's initiation might include a very real and dangerous brush with evil, but she could not imagine the serene surroundings as the setting for anything sinister.

As if he could read her thoughts, he said, "We are merely blind-folded and asked to find our way to the center and back out again without stumbling into the bushes." He grinned down at her. "No bloody sacrifices before the statue."

Allegra wondered if bloody sacrifices were performed in some other location.

He was silent a moment, while he guided her along the path as it turned back toward the outside edge. "My ancestor had this planted several generations back, not long after the original part of the house was built. I can remember my grandfather walking here when I was very young. He said it helped him think. I was too impatient then to walk the path, so I used to jump the bushes to get to the fountain."

Allegra smiled, picturing the boy leaping like a colt to reach his goal. "You must have many memories of growing up here," she said, unable to keep the wistful note from her voice.

"Yes. Most good, some not. What of you, Princess? Do you have happy memories of Auriano?" he asked.

She bowed her head. "Only a few. My brothers sent me away when I was very young, after my parents…" Her throat closed up at the memory.

"After your parents died," he finished. "That must have been very hard."

She swallowed. Then anger surged through her. "Nulkana killed my parents and set fire to Auriano." The hand in the crook of his arm convulsed into a fist. "She is the reason my brothers sent me away. The reason we suffer this curse. I want her dead." Her voice vibrated with her rage. "I know that is a very unladylike sentiment."

"But perfectly understandable," he said.

They had arrived back at the entrance to the maze. Hawksmoor led her to a rose arbor where carved wooden benches were shaded from the sun. He guided her to one deep in the middle of the arbor and sat beside her.

"Tell me," he said.

She looked into those blue eyes, gentle and compassionate. Her own eyes filled with tears. "I cannot," she said with a shake of her head.

He brushed his fingers across her cheek. The gesture made her throat tighten.

"Then show me," he said, placing her hand on his bare wrist.

His skin was warm beneath her fingers. His pulse beat a steady rhythm. He was allowing her to Thought Bind with him, to enter his mind and release her sorrow. The generosity of his offer awed her. The last time she had Thought Binded with him, she had been trying to seduce him, and she felt a stab of guilt, for she had taken advantage of him.

His mouth crooked up. "I don't think we are in the mood for seduction."

Surprise that he could read her so well widened her eyes.

"Thought Bind with me only if you wish it, lovely lady," he said.

His words soothed her guilt. The memory of the first time she had connected with him, when he had been shackled to the wall, came to her. She remembered his kindness, his comfort at her shame and sadness. She remembered that her guilt had been alleviated along with the cravings of the Hunger. She wanted that solace again. Without another thought, she matched his pulse and slipped into his mind.

Sebastian felt her presence enter his head like a warm breeze. He had no time to greet her as he did the last time, for she had placed her memory in his brain like an opened package with its contents spilling out. Completely immersed inside her memory, he stood in a huge courtyard, the vine-covered stone walls rising around him to great height. Some of the vines were mere burnt skeletons, others had their leaves curled and singed. The walls that supported them were scorched, and a large section had crumbled. A coach of understated elegance stood in the space with trunks tied to its roof. Hitched to it, four matched horses shifted, eager to be on their way. In the middle of the far wall, huge studded doors stood open to the countryside beyond, which dipped and fell away. A road stretched into the distance before it disappeared down the slope of a hill. On one side of the track was a field of lavender and wildflowers. Rows of grape vines bordered the other. The rooftops of a village were visible below in the valley. Behind him, a set of tall doors showed dark traces of flames across their surface. He was in *Castello Auriano*, the ancestral home of the Princess Allegra and her two brothers, and it had evidently suffered some terrible misfortune.

"But I don't want to go!"

The tearful words were Allegra's, a little girl of nine or ten years. She was dressed for travel as she stood beside the coach. He felt her distress as she stared up at an older boy, whose hands were heavily bandaged. Beside him, another boy, his twin, looked just as distraught as the little girl. These were her two brothers.

"Alli, you have to go," the bandaged brother said. "We want to keep you safe."

"But, Sandro, who's going to keep you and Tonio safe?" she demanded. Her chin lifted defiantly. "I can use a sword. Gasparo has been teaching me."

The twins exchanged an amused glance.

Indignation tightened her mouth, and she poked her small fan into Sandro's ribs. He jerked away with a shout of pain. Tonio sniggered.

Sebastian remembered the bruise she had inflicted on him with that innocuous accessory. Even as a child, she had been talented with her fan. At the thought, he sensed amusement coming from the woman in his head.

"Don't laugh at me!" little Allegra said.

Tonio went down on one knee and gathered her close. "Oh, Alli, we're not laughing at you."

Sandro joined him and hugged them both. "We're so proud of you. You helped Tonio save me from going after Nulkana when she killed Mama, and you ran and got help when I tried to find Papa under the burning timbers. If you hadn't been so brave, I would have more bandages than these." He held up one wrapped hand.

Wrenching sadness swept through her. "But you couldn't find him," she said through her sobs. "I want Mama and Papa!"

"I know, Alli, but Mama and Papa would want you to be brave now, too," Sandro said. "Luisa and Ernesto will be with you."

Sebastian saw a younger version of the couple who aided Allegra standing a bit apart. Mistress Luisa glanced up at the sky. The vibrant colors of sunset streaked the blue above. A worried frown crossed her face, and she glanced back at Sandro. Allegra reached out a tentative finger and touched her brother's cheek. She drew her hand back with a gasp.

"Sandro! What is happening to you?" she cried.

Sebastian saw the older twin's outline become dark and vague. The boy rose and stepped back, away from his sister and brother.

He pushed up his sleeve to reveal the bare skin above his bandaged hand. His face paled, and he stared at his arm in horror as it became less solid, as it lost color and substance. The phenomenon moved up his neck to his jaw, his cheeks. He opened his mouth, but no words came out. Everyone froze as Alessandro, Prince of Auriano, slowly turned to Shadow.

A disembodied, evil laugh echoed through the courtyard.

"So, it begins again," the voice said. "I do so enjoy a good curse."

"Nulkana," Tonio whispered, as he looked around in fear.

Allegra froze with fright.

"Bring me the pieces of the Sphere of Astarte," Nulkana said, "and I might spare your sister. Disobey me, and she is mine."

"No!" Tonio yelled. "You'll never get her!"

At his words, chaos erupted as servants rushed to surround the twins. Ernesto scooped up Allegra and shoved her into the coach. The vehicle dipped as he jumped to the driver's seat. Luisa stepped inside and caught Allegra in her arms.

"No! No! No!" Allegra yelled as she flailed and struggled, frantic to get to her brother. "Let me go! Sandro!"

The coach lurched forward. Allegra was able to reach the coach window, and she leaned out. But they were already rumbling through the outer gates. She could see the servants hurrying Sandro inside, and she caught one last glimpse of Tonio as the servants surrounded him as well. Before he followed his brother, he turned to watch her leave. He raised his arm in a single wave and blew her a kiss. She waved back, but dust raised by the coach's wheels obscured her view. She collapsed back into Luisa's arms as disconsolate sobs wracked her.

The scene dissolved into a fog of gray-purple mist.

Sebastian understood now a bit more about the Princess Allegra, her inner strength, her deep loneliness. And most likely, her mistrust of anyone who was not part of her family. He wanted to comfort that child who had been on her own for so long.

"Your brothers sent you away to protect you," he said.

Si, he heard in his head.

"And you saw the first time your brother turned to Shadow." He kept his words soft and low.

Si. I was so frightened. Then she added, *I was so lonely without them.*

Sebastian felt her pain of separation like a dull knife carving at his heart. Her fear of Nulkana hovered above, huge and menacing, a black, indistinct shape. He wanted to console her, protect her from the threat of the sorceress. He wanted to be her friend.

Grazie, she whispered in his mind.

He felt a touch, like a warm caress, drift through his head. The sweetness of it melted his heart. And then he felt her withdraw.

He blinked. She was mere inches away. Her soft golden gaze riveted him. He missed her intimate connection. Her fingers still pressed against his pulse, but the touch was not enough. Without thought, he closed the tiny space between them and kissed her, gently, tenderly. Her lips, those sumptuous, delicious lips, opened to him like a flower.

He wanted her more than he had ever wanted anyone before. Besides having her sprawled naked across his bed — a vision that was emblazoned on his brain — he wanted to know her soul. He wanted to know her innermost thoughts and feelings. He wanted to give her joy. But that could not happen. He had too many dark secrets. And she had too many walls. She would never offer what he most wanted. But he would take what little she gave now.

He knew the moment the kiss switched from gratitude to something more, when her return kiss signaled that her blood raced and her skin heated. He felt the gentle pressure when she started to re-enter his mind. He knew what would happen if she did. They would dance the dance of passion, of twining and entangling, of spiraling up until they exploded into a million stars. He wanted that again, the connection with her, the glorious colors and sensations, the tightening and throbbing of his muscles, the delicious release.

This was not the time or the place.

Like pulling curtains across a window, reluctantly, softly, he closed his mind.

Allegra jerked away with an appalled gasp. Wide-eyed, she stared at him, then ducked her head in embarrassment. She had nearly connected with his mind to dance the dance of desire she needed during the Hunger. How could she have been so weak? If he had not closed off his mind, she would have seduced him right in the middle of his gardens.

"*Scusi*," she choked out. "I did not mean to—"

He placed a finger across her lips. "Say no more, lovely lady. The fault is mine. I took advantage." He tipped up her chin. "You have suffered much being away from your brothers. And the threat of Nulkana is always with you. You are very brave, Princess."

She shook her head. "Not so brave. I am always afraid."

"Being afraid doesn't make you weak," he said. "You are brave because you fight even though you are afraid."

He placed a hand over hers. Remembering they were still connected, her fingers against his pulse, she started to withdraw. With gentle pressure he held her where she was.

"Please," he said. "Stay a bit longer. If you would allow me, I would like to be your friend, someone you could turn to for help."

The warmth from his hands comforted and protected. The kindness and solace she felt from him when they were connected through Thought Binding eased her soul. She had never had a true friend, for she could never allow anyone to become close enough to learn of her secret, the terrible curse. She yearned for a friend, but her brothers and Luisa had taught her she should confide in no one. Perhaps this man, with his own secrets, could use a friend as well. But she was not about to agree quite so easily. Danger lurked everywhere, even with those she thought she could trust.

"Friends do not bargain, or threaten with transportation to a penal colony, *Sior* Hawksmoor," she said.

He smiled. "I think you know that threat is an empty one, especially now that the kidnappings have stopped. And all relationships are a bargain of one kind or another. I will be your friend if you will be mine."

While his tone was light and teasing, some darker emotion showed in those blue eyes, something sad and a bit forlorn. She wanted to wipe that sadness away. The desire to do that made her realize that this man had become more than a male who could ease the cravings of the Hunger, more than a tease, more than a thorn

193

in her side. He had rescued her from Nulkana, had healed her arm. He had come to her during the Hunger, protecting her from exposure. Perhaps he was someone she could trust. If she left England to return to Auriano with her brothers, she would miss him terribly—his eyes, his smile, his teasing, his touch. A hole would be left in her heart.

"*Si*," she said with a smile. "I will be your friend." And then in a whisper, "Sebastian."

His smile lit up his face. That smile made her heart soar. He placed a tender kiss on her fingers.

"Thank you, Allegra," he said.

She heard someone clear his throat, then the butler said, "My lord, my apologies for interrupting, but your lady mother has requested you join her for tea."

Sebastian nodded. "Thank you, Quint." With a humorous glint in his eyes, he said to Allegra, "It seems my mother has recovered, and we are being summoned into her royal presence."

She smiled. "Then we must obey."

They rose together and began to make their way toward the house. Luisa was ahead of them, halfway to the steps. As they strolled, warmth flooded Allegra at their easy banter. She decided she liked having Sebastian Fox, Earl of Hawksmoor, as a friend.

They were just passing the maze when despair and pain twisted through her chest. The sensations overwhelmed her, and she fell heavily against Sebastian.

"What is it?" he asked, concern lacing his voice. "What's wrong?"

"Hurt," she gasped, as she pressed her hand to her chest.

This pain was emotional, manifesting in the physical. And it was not hers. It came from someone, somewhere, else. With effort, she glanced across the gardens, across the rolling land, to the folly on a rise at the end of an alley of tall, thick bushes. A hooded figure, dark and brooding, stood in the middle of the delicate structure.

"There," she whispered. "It's coming from…him." Somehow, she knew it was a man, not a woman, and definitely not Nulkana, although she sensed this person was connected to the sorceress.

Sebastian swung her away, putting himself between her and the figure. "Quint!" he called. "Gather some men!"

"No." Allegra clutched his sleeve. "He means no harm. Oh, *Dio mio*," she moaned. "He is in such agony." She turned her face to Sebastian's shoulder. Tears wet her cheeks as despair dripped through her like acid.

He held her close and murmured words of comfort. Luisa hurried back to them. Quint came running from the house followed by several large footmen. They all bore some sort of makeshift weapon—a fireplace poker, a carving knife, a heavy candlestick, an ancient pistol. Quint was the only one who wielded a modern rifle. As their rescuers rushed toward them, Allegra peeked back at the folly. The cloaked figure was gone, and with it the terrible sense of hopelessness and grief. Of emptiness. In relief, she sagged against Sebastian.

"What was that?" he asked Luisa.

"I do not know, but something very strange," she said. "Something that I think we will have to investigate."

Allegra shivered, trying to dispel the horrible sensations she had felt. "I don't want to know anything about it."

Luisa gave her a hard stare. "This has nothing to do with what you want or don't want. This may have to do with your life and those you care for."

Allegra straightened. "You did not feel the agony I felt, the pain."

Her Guide narrowed her eyes. "Did you think you could get through life without pain?"

"Please, Mistress Luisa," Sebastian said. "The princess is distraught. Let me take her inside where she is safe."

"She will never be safe as long as—" Luisa's words halted. She nodded and gave a small curtsey. "Of course, *Sior* Hawksmoor." Without another word, she turned and walked back toward the house.

"She cares for you a great deal," he said, as he placed a supporting hand under Allegra's elbow.

"*Si*, but sometimes she is very hard." Allegra leaned into his arm. She knew she should stand on her own, but she wanted to indulge in his strength, his comfort for just a while longer.

"Perhaps that is why you are so brave." He began walking her back toward the house.

She sighed. He had already tried to convince her of that. She wanted to believe him, but if she were brave, why were her insides trembling so badly? Why did she want to lean on him? "Not brave, *Sior* Hawksmoor," she said. "Just foolish."

He stopped and turned to her. "Then remain foolish so that you may stay alive. I would not want to lose a friend so soon after I have found her."

Awestruck at his words, she stared up at him. Warmth flooded her, replacing the horrific hopelessness she had felt. Reaching up, she touched his cheek. "*Te lo prometto*," she whispered. "I promise."

Chapter 15

Two days later, Sebastian strolled with Undersecretary Foley along the Royal Crescent. Across from them, Crescent Park beckoned with its clusters of trees and thick foliage, more suited for clandestine conversations. Instead of meeting the undersecretary in concealing greenery, he was ordered to meet with him, here, in the open, in order to report to him about the spy network Allegra had uncovered. Sebastian felt as if every eye were watching, especially those belonging to the Legion of Baal, who would note that The Messenger was in conversation with a member of the government. Foley had reminded him of an axiom he knew well: the best place to hide was in the open. Why wouldn't the Earl of Hawksmoor know a certain Sir Cyril Foley of His Majesty's government and join him in a walk through the city? All the same, Sebastian kept his senses on alert for anyone who might be prying.

"The Vicomtesse d'Amaritz has been detained after she was discovered with information regarding our watch on the French navy in the Mediterranean," Foley said. "How she learned that is a puzzle and deeply disturbing. Someone has been revealing secrets. We will have to investigate that further. The route of the spy network is news, indeed, and Crowley's involvement is most interesting. We haven't arrested him because he could give us more information. You must watch him closely."

Sebastian nearly groaned aloud. He thought he was done with Crowley. Instead, he nodded. "Will that information absolve the countess from any implication?"

"Your mother, as splendid as she is, is still culpable for any information she let slip." Foley took several steps in silence. "Discover the whereabouts of the piece of the Sphere of Astarte, and I will see to it that no mention of her arises in the report of this investigation."

Sebastian's fist clenched on his walking stick. He wanted to be done with the Legion of Baal. He hated the role he played as The Messenger, and he despised the contemptible men who were members of the group, especially the Lord High, but he would need to continue as long as the group threatened the stability of England, her allies, and possibly the world. Beyond that, they were a danger to Allegra, and he would protect her with his life.

As he had the thought, he sensed her nature, luminous and golden. She was near, above him, and he realized she was no doubt looking down on him from her window. While Foley went on about the importance of acquiring the piece of the Sphere, Sebastian flipped his walking stick from one hand to the other. He sensed her essence grow brighter and warmer. For a moment, he reveled in that bright warmth. She intrigued him, aggravated him, soothed his soul, defied him, and made him want her like no other woman ever had. Soon, he would have her sprawled, gloriously naked, across his bed. Finally. With that pleasant thought in mind, he nodded in agreement as Foley lectured him once again on the importance of disbanding the wretched Legion of Baal.

Allegra stood at the window of the drawing room and looked down on the street below. She had returned to her house in the Royal Crescent the day after taking tea with Hawksmoor and his mother. The countess had been delightful company. She told of seeing the actress, Sarah Siddons, and her brother John Kemble on the stage, of balls she had attended, and with a wicked twinkle in her eyes, of the gaming hells where patrons could lose fortunes in one play. A pained expression crossed Hawksmoor's face at that, and he quickly changed the subject.

When Allegra's eyes had met Hawksmoor's, a spark zinged between them. Every time those blue eyes landed on her, she could feel their heat as if his hand cupped the back of her neck, as if his fingers trailed across her cheek. She wanted more than anything to have those hands all over her, to be sprawled naked across his bed as he had once daringly declared.

As she gazed down on the street, as if her thoughts had conjured him, she saw him strolling below her window. He was deep in conversation with another man, older and a bit shorter. She wondered who the man could be, then realized she had met him at Lady Hetherington's garden party—Sir Cyril Foley, Undersecretary of Foreign Affairs. Even though he had been perfectly civil, she had found him a bit disturbing. As she had the thought, Hawksmoor's steps slowed and he raised his head, as if he heard her. With a small flourish, he moved his walking stick from one hand to other. Allegra smiled. He might not have heard her thoughts, but he knew she was above him in the window.

A knock came at the door and Luisa entered, disapproval evident in the press of her lips. "A note for you, Princess."

The folded, sealed paper was cheap foolscap, not heavy vellum or even parchment. Allegra surmised it was from Crowley. She hesitated to open it, feeling both dread and anticipation. This was the note Crowley had said he would send concerning the piece of the Sphere of Astarte. She had the urge to toss it in the fire. She wanted nothing more to do with the man but gaining a piece of the Sphere would help break the curse on her family. Did he really know where a piece was located? She did not truly trust him, but she could not allow any possibility of finding the piece slip away.

"Ignore it," Luisa said.

With a shake of her head, Allegra tore it open and read:

Dearest Princess,

Meet me at the Pulteney Bridge tomorrow evening at ten of the clock. Come alone. The item in question is for you only. This is the single chance you will have to obtain it.

HC

Allegra crumpled the note. Luisa would never allow her to meet alone with Crowley. Her Guide would want to accompany her along with Ernesto. She would have to keep Luisa in ignorance.

"It is nothing, Luisa," she said. "He is merely writing of his admiration."

Luisa sent her a sharp glance. "I hope it is not returned."

With a little shiver of revulsion, she said, "He would be the last person I would admire."

Luisa gave a tiny ambiguous grunt. Allegra hoped it meant satisfaction, not suspicion. She was relieved when her Guide left. The thought of gaining a piece of the Sphere chased all others out of Allegra's head. She immediately began planning how she would sneak out. Of course, she would have to send her regrets to Lady Hetherington's theater party. Since she did not truly trust Crowley, she would take her fan, charmed by Luisa, and possibly that little dagger. And there was the nagging question about what to wear. She definitely did not want to be recognized by anyone when she met Crowley. Perhaps that pair of old breeches that had belonged to Alessandro when he was still a youth...

The next night, Allegra carried a lantern to light her way as she walked to Pulteney Bridge. She had successfully slipped out without alerting Luisa or Ernesto. Few people were out, and those hurried to their destinations, for the day had turned misty and night brought chilly temperatures. Anyone who might otherwise stroll to spend an evening with friends or a gathering at the Assembly Rooms traveled in their carriages or hired a sedan chair or hackney coach. Alessandro's cast-off clothing was heavy enough to keep her warm and his old tricorn hat kept her head dry, besides disguising her. The weight of her fan inside her sleeve and the dagger stuck into her boot gave her comfort.

She had thought of sending a note to Hawksmoor, asking him to accompany her, but then dismissed the idea. She had her fan and dagger. She had learned to defend herself. If she could retrieve a piece of the Sphere of Astarte on her own, she could prove to her brothers she was a full-grown woman who could think for herself. Besides that, she had little respect for Crowley. She could handle him.

She glanced up at the night sky. Behind those clouds, the moon was beginning to wane. In a few days it would be new, a dark moon, and she would be Shadow once more. What if she could gain the piece of the Sphere of Astarte before then and break the curse? A thrill of anticipation ran through her.

Just as she rounded the corner onto Great Pulteney Street, she tripped over a drunk slumped against a building.

"'Ere now, boy," he said. "Watsh where ye goin'." He waved a bottle. The fumes of alcohol and excrement wafted up.

Allegra covered her nose with her sleeve. "Perhaps if you did not block the way, I might not have stumbled across you, *si*?"

"'Igh an' mighty, ain't ye?" He waved the bottle again and some of the liquid sloshed out. "Get on wit' ye then, yer 'Ighnesh."

With a hiss of disgust, Allegra hurried on. Inside, she laughed because the drunkard had no idea that he had called her by her rightful title. The bells of the Abbey rang the hour of ten o'clock. At the end of the road, Pulteney Bridge with its closed shops yawned darker than the rest of the vista. This was where she was to meet Crowley, but she could see no one waiting. She slowed her steps and approached cautiously.

"*Signore* Crowley?" she called softly.

She heard the click of flint and a light flared. A figure stepped out of the darkness. Crowley. He was cloaked and wore a tricorn as well.

"Rather indecent to wear breeches, Princess," he smirked.

She sniffed in disdain. "What I wear has no bearing on why we are meeting."

He sneered. "I knew your craving would compel you to come."

"*Signore* Crowley," she said, "do not be rude, *per favore*. I came because you offered something."

He gave a nod of agreement. "Something offered, something given in return."

Of course, he would want something in return. But how dear would it be? She twitched her arm, allowing her fan to slip into her palm.

"I must see the item first," she said, "but if it is worthy, then you will be handsomely rewarded."

With another nod, he said, "Come with me." He turned and took several steps onto the dark, shadowed bridge.

Besides the fact that he was being a complete boor, the thought of being alone with him on the black bridge made her hesitate. But the reward of finally finding a piece of the Sphere of Astarte propelled her forward, and she had her weapons. She remained two steps behind him so she could run back into the city if he threatened in any way. Logically, he would not want to harm her if he wanted a generous reward.

They were about halfway across the bridge when a tiny sound came from behind. It could have been leaves rustled by the wind or a rat rummaging for scraps. Crowley halted, swung around, and held his lantern high.

"Who's there?" he called. "I'm armed, so don't think to rob us." He opened his cloak and showed a pistol stuck into the waistband of his breeches.

Allegra was both relieved and uneasy at the prospect of Crowley with a weapon. At least he could help protect them from robbers, but that did not guarantee he would not rob her, or worse. They stood in silence for a moment. No other sound came from the darkness, only the sound of the river flowing below them and rushing over the weir.

"There is no one, *Signore* Crowley," she said, wanting this trip to be over as quickly as possible.

Without a word, he turned on his heel and strode away. Allegra hurried after. They came to the other side of the bridge where a small carriage waited. She hesitated when Crowley stepped toward it. She had not foreseen that they would be leaving the city. A ride with the man in an enclosed space made her uneasy.

"Where are you taking me, *Signore* Crowley?" she asked.

He opened the door of the carriage and turned to her. "Did you think the object was in the city?" He shook his head. "That would be much too dangerous."

"I think a ride alone in a carriage with you is dangerous, *signore*." She gripped her fan tighter.

"I would never hurt you, Princess," he said. "Trust me."

Skepticism made her erupt in a short, ironic laugh. "One who says that is usually not trustworthy, *si?*"

Impatience bordering on anger emanated from him in waves. "What reason would I have to hurt you? I'm planning on a large reward at the end."

"Of course, you are," she muttered.

His greed convinced her. She could see no other reason for his offer of the piece of the Sphere if he did not expect a large compensation. As she approached the carriage, she realized it was parked before the bench where she and Sebastian had sat when he had negotiated with her into allowing him to relieve her craving during the Hunger. That night had turned into one of the most extraordinary, sensual, arousing experiences of her life, despite her apprehension and fear. And once again, she had remembered every detail. She wished he was with her now, just for the comfort of his warm hand, because she was very capable of dealing with Crowley on her own.

She stopped before the open door of the carriage and cast a sidelong glance at Crowley. As a member of that vile Legion of Baal, would Crowley offer her to the Lord High? Is that what he planned? What would be his reward for that? She decided not as much as what she would give for a piece of the Sphere. She had her fan, charmed by Luisa, and would be diligently alert. With her mind made up, she entered the carriage. Crowley began to shut the door behind her.

"You will not ride with me, *Signore* Crowley?" she asked.

"I will drive. Where we go is much too secret to hire a whip." With those curt words, he closed the door and climbed to the driver's seat.

With a lurch and a dip as if they had rolled into a depression in the road, they started out.

Sebastian held on to the back of the carriage as it traveled through the dark. He had been languidly observing Crowley all day, per the Undersecretary's orders, keeping track of Crowley's suspicious actions—hiring the coach and horses, parking them after nightfall on the far side of the bridge, and then waiting in the shadows. When Allegra had tripped over him, he had thanked the impulse to disguise himself. Acting the drunkard had made her avoid him, and the excrement he had smeared on his coat had repulsed her.

As soon as he had realized the youth who stumbled on him was Allegra, he knew Crowley was plotting something despicable. He vowed he would do everything he could to protect her. But he wanted to see where Crowley was taking her. In order to rid himself of the man, he needed to catch him in the act of committing a crime. He just hoped this uncomfortable trip through the night, hanging on to the back of the carriage, would not be too long.

Chapter 16

The carriage stopped in front of a ramshackle cottage. Even in the scant moonlight, it looked deserted and overrun with weeds. An uncomfortable tingle washed across her skin, followed by a flash of fear. Nulkana was close. Crowley had tricked her. But Crowley was a member of the Legion of Baal, and they were deadly enemies of the sorceress. Why would he have anything to do with Nulkana? But that puzzle could be solved later. Danger crackled in the air.

She had to escape, run and hide. By the time she threw open the carriage door and scrambled out, Crowley had already jumped from the driver's seat. The pistol in his hand gleamed dully in the light of the carriage's running lamps.

"*Signore* Crowley, what is this?" she demanded, indicating the weapon and pretending brave insult. "We had an agreement, *si*?"

He laughed cruelly. "Did you really believe I would give you a piece of the Sphere of Astarte? You are so naive. The Lord High of the Legion of Baal has the piece. He will bring it out at the conclave at Stonehenge when the moon is full." With an evil smile, he added, "But you'll be dead long before then." He motioned with his pistol. "Into the cottage, Princess."

As he said the words, an evocative summons emanated from the building. It was subtle, but it tickled her mind with an urge to turn in that direction. Her arm — the one that the sorceress had frozen and Hawksmoor had healed — prickled uncomfortably. Nulkana was calling her. The thought popped into her head that if she answered that call, the pain would cease. But that was a lie.

Allegra let the head of her fan slip into her palm. She planted her feet. The sorceress would not trick her again. Crowley would not coerce her, nor would he escape unscathed.

"You brought me here for Nulkana," she said.

Crowley's smile was evil. "Nothing you could give me would equal what that lady has promised."

"She'll give you nothing," she said.

The summons became stronger, whispering through her brain with unspoken words. The prickle in her arm turned to pain. Allegra forced herself to concentrate on Crowley and his gun. Beyond his shoulder, a dark shape crouched near the head of the horses. It appeared to be human, but the night was so dark she could not be sure. It could just as easily be a large animal, or some monster conjured by the sorceress. Whatever it was, she was not about to trust it to help her. She gripped her fan tighter.

Crowley motioned with his pistol again. "Into the cottage, Princess," he repeated, his words flat and cold.

Allegra raised her chin. "You'll get no reward from Nulkana if you kill me, and I'm not going inside."

He sniggered. "I don't have to kill you—you stupid girl. A ball through the shoulder or knee will bring you down without killing you. Then Nulkana can do as she wishes."

She knew he would have no qualms about shooting her. She had her fan as a weapon, but it was charmed to use against the sorceress. Her dagger was no match against a pistol. She decided not to provoke him. A dark mass of weeds and vines lay between them and the door to the cottage. She could pretend to stumble in them in the dark, which might give her the advantage she needed to escape into the woods beyond.

She let out a despondent sigh. "*Si, Signore* Crowley. You have won. I hope Nulkana gives you everything you deserve."

She turned and took a step in the direction of the cottage. Nulkana's summons became stronger and harder to resist, and beneath it ran a gloating thread. Allegra had to fight not to be overwhelmed, to remember she needed to escape. The commanding pull of the sorceress nearly clouded everything else in her mind, wiping out her will.

Just as she took a second step, a rush of air and a strangled gasp behind her made her spin back. In the dim light of the running lamps on the carriage, she saw a figure with an arm around Crowley's throat. With a twisting wrench, the figure threw her kidnapper to the ground. A blow to Crowley's jaw stunned him. The figure held out a hand to her.

"Allegra," he said. "Come on. Run."

"Sebastian?" she squeaked in surprise. At the same time, the stench of alcohol and excrement reached her nose.

Before she could move, Nulkana burst out of the door of the cottage in a dark flash of energy. She was surrounded by a black, billowing cloud that snapped with lightning bolts. The sorceress skimmed across the tangle of weeds.

"You'll not get away from me again!" Nulkana screamed.

With instinct honed from years of training by her Guide, Allegra snapped open her fan. She flicked her wrist and sent the fan spiraling toward Nulkana. It sliced across the sorceress's arm.

"My arm!" the sorceress screamed. "My beautiful arm!"

Black blood spurted from a slash across Nulkana's white skin. She bent over the wound and clapped her hand on it to stop the bleeding. She keened as if she had lost a loved one.

Sebastian grabbed Allegra's hand. "Come on." With a tug, he ran with her in the direction of the woods.

They fled to the trees that beckoned with their dark shadows and places to hide. Just before they swept into the trees, she glanced back. Crowley had risen to his feet and begun to follow. With a dismissive swipe of her hand, Nulkana froze him in mid-step, then surged after them.

"Nulkana," Allegra gasped.

Without looking back, Sebastian said, "I know. Keep running."

They crashed into the undergrowth of the woods. Among the trees, the night was even darker than in the open. Allegra had no idea where Sebastian was leading. She stumbled along blindly, unable to see in the blackness, and wondered how he avoided banging into trees in their headlong rush. Twigs and branches caught at her. She tripped over a root. He slowed long enough to steady her, then hurried forward. His grip on her hand was a lifeline. It was the only thing that kept her from dissolving into a mass of terrified panic. The memory of the sorceress's touch made her nauseated with fright.

Behind her, Nulkana crashed through the woods. The sorceress sounded as if she were huge, the size of a very large bear or perhaps even an elephant. Branches cracked. Trees were ripped up. And then her voice came, booming through the dark.

"Don't think you can escape this time, little girl," she threatened. "This time you're mine."

Nulkana's voice echoed inside Allegra's head so loudly that it brought pain. Allegra whimpered and covered her ear as if that would help.

Sebastian gripped her hand tighter. "We're almost there."

He abruptly pulled her to the left and yanked her down. She slipped into a hollow in the ground behind some bushes and crouched beside him. That impression of the moon in his eyes glowed brightly, reassuringly.

"Stay here," he said.

The sound of tree limbs falling, smashing into the ground, became louder, closer. Light flashed through the trees. In the middle of that light was the dark silhouette of the sorceress, distorted and huge. Spikes of black jabbed from her figure.

Sebastian rose and stepped into Nulkana's path. Allegra was about to warn him, call him back when he raised his hands. His sleeves slipped up his arms and bright runes appeared in the air before him. They were an exact duplicate of the tattoos she had seen on his forearms, a delicate intertwining of lines that formed a sort of square knot. He murmured something that sounded like the language he had used when he had healed her arm.

For a moment, nothing happened. Then the runes began to revolve, slowly at first, then faster. They spun in the air so fast they lost their form and became two small whirlwinds, bright against the black of the woods. With a push of his open palms, Sebastian sent them into the dark and then spread them out with a swipe of his arms. The runes separated and became filaments of fog. They wound through the trees and grew thicker, becoming an impenetrable cloud. The wind picked up, but instead of dissipating the fog, it only swirled the clouds into a boiling, seething mass. Rain pelted down in a loud hiss. Lightning flared. Thunder cracked. But a small area around Sebastian and Allegra remained calm and clear.

He held out his hand to her. "Come. I don't know how long this will hold."

Awestruck at his ability, she took his hand. Nulkana raged and thrashed in the middle of the maelstrom. He smiled, and Allegra knew in her soul he would protect her. Together they ran farther into the woods, away from the sorceress. Allegra followed blindly, trusting in Sebastian to keep her safe. After several minutes, they popped out of the trees into the open area near the cottage. Behind her, Allegra could hear Nulkana searching. The fog, wind, and rain remained in the woods, the edge of the trees acting like a barrier. In the open, a tiny sliver of moon peeked between the clouds. Before them, the carriage and horses stood, the animals calm despite the confusion among the trees. Crowley was gone. Somehow, he had freed himself from Nulkana's magic and escaped.

Sebastian yanked open the door to the carriage.

Allegra shook her head. "I'll ride with you."

In a single motion, he took her about the waist and swung her to the driver's seat, then scrambled up after her. He barked a single command and snapped the reins. The horses broke into a gallop and the carriage sped away from the evil, the danger. Away from Nulkana.

Allegra shivered. Now that they were escaping, her fear overwhelmed her. She clenched her hands on the seat as the carriage bumped and swayed in their desperate flight. She had nearly become a victim of the sorceress. If Sebastian had not been watching, she surely would be dead. How could she ever repay him? She had been impulsive and naive, just as Crowley said. But Crowley had also given her information. A piece of the Sphere of Astarte would be in the open, available for the taking at Stonehenge at the full moon. And she would be Shadow. What if...?

Despite the shivers that wracked her, determination stiffened her spine. She would make a plan. Somehow, she would snatch the piece of the Sphere from the Legion of Baal. The plan would be daring and dangerous. Should she ask Sebastian to help her? She would decide that later and, instead, concentrated on keeping her seat on their wild ride.

Sebastian's firm arm pressed against her as he drove the horses. Even through the layers of clothes they each wore, his warmth penetrated the cold that had settled in her blood. She wanted to lean into him, but that would break his concentration on this wild ride in the dark. They could just as easily end up dead from an accident as from Nulkana's sorcery.

He had saved her and was rushing them to safety. His protection, his bravery, his magical ability, and the risk he took, putting himself in danger to rescue her, opened her eyes to an overwhelming fact: She loved him. Her heart flipped in her chest. She shivered again, not from fear, but from the intense emotion that coursed through her.

How could she love him? He had blackmailed her, forced her to spy. He teased and mocked. He coerced her into using only him when the Hunger consumed her. Only him. She squeezed her eyes shut. That had been another layer of his protection. Overwhelmed by his generosity and the sweep of emotions that tumbled through her, two tiny tears leaked from beneath her lashes.

His arm brushed against her again. The man she loved was sitting next to her and driving like a madman to save her. For now, she would wrap herself in that comfort and deal with everything else tomorrow.

Tomorrow, she would decide what to do about the Sphere of Astarte.

Tomorrow, she would decide what to do about her love for the man who could call on the elements and who had the moon in his eyes.

Nulkana burst out of the woods in an explosion of branches and a shower of leaves. She stood panting, in a rage, as she saw the carriage was missing. Kek emerged from the cottage. She stomped across the weeds and stood before him. He bowed low before her.

"You did not stop them, Kek?" Her voice was unnaturally quiet.

He remained in his bowed position as he answered. "They were gone, mistress, before I could do anything."

With a growl, she raised her hand as if she would fling him to the other side of the planet.

"Your arm, mistress," he said. "It bleeds."

Distracted, she glanced down. Black blood dripped from the wound. Her arm, once beautiful, whole, and young after she had touched that Auriano brat, was now wrinkled and old again. At her feet was the fan that had done the damage. The leaf of the fan was painted with a lovely pastoral scene. But tiny metal claws snapped along the fan's ribs, glinting in the faint moonlight.

"It was charmed, mistress," Kek said, still in his obsequious position.

With a scream of rage, Nulkana kicked the offending piece of deadly frippery into the distance. As it flew through the air, she waved her hand, and the fan exploded into a thousand tiny pieces. She watched them disappear into the dark. "I will have that Auriano bitch, Kek."

"Yes, mistress." Kek slowly rose from his bow.

Her eyes blazed a poisonous green. "Her and those two brothers."

"Yes, Mistress." Kek motioned toward the cottage. "Please. Come inside and let me heal your arm."

The sorceress made a wordless sound of agreement, then she noticed Crowley was gone. She took a step closer to where she had left him.

"Where is he?" She stomped around the space where Crowley should have been, frozen, like a statue. "He couldn't have freed himself."

Kek bowed again. "Perhaps the Auriano woman—"

"That Auriano bitch took him?" she asked incredulously. "Why would she do that?"

"A soft heart," Kek suggested.

"Bah. Insipid. She can have him. He was useless," she spat. "If you want something done right, you have to do it yourself. Don't you agree, Kek?"

"Yes, mistress," Kek said.

With a nod, Nulkana swept toward the cottage, Kek two steps behind. She would get her arm healed and plan how she would trap the Auriano whelps. Perhaps during the full moon… Her eyes narrowed. Yes, the full moon would be perfect.

Dawn was a bright line at the horizon just beneath the clouds by the time Crowley stumbled across Pulteney Bridge. He could not believe his good fortune in escaping Nulkana's clutches. That evil bitch had meant to kill him. She never would have been able to freeze him if Hawksmoor, that sneaky bugger, had not attacked him. Only the frog glyph on his arm had saved him. It had slowly melted his frozen limbs.

He knew now that Nulkana's promises of wealth and power were empty ones. But he still had another avenue open to him. Sebastian Fox would have to die. Then he, Hubert Crowley, could step in as the Earl of Hawksmoor. He would inherit the wealth and influence of that old name. He did not need the sorceress and her magic.

He turned toward his humble lodgings. Soon, he would be living in grandeur. He just had to make a plan. And he knew the perfect person to help him execute it. The Countess of Hawksmoor would never realize until too late that she was the instrument of her own son's death.

Chapter 17

Two nights after escaping from Nulkana, Allegra stood at the foot of a large oak and gazed at the stone walls of Blackbrake. The half-moon had just risen and cast long shadows across the lawns. A few windows on the ground floor of the house were lit, indicating some-one was still up at this late hour. All the windows of the story above were dark. Her gaze moved to a set of windows at the very end of the wing. She knew what lay inside those windows. She had been in that room once before as Shadow. But she was not Shadow now. She was flesh and bone. She could taste and smell. She could touch. Feel. Anticipation rippled through her.

She ran across the open grass, dodged around trees and bushes, and stopped at the base of the wall. She put her hand against the stone. It was cold, as stone should be, but a faint tingle of energy made the stone feel alive. She smiled. The walls had been warded, but only against evil. What she intended was far from that. With a leap, she grabbed the vines clinging to the house and began to climb, glad she had once again donned her brother's cast-off breeches.

The window she wanted was open a crack. She pushed it wider and slipped inside. Moonlight cast bright rectangles on the polished wood floor. A plush Turkish carpet had covered the space the last time she had visited. With a wry tilt of her lips, she assumed the piece was out for repairs, for she had sliced through it when she plunged his dagger into the floor. She searched and found the small groove where the weapon's point had stuck in the wood. No repair had been made to that spot. Her smile turned to a grin as she crouched and ran her finger along the depression. He had been so wary when he had seen her with the dagger, and so surprised at her ability to manipulate it in midair. He would be surprised again, this time, she hoped, pleasantly so.

Footsteps approached in the hall. She did not want to be found yet. In two quick strides, she hid behind the draperies. The memory of the last time she had hidden from him behind draperies came to mind. That time, she was frightened. This time, anticipation made her heart race.

The footsteps passed by the bedchamber door. A door opened farther down the hallway. The rumble of his baritone dismissed his valet for the night. A short murmur answered. The door closed. The footsteps returned and halted. Allegra held her breath. Why did he hesitate in the hallway? Finally, the doorknob turned, and he stepped into the room.

Allegra waited. She wanted the moment when she revealed herself to be perfect, a complete surprise.

Then, from just on the other side of the draperies, he said, "Are you hiding from me again, lovely lady?"

She released her breath on a laugh. Somehow, he had known she was there. But she had one more surprise for him besides her presence in his bedchamber. Slowly, she pushed aside the drapery hiding her and stepped forward.

She watched his eyes widen, those blue, blue eyes catching the light from the moon. His gaze took her in, from the top of her head down to her toes. And then he grinned.

"I can't decide if you are being modest or immodest," Sebastian said.

Allegra smiled and cocked her hip. "Whichever you would prefer." While she had been hiding behind the draperies, she had discarded all her clothes except her shirt, fine lawn and nearly transparent, which ended just above her knees.

He tipped his head thoughtfully. "I'm having trouble making up my mind. I need more information."

"*Si*? What more would you like to know, *Sior* Hawksmoor?" She stepped forward.

"Why did you come here?" He also stepped forward until they were only inches apart. His voice was a seductive murmur.

"Why, to frolic of course." She reached out and placed her finger against the hollow of his throat, then trailed it down his chest to where the closed lapels of his dressing gown came together in a vee.

His eyes darkened. "I thought only kittens and bunnies frolicked."

Hearing her words quoted back to her in his voice caused a pleasurable clenching deep inside her. "Perhaps kittens and bunnies know something we do not. Perhaps we should discover what that is," she whispered.

He cupped her face in his hands. "Ah, Allegra, you bewitch me." He lowered his head and claimed her mouth.

Allegra melted against him. Their tongues dueled and danced. She wrapped her arms about his waist, holding him close, feeling the strength of him, the heat of him. His erection stirred against her belly. She smiled to herself, pleased at his arousal. And then, quite suddenly, he raised his head and held her away.

"Why are you here, Allegra?" he asked, completely serious. "What do you want?"

Surprise widened her eyes. A tiny pinprick of hurt at his somber question, suggesting rejection, stung her heart. She backed from the hold of his hands, turned and walked into the dark of the room where he could not see her. Where she could hide.

"I thought—" She swallowed. "That is, I wanted—"

She could not get the words out. She thought he would want her without question. She thought that he would understand she was offering herself to him because she was grateful for what he had done, saving her. She thought she would not have to reveal the true reason for her presence—that she had fallen in love with him.

She turned to face him. Catching the hem of her shirt, she swept it off. "I thought you wished to have me *sprawled naked* across your bed," she teased, reminding him of the words he had used when he had drawn her to that dark room at the ball. Resorting to the seduction she used during the Hunger, she walked two steps closer, stopping just at the edge of one of those rectangles of moonlight on the floor so he could see her.

His gaze traveled down to her toes and back up to meet her eyes. "I would like nothing better," he said. Then his tone turned calmly logical. "But I would like to know the reason you are offering yourself." He glanced to the window where the half moon was visible.

"You're not in the Hunger. We were very careful the last time you were. So, tell me, lovely lady, why are you here?"

Frustrated and wounded by his cool response, she grabbed her shirt from the floor and jerked it on. "I can see that you do not wish to frolic, *Sior* Hawksmoor, so I will leave." She brushed past him to where her clothes lay in a pile behind the drapery.

He stopped her with a word and a hand on her arm. "Allegra."

She would not look at him. If she did, she might burst into tears. A tangle of emotions crowded her heart—embarrassment, anger, hurt.

He dropped his hand and stepped in front of her, so close she could feel the heat of him. "Allegra," he murmured. "I care for you. I want you to be sure this is what you want, because I'm not sure I can hold back." He paused, took a breath. "You unglue and unseat me. You hover at the edge of my thoughts during the day. You are present in my dreams at night. Allegra, lovely lady, you unmake and undo me." He paused again, as if giving her time to absorb his words. "So, I'm asking again if you truly know why you are here."

Wide-eyed, Allegra stared at him. His words took her breath away. He asked, not because he was suspicious or because he did not want her, but because he cared. Perhaps, he might even love her a tiny bit.

The silence between them stretched out. He was waiting for her answer.

She placed her palm against his chest. Beneath her hand, she could feel the thump of his heart, and like a stream within a stream, his power coursing through his blood. This man turned her knees to porridge, her insides to mush. He heated and melted her in a plume of desire.

She'd warred with herself about her decision to come here. Her brothers had lectured her countless times on not trusting anyone outside the family. Nulkana could twist anyone to do her bidding, and the insidious branches of the Legion of Baal reached all corners of the world. But the man standing before her had protected her, cured her arm, risked his life to save her.

She looked up into those blue, blue eyes, dark now in the shadows. "After you cured my arm and saved me from turning to ice, you left so suddenly. You seemed different, and I think you took some of

Nulkana's evil sorcery into yourself. For me. When I slipped on the riverbank and you caught me, I saw the rune appear in the air. And when you came to me while I was in the Hunger, I saw the runes on your arms. They hadn't been there before. So, I understood that they were *your* protection against Nulkana. But you used them to save my life." She glanced at her hand still resting against his chest. "I trust you." Meeting his dark gaze again, she whispered, "I want you. I want you to be the first."

Her words arrowed into his heart. They humbled him. Sebastian understood what she was offering. Even in the throes of the Hunger, she had been careful. But now, she was throwing away caution.

For him.

He wanted her more than anything he had ever wanted. He wanted to bury himself inside her, feel her wrap herself around him. He wanted to hear her sigh and moan in her passion. He wanted to see her fly apart in ecstasy and then come together. He wanted to hold her, sated and boneless. And then he wanted to do it all over again.

He should not want this, not that much. He was damaged — had done things in his life that no decent man would ever do — monstrous things. He had too many secrets, one in particular that would drive her away screaming — that he was The Messenger of the Legion of Baal. Those secrets couldn't be kept hidden forever. But for this one night, he could pretend to be the good man she thought he was. Just one night. He would hoard this memory and keep it in his soul — the night a beautiful, brave woman loved him.

His body clenched. His blood heated. Without another thought, he reached for the hem of her shirt and pulled it over her head.

Her fingers trembled against his chest. Then her hand slowly slipped down to the tie of his dressing robe. It left a trail of fire in its wake. He wondered how such a delicate touch could make his skin so sensitive that it tingled everywhere she made contact. She pulled the tie apart. Her hand slid inside and came to rest on his hip.

He wanted to touch her all over, but he forced his hands to remain at his sides. He would let her set the pace, however slow and agonizing that might be. She was not in the Hunger, and not ruled by its cravings and demands. He would not frighten her with his impatience.

She raised her head and met his gaze with those glorious golden eyes. "I want to make love with you, Sebastian," she said.

Her words shot from his brain to his groin. He could wait no longer. He scooped her up and carried her to his bed.

She giggled. "I knew I would be sprawled naked across your bed tonight." She twitched to the side and held out her arm. "Come, sprawl naked with me."

He needed no further urging. He shed his robe and lay beside her, this luscious woman who had invaded his soul.

Allegra watched as he revealed his body. She loved the long lines of him, the planes of his muscles, the shadows of his sinews and joints. When he lay beside her, she turned to him and ran her fingers across the contour of his cheek, over his jaw, to his mouth. She traced those sculpted lips. She wanted to memorize every bit of him. For this one night, he was hers as a normal woman, not one who was cursed. She would never have a normal life, despite what her brothers said. Even with the moonstone pendant they had brought her to dampen the Hunger, she still turned to Shadow. No man would want a woman like her. Even someone like Sebastian. How could he? He was a peer of the realm. How could he explain his wife's frequent absences from official functions or events? Any children they might have would be born with the curse over their heads. He would worry that they would be just like her. The danger of Nulkana would always be hanging over their heads. Even though he cared for her now, even though he wanted her now, eventually he would come to resent her – her difference—the fact that she wasn't a normal woman. The fact that she was cursed.

But tonight, she would know what a normal woman felt when she was with the man she loved. She would know all his secret places, everywhere that made the breath leave his lungs, that made the growl rumble in his chest. Her fingers trailed down his throat. She followed with her mouth, kissing, tasting, sucking on his nipple. He lay still, allowing her to do as she wished.

"I love the taste of you," she whispered. "You taste like apples."

A laugh rippled through him.

She kissed lower, following the arrow of hair that led to his manhood, erect, pulsing. She licked up that silky shaft.

His breath hissed through his teeth, and his fingers tangled in her hair, cupping her head, halting her.

"Do you wish me to stop?" she asked.

"Only if you wish this night to be over before it begins." He drew her up along his body. "Let me give you pleasure." He rolled her over, covering her with his body.

She was a bit disappointed that her exploration had been halted, but that quickly dissipated when his mouth fastened on her breast and he sucked. His fingers danced down across her ribs to her hip, stroking, then back up to her other breast where he played with her nipple. A moan escaped her. His touch was delicious. Her skin became sensitive, but this was different than during the madness of the Hunger. This time, she knew his touch was for her because he wanted it to be, not because she had entered his mind and seduced him.

He kissed his way down across her belly. His tongue lapped between her thighs, where she was warm and wet. A pulse of desire made her squirm. She sucked in a breath. His lips and tongue played her like an instrument until her insides were wound tight with pleasure. She thought she might go mad. And then he stopped.

She made a wordless complaint.

"Patience, lovely lady," he said as he covered her with his body.

He kissed her, and she tasted herself on his lips. It mingled with the taste of him as their tongues danced. Then he propped himself above her. She looked into his eyes, soft and dark as the night sky. While he held her gaze, with a sudden thrust, he was deep inside her.

She gasped in surprise. Compared to everything she'd experienced from the curse, this was only a minor sting. But the feel of him inside her was unlike anything she had experienced. He filled her. He made her whole. He made her a woman.

When he began to move, she groaned her delight. Her hips moved with him — as though she had been loving him her entire life. Her insides pulsed. Her desire built. With a cry, her release burst into a million stars.

Sebastian barely had enough mindfulness to pull out of her and spill his seed on her belly. This woman made him mad with need. She unbalanced him. He wanted nothing more than to be with her, like this, every day and night. He wanted to have her breathless, moaning, squirming beneath him in passion, not because she was in the Hunger, but because he aroused her with his touch.

He did not deserve her trust, this brave, cursed woman. He did not deserve the gift of herself that she bestowed on him. Whatever happened after this night, he would cherish these few hours with her forever.

But he had to be careful. He was an agent of the government, working in secret, and he was The Messenger of the Legion of Baal. She most likely suspected the first, but he could never reveal the second. She would hate him for working for her enemy. And she was in danger by being with him. The Lord High wanted her as a sacrifice. Somehow, he had to keep her safe, and the best way to do that was to send her back to Auriano with her brothers. The last thing he wanted to do was send her away. Nor did he wish to reveal himself to the twins. They would look upon him as an enemy, The Messenger of the Legion of Baal, and that would surely complicate the situation. They would want his death. He wouldn't be able to help Allegra if he were dead. If he could find no other solution, then he would grab his honor and courage in both hands, reveal himself and send her away. But in this moment, he could not bring himself to part from her.

For tonight he would hold her. He gathered her in his arms and held her, boneless and sated, as she cuddled against him.

Chapter 18

The next night, Sebastian rode in his coach with his mother. She had tried to make conversation with him several times, but part of his attention was on memories of the night before, when Allegra had come to him in all her deliciousness. When she had offered herself like a luscious morsel. When she had aroused him to the point of mindlessness. When she had made him see that he would never want another woman as much as he did her. When she had given him her trust.

"Sebastian, I am so grateful you decided to accompany me," the countess said for at least the fifth time since they had left Blackbrake. "You know Mrs. Fiddick has *the* most exquisite bonnet designs, even though her shop is not on Milsom Street. I must get her to move. She would have so many more customers. But to get new designs from Paris and invite me to be the first to see them…Well, that is just too good to pass up. I wonder if there will be bows. Or birds. Or flowers. You know I adore flowers on a bonnet."

Sebastian controlled a grimace. "Mother, I said I would come with you so you could indulge yourself with a new hat. But please spare me from descriptions of gewgaws."

"Of course." His mother plucked at a bit of something on her skirt. "You know, I could not contain my delight for this special event, so I invited the lovely Princess Allegra to meet us at Mrs. Fiddick's shop. I thought she might enjoy seeing the latest before anyone else in Bath. She is always so up to the mark." A mischievous twinkle lit her eyes.

Sebastian's attention riveted on his mother, seated across from him in the coach. "The princess?" he croaked. Mere mention of her made his pulse race and his body stir. He cleared his throat, then said, as nonchalantly as he could, "That was quite thoughtful of you."

His mother's glance was sly as she said, "I did so enjoy her company at tea. I thought she and I could try on bonnets and be silly women together while you go off and amuse yourself until we are done."

For some inexplicable reason, the idea of watching Allegra try on bonnets seemed to be the most erotic amusement he could imagine and definitely not silly. His mother prattled on about Mrs. Fiddick's clever designs while his mind took him back to the night before when he had entered his bed chamber to discover the nearly naked, deliciously lovely princess. He had finally gotten his wish to have her sprawled naked on his bed. The experience was everything he had imagined and quite a bit more. For he had found himself sprawled naked on his bed as well. And perfectly comfortable. More than comfortable. Aroused, absorbed, enamored. They had made love several times, each one better than the last. He could hardly believe he'd had such stamina. But he could not get enough of her, the feel of her, the taste of her. They had finally fallen asleep just before dawn. When he awoke, she was gone, as if she had never been. Except lying on the pillow next to him was his torc.

He wore it now beneath his shirt, reached up and touched it as if positioning his neckcloth. The feel of it around his neck was both familiar and strange, for he had not had it for some time. He felt the subtle hum of his power running through it. A faint smile touched his lips. The woman who had stolen and then returned it was subtle as well. Intelligent. Brave. Honorable. Sensuous. He shifted on the seat to cover his arousal. After all, his mother sat just across from him.

The carriage jolted to a stop. He glanced out and discovered they had reached their destination. Mrs. Fiddick's shop, nearer the city end of the bridge rather than the Sydney Garden end, was well-lit in contrast to the other shops, all closed up for the night. The bridge itself was nearly deserted. Only a single barouche passed them as it traversed the span, then turned onto the Grand Parade, most likely on its way to the Lower Assembly Rooms. The countess watched the vehicle with suspicion until it was out of sight. This visit to the milliner's was a clandestine affair, for being the first with a new fashion was a coup for the countess. He handed his mother down from the carriage, then told his whip and tiger to take themselves off for some refreshment.

His mother looked at him in surprise. "Are you not taking yourself off somewhere?"

"I find I am intrigued by your discussion of Mrs. Fiddick's new designs," he said, trying to find a middle road between trumped up enthusiasm and sardonic boredom.

"I see," the countess said, accepting his explanation much too readily. She swept into the shop.

Sebastian sighed. His mother was not fooled at all. She knew exactly why he had chosen to remain. Resigned to her meddling, he followed.

Mrs. Fiddick greeted them in the middle of her shop. Hats and bonnets on stands stood like fashionable, bodiless soldiers on shelves lining two of the walls opposite each other. Against the third wall were two dressing tables with mirrors above, and a window between them that looked out over the rushing river below. To the left of the entrance was a counter with spools of ribbons, boxes of silk flowers, vases of multi-hued plumes, and rows of tiny birds with feathers like jewels.

The milliner was a not a young woman, but neither was she old. She had a pleasant countenance and was neatly but plainly dressed. Spectacles sat primly on her nose. She clasped and unclasped her hands repeatedly at her waist. Sebastian wondered why she was agitated.

"Please," she said, opening a door in the middle of the wall to the right, "come into my private showroom."

"Has the Princess Allegra arrived?" the countess asked.

"Yes. Yes, she is already inside." Mrs. Fiddick bobbed her head several times.

His mother stepped through. "Oh!" She sounded overcome with emotion and as if she were about to faint.

Sebastian tamped down the dread of listening to her exclaim and twitter all evening with the pleasant expectation of seeing Allegra. He stepped through the doorway. And halted. The sight which met him turned his blood cold. Then hot with fury.

Huddled in one corner of the room was a young girl, most likely the milliner's assistant, bound hand and foot incongruously with beautiful satin ribbon. Next to her was the indomitable Luisa, also bound and gagged as well. To the other side stood Crowley holding a knife to Allegra's throat. Her hands had also been tied with satin ribbon. Now he knew the reason for the milliner's agitation. Crowley had lured them into a trap. He was very glad the princess had returned his torc. And that he had thought to bring the walking stick she had given him. She trembled, but after meeting her gaze, Sebastian realized it was not from fear, but rage.

"We meet again, Hawksmoor," Crowley said with a nasty grin.

I want to kill him, Allegra said in his head. *He has tricked me twice.*

Sebastian acknowledged her declaration with a nod, admiring her bravery and determination.

She wriggled in Crowley's grasp. He tightened his grip and pushed the knife closer to her throat.

"Stay still, woman," he growled.

I can't Thought Bind with him. Frustration threaded through Allegra's silent complaint. *If I could reach his wrist, I could connect with him and put him to sleep.*

Sebastian frowned and gave his head a tiny shake. He did not want her anywhere near the inside of that man's head. "Release the princess, Crowley. She does not need to be involved in this."

Crowley snorted a laugh. "I'm not releasing my prize. I'm not addle-pated."

"Really, Crowley," Sebastian drawled, "you are quite addle-pated, and you are becoming very tiresome."

"How tiresome will I be when you are dead, and I take over Blackbrake and the Hawksmoor title?" Crowley sneered.

The countess gasped. "Sebastian, whatever does he mean?"

"He believes he is my half-brother," Sebastian said as he edged between his mother and Crowley.

"But that's not possible." His mother looked very confused. "Your father never kept a mistress. I would have known." She peered at Crowley. "And you are so much older than my Sebastian."

"God's blood, you're even more bird-witted than I thought," Crowley ridiculed. "The old earl sowed his seed in the wrong field. My mother wasn't good enough to become his countess."

Shock crossed her face. "Oh." She put a hand to her forehead. "I must sit down. I feel quite unwell."

The only chairs were behind Crowley. Before Sebastian could stop her, she plowed forward toward the chairs. Toward Crowley. She bumped him hard as she passed.

"Be careful, you old hag," he snarled.

The countess turned on him. Her cheeks were pale. "I beg your pardon?" Her question came out cold and haughty. She did not wait for a response. "After all I have done for you, you dare to insult me?" She hit him with her reticule. It landed with a heavy clink against his arm, the one holding Allegra. "I let you into my circle." She hit him again. "I gave you coin to gamble." Another blow. "I paid your haberdasher chits." And then the blows rained down on him, one after another after another. "You cad. You weasel. You insignificant little worm."

Crowley tried to protect himself from the blows, turning this way and that, at the same time attempting to hold onto Allegra. "Stop that," he cried.

Sebastian watched his mother in awe.

The countess landed one well-aimed blow at Crowley's head.

"Damn you, woman!" He pushed Allegra at the countess.

Allegra stumbled against her. They landed in a heap on the floor amid tangled limbs and billowing skirts. Crowley paid them no attention. As Sebastian moved to help them, Crowley lunged at him with his knife. Sebastian jumped back, barely escaping a sliced sleeve.

"Come on, you bastard," Crowley taunted, waving his knife before him, focused on Sebastian.

"I believe you speak of yourself, Crowley," Sebastian said. "You're the one born on the wrong side of the blanket." His gaze flicked to Allegra and his mother to assure himself they were unharmed. He turned back to Crowley. "Now, put down the knife and let us discuss terms. Perhaps we can come to some understanding." He had no intention of coming to any understanding with the bloke.

"The only understanding I want is for you to be dead." Crowley lunged again with the knife.

Sebastian deflected the blow with his walking stick. Then he struck the man on the shoulder. Crowley swiped the knife in an arc.

The walking stick fended it off again. Slowly, Sebastian backed out of the room, drawing Crowley with him away from the women as the man jabbed and thrust. Finally, with a flick and twist of his wrist, Sebastian used the walking stick to disarm him. The dagger flew out of Crowley's hand and skittered across the floor into a corner. Sebastian unsheathed the sword hidden inside the stick and pointed it at Crowley's heart.

"You are finished here, Crowley," he said. "Admit defeat."

Instead of surrendering, the man grinned evilly. He raised his arm and made a fist. His sleeve fell back, revealing the frog glyph on his wrist. "You forget I have this. I know you don't have one."

Irritated, Sebastian sighed. As The Messenger of the Legion of Baal, he had been the one to place the glyph on all the members, giving them a token amount of protection against Nulkana. But it did not nearly equal his own abilities as a Druid priest. "No, Crowley, I don't have one of those."

Crowley sniggered. "Careless of you, Hawksmoor."

Sebastian hated this man. He was furious that the bastard had duped his mother and had tried to give Allegra to Nulkana, besides twice holding a weapon on her. But he did not wish to kill him. He had enough blood on his hands. Besides that, the man might be his half-brother. What he wanted for Crowley was something far more punitive and degrading. Sebastian wanted to put him away into prison for a very long time. For a man like Crowley who craved the trappings of society, that would be dire punishment.

"I don't think you understand, Crowley," Sebastian said. "I can hurt you very badly."

Crowley shrugged and wiggled his arm with the tattoo. "I've been practicing with this. I've become very good. Would you like to see?"

Without waiting for an answer, he swung his arm and a stream of energy shot from the frog glyph. Sebastian blocked it with the sword. The bolt struck the metal with a loud ping and sizzled up its length in a current of green light. The surge zapped through Sebastian's fingers, into his hand and traveled up his arm in a pulse of pain, surprising him. The torc around his neck heated. In an instant, before he could suppress it, his own power answered, coursing down his arm, through the sword and out its tip. An arc of blue energy seared through the air between them and hit Crowley in the chest. It threw him back against the window. The glass exploded. He teetered for an awful moment on the sill. Sebastian grabbed for him, catching the lapel of his coat with the tips of his fingers. But the weight of Crowley's slack body was too much. The material ripped away. Without a sound, Crowley fell back and disappeared down into the dark. Sebastian heard the splash as he landed in the river.

If he were still alive, Sebastian was not about to let him escape by floating down river. He wanted him to answer for his crimes. Spinning about, he raced out of the shop, to the end of the bridge, onto Grand Parade. He skidded to a halt at the very spot where Allegra had slipped on the embankment. Crowley was already bobbing past, his face a pale blur, a dark irregular burn in the middle of his white shirt. He was still alive, struggling weakly against the current. Sebastian slid and slipped down the bank to the river with the thought he might be able to snag him, but the current was too swift. By the time he got his feet under him, Crowley was already bumping over the weir. And then he disappeared beneath the churning water.

Sebastian ran along the river's edge through the mud and slippery grass. He cursed the tangled vines that caught at him. If he had been on the other bank of the river, he would have been free to run along the walk that had been built for the ease of strollers. Instead, he nearly slipped into the rushing water several times. He strained in the dark to see any sign of Crowley, but he saw only the black water, deceptively smooth on the surface once it passed the weir. And then several yards away, an arm emerged from the surface of the water as if waving at him. The frog glyph glowed dully, then faded. Crowley's arm slowly sank, leaving behind a few bubbles that reflected the moonlight. A few moments later, something looking very much like a bundle of laundry surfaced farther down river. It floated away on the current.

Sebastian stopped, panting, as he scanned the river. Crowley was gone. No doubt his body would wash up miles downriver. Sebastian would have to alert the authorities. With one last searching glance at the water, he trudged back along the river.

He had mixed feelings about Crowley's death. Relief that he would not have to deal with him and his evil schemes to turn Allegra over to Nulkana, or his dastardly plan to gain the Hawksmoor title. Regret that the man would not be able to answer for his crimes. And guilt—one more death to add to the list that weighed on his soul. The deaths had all been executions, some for the undersecretary, some for the Lord High, and the men had all been depraved or evil. But each one had changed him, made him harder, colder, one more bite taken out of his soul. He was afraid he was finding them too easy to carry out, despite his loathing of what he did.

Allegra was waiting for him when he reached the top of the embankment.

You killed him, she said silently. *Thank you.*

His regret and guilt at Crowley's death lifted a little with her words. The man would have never let her alone. Even if he had been put into prison, his threat to her would have remained. Crowley would have found a way to escape, and somehow, he would have sacrificed her to Nulkana.

Sebastian smiled. His conscience was quiet.

"Are you hurt?" Allegra asked as she stepped closer.

"No." He reached out and touched her cheek. "Are you?"

"Just my pride," she said with a wry twist to her lips. "He surprised me."

"He will never bother you again." Relief at that flooded him as he tucked her hand in the crook of his arm and strolled with her back to the shop. "Thank you once again for the walking stick. It was quite handy."

She grinned. "The Druid's Sapphire for a Druid."

Her flippant remark was made in innocence, but he wondered if she truly knew the power of the gem. In combination with his torc, his abilities seemed to be magnified. Perhaps they even equaled those of the sorceress. What if he could destroy Nulkana and end the deathly threat against Allegra and her family? What if he could end the threat of the Lord High and the Legion of Baal? What if he could find the remaining pieces of the Sphere of Astarte and turn them over to the lovely, tortured lady beside him? A plan began to form in his head, one he would have to plot carefully.

As he planned, he realized that accomplishing all those goals would mean that Allegra would learn who and what he was, what he had done. She would want nothing more to do with him, for what woman worth having would want to associate with an assassin? The thought brought a wrench to his heart. With that pain came a realization so sudden and strong he nearly stopped walking. He loved this woman. This woman who had drugged him, kidnapped him, chained him to a wall, and then connected to his mind in the most sensuous way imaginable. This woman who fought demons in her soul at every change of the moon. This woman who bravely faced down her enemies. This woman who had willingly given herself to him.

He would do everything in his power to make her whole and then send her on her way. He was not worthy enough to ask her to remain with him. But her exit from his life was days away. Until then, he would enjoy her company as often as he could. As they entered the bridge, he pulled her into a dark doorway.

She laughed. "*Sior* Hawksmoor, this is most inappropriate," she teased.

He cupped her face in his hands. "Not as inappropriate as being sprawled naked across my bed," he murmured. Then he kissed her.

At the touch of his lips, Allegra melted against him. His solid body calmed her, and at the same time it evoked a delicious tingle that curled her toes. She had not realized how frightened she had been when Crowley held that blade to her throat. Unable to use her fan as a weapon, unable to Thought Bind with him to persuade him to let her go or to put him to sleep, she had felt helpless. That had made her angry.

She was awed by Sebastian's power that had sent Crowley crashing through the window. He had saved her. Again. He had become the man who protected her rather than the man who threatened with exposure of her secret. He made her feel safe, a sensation she had not experienced in a very long time.

Sebastian's mouth against hers, the sweep of his tongue, and the bands of his arms brought her comfort as well as a delightful throb deep within her. The night she had gone to him had been extraordinary. Spectacular. Dazzling. He had made her feel like a normal woman, not some tortured, deformed creature, not a woman who was cursed. She wanted that again. Soon.

His kiss deepened. His arms tightened. His arousal pressed against her. She squirmed against him, his hard erection making her body remember the pleasure he had given her. She went moist and limp in response, forgot they were in a dark doorway on the Pulteney Bridge, visible to anyone who happened by. If he wanted, she would give herself to him right there and then, as if she were some wanton who had no control. As if she were in the middle of the Hunger, crazed with need. But something nagged at the edge of her mind.

She sensed a desperation in him that seemed unusual in a man so sure of himself. His kiss felt like a farewell, rather than a connection. Slowly, she pulled away.

His eyes were hot and dark, hungry, his breath ragged. A line formed between his brows, half confusion, half annoyance.

Before he could speak, she placed her hand against his cheek. "Something troubles you, *caro mio*," she whispered.

He blinked. A dark emotion flashed through his eyes, but then was gone. In its place was the urbane, ironic English earl.

"I was kissing you, and then you stopped," he said. "That is most troubling."

She gazed at him earnestly. "You know that is not what I meant."

He took a breath and let it out slowly. "You will be Shadow soon. How can I survive without holding your luscious body or kissing your delicious lips?"

She smiled, charmed by his words but knowing he was attempting to distract her. "I'm sure you'll live. Besides it only lasts a short time. Think of what we can do when I return to flesh and bone."

He became very serious. Reaching up, he tucked a stray strand of hair behind her ear. "Alli, I have come to care for you. Promise me you'll not do anything foolish while you are Shadow."

Her breath caught. Had he deduced what she was planning? That she was going to the Legion of Baal's gathering at the full moon? She had told no one, not even Luisa. Perhaps during their night of passion, she had inadvertently connected with him through Thought Binding and he had discovered her intent. No, she would have remembered if they had connected that way. She decided his words were only the result of a general concern for her safety. And a declaration that he held tender feelings for her. It warmed her heart.

But he had not mentioned love.

Of course, he could not love her. She was cursed, doomed to a life of hiding what she truly was. No man would want a woman with such an affliction. She ignored the twinge of pain through her heart. She would accept what he offered and hold it close. But she would never reveal her own feelings, nor that she intended to risk everything to retrieve a piece of the Sphere of Astarte.

"When I am Shadow," she whispered teasingly, "is when I can be as foolish as I want."

He blew out a breath in exasperation. "You will be the death of me, lovely lady."

She smiled. "Only when we make love. The French call it *la petite mort*."

With a chuckle, he nuzzled her neck. "Of course. The little death. I want to do that now."

Allegra silently agreed, but instead, she said, "Luisa and the *contessa* might wonder where we are, *si*?"

His eyes widened. "My mother! Good God, she will have bought out all of Mrs. Fiddick's shop by now."

Allegra laughed as he tucked her hand into the crook of his arm. "Your mother was quite formidable against Crowley. She should be allowed a reward."

"She was brave, wasn't she?" he reflected as he led her back to the shop.

Something in his tone made her think he was quite bemused by his mother's courage. But she put it out of her mind because she was distracted by his warm hand covering hers and his fingers that gently stroked in circles.

Sebastian stared out the window of his coach as it rolled out of the city toward Blackbrake. Across from him, his mother sat subdued and staring out her own window. After Allegra and a very disgruntled Mistress Luisa were collected by Ernesto, he had informed the authorities of Crowley's death. They had exclaimed over the violence visited upon him, his mother, and the lovely Princess Allegra, and murmured their concerns over everyone's welfare. They assured him they would alert the villages down river, told him they would check on Mrs. Fiddick, and then allowed him to leave with few questions.

Relieved that the matter was settled, his thoughts jumped from the death of Crowley to the kiss he had shared with Allegra. The memory made his body tighten. He shifted to get comfortable. The motion brought his mother's attention from the window. This was a good time to bring up her sudden bravery and have her answer some questions.

"Your attack on Crowley saved the day, Mother," he said.

She flashed a pleased grin. "Thank you." Then she made a moue of distaste. "I cannot believe I befriended such a disagreeable person."

"You could not have known."

"I should have known." Her words held a tone of self-reproach.

"Why?" he probed gently.

"I—" she began, halted, and shook her head. "I just should have known."

Her statement suggested more than a failing of her social skills. "Mother, I think you need to tell me how you learned to fight and distract."

With a tiny gasp, her eyebrows shot up. "Fight? Distract? Oh, my goodness, where would I have learned such things?" She gave an amused chuckle.

Sebastian's eyes narrowed. His mother was dissembling. He needed answers because Nulkana was in the vicinity. Although he did not think the sorceress would have any interest in his mother, just the fact she was related to him could put her in danger. His mother's skills, if she had any, could be either a help or hindrance if Nulkana attacked.

"Mother." His single flat word was a warning.

The countess's shoulders slumped. She turned to gaze out the window and the corners of her mouth drew down. When she turned back to him, a line appeared between her brows.

Before she spoke, he said, "No megrims, Mother. I need to hear the truth."

A bit of temper made her eyes flash. "There are some things that parents should not have to reveal to their children."

"There are some things that children need to know in order to keep their parents safe," he returned gently.

His mother's features softened. "You have always kept me safe, Sebastian, especially after your father died. Allow me this one time to help you."

Sebastian toyed with pressing her, but he could see she was still a bit shaken by the experience, despite the pile of hat boxes on the seat beside him. He decided to concede to her wishes for now. But sometime in the near future, he meant to discover how his gently reared mother suddenly demonstrated the skills of someone who was acquainted with danger.

Chapter 19

Sebastian stood on the veranda just outside the doors that led into the ballroom. His mother's masquerade ball appeared to be a success, for the guests were dancing and chatting and apparently enjoying themselves. The countess herself was holding court at the far side of the room. She laughed, accepted compliments, and flirted outrageously. But he knew she was disappointed. The Princess Allegra had not appeared, nor had either of her brothers with their wives. Besides the discourtesy, she was hurt, for he sensed his mother truly liked the princess. For that, he was angry. But he was also relieved. Allegra's brothers knew him only as an adversary, The Messenger of the Legion of Baal, despite the fact that he'd helped one avoid a dangerous threat and saved the other's life. He had not looked forward to dodging them all evening. But he also keenly felt Allegra's absence.

For the past two days, all he had been able to think about was her. He went through the hours in a blur, speaking with his estate agent and not remembering what he had said, going for a ride and finding himself gazing down at the priory without knowing how he came to be there. He had to stop this madness. He needed to take control of his life, something that seemed to have eluded him since finding himself naked and chained against a stone wall with a delectable woman seducing him.

He turned away from the ballroom and gazed up at the sky where the moon hung heavy and pregnant, nearly full. This would have been the last time he would ever see her. The conclave of the Legion of Baal was in two nights. It could either be the night when he would take possession of a piece of the Sphere of Astarte and send Allegra back to Auriano with her brothers, or it would be the last night of his life. He had wanted one last touch of her hand, one last delicious kiss.

Something, a ripple through the crowd, the sweep of a murmur made him turn back toward the ballroom. New arrivals. The Auriano twins and their wives, along with their sister. The evening, which he thought would be dull and lifeless, became one of anticipated pleasure. He felt his heart skip and his body stirred. Bemused at his reaction, he watched them slowly make their way into the ballroom. He had told Allegra on the Pulteney Bridge two nights ago that he cared for her. With a jolt, he realized those words were pale in comparison to what he actually felt. He loved her. He would do anything for her, including the wrenching idea of giving her up to keep her safe. In two nights, one way or the other, he would never see her again. The thought pressed down on him, and he pushed it away. She was here, and he would enjoy his time with her.

His mother, regal in her Elizabeth I costume, approached them, and he watched the interplay of greetings and compliments, each one of them playing the role of their costumes. The twins were dressed identically. Both wore the *bauta*, the traditional costume of the Venetian *Carnevale*. It consisted of black cape, tricorn hat, and plain white full mask. But he noted a slight difference in one mask. At the outside point of one eyebrow was a design, made of small diamonds, of a circle broken into three arcs with a lightning bolt through its center. He had seen the device on the side of the prince's coach in Italy and knew it for the coat of arms of the House of Auriano. The wearer of the mask was the prince, Alessandro. At least now he would know which twin he had held at sword point and knocked unconscious, and which twin he had brought back to life. He could sense their essences, both golden like their sister's, but the prince's was dimmed by shadows. He wondered if the man might be experiencing some effects of the curse.

The prince's wife was wearing a milkmaid costume of black silk bodice with a white lawn chemise beneath, so thin and fine that it was nearly transparent and revealed the warm skin of her arms. Her dark blue satin skirt had a hem mimicking tatters, and a gauzy petticoat, cut in the same fashion as her skirt, peeked from beneath it and dragged behind her. Her half mask was made of brown and gold feathers, the tips flaring up and away from the sides. A lacy kerchief was tied over her rich, dark hair. The duke's wife was dressed as a highwayman in black silk breeches, dark brown velvet frock coat, and a tricorn hat trimmed with braid and sporting a white plume. The costume consisted of rich materials that were never part of her clothing when she was a thief in France. Rather than a scarf covering the lower part of her face, she wore a strip of black velvet across her eyes. He was sure some of the company were scandalized by her breeches. But his attention was centered on Allegra, who was dressed as a nun, but a nun whose simple gown was of luxurious black silk. Her white satin wimple covered her shoulders and draped across her chest, but rather than the severe head covering nuns wore, she wore a veil of black Venetian lace. Her half-mask was red satin with gold embroidery, a startling contrast to her subdued costume.

He waited until his mother had waved her fan, inviting them to partake of the dancing and entertainment, then he threaded his way across the ballroom. If the twins and their wives recognized him in his costume, he was hoping decorum and courtesy would prevent them from challenging him to a duel, or at the very least from creating a scene.

He had never felt so anxious, not even when he had been on his first assignment for Sir Cyril. That night, long ago, he had been tasked with retrieving a document from an American who had stolen it from a careless clerk in the Foreign Office. Of course, the only way to get the document back was to creep into the American's rooms and steal it while he was sleeping. Fortunately, the task had been a success.

That memory made him think of the night he had encountered Allegra in Crowley's rooms. She had been annoyingly stubborn and insightful. And beautiful, sensuous, and luscious as Shadow. She was flesh and bone now, just as beautiful, sensuous, and delicious, but surrounded by her family, she was aggravatingly remote and inaccessible. He wanted to get her away from them. He wanted her all to himself. And when he did... He halted those thoughts immediately.

He reminded himself this was a social event and many eyes watched. With a discipline born of years of practice, he took a breath and stopped before them.

"Good evening, gentlemen and ladies," he greeted. "Welcome to the masquerade ball of the Countess of Hawksmoor. All identities will remain secret until midnight, but please feel free to partake of the entertainments."

Allegra recognized the Earl of Hawksmoor immediately, despite the black silk half-mask he wore. He moved with a sleek grace she had come to recognize as his alone. He wore a kilt of dark green plaid, a short, black velvet jacket, and white shirt ruffled down the front. White lace frothed over his wrists. His stockings ended at the knee and revealed his powerful legs. He had braided his hair into a single heavy plait which hung down his back. The vision she'd had of him when he cured her arm came to mind, but no scrolling tattoos were visible beyond his lacy cuffs and neckpiece. She wondered if he wore undergarments beneath that kilt or nothing at all. Her thighs clenched at the thought. Reminding herself they were supposed to be strangers, she solemnly bowed her head and kept her hands demurely clasped within the wide sleeves of her nun's habit. But she could not wait for him to discover that beneath the modest wimple that draped around her neck and across her chest, her gown had been cut to a nearly indecent décolletage.

Just before Sebastian reached them, Alessandro murmured as he glanced around at the large gathering, "I thought you said the earl was a recluse. This masquerade seems to indicate the opposite." His voice sounded hollow behind the mask, but also because he was experiencing part of the curse, mitigated by the piece of the Sphere he had found.

"I must have been mistaken." Allegra shrugged. "I had heard that he shuns society." She did not lie because she had heard that about him when she first arrived in Bath.

Solange cocked her head as she watched him through the crowd. "He seems familiar for some reason, like I have met him somewhere else." She shook her head. "But that is impossible."

Allegra was relieved she did not have to answer, for Sebastian, handsome, tall and elegant, stood before them. Her brothers and their wives acknowledged Sebastian's greeting. She was so taken by the sight of him and so afraid that her brothers would discover her unorthodox and highly improper relationship with him that she froze and was unable to respond. Words flowed around her as merely sound with no meaning. She felt shy and unsure, as if this were the first time she had ever seen him, and so she lowered her eyes to the polished floor just beyond her toes. Abruptly, an elegant hand appeared within her sight. His voice caressed her ears, and she realized he was speaking to her.

Her head snapped up. "I beg your pardon?"

A tiny smile curved his lips. "May I have the honor of this dance, good sister?"

On her left, Alessandro bristled. On her right, she sensed Antonio's predatory gaze. Rebelliously, she decided since this was a masquerade, rules of propriety did not apply. Before either brother could object, she placed her hand in Sebastian's.

"Since I have lived most of my life in a convent, good sir, I have little knowledge of the steps of the dance," she said, playing her part as a nun. "Perhaps you would be good enough to teach me, *si*?"

His eyes behind his mask warmed at her words. "I would be pleased to lead you through all the steps."

Allegra felt the heat rise in her cheeks and her nipples pucker. Their innocent words echoed those she had used when she had kidnapped him and seduced him with Thought Binding, and again at Lady Hetherington's lawn party. How far they had come since then. First, adversaries in an intricate game and now, secret lovers.

She had never felt so drawn to a man. Before, men, not including her brothers, were a foreign race who coexisted in the same world. She conversed with them, sometimes flirted with them, yet they never interested her as anything more than the means to calm the Hunger. But Sebastian had drawn her attention like iron to a magnet. Like the iron, she wanted to cling to the magnet that was him. She wished there could be more between them. At some point, she would have to pull away.

Both of her brothers stiffened when she accepted Sebastian's invitation. She blithely ignored them as she allowed Sebastian to lead her to the middle of the ballroom where couples formed up for a reel. He smiled, a secret little sly smile. To anyone observing, he appeared merely friendly, but to Allegra, the smile implied the touch of his lips, the slide of his fingers, the stroke of his body. Her cheeks flushed with heat.

The music began, and when they came together, he murmured, "I've missed you."

The steps led them apart too quickly for her to respond.

Once again, they came together, and he whispered, "I want to hold you."

As a smile curved her lips, they separated.

"I want to kiss you," he said at their next meeting.

Her breasts grew sensitive as they rubbed against her chemise.

Five steps later, he whispered, "I want to suck on your toes."

All the tiny hairs on her arms stood up.

The next time they met in the dance, he said, "I want to undress you."

She had to fight to keep her knees from collapsing.

Once again, they came together. "I want to touch all your secret places," he said.

Her breath caught in her throat. Moisture gathered between her thighs. Every nerve ending in her body tingled. She prayed for the dance to end quickly. His seduction was torment, for her brothers watched. If she did not want them to drag Sebastian out of his house and skewer him with a rapier or stiletto, then she had to pretend she hardly knew him, difficult to do when all she wanted was to grab him and put her mouth all over him.

Each time they came together, he whispered words of seduction, or allowed his fingers to linger a bit longer than was proper, or caressed her palm or wrist. Allegra thought she might go mad as she fought to appear cool and polite. Part of her wanted to scream at him to stop, while another part wanted him to tear off her clothes. She felt as if the Hunger had taken her over.

After an eternity, when her body vibrated and her blood heated every time the dance brought them together, the music ended with a flourish. In proper fashion, he bowed to her.

"Meet me outside," he murmured before he led her back to her family.

Her brothers glowered at him behind their masks.

"Thank you for honoring me, good sister," he said, once more bowing to her. He turned to her brothers with a charming smile, ignoring the belligerence rippling off them. "And thank you for allowing me the pleasure of the good sister's company." He calmly turned and sauntered away.

Allegra felt her brothers' annoyance and her sisters' curiosity.

You will not dance with him again, Alessandro said silently.

"It was only a dance," his wife, Sabrina, reasoned.

He is much too forward, Antonio added.

"He was being polite," Solange, Antonio's wife, retorted.

Allegra remained quiet while they squabbled about Sebastian and scolded her. Their words, both silent and spoken, became background noise in her head as she watched the dancers form up for a quadrille. Sebastian had invited a fairy, lovely in her flowing pastels and diaphanous wings, to partner with him. A prick of jealousy stung her. Until he turned in the dance, met her gaze, and smiled a secret smile. The tightness in her chest eased away. Of course, he had to partner with others, or their secret connection would become known. He danced to protect her. Her heart melted.

Alessandro and Antonio still scolded. Sabrina and Solange still defended.

Then Alessandro declared, *You will dance only with us.*

Allegra gasped. *I will not. This is a masquerade, Sandro, where no one knows who I am. I am safe behind my mask. You have left me on my own for too long to decide what I may or may not do.* Abruptly, she moved away through the crowd.

Alli, Sandro called, but she ignored him.

She knew her brothers were trying to protect her, but their sudden overbearing attention annoyed her. She had lived apart from them for too many years. Besides, she was not about to let them interfere with her relationship with Sebastian, no matter how scandalous.

Her irritation brought her to the long veranda outside the ballroom. A wide set of stone steps led down into a garden lit by the nearly full moon. She stood at the carved stone rail and breathed in the cool air while she let her emotions calm. In two nights, she would be Shadow. And with a little luck, she might be able to snatch the piece of the Sphere of Astarte at the gathering of the Legion of Baal. The magical piece might dispel the curse, and she would be a normal woman. And perhaps, then she might be able to reveal her true feelings to Sebastian.

As she fantasized about that moment, she sensed someone exit the ballroom. She heard a step behind her and then a light brush against her hand, the slide of fingers across her skin. Footsteps moved away into the dark end of the veranda. Sebastian summoned.

She wandered farther down the veranda to its end where it curved around the side of the house. A hand caught her and pulled her into the dark, away from the light of the torches. Sebastian's tall form was a black silhouette against the night sky.

As he trailed his fingers down her cheek, he said, "I thought I might go mad in there, not being able to hold you."

Allegra cupped his face and drew him down. "My brothers were watching," she said against his lips.

"But not now," he murmured, then dragged her tight against his body and kissed her.

Allegra gave herself up to the gentle onslaught. She loved the feel of him against her, his hard planes pressing on her soft curves. His tongue swooped and caressed, and his hands wandered over her, pressing, kneading, stroking. Time flew away. She drank him in, drugged on his touch, his scent of piney woods, his taste like apples.

The sound of laughter from the ballroom reached her, and she became aware of where she was, and what she was doing. Her attention had been all on him, on his mouth, his hands, his body. Reluctantly, she put a tiny bit of space between them. Sebastian protested with a growl. She stared up into those blue, blue eyes, glowing with color even in the dim light.

"My brothers will wonder where I am," she said breathlessly.

His hands roamed over her, and his gaze focused on her mouth. "Let them wonder." As his fingers trailed beneath her wimple, they followed the neckline of her gown and slipped down to the bare skin of her breasts. His eyes widened as he realized how low her décolletage was. "Lovely Alli, you will destroy me," he whispered.

With barely a tug, he freed her breasts and cupped them in his hands. His thumbs stroked her tight buds and sent delicious tingles through her. A half-sigh, half-moan escaped, and her head dropped back. She could barely stand. As his hands caressed, his lips traced a trail of kisses up her neck, to her jaw, her cheek, until they claimed her mouth once more. She was lost.

Sebastian drowned in her. The feel of her satiny skin beneath his fingers, the warmth of her lips made him forget where they were. He was delighted at the secret seduction she wore beneath her demure exterior. Her breasts were a delectable handful, the tips tightened into small knots. As he kneaded and squeezed, she made tiny whimpering noises that made him clench and harden. He backed her up to the support of the wall of the house. Her body was a supple delight beneath his fingers. Allegra's lips beneath his, her luscious breasts in his hands drove everything else from his mind. The masquerade ball and her brothers were far from his thoughts. But then her attention wavered.

"Allegra," he murmured, still absorbed in her.

She placed her hands against his chest and put some space between them. His concentration broke.

"Listen," she whispered.

His mother's voice, low and vibrating with anger, came through the open window beside them. "You promised me that he would not be in danger," the countess said. "You told me he would only be involved in diplomacy."

"My dear Evelyn, I never thought you would be so gullible." Sir Cyril's smooth barb came clearly through the window.

Sebastian froze, riveted by the conversation.

"Gullible?" His mother's voice rose. "Cyril, I was never gullible. I've always known you were a devious snake, but I always believed you to be truthful with me."

Allegra's lips parted as if she would speak. Sebastian warned her to remain quiet with a shake of his head.

The rustle of silk petticoats approached nearer the window. "I put myself in danger for you many times because I believed that you would keep me safe," the countess said. "All those times I traveled to France for you so I could bring back information."

Despite Sebastian's warning to silence, Allegra said silently, *Your mother was a spy!*

Helplessly, in shock himself, Sebastian merely stared and nodded.

"You betrayed me, Evelyn." Sir Cyril's voice was hard. "You, merely the farmer's daughter, married the wealthy earl."

"I was a squire's daughter," his mother said, her tone insulted.

"You tossed me aside," Foley sneered.

"I fell in love with him." Frustration twined through her statement.

"You broke our engagement," he growled.

"We had no engagement," she said with a sniff. "You assumed something I never agreed to."

"When I asked if you would stay with me—"

"That was such a romantic proposal." The countess's words dripped sarcasm. "'Stay with me, Evelyn, and you can travel the world,'" she quoted in a deep voice. "You never mentioned marriage, Cyril. But I did stay with you. I allowed you to visit, especially after my husband died, to develop a relationship with my son." The rustle of her petticoats moved away from the window. "I encouraged him to work for you."

Allegra gasped.

Sebastian's teeth clenched as he learned how he had been manipulated.

"And now," his mother went on, "I find you have him in the middle of danger. I can't even imagine what atrocious things you have him doing."

"What can I say, Evelyn?" Sir Cyril's tone suggested smug dismissal. "He's working for me, and I can send him anywhere I see fit, even into danger."

"You monster!" the countess hissed. The crack of a hand against flesh came clearly through the window.

Sir Cyril chuckled coldly. "Yes, I am." He paused, and his next words were low and deadly. "I hated you for throwing me over. He should have been my son. But he's not, so I can use him any way I wish. And if something happens to him, I know it will pierce your heart, just like you pierced mine when you married his father."

"Go to Hell," his mother snapped. Then her angry footsteps receded across the floor and a door slammed.

"I'll go to Hell right behind you, Evelyn," Sir Cyril growled. That same door opened, then closed quietly.

Stunned and enraged, Sebastian's focus shrunk to a tiny dot of black fury. All he wanted was to kill the man whom he had looked upon as a mentor. He needed a weapon, a pistol, a sword, anything. He tried to move. Two hands clutched at his coat.

"No, Sebastian. No." Allegra's urgent whisper was accompanied by a rough shake.

"Let me go," he said, the words toneless in his dazed state.

"Sebastian." Allegra shook him again. "Do you think your mother wants you to know where she came from? That she used to spy for Foley? Why do you think she never told you?"

He stared down at her, unable to form an answer.

"Sebastian." She spoke his name like a command. "She is ashamed of who she is. He forced her—" Her words stopped as if she could not bring herself to finish.

He wilted at her words and placed his hands against the stone wall on either side of her to keep himself upright. His mother had always been vague about her background, claiming that her noble family was defunct, that she was raised by a maiden aunt in Ireland. Now he knew the reason for her evasion. He did not think any less of her, but he understood her better.

Allegra's eyes narrowed, and she pressed back against the wall, away from him. "*Madre di Dio*," she whispered. She muttered something else in Italian, but his brain was focused on Foley.

"One of these days, I'm going to kill that man," he muttered. "But first, I'm going to get my revenge."

She sucked in a breath. "*Si*. He taught you well. You are just like him." Her glorious golden gaze glittered in anger.

"Pardon?" Sebastian felt like he had just stepped into nightmare. Sir Cyril, the man he had looked to for guidance for most of his adult life, was a cruel, vengeful fiend. And now Allegra was accusing him of being the same.

"No," he said, scrambling to collect his thoughts. "That's not true."

"You threatened transportation if I did not spy on Crowley. You used me in return for your silence." Her words hissed at him.

He shook his head. "No, Allegra, I never meant to—"

"*Si*." Her hands clenched on his coat as if she would tear it apart.

"No." His mind flailed in a hundred directions. "I didn't...You weren't..." He shook his head again. "I told you to stop."

"How could I believe you? You knew too much. You knew about the curse!" she spat.

"Allegra," he pleaded and pulled off his mask in desperation. "Please understand."

"No." She squirmed away from between him and the wall and rearranged her clothes. "Please take me back to my brothers."

Sebastian stared, appalled at the abrupt turn the night had taken. All he wanted to do was hold her, to absorb her warmth after the shock of learning about his mother and how Foley had used him. But she had become distant, unreachable. She did not understand he had been trying to help her and keep her safe with his threat of transportation. He knew no matter how much he explained right now, she would not believe him. She was furious. Perhaps later, when she had been able to look back at how he had protected her, she would forgive him.

Gathering his dignity, he backed away. "Of course."

He watched her straighten her veil and twitch her skirt into place. His fingers itched to help her, to smooth the wimple over her shoulders, to tuck a curl beneath the lace of her veil. He wanted to explain that he had never intended to carry out his threat. He should have told her that, but he never had. Perhaps he *had* learned too well from Foley. Perhaps he had become a cruel, vengeful fiend as well.

With his heart a knotted lump in his chest, he escorted a tight-lipped, stiff-backed princess back to the ballroom. They had no sooner rounded the corner of the house onto the long stretch of veranda when the twins and their wives emerged from the ballroom. The expressionless masks of the men's *bauttas* looked ominous, even without the aggressive anger rippling off them. Sebastian knew they were fuming that he had whisked their sister away. He was about to be punished for his rash behavior. Resigned, he could only hope they would not challenge him to a duel.

Solange, wife to the duke, Antonio, came to an abrupt halt. "*Sacré bleu!*" Her eyes widened behind her mask. She took a step forward. "It is you! *Merda!*" She turned to her husband. "He is The Messenger of the Legion of Baal."

Sebastian froze. At first, he could not understand how she'd recognized him. Then he realized he had removed his mask. She had seen him in Paris, as a witness to the duel she had been forced to fight with her husband, Antonio. Time seemed to slow. The twins, their wives, and Allegra beside him became statues in their shock. He wanted to deny, to explain. He was not truly that man known as The Messenger. But his throat was paralyzed. No words emerged. He was trapped in an ugly masquerade that had nothing to do with playful flirtation or giving rein to wild desires. His masquerade was deadly, a knife-edge walk between life and death.

But even that danger faded when he saw Allegra's face. She took a single step back. Cold rage and betrayal turned those glorious eyes to hard metal.

"*Bastardo. Stronzo. Vaffanculo.*" She delivered each swear word as if it were a hammer blow. Then she slapped him.

She turned on her heel and walked with her head high to her family, stepped between them and disappeared into the ballroom.

The twins in their identical *bauttas* turned to look at each other, no doubt communicating silently. Then, together, they faced him again.

"You have dishonored and endangered our sister, *Sior* Hawksmoor," the prince said. "We will do nothing now for the sake of your mother, the countess, but this is not the end. The Legion of Baal is our enemy. No matter what you have done to help us in the past, *you* are our enemy. We will have your death."

As a group, they all turned and entered the house.

Sebastian stood, stunned and stupefied. His heart felt like a shriveled mass in his chest. He was The Messenger of the Legion of Baal, but he was not that man. He was Sebastian Fox, who had taken on that other identity to please his mentor and fulfill the assignment given to him. He would never hurt Allegra or any of her family. But how could he get any of them to believe him?

He closed his eyes and took a breath. The only way to prove that he had any honor was to acquire the piece of the Sphere of Astarte. In two nights. Perhaps then Allegra might forgive him. Provided her brothers did not kill him first. Or he did not die at the hands of the Lord High.

Allegra felt as if her heart had been ripped from her, pummeled into a bruised mass, and then pushed back into her chest. Yes, he had used her in the beginning as she had used him, but she believed they had moved beyond that. She had trusted him. She had even fallen in love with him. She wanted to be cured from the curse so she could declare her feelings to him as a normal woman. But she never expected him to be her family's enemy. He was no better than Crowley! Worse! She had fled Paris to escape the members of the Legion of Baal. She thought she would be safe at the priory between Bath and Stonehenge, both places of mystical power. She never expected her enemy to be her landlord. She never expected her enemy to be the one who would assuage the Hunger. She never expected her enemy to be the man she loved. Shame washed over her. She wanted to run and hide.

Blindly, she wound through the crowd in the ballroom. Without stopping to express her regrets, she fled outside. Somehow, she found their coach. Ernesto was there, and without a word, he helped her inside. She ripped off her veil and mask and curled into a corner. No tears came. She felt hollowed out and dry as chaff.

He had used her. Tricked her. Betrayed her. The man she loved, the man who had awakened her body, who had captured her soul. He was her enemy. *Her enemy.* Remorse made her insides cringe.

What would she tell her brothers?

Nothing.

She would tell them nothing. She could not bear to face them. They had fought so hard to protect the family, and she had let them down. She had blithely danced into the enemy's web. Now, she had to extricate herself.

In two nights, she would be Shadow. In two nights, the Legion of Baal would convene at Stonehenge. A piece of the Sphere of Astarte would be there. Somehow, she would steal it. She would retrieve what belonged to her family and take her revenge on the man who had wormed his way into her heart and then punctured it with holes.

Her family arrived and climbed into the coach. She barely acknowledged them. Her brothers were tight-lipped in their rage. Their reproach would come later. Her two new sisters tried to console her, but their words were meaningless murmurs. Her mind had closed down, spinning in a closed whirl of guilt and shame. She could not face them. Staring out the window as they rode down the long drive, she wanted nothing more than to fade into the night. She shut her eyes, walled off the world, and prepared to endure the hours until she could repair the damage she had done.

Chapter 20

Allegra stood hidden in the line of trees and looked out across the plain spread before her. Darkness had fallen and the ground was an ebony smudge spreading away into the distance until it met the star-studded sky. The moon was halfway up, huge and orange. Between her and the moon, the enormous standing stones of Stonehenge poked up, creating black voids in the nighttime sky and looking like the claws of some monstrous creature that lived beneath the surface.

She had already turned to Shadow. Her senses of taste, smell, and touch had faded to nothing. She expected to be back at the priory before she experienced the Hunger. But hanging from her horse's saddle was her moonstone pendant that would dampen those wild cravings if her return was delayed. Her clothes were a neat pile at the foot of the tree.

She had stolen out of the priory to be here at Stonehenge for the gathering of the Legion of Baal. Since that terrible night of the masquerade ball, she had locked herself in her room and refused to speak to anyone. Her brothers had knocked on her door. Her new sisters had knocked on her door. Antonio's wife, Solange, had even told through the wooden panels some fantastical story about a Crystal Dagger, and how The Messenger had saved her life, and possibly Antonio's.

"Allegra," Solange had said quietly from the other side of the door, "I think he returned a piece of the Sphere of Astarte to Antonio. I think he brought Antonio back to life."

Allegra's heart twisted and cringed painfully in her chest as she listened to the story. She didn't know what to believe. She only knew he had used her, betrayed her. How could she ever forgive him? He had known he was her enemy, yet he had kept his secret. He had lured her in, pretending protection. She had been stupid, giving herself to him. Perhaps even the times he had saved her he was manipulating her into trusting him, becoming pliant for his seduction. Tonight, she would get her revenge. She would sneak into the stone circle, invade the gathering of the Legion of Baal and steal the piece of the Sphere. Then she would disappear.

The drone of chanting echoed in the distance. Beyond the thin line of trees, two rows of men carried lit torches. They wore dark green robes, the hoods shadowing their faces. At the head of the line, two torchbearers flanked a figure in a black robe carrying a tall staff. The gait of the procession was solemn, slow and steady, in rhythm with their low, deep chant. They looked like evil monks.

Allegra shrank back as they passed the tree line, even though she knew they would not be able to see her. With a touch of her mind, she soothed her horse, making sure it would not give away their presence. She watched them pass her and continue to the stone circle. Silently, she followed at a discreet distance.

Despite her fury at Sebastian, she searched the line for his familiar figure. She thought she would be able to pick him out, even though the robes were identical, but no figure carried himself with the same elegance, nor walked with the same grace. A tiny tickle of disappointment itched in her chest. She ignored it. She was there for the piece of the Sphere, not to see the man who had betrayed her.

As the head of the procession reached the outer ring of stones, it halted. Allegra dropped to her belly. The ground was relatively flat, and she hoped her shadowy form appeared to be only a dip in the contour of the earth if anyone happened to glance her way.

A single torch flared within the stones.

"Who enters the sacred circle?" a voice called out.

Chills ran down her spine at the words, for the voice belonged to the man who had whispered words of seduction in her ear.

"It is the Lord High of the Legion of Baal," the man at the head of the procession answered in a high, sing-song voice. "We come to pay homage to the god."

"Then enter and yield all connection to this earth," Sebastian said.

The procession moved forward. Between the stones, she watched the robed figures arrange themselves in a circle. She crept forward and hid behind one of the stone pillars to watch.

As soon as she touched the rock, the force of the stones, older than time, like a deep, low throb, thumped through her bones. This was ages-old power that drew its might from the earth, the stars, the planets, the universe. It slumbered, neither good nor evil, only awakening when something disturbed its rest. Like a sleeping dog, it allowed her to nestle within its warmth. She ran her hand down the stone. A friendly rumble, more sense than sound, answered.

She turned her attention to the men inside the pillars. The Lord High stood at the head of the circle behind the altar stone. Sebastian, distinctive in a deep purple robe, but also identifiable by his posture, stood at the foot of the circle. All the robes were embroidered with a frog glyph in red, the symbol of the Legion of Baal.

Allegra closed her eyes against the sight of the man she loved taking part in this gathering of men who wanted her death and the destruction of her family. Despite his betrayal, her body yearned for him, even though she was Shadow and had no sense of touch. She felt as if every inch of her strained toward him, like flowers reaching for the sun. She wished she had never seen him walking down the streets of Bath. She wished she had not cajoled Luisa into kidnapping him to appease the Hunger. She wished for this night to be over quickly, so that she might steal the piece of the Sphere and be gone from this country forever. And never see him again.

Sebastian held up a gold chalice embellished with gems. "We drink to the god Ba'al this night. May he infuse us with his spirit and give us power over our enemies."

He handed it to the man at his right. The man drank and passed it along. Everyone sipped from the chalice except Sebastian and the Lord High. When it returned to him, he poured the remaining few drops of liquid on the ground.

"We offer refreshment to the goddess Astarte, that she may join with her god in pleasure and joy," he intoned.

The group responded with a single wordless syllable of agreement. The ceremony proceeded with the Lord High invoking the god Ba'al and reciting petitions. The members responded, repeating the single phrase, "As the god pleases." Allegra paid little attention to what was said and waited impatiently for the piece of the Sphere to be produced.

She heard rustling to her right. A shadowed form flitted between two of the outer standing stones. Someone in a dark cape watched. It appeared to be a woman.

Stay away, she sent silently.

She heard a tiny gasp that was immediately smothered. The other watcher swung around and disappeared behind one of the opposite stones. Allegra wondered who it was, how the woman knew about this secret conclave, and why she was present. She sensed no hostility from her, but even the most evil of creatures could hide their true intent. No matter who she was, she would not get the piece of the Sphere. It belonged to Allegra's family. No one else.

Allegra turned back to the ceremony but kept part of her attention on the cloaked figure. The woman hid herself well and seemed interested only in the ceremony taking place. The rite proceeded with the gravity of a church service. Finally, at the end of a long tirade about power and magic, with a flourish, the Lord High held out a dull bit of carved amber in his palm. Sebastian swung his arm wide and a streak of light swept across the circle. It disappeared into the amber, and then the piece began to pulse with a soft yellow glow.

Murmurs of appreciation passed among the participants. Solemn silence fell as the Lord High turned to place the piece of the Sphere of Astarte on the altar stone at his feet. Somehow, Allegra knew that pulsing light was a sham. Sebastian had used his power to light it up, but the piece had not awakened. Something would have happened to her if it had.

She flitted from pillar to pillar to get nearer. Only about a third of the stones in the outer circle was still standing, and only a few of the inner circle. But the altar stone was near two of the standing pillars. The piece of the Sphere beckoned. It called to her, like a faint vibration in the air. Desperate to hold it, she grasped the stone pillar before her, so she would not reveal herself.

She was nearly invisible as Shadow. If she could get close enough and be quick enough, all she had to do was snatch the piece and then disappear into the dark. She just had to wait for the right moment.

Sebastian had seen Allegra as she followed the procession to the stone circle. She was invisible to the members of Legion of Baal, but when he stood alone in the black circle and waited to play his foolish part in this ceremony, he had caught a glimpse of those glorious eyes that glowed like molten gold. And then he had seen her lithe, shadowy form flitting across the moonlit plain like a dark nymph.

Fear for her tightened his gut. She should not have ventured to this gathering. She had no idea how ruthless the man was who called himself the Lord High. But he could not warn her away, for that would reveal her presence. Of course, the reason she was here was to steal the piece of the Sphere of Astarte. He wondered how she knew it would be present. Then he remembered overhearing Crowley at Nulkana's shack brag to her that the piece would be shown at tonight's conclave. She had to be desperate to retrieve it, to put herself in such jeopardy. His resolve hardened to steal the piece for her, no matter how dangerous. And he had to do it before she revealed herself.

Allegra hid behind the stone nearest to the piece of the Sphere. It was so close. The Lord High was reciting a supplication to the god Ba'al. His arms were raised over the piece and he faced away from the circle of men. If his head were not thrown back to the sky, if he glanced a bit to his right, he might see her. She plastered herself against the upright stone and kept her gaze lowered to hide her eyes. Her heart sped up in anticipation. As soon as he turned away, she would snatch the piece. It was only a few steps from her.

From where he stood at the foot of the circle of men, Sebastian saw Allegra pressed against the stone, her shadowy form blending in with the darkness. He knew what she was thinking—that she could take those few steps, snatch the piece of the Sphere and disappear into the night. But she did not know the Lord High and how perceptive he was, how canny he was. How ruthless. How cruel. He would catch her, torture her, and sacrifice her to the god. Sebastian could not let that happen. Besides, he had planned on stealing the piece for her. But there was no way to warn her. If he did, he would give himself away and they could both die. Despite being a Druid, he was still human.

He felt his power gathering in his fingertips. In frustration, he curled his hands into fists, shutting down the surge that would erupt if he allowed it. Inside the sacred stone circle, his power was stronger, nearer the surface. He had to keep it tightly in check. This was not the time to let it loose. Allegra was too close to the Lord High. She might be hurt. Besides, the time for revealing himself had not yet come. But soon. The wine he had passed in the chalice had been laced with a drug that would create hallucinations, and with a bit of magic to enhance those visions. He just had to wait for it to take effect. And then he could be done with this madness of playing the part of the Lord High's Messenger. His lackey. He only hoped Allegra would not try to grab the piece of the Sphere before his plan played out.

Relief flowed through Allegra when the Lord High finished his benediction over the piece of the Sphere. He turned back to his circle of followers. Away from her. Away from the piece.

Now.

She crept forward, keeping out of the flickering torchlight. One step, two. Another. One more. No one had seen her. She glanced up. Only those blue, blue eyes of The Messenger of the Legion of Baal tracked her. But she hoped he would not give her away.

Please, let me take it, she pleaded silently to him.

He made a tiny gesture with his hand. Permission or warning? She could not decide. But she had no time. Reaching out, she scooped up the piece of amber that was her fate. And froze.

A shockwave passed through her. Her body arched. Pain exploded in every nerve. Fire beneath her skin. A scream, silent at first, then ear-shattering, ripped from her throat. Blindness blocked her vision. An unintelligible roar assaulted her ears.

And then it all faded away.

When she could think again, she found herself collapsed on the ground and clutching the piece of the Sphere tightly to her chest. She could sense the eyes of the men surrounding her like an uncomfortable palpitation on her skin. How could they see her?

A hand curled tightly around her arm and pulled her to her feet. She was dragged a few steps then tossed to the ground. Her brain could not process what was happening.

"We have an intruder!" the Lord High exclaimed. "A member of the House of Auriano! She steals our piece of immortality."

Allegra heard the murmurs of discontent around her. Confused, bewildered, she shivered in the cool night air and huddled on the ground, surrounded by men whose gazes made her skin twitch. Her glance fell on her bare knees. Skin, scratched and bleeding. Solid muscle and bone. She blinked, not quite understanding what she was seeing. What she was feeling. The chill of the air. The hard, pebbled ground beneath her. The sting of the scratches on her knees. Then she knew. She had transformed. She was human. Not Shadow. Her curse was broken.

Despite the danger, despite her fear, despite her embarrassment at being naked before so many male eyes, exultation swept through her. The piece of the Sphere of Astarte had worked its magic. And it was hers. She clutched it tightly to her chest.

Sebastian saw her transform like every other man standing in the circle. Unlike the others who gaped, uncomprehending, he knew what was happening to Allegra. But he was as frozen as the rest, transfixed by the beauty of her, the turn from dark Shadow to glowing skin. Her scream of pain pierced him. Her agony cut his heart. He wanted to go to her, enfold her in his arms, soothe her anguish. But he did not want to hurt her with his touch. Nor did he wish to put her in any more danger by revealing himself. By remaining silent, keeping his secret, he still might be able to save her.

The others stared at her. He saw their lascivious greed, their lust for her in ugly purple swirls above their heads. They would defile her before they sacrificed her to the god. He would do anything to prevent that from happening.

This was not how he had planned the night. A touch of exasperation at this headstrong woman whom he had come to love made him clench his teeth. Admiration for her bravery warmed him. He would have to make a new plan. But first, he would protect her from the leering stares. Unclasping the robe at his throat, he strode to her and draped the garment around her shoulders.

"Messenger." The smoothly calm voice of the Lord High cut through the murmurs. "Do you protect the Auriano baggage?"

Sebastian stood tall and gazed serenely back at the man while his mind raced with one plan, then another. "She is for the god, Sire. If she is to be given to him, then we must prepare her for the ritual."

Allegra gasped and started to rise. Gently, he pushed her back down.

"Then take her and prepare," the Lord High said. "But first, give the piece of the Sphere to me." He held out an imperious hand.

Sebastian forced himself not to smile as he came up with the prefect argument. "Sire, if I take the piece, then she will return to Shadow, nearly invisible. No one here would be able to restrain her."

The Lord High dropped his hand. "Not even you, my Messenger?" His silky question taunted dangerously.

Sebastian bowed his head, miming respect. "As you say, Sire." He would humble himself a thousand times if it would help him save Allegra and allow her to keep the piece of the Sphere.

"Sacrifice." The word came from one of the men in the circle.

"Sacrifice." Another man opposite echoed it.

A third man called, "Sacrifice!"

And then a fourth man, a fifth, a sixth. Until the word was chanted by everyone in the circle. They banged their long-handled torches on the ground in cadence. Their mood had turned ugly.

Sebastian watched their essences turn from the purple swirls of lust to violent red with slashes of black. The drug he had put in the drink was having the opposite effect of what he had planned. He glanced at the Lord High. Even behind the gold mask, he could sense the man's smile.

The Lord High held up his hand. The chanting stopped. Silence descended like a knife.

"The moon is ripe, Messenger," he said in his weird, high-pitched voice. "The god calls for sacrifice. He hungers."

A howl went up from the throats of men drugged with magic and lust. As if bindings had suddenly been cut, without warning, the circle closed in with a rush. Hands grabbed and clawed for Allegra. He tried to protect her but was shoved aside. A mass of bodies separated them. He tried to push his way to her, but an elbow to the face, another to his ribs dazed him. A boot to the back of his knee made him lose his balance. A flurry of fists pummeled him to the ground. His power scattered. Feet kicked him and stomped over him. He caught a glimpse of the top of Allegra's head, the golden highlights silvered beneath the moon. Then she disappeared behind the wall of robed men. He heard her cries for help, her screams. He had to stop this rampage. She would be torn to pieces.

He fought his way free and staggered to his feet just outside the melee. Taking a breath, he centered his power. And then, using his Druid voice, he shouted "NO!"

The sound bounced off the stones and reverberated back as if it were something solid. Everything stopped. The men stood motionless, stunned. Sebastian knew their shock would only last a moment before they resumed their assault on Allegra. She was quiet, and he prayed she was still alive. He had to divert their attention so she could escape.

"She is not the proper sacrifice," he said. "You will take me instead."

As if they were a single entity, the men turned to him. He could not see their faces within their hoods. Many of the torches had been tossed aside in the frenzy and their light flickered erratically, barely enhanced by the moon, now high in the sky. Even in the dim light, he saw their eyes, greedy for sex and blood. If he could not escape, his death would not be easy.

"Messenger." The Lord High's voice opened a path through the men. "You have feelings for this abomination of the House of Auriano."

Sebastian caught a glimpse of Allegra huddled on the ground amidst the men. The robe he had thrown over her was torn and dirty. A tiny tremor ran through her, so he knew she still lived. As relief flowed through him, he glared at the man standing opposite and allowed his hatred to show. He said nothing.

"Traitor." The Lord High flung the word at him. "Traitors feel the wrath of the god. He does not give them an easy death." At Sebastian's silence, the Lord High tipped his head as if in thought. "Very well," he said. "We will have a double sacrifice."

The moment hung suspended. No one moved. No one breathed.

Sebastian gauged the distance to Allegra. He would seize her and run. He inched forward.

And then, the Lord High's voice rang out. "Take them! Bring them before me on their knees!"

Hands grabbed him, mauled him, so many he was nearly lifted from his feet. As if he had flown, he found himself kneeling before the man in the gold mask and black robe, the man he hated, the man whom he had vowed to destroy for England. His only consolation was that Allegra, alive, knelt next to him. A bruise darkened one cheek. Her lip bled. The robe, torn at the shoulder, showed an ugly scrape down her arm. She swayed a bit.

"Are you all right?" he murmured. Even as the words formed, he knew the question was foolish. Of course, she was not all right.

You tried to save me, she said inside his head.

"Yes."

Grazie.

"*Non c'é di che.*" You're welcome.

His Italian words made something shift inside her. Tears threatened, and she blinked them back. She wanted home, safety. She wanted her brothers, but they had no idea where she was. Not even Luisa or Ernesto knew. She was alone except for this enigmatic, charismatic man beside her. A man who was The Messenger of the Legion of Baal. He had tried to protect her, had offered his own life in exchange for hers, and she was grateful. But they had ended up in the same dangerous place, both about to be a sacrifice to the god Ba'al.

Confusion swirled around them. Two men stood over them as guards. The Lord High directed others to this task or that, sharpening a large knife, setting the torches into the ground, brushing off the sacrifice stone.

Sebastian leaned a bit toward her. "If you give me the piece of the Sphere, you'll turn back to Shadow," he whispered. "Then you can escape."

Allegra cast a glance at the guards to see if they'd heard. They seemed distracted by the activity around them. She curled her fist into her chest. The bit of amber pulsed warmly and dug into her palm. What he said made perfect sense, but this was her legacy, her talisman to normalcy. If she gave it to him, she might never see it again. He could be tricking her into giving it up. He was, after all, The Messenger of the Legion of Baal. Her enemy.

She peeked up at him.

Those blue, blue eyes met hers. The image of the moon shone brightly in them. He was The Messenger, but he was also a Druid priest. Did one set of loyalties contradict the other? Or were loyalties not involved at all?

"I will return it to you and your family," he said. "It belongs to the House of Auriano."

She wanted to believe him, but he had kept his identity as The Messenger of the Legion of Baal a secret, a lie of omission. How could she trust him? If she gave him the piece of the Sphere and became Shadow, the piece would go back to the Legion of Baal. Even if he did not return it to the Lord High, it would be taken from him. He would be sacrificed, despite his Druid powers. She suspected it would not be a quick or easy death. That made her stomach churn. Not even her enemy deserved such an end, especially one who had been her lover. More than that, the man she loved.

"You do not believe me," he said.

She said nothing, not sure herself.

"I give you my word, I will flee from here and return it to you," he said.

Her response was to glance at the two guards who were distracted. But that could change in an instant.

She saw him arch a single, dark brow.

"Do you doubt my ability to escape?" His words challenged.

This was the confident, teasing man who had first enticed her. But he was not sauntering down a street nor at a ball. He was in terrible danger.

"*Si*," she said with a single nod. "I doubt you can escape on your own."

He huffed a laugh. "My brave Shadow."

She hissed her annoyance at his possessive. "Not *your* anything." She slipped the piece of the Sphere into his hand. "I will help you escape. Then I will take back what is mine."

His fingers curled around her hand as he accepted the piece. She felt herself slowly begin to fade.

"Everything I am is yours, dearest Alli," were his words just before she lost her sense of touch.

She was Shadow.

She slid her fingers from his hand, regretting the loss of that special tingle of his skin against hers. The robe covering her fell to the ground. Before the two men guarding them understood what had happened, she slipped between them, beyond the activity within the stones, and out into the night. She smiled at the surprised shout that sounded the alert at her disappearance. But a growl of anger, the crack of a fist against flesh and grunt of pain made her cringe and resolve she would do everything she could to save Sebastian, enemy or not.

His words had warmed her, touched her soul, whether they were true or not.

Chapter 21

The fist that cracked across Sebastian's cheek sent him sideways into the dirt. He lay stunned for a moment. Before he could rise, his arms were pulled back and his hands tied behind him. Then he was jerked to his knees. One of the men tried to wrest the piece of the Sphere from his fingers. Sebastian's growl, enhanced by his Druid power, made the man jerk away.

"Messenger." The Lord High's voice scraped across his nerves. "You have revealed yourself as a traitor. Your sacrifice will be an appeasement to our god who is angry. We will offer him your heart."

From his position on his knees, Sebastian glared at the eyes behind the gold mask. He loathed this man whose essence swirled with putrid greens and foul yellows. He vowed to himself he would discover his identity and kill him.

Sebastian raised his chin in challenge. "You may take my heart from my chest, but it will never belong to your god," he said. "I have already given it to another."

"The Auriano bitch? Bah!" The Lord High swiped his hand as if chasing away an annoying insect.

"She outwitted you, Lord High of the Legion of Baal, and escaped," Sebastian taunted. "Perhaps you are nothing more than a pathetic creature who preys on the weaknesses of others."

He sensed the held breaths of the men surrounding him.

He pushed further. "Perhaps you are no one, a lowly man and insignificant."

The Lord High stiffened. Then very slowly, he raised his hand to his mask. Just before he pulled it off, a voice rang out from atop one of the stone pillars.

"You are all insignificant!"

Allegra, hiding behind one of the pillars, gasped and pressed against the stone. Nulkana! Where had she come from? How did she know they were here?

She slipped to the next stone and peeked around it. Across the open space inside the ring, the sorceress stood on top of the lintel stone resting atop two of the pillars. She wore a flowing black gown and her black hair hung loose around her shoulders. The members of the Legion stood aghast, rooted and open-mouthed at Nulkana's appearance. The flames from their torches threw flickering light across the sorceress, reflecting red in her eyes, making her appear diabolical. In the shadow beneath the stone where she stood, a somberly clad, cowled figure stood. It was the same tortured figure she had seen in Sebastian's garden.

As Allegra ducked back behind the pillar, she bumped something that clattered to the ground. Glancing down, she saw Sebastian's walking stick. She surmised he had left it hidden while he performed his duties as The Messenger. The Druid's Sapphire glowed faintly. His power must have lit it up. If only she could get it to him without Nulkana noticing.

Movement just behind the next pillar caught her attention. The woman she had seen before watched the scene within the circle of stones, transfixed. She thought the woman had fled to safety, but something must have drawn her to this place, something that kept her riveted despite her fear.

Go away, Allegra sent silently. *You are in danger.*

The woman swung around in surprise. Allegra, forgetting for the moment she was Shadow, motioned for the woman to leave. The woman stared, her mouth agape, then she flitted away, to hide behind another pillar.

"Such little men!" Nulkana crowed. Her laugh rang through the space. And then the snap of the sorceress's power crackled through the air.

The members of the Legion of Baal scattered as the sorceress's power blazed and banged among them. Some were hit. Their screams of pain and fear mingled with Nulkana's mad laughter and the deafening echoes of the explosions.

Allegra tried to see Sebastian through the confusion. Men zigged and zagged as they fled, trying to escape Nulkana's wrath. Some of the torches toppled, flaring, then died to embers. Men rushed beyond the circle of stones out into the night. Some ran past Allegra, but they either did not see her or they did not care. The sorceress targeted Legion members who were too slow to escape. Allegra watched in horror as men fell, some writhing in agony as their robes caught fire. Some dropped dead as they ran.

"Papa," the woman who was hiding gasped.

Allegra could see the woman's wide eyes in the bright flashes, her hand to her mouth. Then, with a whimper, she turned and fled into the night.

The light from the power bursts was blinding. But then she saw Sebastian, standing still and calm in the middle of the chaos, his hands still bound behind him. Without flinching, he faced Nulkana. Despite the pain he had caused her, Allegra feared for him. With a single thought and a flick of her fingers, she untied the rope binding his wrists. Without diverting his attention away from the sorceress, his head dipped in thanks. Then he straightened, appearing to grow several inches. He held out his fist and opened it, revealing the piece of the Sphere of Astarte to Nulkana.

"Is this what you want, witch?" he called.

Allegra's heart stopped. Would he give the piece to the sorceress? Even after she had freed him?

Nulkana's attack subsided as she focused on the bit of amber Sebastian held in his palm.

"I can burn you to ash," she hissed.

Sebastian smiled. "You can try."

Just as he closed his fingers around the piece, the Lord High stepped up and tried to snatch it away. "That is mine!" he cried, but Sebastian had it securely in his fist.

Energy snapped out from Nulkana's hand. "Get away, you bug!"

The Lord High jumped back and threw up his arm. The frog glyph on his wrist deflected the blow, and he let loose his own stream of power. Nulkana's energy flashed again and again, scorching the earth all around them. The Lord High deflected them all. Then he sent his own power whizzing toward the sorceress. A battle raged as each tried to destroy the other.

Through it all, Sebastian stood still, his eyes closed, his lips moving. A haze surrounded him. Even though Nulkana repeatedly shot her energy at him, nothing seemed to touch him. Clouds began to gather in the sky and scudded across the moon. A wind swept through the stones and created dust devils. As the clouds thickened, a spear of lightning crashed into the clearing. Rain began to fall.

Allegra heard a very faint hum in the stone that hid her. It seemed to sing to her. And she realized she could use the power of the ancient stone circle to help defeat the sorceress. Placing her hands flat against the pillar, she concentrated as if she would lift the massive stones. They were heavier than anything she had ever tried to move with her mind. She would never be able to raise them, but if she could jostle them a little, she might dislodge the sorceress from her advantageous position.

A deep rumble and a shiver ran through the stones. They shifted and wobbled just a tiny bit, enough to make Nulkana halt her attack as she tried to maintain her balance. The stones settled. But the sorceress did not fall.

Allegra slumped against the stone, drained and disappointed. But at least she had given Sebastian a bit of a reprieve.

The sorceress stood firmly on the lintel stone with a ball of spitting, deadly energy in each hand. "You'll not distract me with your tricks, Druid," Nulkana yelled out, then she resumed her onslaught.

As the sorceress's energy flashed and banged and she concentrated on Sebastian, the Lord High eased away, attempting to escape. Allegra would not allow him to flee. She hated him and what he wanted to do to her and her family. She hated what he had done to Sebastian. Fighting her exhaustion, she gathered her reserves. With a flick of her fingers, she flung a cloud of dirt and stones at him. He ducked and threw up his arms to protect himself, but he caught Nulkana's attention. With a growling hiss, the sorceress sent a shaft of power at him. It hit him squarely in the chest, and he fell to the ground, motionless.

While Nulkana's attention was on the Lord High, Allegra held her hand over the walking stick and concentrated. She lifted it into the air and sent it to hover in front of Sebastian. Without opening his eyes, he grabbed it and pulled out the hidden sword. The metal glowed white-hot. Blue light pulsed between his fingers from the Druid's Stone. He raised the tip to the sky. Lightning flashed and ripped down the blade with a tremendous bang.

"*Imigh uaim a dheamhan!*" he shouted and pointed the weapon at Nulkana. *Be gone evil spirit!*

A stream of power arced through the air and hit Nulkana in the chest. Her shriek echoed and bounced within the pillars.

"*Imigh uaim a dheamhan!*" Sebastian repeated, using his deep Druid voice.

Nulkana screamed again. And fell from the lintel stone.

In the sputtering light of the fallen torches, Allegra could see the sorceress standing on the ground between two of the stone pillars. She was bent over in agony.

"You have won this time, Druid," Nulkana said, her voice ravaged and thin. "Take your Auriano bitch for now. But I'm not done with her."

Allegra was not done either. Fury energized her. With a swipe of her hand, she sent a large rock through the air. It hit Nulkana in the chest where she was already wounded. The sorceress cried out and staggered. When she regained her balance, she was hunched over, her hand at her chest, and black blood oozed between her fingers. The hooded figure who stood beneath the lintel stone nodded in Allegra's direction, as if he approved of what Allegra had done.

"Bitch!" Nulkana snarled. "I'm coming back for you."

With a sharp wave of her hand, Nulkana opened a void behind her. She stepped back and disappeared. The hooded figure was dragged back with her. The void snapped shut with a pop. She was gone.

Chapter 22

Sebastian allowed the wild storm to calm. Silence dropped into the circle of stones. The rain stopped. The lightning ceased. The only sound was the slow drip of water. The scent of wet earth and damp ashes filled the air. His energy was spent, and his legs wobbled. He dropped to one knee. His head drooped.

"*Are you hurt?* Allegra's concerned voice whispered in his head.

"No." He glanced up and saw she was standing beside him. "At least I don't think I am."

You drove away Nulkana, she said, her golden eyes blazing.

He smiled. "You helped."

She gave a dismissive shrug. *Not very much.*

He nodded. "*Si*. Very much."

A groan came from near one of the upright stones. At first, Sebastian could see only black, shapeless forms, then something moved. It was the Lord High in his black robe.

Sebastian pushed to his feet. Hatred squeezed through him. Whoever the Lord High was, all Sebastian wanted to do was kill him. His vision narrowed, red-rimmed with animosity. Intent on murder, he strode to the prostrate figure.

"No," the man whined. "Don't hurt me."

Sebastian caught him by the shoulder as he tried to crawl away and flipped him to his back. As the moon broke through the clouds, he could see a large hole burned through the man's robe. Beneath it, his skin was blistered, oozing, and singed black. So, the frog glyph had not protected him after all. Satisfaction brought a cold smile to Sebastian's lips.

He sensed Allegra move up beside him. "Stay back," he warned and wrapped his hand around her arm. Those delightful tingles erupted on his palm, reminding him of her allure, but also her vulnerability. He would protect her with his last breath from the man laid out before him.

The Lord High groaned again. "Help me, my Messenger."

"I'm your Messenger no more." Sebastian's words were chilly. "Let's see who you really are."

With a flip of his fingers, he ripped off the golden mask of the Lord High. His breath left his lungs. Cold rage suffused him.

Madre di Dio, Allegra gasped inside his head.

The man laying injured and dying before him was Sir Cyril Foley, his mentor, the man who had saved him from a life of debauchery and dissipation, and then taught him subterfuge and coercion and other dark skills. This was the man who had threatened and used his mother, and then used him.

Sebastian wanted to kill him.

He dropped to his knees. As if his hands belonged to another person, they closed around the man's throat, squeezing the life from him. Foley fought for breath and he clawed at Sebastian's fingers.

"You deceived me," Sebastian said through his teeth. "You tricked me and used me for your own ugly needs."

Foley's face started to turn purple.

Sebastian. Allegra's voice whispered through his brain.

He ignored it.

Sebastian, you're killing him.

Her words flashed through his head. He realized what he was doing. Abruptly, he released the man's throat. If he had killed Foley, he would have been no better than the man who had manipulated him into doing unspeakable things. His murder would have been one more dark smudge on his conscience. His conscience was already black enough. Besides, Foley would most likely die from the wound inflicted by Nulkana.

Foley coughed. Blood appeared at the corner of his mouth. But he smiled, an evil, cold smile.

"I almost had everything," he rasped. He turned a cruel gaze on Allegra . "The death of one of the Auriano abominations." He turned

274

back to Sebastian with a chuckle. He coughed and more blood speck-
led his lips. "And your death, dear boy. A perfect revenge on your
mother." His gaze turned inward, and he mumbled, "That deceitful
bitch, she should have been mine. Mine." His eyes closed. "Mine,"
he whispered. His chest filled once, his breath escaped in a burbling
sigh, and he breathed no more.

Sebastian watched him for a moment, expecting him to return
to life, to torment him with some other devious scheme. Finally
accepting the man was truly dead, he slowly rose to his feet. He
was numb. He had been two men for so long he had trouble envi-
sioning living a life as only one. He was no longer The Messenger of
the Legion of Baal, but he was not sure he was Sebastian Fox, Earl
of Hawksmoor, either.

He glanced at the woman beside him. She watched him with
those glorious molten eyes. She was beautiful, his Shadow. No, she
was not his, could never be. He had deceived her. She hated him.
But she had helped him vanquish Nulkana, at least for now. And he
could at least give her one thing.

He strode to the middle of the stones where he had dropped
his walking stick and had called down the power of the Druids. A
torch, shielded from the rain by a tilted rock, sputtered nearby and
he scooped it up, then searched the ground. When he found what
he was looking for, he closed his fingers around it, then returned to
where Allegra still stood, her lovely feet barely touching the earth.
He braced the torch against a nearby stone. Taking her hand, he held
it, palm up. Those incredible tingles tickled where her skin met his.
This would be the last time he would ever feel them, and he mourned
their loss. Then he dropped his gift into her palm. The piece of the
Sphere of Astarte. The artifact that would help break her curse and
give her back her life. A life without him.

As soon as the piece of the Sphere landed in Allegra 's hand, pain
whipped through her. Fire. Burning. Scorching beneath her skin. Her

bones throbbed. Her sight went blank. A roar engulfed her ears. She fought for breath. She thought she might be dying. Not like the last time, when she had grabbed the piece of the Sphere herself and been roughly dragged back to flesh and bone by the rough handling of the men of the Legion of Baal. This time, her torment was prolonged. And then faintly, like a thin lifeline, she heard her name.

"Allegra." The voice seemed to come from very far away.

"Allegra." It came again, dragging her back from the torture.

The pain was gone. She drew in a breath and let it out. Opened her eyes. Sebastian stood before her with concern clouding his eyes, those dear, blue, blue eyes. He had returned the piece of the Sphere to her.

Speechless, she gazed down at the piece of the Sphere in her hand, then down at herself, at her body, flesh and bone. She was naked, and her skin puckered into goose bumps from the chill night air. But she was whole, not filmy, not Shadowy. She looked up at the moon, high in the sky now and spilling its silvery light onto the earth. It seemed to be smiling down on her.

Sebastian draped his coat across her shoulders. It held his warmth and she snuggled into it.

"*Grazie*," she said.

The hint of a smile touched his lips. "You're welcome." Then he turned very serious. That imprint of the moon appeared in his eyes. "I never meant to hurt you, Princess. The piece of the Sphere of Astarte was always yours." Pain crossed his face. "I've done some terrible things. I thought I was being honorable. Now I know differently." He glanced away, took a breath, and met her gaze. "I love you, Princess Allegra of the House of Auriano. I think I fell in love with you the first time I heard your voice when you had me chained to the wall. I hope, someday, you can forgive me." He reached out and touched her cheek. "Find pleasure in your new life, dearest Alli."

Stunned into silence, Allegra could only stare at him. She could not find words to express the tumult of emotions swirling in her chest.

The sound of a coach just outside the circle of stones distracted her. She watched it come to an abrupt halt, and then her family tumbled out. They rushed to her with exclamations of dismay and concern, then with surprise and delight as they surrounded her.

"Are you well?"

"Are you hurt?"

"You are cured!"

"The curse is broken!"

"You should have told us…"

"We were so worried…"

They had figured out where she had gone on this night of great power. Allegra stopped their questions when she opened her palm to show them the piece of the Sphere. Out of the corner of her eye, she saw Sebastian collect his walking stick and then head toward the open plain beyond the stones. He appeared to be heading into a dark place where he might disappear forever. A hole opened in her chest. Evan's words echoed through her head: *You will find the truth within the stones.* She ignored her family and stepped away from them.

"Wait!" she called to the man walking away from her.

He stopped and turned.

She strolled toward him. "I think you have forgotten something, *Sior* Hawksmoor."

A line of confusion appeared between his brows. "Have I? I don't seem to recall…" He shook his head.

"Perhaps in the confusion, it slipped your mind." She stopped halfway between him and her family.

"Perhaps it did." He appeared rather unsure.

"*Si.*" She gave a definitive nod. "My family is most concerned about my reputation."

"Are they?" He sent an apprehensive glance in their direction.

Allegra knew her brothers were beginning to bristle and would pounce on Sebastian if she merely flicked an eyelash in their direction. She also was aware her new sisters were holding them back. She hid her smile.

She took a tiny step forward. "My family knows of your reputation as a blackguard and a rogue. They have come to rescue me. It seems they have found me, unclothed and wearing only a man's coat. Your coat, *Sior* Hawksmoor."

Those blue eyes narrowed. "I see."

She shook her head. "No, I don't think that you do."

"No?" He looked quite confused.

She sighed. "You see, the man who ravished me, who left me in this deplorable condition, the man I *love*, seems to be running off."

He appeared a bit uneasy and disconcerted. Then his gaze focused on her. "I beg your pardon, but could you repeat that please?"

She frowned. "You seem to be running off."

"Ah, I meant the part before that," he said.

She tipped her head. "Do you mean the part about the man I love?"

His eyes widened. His mouth opened and closed. He swallowed.

Before he could speak, she advanced another step. "I have a question for you, *Sior* Hawksmoor."

Alarm crossed his face, as if he thought the earth at his feet might open at any moment. "Yes?" He sent a calculating glance across her shoulder to her brothers.

"Will you marry me?"

Her words had the same effect as the deep pause before a thunderstorm. She sensed her family's shock behind her. Sebastian looked like he had been shot. Right through the heart.

He recovered before her family. His smile warmed her from the inside out. At the same time, both her brothers blustered behind her, and their wives shushed them.

"Yes," Sebastian said. He strode to her and took both her hands, the one clutching the piece of the Sphere warmer than the other. "Yes, dearest Alli. I will marry you."

And then he took her in his arms and kissed her, right there in front of her brothers.

Epilogue

Sebastian held his torch high as he trailed the Prince of Auriano and the Duke of Auriano, along with their wives, down the steep rock stairway. Each of the other two men also carried a torch. It appeared they were heading into the bowels of the earth. Allegra followed him with a hand on his shoulder. She placed it there to steady herself on the steps, but it also steadied his nerves. He covered it with his own hand, needing the comfort of the connection.

A month had passed since that terrible, wonderful night at Stonehenge, a month of teas with his mother and dinners with Allegra's family, of fencing matches, drinking bouts, and hard rides through the countryside with her brothers, of stolen interludes with Allegra. Finally, the time had come to travel to Italy. A week had passed since their arrival in Auriano, a week when he'd had barely a chance to be alone with her. The twins had kept him occupied with much the same as in England—rides through the glorious countryside, reckless matches with sword and stiletto, games of chess and whist where he was sure the brothers cheated a bit, and long nights of sampling the very excellent vintage produced by the Auriano vineyard. But the week was over. Behind him, through the open doorway, he could hear the revelers celebrating his wedding to the Princess of Auriano.

His mother was out there, dancing, drinking the wine, and thoroughly enjoying herself. They'd had a long conversation the day after the battle at Stonehenge. She explained how Foley had lured her to spy for him while she was in her first season in London. Then she had met Sebastian's father. And fallen in love. Like he and Allegra had. But his mother had been unable to separate herself entirely from Foley, for she had done some scandalous things for him, and he threatened to tell the earl and ruin her. He'd made her promise to send Sebastian to him when he came of age. In tears, she begged Sebastian to forgive her. Of course, he did. She was his mother and Foley was dead. And because of those circumstances, he, Sebastian, Earl of Hawksmoor was now wed to the Princess of Auriano.

She looked glorious, his Allegra, like a goddess in her gold satin dress. She wore a simple gold circlet studded with diamonds to hold back her flowing hair. At her throat was the large solitaire diamond he had given her that was part of the Hawksmoor family jewels. He could not believe that she was now his wife, this brave, delicious woman.

"Stop staring at me or you'll fall down the stairs," she whispered in warning.

Despite her subdued tone, her words echoed against the stone.

"Behave yourself, Hawksmoor," Alessandro grumbled, halting their progress down the steps.

Antonio gave a nod. "*Si,* show some restraint."

Solange gave a delicate snort. "He's showing more restraint than you, Tonio."

"Or you, Sandro," Sabrina added with a grin at her husband.

"Can we just get on with this?" Allegra pressed.

Alessandro and Antonio glanced at each other.

"She is much too anxious for her wedding night," Tonio said.

"I believe she has developed some very bad habits," Sandro said.

Allegra hissed. "*Madre di Dio!* If you two don't stop, I will do this thing by myself."

Appalled, the brothers stared at her. Solange gave her husband a tiny shove. With a grin, holding his torch high, Antonio turned and led them the rest of the way down the steps.

As he reached the bottom, he mumbled, "My sister has wed a man who wears a skirt."

"What do you suppose he wears beneath it?" Alessandro asked, as he placed his torch into a wall bracket.

"I think he looks very handsome in his kilt," Allegra said, and the two other women murmured their agreement.

Sebastian tried to ignore the taunts. He had never had siblings, but he had observed the same behavior with his friends at school and their brothers. This was part of the reason he was anxious, for he wanted Allegra's brothers to accept him. After Antonio had placed his torch in a bracket, he heaved a great sigh and solemnly studied Sebastian.

"I suppose we'll have to keep him, since our sister thinks so highly of him," he said.

"*Si.*" Alessandro sighed as well. "A shame to waste all that training this past week."

"Training?" Allegra stamped her foot. "You were *testing* him!"

Sebastian put a calming hand on her arm. "It's all right, Alli." He was warmed both by Allegra's defense and her brothers' acceptance.

"Perhaps we should get started," Sabrina suggested mildly.

Without another comment, everyone arranged themselves in a circle on the stone floor. Allegra tugged him into place beside her. This was the other reason for his anxiety. The Auriano siblings were about to conduct some sort of ritual with the piece of the Sphere of Astarte. This time, the ritual was real, not some dramatic charade the Lord High of the Legion of Baal had dreamed up. He hoped he could keep his power in check.

He glanced around at his surroundings. They were in a small circular chamber that was deep beneath the *Castello* Auriano. It appeared ancient. Its rock walls were roughly chiseled, and paving stones covered the floor. A large flat stone that would need many men to move lay in the center of the space. Alessandro, Antonio and Allegra stepped forward and arranged themselves around it. They closed their eyes. Their fingers twitched. After a moment, the huge stone shifted, floated up and sideways, then landed with a loud thud. The floor below looked no different than the rest of the space, and Sebastian wondered why such an effort had been made to protect it.

Alessandro and Antonio stepped back. Allegra held out a hand over the middle of the paving stones and walked in a counterclockwise direction. A round section of the floor moved with her. With a flick of her hand, a vault opened in the bedrock of the cavern. It was lined with gold, and in its center was an intricate golden pedestal holding two pieces of the Sphere of Astarte. Sebastian watched, amazed, as the pedestal slowly rose and stopped as its base reached floor-level. Allegra scooped up the incomplete Sphere. Sebastian dug in his pocket for the third piece that Allegra had asked him to hold. He handed it to her, and the three siblings connected the piece to the others. She placed it back on its pedestal, stepped back to his side, and twined her fingers with his.

They waited in silence. Sebastian counted the breaths. One, two. Five. Nothing happened. Six, eight. Allegra gasped and her grip tightened. The Sphere began to glow, and tiny beams shot out from its center. The added piece grew brighter than the other two, and slowly, it fused with them. The bright light faded back, but the Sphere glowed softly amber. It pulsed — once, twice, three times.

Sebastian felt the pulse ripple through him like a cool wave. The three siblings gasped, obviously affected more than anyone else. The power spread out into the walls of the cavern and through the bedrock of *Castello* Auriano. He heard a low heartbeat in the stone, followed by another, and a third. Then silence.

Antonio spoke first, confusion and disappointment running through his words. "Shouldn't it still beat?"

Alessandro appeared just as confused. "*Si.*"

Allegra stepped forward and peered at the Sphere. When she straightened, her eyes were wide with surprise.

"There's a piece still missing," she said.

Some instinct caused Sebastian to consider the essences of the three Auriano siblings. They were all similar, golden and true, Allegra's a bit softer than her brothers', but when he put them together in his mind's eye, he saw a space where something was missing.

"There is someone else," he said. He examined the space again.

And then he knew.

"You have another brother."

About
Patricia Barletta

Patricia Barletta is an award-winning author of historical and paranormal romance fiction. After a fulfilling career teaching English Literature in high school, she decided to go back to school herself, and obtained a Master of Fine Arts in Creative Writing at Stonecoast (University of Southern Maine). When she's not at a yoga class doing her best downward dog, Patricia is usually tending her hydrangeas or hosting a brunch for her writing group. Patricia loves to travel, and often finds the inspiration for her dark heroes, feisty heroines, and romantic settings while on a research trip. At the end of each journey she loves going home to her cozy, historical old house outside of Boston where she weaves her magical tales.

Find out more about Patricia and her books on her website: patriciabarletta.com and on Facebook.